CAPTURED
by *Twilight*

TAWNY
TAYLOR

ELLORA'S CAVE
ROMANTICA PUBLISHING

$\mathscr{W}$hat the critics are saying...

$\wp$

"*Burning Hunger* was so much fun to read. The author Tawny Taylor manages to combine the perfect erotic elements of a story into a fun adventure. *Burning Hunger* is definitely a must read for vampire erotica fans. As a matter of fact, if you weren't one before, you will probably become one after reading this story." ~ *Reader Views*

5 Tombstones "Tawny Taylor writes an excellent story. She draws the reader deep into the story. […] I enjoyed Ms. Taylor's BDSM scenes, which were very tastefully done. Ms. Taylor writes a very erotic and steamy story. *Everlasting Hunger* is the third book in the *Twilight's Possession* series. While I have not yet read the first two books in the series, after reading this one, I will be sure to check out the other books. I will also look forward to the next one in the series. If you have not yet checked out any of Tawny Taylor's books, I recommend picking this one up. It is another book which will keep you warm on a cold winter night." ~ *Bitten by Books*

An Ellora's Cave Romantica Publication

www.ellorascave.com

Captured by Twilight

ISBN 9781419959998
ALL RIGHTS RESERVED.
Burning Hunger Copyright © 2007 Tawny Taylor
Carnal Hunger Copyright © 2008 Tawny Taylor
Edited by Sue-Ellen Gower.
Photography and cover art by Les Byerley, Syneca.

This book printed in the U.S.A. by Jasmine–Jade Enterprises, LLC.

Trade paperback Publication August 2009

CAPTURED BY TWILIGHT

ℰᴑ

BURNING HUNGER
~13~

CARNAL HUNGER
~147~

BURNING HUNGER

&

Trademarks Acknowledgement

☙

Outback: OS Asset, Inc.

Pirates of the Caribbean: Disney Enterprises, Inc.

Pop-tart: Kellogg Company

Q-tips: Chesebrough-Pond's Inc.

Radio Shack: Technology Properties, Inc.

Raisinets: Ward-Johnston, Inc.

Serta: Serta, Inc.

Shelby: Carroll Hall Shelby Trust

Starbucks: Starbucks U.S. Brands, LLC

The Body Shop: The Body Shop International

Uzi: Israel Weapons Industries Ltd.

Van Helsing: Universal City Studios LLLP USI-UCS Holdings LLC

Xanax: Upjohn Company

The Cytherean Guard

We are the protectors of our king, a secret brotherhood of
warriors.
We are strong, loyal and dedicated, the sworn keepers of
the Secrets.
We are defenders of justice, guardians of the Sons of the
Twilight.
We show no mercy to the enemy.

Chapter One
∞

Oh yes, she'll be perfect.

Marek Setara stood in the shadows and watched as the woman unfolded her lush form, stepped out of her vehicle and sashayed up the front walk. The way she moved. Smelled. Looked. He was ready to take her then and there. But he couldn't. All he could do was watch and wait.

Soon. Very soon she would be his.

Petite yet strong, her body was the picture of feminine perfection. Curvy and compact. Full breasts. Wide hips. Shapely legs. He couldn't wait to feel her satin skin, sweat-slicked and sweet-scented, glide against his. To hear her moan in ecstasy. To taste her.

Raw, burning hunger seared his insides when her scent, carried on a gust, teased his nostrils. As she stepped onto her front porch, she lifted a hand and pulled the clip out of her hair, letting the golden-brown tresses fall in a moonlit cascade of lilac and woman-scented glory. Did she have any idea how seductive she was? How her every movement stirred his lust? She would. Soon. Very soon. He forced himself to leave, to search out a willing female for one more night. Tonight, he hunted for mere sustenance.

Tomorrow, he would have rapture.

* * * * *

After nearly five hundred years of taking certain things for granted, Dayne Garrott knew time had run out.

So much to do. So little time to do it.

Skydiving. Sun-worshipping on the beaches of Maui. Climbing to the peak of Mt. Everest...serving up a cold but well-deserved dish of revenge to his enemies.

Granted, he'd never be able to do most of those things since, being a vampire, he had a slight issue with being in direct sunlight for more than a half-hour. But he still wasn't ready to call it quits and take a permanent dirt nap, if only for the vengeance thing.

But damn if the fates hadn't just thrown a friggin' mountain in his way. Or rather Marek Setara's older brother, who happened to be King of Sons of the Twilight.

He crossed his arms over his chest and glanced at Marek, the former target of his quest for revenge. His mortal enemy. They'd met at an underground—*literally*—vampire hangout called Carpe Nocturne over a year ago. He'd spent the last twelve months preparing to kill Marek. He was ready. His plan had been put into action.

And just like that, he'd been thrown back to square one. By royal effing decree he would join with his enemy in a blood-bond before the new moon. A vampire couldn't kill another vampire if they shared a blood-bond.

Although he hadn't yet completed the binding, he had no choice. At least not if he didn't want to die.

"I have a few ideas where to go." Still in bed, Marek stretched, his thickly muscled arms flexing, and gave Dayne a lazy smile. "I'm so tired. Wish we could wait one more day."

"Yeah. Me too." Dayne was so lethargic he felt like his body weighed at least a hundred times more than it did. The signs were all there. Second death was imminent if they didn't start the binding within the next few hours. "But if we put it off another day, we'll both be too weak."

"Yeah." Visibly weary, Marek rolled off the bed and dragged his heavy body to the closet. He pulled out the pre-selected garments, identical to the ones Dayne was wearing. "We only need one human woman. I did some thinking last night and made up a list where to find one fast. Places where there are hundreds of human females." He dressed as Dayne stood in the doorway, waiting.

"Good." Dayne nodded. "But what if we pick one and she won't come with us?"

Marek reached into the closet, gripped a duffle full of supplies and smiled. He lifted a roll of duct tape. "We'll make her." He dropped the tape in the canvas bag emblazoned with a huge white Nike "swoosh" on one side and went back to dressing.

"And what if she refuses to stay?"

"We'll convince her?" Marek shrugged, tying a shoe. "Can't be too hard." Now fully dressed in head-to-toe black, he strode toward Dayne, the black bag in one fist. "If not..."

They both knew the consequences. Neither could say it aloud.

Dayne followed Marek out of the house they were now forced to share, his gaze fixed on his enemy's back, wishing he could simply plunge a stake through the bastard's heart.

It was what he deserved.

This was a major setback but Dayne was determined. His family would have justice. His mother, father, and sister, who'd only been a child when the motherfuckers had slaughtered her. Dayne knew it was him—Marek's brother, then a high-ranking officer in the military and now king—who'd ordered the assassination. He'd been hidden inside a kitchen cabinet, watching the whole thing, too horrified to move. To scream. To forget.

To forgive.

The reigning king at the time had denied Dayne's family the justice they deserved. After all, that would require His Majesty to order the death of his son, and at the time the sole successor to crown. To have his only son put to death, His Majesty risked the crown falling into the hands of a longtime rival. Politics always took precedence over justice.

So it was up to Dayne. His family's death would be avenged.

He would not fail.

* * * * *

Brea Maguire died on Friday the thirteenth.

That was, she died Friday, September thirteenth, 1996, in a white-water rafting accident. Obviously, by some miracle, she'd found her way back from the "other side". Regardless, that day changed her life forever.

The minute she woke up from her three-month-long snooze, she vowed to avoid doing, eating or even thinking about anything dangerous, especially on a Friday the thirteenth.

The day was bad, bad, bad luck.

Take today, for instance. The neighbor's backfiring Buick rudely interrupted the best dream of her life. Unfortunately, she was supposed to wake up two hours earlier to attend a vitally important meeting with her new boss. Not the best way to begin a new job, especially a new job that had taken her six months to find.

That was just the start of things. She discovered her "fat days" pair of black all-purpose pants had mysteriously acquired a hole in the ass while at the drycleaners. Her Mr. Coffee was spitting gnarly, foul-smelling gook instead of *Good-to-the-Last-Drop* Maxwell House Vanilla. And her cat Princess had kindly deposited a slimy hairball on her last run-free pair of nylons.

If Brea had been given any choice in the matter, she'd have opted to stay home and ride this one out in the relative safety of her Queen Serta. It wasn't like she hadn't done it before. She'd have Princess, an assortment of safe comfort foods and the Discovery Channel for company. Twenty-four hours would go by in no time.

But thanks to a threatening message from her angry employer, Uncle Andy—who wasn't really a blood relative but rather a lifelong friend of her deceased father's—she had no choice. She'd have to risk life and limb to brave the big, bad, dangerous world...or rather, dangerous metropolitan Detroit.

He had no idea what he was asking.

Uncle Andy didn't believe in superstitions. He regularly tempted fate by not just walking but dancing under ladders...while holding black cats. He also broke mirrors just for kicks. Spilled salt. The list went on. Yet the man had the most sickening good luck of any human being on the planet.

Life was so unfair.

After a hair-raising drive down I-275 in her black Shelby Cobra, and a blustery lecture from her Uncle Andy, which thankfully quickly segued into a brief discussion of her first case, Brea was free to go about her business. Since the past couple of hours had gone relatively okay, she opted to make a pit stop at the mall to pick up a few essentials.

Tomorrow, she'd depart for her first trip as a private investigator, a quick trip to Nebraska to follow up a lead. She had to be prepared. Uncle Andy had told her a good PI knew how to become invisible, to blend into her surroundings. With her vintage mink-trimmed suit, he'd pointed out, that wasn't going to happen. In New York, maybe. But probably not in a place like Broken Bow.

She had to agree. Didn't hurt that he'd given her a company credit card and carte blanche to buy whatever she needed.

A girl simply could not launch a new career as one of Charlie's-lost-Angels without the proper accoutrements. There was the always-fashionable black trench coat. The classic fedora. Oh and the Audrey Hepburn sunglasses. Besides, a to-die-for pair of Kate Spades was on sale at Bloomies. She simply had to have them. She hadn't spent a penny on shoes since she'd been fired from her last job.

Uncle Andy's Visa card burning a hole in her pocket, she pulled up to the mall's valet station, shifted her car into park and stepped out, glaring at the pimply teenager eyeballing her '66 Cobra with gape-mouthed awe.

"If there's a scratch on my daddy's baby when I get back, I'll have your ass. He's the City of Detroit's prosecuting attorney," she lied with a cheery smile as she stepped around the front of the car. She leaned closer and added, "If you happen to have any...unfortunate secrets...you'll want to be extra careful."

The kid visibly gulped then gently lowered himself into the driver's seat, reluctantly wrapped his fingers around the steering wheel and pulled the door shut.

She gave him an approving nod then headed inside.

At least she'd be relatively safe at this mall. In the heart of the 'burbs, and at the center of one of Michigan's highest-rent districts, its high-end designer stores didn't attract the troublemaking kind of clientele some of the other malls did. It was a fair gamble for a Friday the thirteenth.

Or so she thought. About twenty seconds later, she knew she'd made a terrible mistake.

This enormous man dressed head-to-toe in black jumped out from a narrow corridor between the Cracker Barrel and The Body Shop, wrapped an iron fist around her wrist and yanked her off her feet. Before she was able to belt out a scream for help, he had a palm pressed tightly over her mouth and an arm snaked around her waist.

It took one, two, three heartbeats before she fully realized what was happening. And by then it was too late to do anything to stop it. She tried to fight herself free but the guy was so incredibly strong his grip didn't shake loose. Not even a smidge. Nor did he let go when she kicked his shins hard enough to make the average guy howl like a wounded hound.

Powerless to stop him, and worn out from the struggling that had gotten her nowhere, she concentrated on catching her breath as he hauled her through an emergency exit. Hopefully, she'd have one last chance to get away when he put her in his car/truck/whatever.

One of those plain white delivery vans pulled up to the curb, the kind you see in the movies carting around bad guys or hauling stolen automobile parts or illegal Uzis. The tires skidded on wet pavement when the driver punched the breaks, bringing it to an abrupt stop. Another guy, dressed identically to the one holding her hostage, jumped out of the driver's seat and ran to the vehicle's rear doors. He gave her a quick up-and-down look as Kidnapper Number One dragged her to the van.

"She's strong. Secure her extra tight."

She sent Kidnapper Number Two, who was now wrapping duct tape around her wrists, a dose of mean eyes that should've made him question whether trussing her up like a Thanksgiving turkey was such a good idea.

Her hands secured, he worked at her feet while she tried to shout, kick or otherwise cause some kind of scene. This wasn't supposed to happen! Not here in the middle of Birmingham! In broad daylight!

Where the heck was mall security when a girl needed them? Not that an unarmed security guard could've stopped these guys. It looked like they'd planned this carefully, which made her wonder what the heck they were kidnapping her for.

Was it somehow related to her case? Or were they hoping for a ransom? If so, they were in for a surprise.

Once they had her legs bound at the ankles and knees, and her mouth taped shut, they tossed her into the van's lumpy, cold cargo area—they couldn't at least throw a mattress or something on the sheet metal floor?—slammed the doors and headed for the driver's compartment.

The van sped off.

Her heart sank.

A steel grid gate separated the cargo section from the driver's. Not soundproof, so she was able to overhear bits and pieces of their conversation as she bounced around the back of the van.

"...she should do..."

"...I told you she was...a good choice..."

"...hope she doesn't have any..."

Hardly any decent clues in those little snippets. She tried to heave a weary sigh but the duct tape over her mouth made it impossible. A sigh through the nose was simply not as satisfying.

They drove and drove and drove...and drove some more. She bounced and slid and bounced. And bounced some more.

Didn't they have shocks on this heap? And where were they taking her, Timbuktu?

After at least a couple hours—or so she guessed—the vehicle's lulling motion stopped. The doors opened, revealing inky blackness outside.

It was nighttime? Wow. She'd headed to the mall at about two. It got dark around six at this time of year. That meant she'd been riding in the back of that delivery van for as many as...four hours? Four hours!

That was so not right! These guys were animals, making a girl ride on that cold, hard metal for that long. Not stopping to get her something to eat. Or letting her use the bathroom. Neanderthals!

Outside, they bent forward, grabbed her by the feet and dragged her toward the gaping set of rear doors. She tried to fight but it was no use. The tape was doing its job.

As she slid forward, she realized the darkness was not because of a lack of sunlight but because they were parked inside an unlit garage. A garage attached to a home. And a garage that was empty, save the white van.

So maybe it wasn't six o'clock? And maybe they hadn't made her lie in the back of that van for four hours. Maybe they hadn't starved her. Or made her risk a bladder infection.

That didn't raise her opinion of them much. They were still kidnappers, though perhaps not quite as inhumane.

They cradled her body between their bulky frames as they carried her through the doorway that bridged the house and the attached garage. She was surprised by how gentle they were as they worked their way through the narrow kitchen, wove around the dining room table, shuffled between a couch and coffee table in the living room and clomped up a set of narrow steps. They even lowered her onto the massive king-sized, four-poster bed with unexpected care.

Obviously, they didn't want to hurt her. At least not yet.

What did they want from her?

Her stomach growled loudly and two sets of dark-as-night eyes settled on her body in the general vicinity of the sound. One of them scrunched up his face in disgust.

Well, what did he expect? Starve a girl, and he's going to hear some unpleasant noises. She was tempted to let him hear a couple more—from a different part of her anatomy.

"What's that?" the one with the scrunched-up face murmured.

"She needs to feed."

Disgust gave way to wide-eyed shock. "Oh no."

"They have to feed at least three times a day. I read about it in the Book of Secrets."

What was all this talk of "feeding"? As if she was a baby…or the whole idea of eating was foreign to them. And what was with the Great Big Book of Secrets? Was it a rule book of some kind? Were they frat boys playing some kind of game?

Or aliens? She'd read about alien abductions in *The Globe*.

She gave them a closer look, just to make sure.

No weird, buggy eyes or extra appendages. No scales, antennae or other glaring signs. And so far they weren't threatening to shove a metal probe up her ass.

She'd give them this though—they were larger than any of the human males she'd personally known. Huge. As near as she could tell, around seven feet tall. Granted, guys that size were probably a dime a dozen in the NBA.

They were fairly solidly built too. Wide shoulders. Broad chests. Thick arms and narrow waists. The kind of physique a guy got by spending all his free time pumping iron in Gold's Gym.

She took another good, long look. Chest to toe then back up, toe to chest. Nope, nothing alien about them. She had to admit, they had drool-worthy bods for a couple of cold-hearted, non-alien kidnappers.

She let her gaze wander higher, to the first kidnapper's face.

Wow.

Since she'd spent the bulk of their intimate together-time in the mall facing away from Kidnapper Number One, and she'd been too busy trying to bust loose when he'd put her in the van, she hadn't noticed how gorgeous he was.

Chiseled features that were masculine but not severe. Dark mocha skin—obviously he had a membership to a tanning salon—and black wavy hair that skimmed the collar of his snug black t-shirt and fell in seductive layers around his face.

She stole a glance at the other guy. His features were equally breathtaking, although his hair was more a golden-brown than inky black.

Two gorgeous human men.

Had she been kidnapped by a couple of Chippendales?

Why? Was this some insane person's idea of a gift...or a joke?

Uncle Andy?

A distinct possibility. He had a weird sense of humor, had played dozens of pranks on her father. Exploding salt shakers and fake cops. If she believed the stories, there'd been countless, half of them taking place when they'd roomed together in college. Her father had always warned her not to trust Uncle Andy.

Hmmm. Uncle Andy gave her the credit card, knowing she'd head straight for the mall. Yes, this made sense.

Chippendale Number One—yes, a new moniker was in order now that she knew the truth—reached forward and gingerly picked at the tape covering her mouth. The glue held, which made the process pretty damn painful. But on the bright side, she wasn't going to need an upper-lip wax for the next several decades. Or a chemical peel. Damn stuff took off a few layers of skin too.

On the bad side, she'd need some antibiotics pronto. And some painkillers.

"Ow! Owwwwww!" she said, once her mouth was finally uncovered. "That was so not nice, putting tape on my mouth."

Chippendale Number One removed the inch or so of tape still stuck to her cheek with a quick jerk, balled it up and lobbed it across the room. "It was necessary."

"Says you. I say this whole kidnapping thing was totally unnecessary. What's wrong with you two? Who doesn't know kidnapping's illegal? Duh." She paused mid-rant to stretch her facial muscles. Thanks to the remains of adhesive, her skin felt funny when she talked. "So prank's over. Why don't you go ahead and get rid of the rest of the tape and we can talk about how you're going to take me home?"

The Chippendales looked at each other and then turned their collective gazes at her.

"We can't let you go yet," Chippendale Number Two said, not sounding the least bit apologetic.

Urgh! Another fucked-up Friday the thirteenth!

23

Should have gone home. She should've known something was up when he'd given her that credit card. "Uh, why would that be?" she challenged.

"Because we can't," Chippendale Number One answered evasively.

Based on that ambiguous answer, she decided he must be an attorney by day and moonlight as a dancer. Probably had some hefty law school loan payments to make.

"I see a career in politics for you." Fuming, she turned her meanest glare on the quieter Chippendale standing behind him, the expression she reserved for anyone who dared to cut in front of her at the grocery store. Or Starbucks. "This joke's gone too far. You do know that kidnapping is a federal crime? I think it's even punishable by death."

Chippendale Number Two burst into a belly-busting guffaw.

What the heck was so funny? "I will press charges."

Chippendale Number One joined the doubled-over Number Two, laughing his ass off as well.

"You laugh now but I promise you'll be sorry."

Yeah, yeah, she knew that was tough talk coming from a chick who at the moment couldn't scratch her nose. But she had to get her point across. This was an issue of personal liberty. And more importantly, it was an issue of safety. Trussed up like a pig headed for slaughter, she was defenseless. What if there was a fire? Or tornado? Or tidal wave?

With her luck on Friday the thirteenth, any or all of those were possible, regardless of the fact that they were currently a bazillion miles from the ocean and the forecast didn't even include a drizzle of rain.

"You won't get away with this."

After enduring several more minutes of their snorting and chuckling like Beavis and Butthead, it became clear the Chippendales were not going to take her threats seriously. Too bad for them. She pulled out her ace, "My daddy's the prosecuting attorney for Detroit."

More annoying laughter.

Cads!

Jerks!

Egotistical assholes.

There was one surefire way to take these guys down a notch. "I bet you stuff your shorts. And your weenie is limp because of all the 'roids you shoot into those over-inflated muscles of yours."

The laughter ceased. The room fell into an eerie silence. And two egotistical assholes shot death daggers at her with their eyes.

Maybe that hadn't been such a good idea.

She'd wanted to annoy them, to let them know she wasn't playing along with the joke, assuming that was what was going on. But more than anything, she needed to show them she wasn't scared. Just in case this was for real.

She'd taken self-defense. Three times. All three teachers had told her that it was important to not show fear.

Chippendale Number One ripped his t-shirt off with the muscle-bunching yumminess that only male strippers possessed. "She called our muscles overinflated."

Awwww. She'd wounded his fragile ego. Poor baby. Not!

"Should we show her what our muscles are capable of?" Number One grumbled.

She heaved the first satisfyingly heavy sigh she'd enjoyed in quite some time. "Listen, I really don't get what's going on here. Whether you're trying to charm me...or whether Uncle Andy hired you as a joke...or whether a recording of this whole insane thing is headed to Hollywood for some reality television show. But I'm not game. So kindly quit with the flexing," she said and nodded toward Chippendale Number One, shirtless and tensing his pecs and abs. The sight of

25

bulging, rippling muscles under smooth, tan skin was uber distracting. She set her face in a scowl. "If you're trying to scare me, it's not working. Nor are you impressing me."

Number One leaned toward Number Two. "I thought these females were supposed to fall all over us when we did this?"

Number Two shrugged. "First time for me too."

Number One's shoulders sagged. "Great."

"Oh, isn't this fun? I've been kidnapped by two clueless first-timers. Swell. Peachy. Just my luck. Let me go."

"Can't."

"Must," she shot back.

Number Two shook his head. "Must not."

This was going nowhere. And as long as that was the case, neither was she—going anywhere, that was. Time for a new tactic.

Think. Think... "I have to pee."

Number Two groaned.

Number One grimaced.

"Come on, guys. Do you know what holding it does to a woman? Ever pissed hydrochloric acid? It's no fun, let me tell you."

Number Two blanched. "Maybe we should take this one back?"

"Oh yes! That's a great idea. Take me back to the mall. I have personal issues you don't want to know about. Infections, personality disorders—"

Number One glared at her with those wicked-cool dark eyes. "No. There's no time. She'll have to do."

Damn. "Speaking of haves. I have to pee."

"Yes, fine." Looking like she'd asked him to get his testicles waxed, Number One started unwrapping the tape from her wrists.

Number Two went to work on her legs.

The second she was free, she scooted off the bed and made a break for the exit.

They didn't even attempt to stop her.

She learned why in exactly three seconds.

The effing door was locked! Bastards. She turned around. "Unlock. Now."

"The bathroom's that way," Number Two said from behind her.

She yelped in surprise. How the heck had he crossed the room without her seeing him? She looked at him then at the spot where he'd been standing less than a second ago. And then back at him again.

He smiled like there was nothing weird about a guy magically transporting across a room. "There. Bathroom." He pointed at a second door, on the other side of the room.

"How'd you do that?"

He looked genuinely confused. "Do what?"

Bold-faced liar! "You're messing with me. Funny. Ha. Ha. I'd rather use this door."

Number One's mouth pulled into a lopsided grin, flashing a dimple. He crossed his arms over his yummy chest. "Sorry. Can't let you. At least not yet."

"Can I ask why? Why are you kidnapping me? Of all people? If Uncle Andy paid you, what'll it take to hire you to go kidnap him instead?"

"Who's Uncle Andy?" Number Two asked.

Uh-oh. "Andy O'Byrne?"

Two Chippendales shook their heads.

Oh shit. Were they lying? "I have no bank account to speak of. No rich relatives. You're not going to get a penny in ransom if that's what you're after."

Number One slanted one ebony eyebrow. "It's not. Didn't you have an urgent matter to take care of?"

"Is this about my case then? Are you trying to stop me from solving it?"

"What case would that be?" Number Two asked as he muscled her toward the bathroom.

"So that's it! You're going to hold me here until the Sacred Triad can be sold on the black market."

"The Sacred Triad? The sculpture?" Number One said, magically appearing at her side.

Once again, she screeched in surprise. How the heck did these guys do that trick? Magical Chippendale kidnappers? "Who hired you?"

"No one," Number One answered. "Why are you looking for the Sacred Triad?"

"Duh. You know why. Because it's my job."

An extremely unsettling smile crept across Number One's face. It did all kinds of things to her insides, like simultaneously chilling and searing them. He crossed his thick arms over his chest.

"I have a proposition for you," Number Two offered.

"A proposition involving letting me go?"

"Yes."

"I'm all ears."

"You stay here with us for seven nights and...serve us...and we'll give you a clue each night. By the seventh, you'll know exactly where the stolen sculpture is."

Was this for real? She narrowed her eyes and gave him an intimidating stare. "You're not playing me?"

"No, not at all."

Sounded sincere.

Wow, this was a weird turn of events. But it did raise a few compelling questions. The first being, "Why help me if you kidnapped me to stop me from finding the statue in the first place?" she asked, trying to sort it out. Nothing about this made any sense.

"We didn't kidnap you to stop you."

"Then why did you kidnap me?"

"Because we need you," Number One said.

She recalled Number Two's so-called proposition. What was the word he'd used? Serve? "What exactly do you need me to do over the next seven nights? I'll warn you, I don't like surprises. So you'd better give it to me straight."

Was she really thinking of going along with these guys?

Was she insane?

Then again, did she have any other choice? Other than perhaps lock herself in the bathroom until she starved to death?

Even if she were to escape, every day's delay meant the trail for the stolen artifact would grow colder. Once it was sold on the black market, she knew the chances of finding it were nil.

"Serve us," Number Two stated.

"Serve you what? Food? 'Cause I have to tell you, I'm not the best waitress in the world. In fact, I'm a really, really bad one. My last boss would testify to that. But if that's what you want, a personal waitress for a week, I might be willing —"

"Waitress?" Number One said, a slow smile drawing his lips back. "No, that's not exactly what we had in mind."

His smile widened, revealing a set of chompers straight out of *Van Helsing*.

Gasping, she spun around and ran smack dab into Number Two, also sporting a set of fangs that made her blood run cold. She did a quick one-eighty and smashed into Number One. She stumbled back a step.

"So what do you say?" Number One said, his fists wrapped around her upper arms, the glint in his eyes making her feel small and defenseless. "Serve us and you'll solve your case."

"Oh my God," she mumbled, too terrified to put together a more appropriate response.

"We promise you'll enjoy every minute," Number Two said, pressing against her back.

"Wake up!" she yelled, wincing as Number Two pulled her hair to one side. "This is just a dream—correction, a nightmare. Wake up! I-I've just watched too many *Buffy* reruns. They've come back to bite me—"

"We thought you'd never ask!" Evidently taking her last words as an invitation, Number Two spun her around, dragged her body against his, lowered his mouth to her neck...and bit.

White-hot pain blasted through her body like a nuke exploding in her head.

Oh my God, this is one nightmare I'm not going to wake up from. The worst Friday the thirteenth ever.

The most unexpected sensation followed the breath-stealing pain—sexual hunger. Raw, unbridled lust. It sizzled and sparked like currents of electricity, charging up and down Brea's limbs and swirling between her legs like a gathering summer storm.

Her thoughts and fears raced from her mind, swept away by a tsunami of need so powerful there was nothing she could do to stop it.

Questions vanished. Only one thought remained.

Correction. This is the best Friday the thirteenth ever!

Chapter Two

ଽ

Hot, sweet blood streamed down Marek's throat, sending pulsing waves of raw energy through his tired body and urgent need to his groin. He jerked the woman closer, eager to take his fill of both her blood and her body. Yet no matter how firmly her softening form molded to his, and no matter how eagerly he drank, he could not get his fill of either.

More!

He drew in another mouthful of her blood. The unfamiliar sound of his heartbeat, slow and wavering but growing steadier, thumped in his ears. Strength returned to his arms and legs. The overwhelming weariness that had nearly overtaken him slowly lifted.

More!

He pulled in a third mouthful of energizing blood. She whimpered, lifted her arms and draped them over his shoulders. Her legs straddled one of his and her hips ground into his thigh as his heat burned into her.

"Ohhh..." she said on a sigh.

More, more, more!

Dayne's growl of protest stopped him from taking what his body demanded. He would kill her if he didn't stop now. They had seven nights to get their fill. Although he craved complete and immediate satisfaction, he knew receiving it would come at a great price. To all three of them.

Meeting Dayne's gaze, Marek gently pushed the flushed, dazed woman toward him, encouraging Dayne to take what he needed. She cried out, visibly disappointed by his apparent rejection. But when Dayne eased her around, swept her hair aside and sank his fangs into her porcelain skin, her expression turned wanton once more.

Agonizing lust simmered in his veins as he watched his new blood-mate drink. The expression in Dayne's eyes turned fierce, erotic, as he pulled in a second mouthful of the woman's blood, stirring Marek's lust to even more painful heights.

Driven by his need, he ripped the back of the woman's shirt down the center, revealing a stripe of silky skin marred by an ugly black strap.

He groaned.

The woman whispered, "Oh yessss…"

He unfastened her bra and gently lowered her arms, pressing his length against her back. His hips rocked as he removed her clothing from her upper body, driven by a different kind of hunger surging through his system. A sexual hunger.

Dayne lifted his head, releasing her neck. The bloodstained mark on her skin vanished instantly. His tongue swept over his lips, an invitation.

It was done. Dayne was now bound to him, and he to Dayne. For the first time in his life, he was overcome by sexual hunger for another man.

Driven by instinct, Marek hooked a hand behind Dayne's head and with the woman's writhing body between them, claimed his mouth. Their tongues battled, stabbing, stroking while the woman's soft derriere pillowed his cock and balls, the scent of fresh spring air and delicate flowers teased his nostrils and her feminine whimpers and sighs filled his ears.

The agony and ecstasy.

Senses that had slowly faded over the centuries were suddenly painfully sharp, a contrast so severe it nearly drove him mad. He could hear the gusting of air as she exhaled. Could smell the musk of her need. Could feel the cool silk of Dayne's hair twining around his fingers.

He broke the kiss, instead turning his attention to the woman who'd given him so much. By the simple act of being there, submitting to their needs, she'd given both of them a chance at another five hundred years of life. She would get her reward.

The clue she wanted. The dominant lovers she craved. And the release she demanded.

* * * * *

Oh my God! They're kissing each other? They're bi? That is so hot.

Brea's body was burning up. She was the meat in a Chippendale sandwich and God help her, she was loving it! Smooshed between two hot, impossibly sexy bodies, her shirt gone, her bared nipples teased to aching erection by the delicious friction against Number One's shirt. Two sets of hands were exploring each other then her body, easing her out of the rest of her clothes, smoothing up her arms and down her sides. Two mouths were tickling her neck and shoulders with teasing kisses and soft nips.

Two voices murmured seductive promises.

Who would have thought it was possible? To be so lost? To experience such overwhelming need?

Before she fully realized it, she was unclothed and so were they.

Two perfect bodies. Toned, tanned and both possessing a latent power that stole the oxygen from her lungs.

Their expressions mirrored each other's, both dark with desire. It was their looks, the heat she saw simmering in their eyes that drove her backward, until the back of her legs struck what she quickly realized was the bed.

That was one enormous adult playground.

Number One caught her hands in his fist and lifted her arms over her head. He stepped closer until his huge frame completely invaded her personal space, both driving her crazy with desire and making her feel slightly uncomfortable at the same time.

It was a bizarrely thrilling combination—discomfort and desire.

"I can smell your arousal," he murmured, his eyes searing her skin as his gaze swept over her face. "The fear intensifies your reaction."

Did it ever!

Was that why she wasn't screaming for her life? Was that why she wasn't kicking him in the gonads or at least begging him to stop? She'd never had sex with a complete stranger, let alone two. She didn't even know their names.

God, how bad was that?

"You have been secretly yearning for this for a long time." He pulled slightly, forcing her hands higher in the air. Her biceps sandwiched her head, pressing against her ears and muffling sounds, his voice. Her racing heartbeat pounded in her head. "You want a man to take control in the bedroom."

She did. She really, really did.

No. This was so wrong! Control? Absolutely not. Sleeping with men she didn't know. Kidnappers. Bad men. They were bad.

But they looked soooooo good. And felt soooo amazing.

He gathered both of her wrists into one fist and twisted, forcing her to turn her body to the side, where Number Two was kneeling.

"Spread your legs," Number Two demanded.

No doubt what would happen next. A gush of heat pulsed to her core as she met his gaze. A split second later, a spike of guilt stabbed her insides. She was crazy if she did anything with these guys. A shameless hussy. She hadn't been raised like this—to fuck the first kidnapping Chippendale she stumbled upon...or first pair of kidnapping Chippendales.

34

Time to reclaim some of her scruples, to recover her brain out of the thick fog that had somehow enveloped it.

How had she gotten to this point anyway?

One minute she'd been talking about a job as a personal waitress...or something like that. And then what?

She looked down at her clothes, lying in a heap on the floor. How'd her shirt get ripped? Why couldn't she remember? Was there anything to remember? Of course there was.

Her neck tingled, burned like she'd scratched it. After Number One released her wrists, she pressed her fingertips to the sore spot, the chill easing the pain.

As she struggled to gather her thoughts, she lifted her chin, an intentional show of defiance. "No."

Number One's formerly charming smile turned wicked and a little threatening, utterly sexy. "But you've given us so much. Don't you wish to receive your reward?"

"Given you what?" Why did she feel like she'd missed something important? Like she'd stepped out of a movie theater to buy some Raisinets, seconds before the Big Murder Scene and returned seconds after it was over?

"We'd like to show our gratitude," Number Two said, his eyes telling her exactly how he intended to say "thank you".

"Gratitude for what?"

Number One ran one hand down her arm and along her side. She flinched when his fingertips brushed the side of her breast. "Serving us. You promised. Remember?"

"Ummmm...not sure." She could remember what had occurred after she'd backed into the bed clearly enough. But before that...she remembered the van ride. Being carried into the bedroom. And she recalled trying to escape. Had something else happened between then and now?

How had her clothes gotten torn?

Her thoughts were cloudy, like she'd just woken from anesthesia. She glanced at the clock. The last time she'd looked it had been around four-thirty. It was after five now. A half hour had passed? She could swear they'd only been here a few minutes.

Oh. My. God. Had they drugged her? That had to be it.

Did they rape her? Her pussy, wet and ready, clenched around aching emptiness. No, she was pretty positive there'd been no penetration. At least not yet.

What was going on? She jerked sideways, tripping over Number Two's knee.

Space. She needed space. She needed to think. To try to sort through the scrambled pieces of the puzzle she wasn't quite able to see clearly. "Stop it! What's happening? What'd you do to me?"

Before she could blink, she was flat on her back, on the floor, Number Two on top of her. His hips were resting between her legs, his rigid cock grinding against her clit.

"Why are you fighting us?" Number Two asked, his mouth so close to hers his breath gusted her lips with sweet, warm air. "We know you want us."

"I-It's wrong," she stuttered.

"What's wrong?" Number Two shifted his hips, making that rigid erection of his rub her pussy in a slow, erotic rhythm. "Is this wrong?"

"Uh." *No.* "Yes." Her eyelids fell closed, shutting out the sight of the gorgeous man on top of her. She'd never had a guy who looked that good want her. Was he blind? She was plain old Brea. Nothing special to look at. Nothing special to talk to. Nothing special, period. "I don't even know your names," she heard herself say.

"I'm Marek," Number Two whispered in her ear. "And that's Dayne."

She shivered when his breath tickled her ear. "Marek. Dayne. Unusual names." She felt someone's hands on her ankles, pushing them up, forcing her knees to bend. Marek angled his hips down until the head of his cock was prodding at her slit.

They were going to rape her.

Was it technically rape if she secretly, kind of — correction, *really, really* — wanted it?

"Wait!" She forced her eyelids open and shoved his chest. "Ohhhh!" His cock inched inside her, and she screeched. A ripple of lust pulsed through her body. "Noooo...ooooohhhh! Yes!"

What was she saying?

"Ohmygod. Wait!" She tried to scoot up, to keep him from fully penetrating her, but he thrust his hips, seating himself to the root.

Her blood turned to liquid fire. Wild, wicked lust raged through her body, flaring along her nerve endings like TNT blasts. Her senses amplified, the sounds of her own breathing and Marek's guttural moan. His scent burned her nostrils, sweet and tangy and intoxicating. His skin, hot and smooth, gliding against hers.

For the first time in almost ten years, she felt fully alive.

"Ooooohhh." She rocked her hips back then forward, clenching her inner muscles and taking him deeper. Her fingertips clawed at his chest. Her heavy eyelids fell, closing her in a black world of aching, powerful need and breath-stealing sensations.

"Yes. Accept what's yours," Marek murmured. He slowly withdrew then slammed deep inside again.

She cried out in gratitude and agony. It was beyond words. Beyond understanding, the sensations he stirred. The sexy slap of skin striking skin as he fucked her. The erotic feeling of his heavy balls bouncing against her ass.

Someone was holding her knees, pulling them out and back. She was losing control — no, relinquishing control. It was a willful surrender.

Yes, take me! Take control. Deeper! Harder!

For once in her life, she had no choice. She could no more resist following her impulses than she could resist sucking in her next breath. The nagging voice in her head screamed dire warnings. But for the first time in nine years, she tuned it out.

The last nuggets of her guilt squashed like ants trapped under an elephant's foot, she submitted fully, allowing the sensations battering her body to carry her away. Marek sat back, his body perpendicular to hers, lifting her hips to line up with his groin. The position both intensified his intimate strokes against the super-sensitive upper wall of her vagina and left her entire upper body exposed to both Marek and Dayne. Men's hands explored her breasts, her stomach, her face. One mouth teased a nipple until she was almost crazy with need. Another plundered her mouth. A tongue thrust in and out, tasting and taking and mimicking the movements of Marek's cock gliding in and out of her slick pussy. Her juices ran between her ass cheeks, scenting the air musky sweet.

Dayne teased her clit, drawing slow circles, round and round with a finger. Quivering with pent-up tension, she moaned her answer, "Yesssssss…" and shuddered. The combination of Marek's thrusts, the strokes to her clit, launched her toward a powerful climax. Her body shook as spasms pulsed through her muscles. She reached up, wrapped her arms around Marek's neck and clung to him. Her breasts flattened against his sweat-slicked chest. Strong arms circled her, pulling her into a tight embrace. Deep, masculine moans filled her ears. He log-rolled, taking her place on the floor and pulling her on top of him.

Thanks to her change in position, Marek's thrusts deepened, lengthening the pleasure of her climax. Sensing he teetered on the brink of release as well, she angled her body up and rocked her hips back and forth, riding him hard and fast. She felt the muscles of his thighs trembling, his shoulders quaking. A second male body, Dayne's, crushed against her from behind. His mouth grazed the back of her neck, birthing a coat of gooseflesh over her upper body. His hands slid around her sides and flattened against her breasts. He pinched her nipples hard. The bite of pain mingled with the ecstasy of Marek's intimate strokes, bringing her to a swift second climax.

Riding the waves of bliss as Marek growled his release, she tossed her head back onto Dayne's shoulder. "Oh, yes!" She felt Marek's hot cum shooting inside her, welcomed it with rough, desperate, grinding motions that forced him deep inside her.

Dayne released her nipples. The pain was gone instantly. The pleasure took longer to fade, thankfully. She flopped forward, buried her head in the crook of Marek's neck and relaxed, soothed by the warmth of two hard male bodies and deep, rumbly voices cooing promises of more pleasure for the next six nights.

When she tired of being in the same position, her muscles screaming in protest, legs aching to be stretched out, she started to squirm. Marek's now limp cock slipped out. He grumbled something she didn't quite comprehend.

Dayne helped her stand.

Her legs were as wobbly as a newborn foal's. She teetered to the bed and let the Chippendales tuck her in.

Smooth, cool cotton sheets. Pillows that felt like clouds. And covers that cocooned her exhausted body in warmth. She knew she was smiling like a goon as she drifted off to sleep but she couldn't help it.

That had been the most amazing, mind-blowing sex ever.

"That's it," Marek said. She felt the mattress sink as he sat beside her. He caressed her cheek. "Sleep now. You need rest. Your clue will be here when you wake." He bent down and gave her a sweet, soft kiss on the cheek.

Despite her determination to stay awake and see the clue, she was asleep before they walked out of the room. The last thing she saw were her two Chippendales looking down upon her, satisfied smiles on their faces, their arms crossed over broad, tanned chests, muscles bulging and bunching and flexing.

Now that was a dream!

Chapter Three

ဢ

The end is only the beginning.

What kind of clue was that? Sounded more like a bit of worthless wisdom she might find inside a fortune cookie from her fave Chinese restaurant.

Brea wadded the scrap of paper into a ball and lobbed it across the room. She should've known they wouldn't keep their word. Kidnappers? Moral? What had made her think they'd help her solve her case? After all, they'd stooped to breaking the law to bring her here. And damn near raped her too.

Why did they bring her here? She had to believe it was because of her case. That was the only explanation that made any sense.

Although that didn't explain why all that other *stuff* had happened. The naughty but kind-of-yummy stuff. Surely there was no need to seduce her if they were merely trying to keep her from her case until the artifact could be sold on the black market.

Or was there?

God, she felt used. Dirty. Ashamed. Just like she had years ago, when she'd been drunk and asked her best friend Steve to blindfold and tie her up. Just for fun. It had been naughty and exciting. At first. He tickled her. Teased her. Kissed her. But then something happened. The teasing and laughter stopped. He told her only sluts liked that kind of thing. He ripped her clothes. Climbed on top of her. Forced her to do things she hadn't been ready to do yet. Thanks to the bindings, she'd been powerless to stop him.

Her first time. The loss of her virginity.

Even though she'd enjoyed parts of the experience, she'd called it rape because she couldn't accept the alternative. He'd called it something else. The immediate effect—their friendship was over. The long-lasting effect—she had very mixed feelings about herself, her desires and her curiosity about being dominated, seduced, forced.

Her body tended to take a full-steam-ahead attitude. Her brain tended to put on the brakes. Like now. All the tingly, achy parts were pretty happy with what had occurred. But her mind wanted to deny all that *stuff* had even happened. God, what had she done? She grimaced as she scooted to the edge of the enormous mattress and wobbled across the room on rubbery legs to the bathroom.

Her issues with sex aside, this was all so unlike her. Since she'd drowned in that icy river those many years ago, she'd lived a life of caution, determined to never again put herself in harm's way. Yet contrary to what some people said, her fears did not rule her life. Those people just didn't understand. Once you die, nothing's the same.

So why had she acted so out of character earlier? Sex with a stranger? No rubbers? Talk about putting oneself in harm's way. She'd willfully walked into a swirling whirlpool of potential disaster. There's no way she'd do that if she'd been in her right mind.

They had to have drugged her.

She took a quick shower, scouring away the odors of man and sex. The guilt didn't wash away as easily.

A half hour later, she was clean and wet but still full of regret. Wrapped in a fluffy white lilac-scented towel, she checked the clock as she padded barefoot into the bedroom. It was a little after five a.m. The Sacred Triad had been stolen over twenty-four hours ago. Instead of goofing off here, playing hide-the-sausage with a couple of conniving kidnappers, she should've been at home, doing research, preparing for her trip. If she didn't get cracking, the case would be stone cold before she'd even gotten started.

She rummaged in the closet for some clothes that fit her reasonably well—meaning they didn't fall off. She then eased into the cozy wingback chair parked in front of a round table to pull on some socks. As she stuffed her feet into the socks, she eyed the silver tray on the table. A covered plate of something that smelled scrumptious sat in its center. In addition, several glasses of liquids, plus a can of Diet Coke and a small container of milk, crowded the upper edge of the dish, competing for real estate with several covered glass bowls.

She'd been starving hours ago, when her captors had first brought her here. So she was grateful for the food. But evidently her kidnappers expected her to be thirsty as well. Way thirstier than normal. Probably a side effect of the drug they'd given her.

Bastards.

Out of nowhere, a little frisson of desire sizzled up her spine.

Where the heck did that come from? She'd had so few lovers in her life she could count them on two fingers. And not once had they affected her like those two snorting, overmuscled lawbreakers. What was her deal?

She'd paid weekly visits to her counselor, Bob, since she'd gone home from the hospital after the accident. After nine years of picking her brain and scrutinizing her every thought under a microscope, he figured he knew her inside and out. She'd love to hear his take on this. Knowing him, he'd suggest it was some kind of subconscious reaction to the many years she'd played things safe.

Shrinks. Everything was a subconscious something-or-other. Penis envy. Whatever.

Her take—it was simply a moment of insanity brought on by stress. Yeah. That made sense.

Or maybe they'd given her that date-rape drug?

That made even more sense, considering the little jolts of erotic heat buzzing and zapping through her system hours afterward, and despite the guilt and regret and anger.

It had been quite a long time, over twelve hours since they'd kidnapped her from the mall. Twelve hours was a long time for a drug to stay in a girl's system. Still, all in all, out of the three explanations that one made the most sense.

Suddenly aware of how ravenous she was, her mouth flooding with saliva, she lifted the metal lid off the plate. She'd need her strength if she was going to escape.

But what if they'd seasoned the food with Xanax? Or worse? Shoot, she was so hungry she was dizzy. Wouldn't hurt to take a look. Right?

Steak. Baked potato with the works and string beans smothered in butter. Oh, she was in heaven! Who needed eggs and toast for breakfast?

She checked the bowls circling the plate, lifting little paper covers. A tossed salad with ranch dressing. A second bowl cradled steamed veggies. And lastly, a brownie topped with chocolate ice cream, the whole thing smothered in chocolate syrup, sat in a third bowl.

She saw no traces of white powder, sensed no suspicious smells. She dipped the tip of her finger in the sour cream and took a tentative taste.

No funny flavor. Tasted like sour cream.

She picked up her fork and knife and cut a piece of the meat. She chewed slowly, moving the meat around in her mouth, alert to every nuance of the flavor, texture and smell. Again, no red flags.

Giving herself the *All Clear*, she dug in.

So this was how a girl "served" the Chippendales? Sleep, eat like there was no tomorrow and…and play?

If she could convince them to one, give her some useful clues, and two, leave out the sex part, it might be tempting go along with their plan.

Drugs, a subconscious rebellion or simple madness, she wondered what it might be like to spend some more time with her kidnapping Chippendales, Dayne and Marek.

Wouldn't Bob her therapist have some fun delving into her subconscious now?

Savoring a mouthful of vegetables, she shook away those silly thoughts. Time to get serious. She couldn't afford to sit around this place, playing Queen of the Chippendales while some thief was out there trying to sell her statue—or rather, her client's statue.

This was one job she needed to keep for a while.

She scampered across the room, uncrumpled the wadded clue and plopped in her seat. While consuming a steak more tasty and tender than the Outback's very best filet, she pondered the puzzling clue.

The end is only the beginning.

Uhhhhh… Would that imply the converse—the beginning is the end?

Ack. What did it mean?

The end. The beginning.

She was so NOT into riddles. The classic *What's black and white and red all over?* still stumped her.

Naturally, a job solving cases—a.k.a. following clues and riddles—was far from a logical choice for a girl who couldn't solve her way out of a paper bag to save her life. But she was far from stupid. And after having lost her last job, and starving through close to six months of unemployment, she had no other choice. The economy was tight these days. Jobs were hard to come by. Beggars couldn't be choosers.

Heck, she'd even been turned down by all the local fast-food joints. Seemed she was overqualified to nuke frozen hamburgers. Underqualified for the better jobs, like nurse anesthetist or certified public accountant. She was kicking herself now for not listening to her grandmother and going to nursing school.

Which left her back at square one—a job she needed.

And beginnings and endings.

As far as her case went, what was the end? She knew what she'd like to see in the end. The statue would be returned to the owner and everyone would live happily ever after.

What was the beginning? The crime? The statue was stolen from the client's home. Did this clue mean the owner had the statue? Or the owner was the thief? Or...what?

Okay, if her client had stolen the statue, why would he make a police report?

Insurance?

A distinct possibility. It wasn't like that had never been done before. Definitely worth checking out.

But why hire a private investigator if he'd faked the whole thing? He was risking being caught. In her book, hiring a private investigator to solve a crime you'd committed had to be one of the top three stupidest things to do. If she'd stolen her own statue for insurance money, the last thing she'd consider doing is hiring someone to poke around. She'd rather rely on the overburdened police department to fail, and merrily skip to the bank with the insurance check.

That was it. She needed access to a computer. She needed a phone. And she needed to get the heck outta here.

By the time she'd polished off the last bite of the ice cream and brownie sin, she'd determined her hosts owed her another clue and her freedom. They'd give her both, or something unpleasant was going to hit the fan.

* * * * *

Smiling to himself, Marek shut down his laptop and scribbled down the second clue on a piece of paper.

As he'd hoped, Brea would serve more than one vital purpose. His plan, which had involved a call in to her employer and a morning tailing her, waiting for the perfect opportunity—while keeping the truth from Dayne—had gone exactly as he'd hoped. She'd prolong his life, and she'd lead him to the Sacred Triad, thereby helping him save his brother's life.

If only he had some better clues to give her! Whoever was feeding his security team these vague bits of evidence needed to give them something useful. That riddle—found by the relic's last know owner, scrawled on a scrap of paper left in the artifact's storage case—was hardly the smoking gun he was hoping for. But Marek's brother Kaden had been absolutely certain it would somehow lead them to the Triad.

This was going to take some time.

He only hoped the thief didn't know the true power of the Triad.

If he did, all Immortals were in danger, especially the brother he loved more than life itself.

* * * * *

Dayne punched the power button, cutting off the call.

He would have his revenge. A new plan was in motion and by the gods, this one wouldn't fail. His family's death would be avenged. He'd give his own life if necessary.

Fortunately, it didn't look like that would be needed.

He grimaced as he adjusted the front of his pants. No one had warned him about the secondary effects of the blood-bind, the overwhelming erotic hunger. Insatiable and relentless. He could barely think of anything else. Marek. Brea. He wanted them both. Now.

If only he'd known.

What an ironic and annoying twist. The focus of his hatred was now the object of overwhelming desire. For the first time in his life he longed for a man. And not just any man. His enemy. He could do nothing to ease the desperate craving but surrender to it.

He had a new appreciation for Marek's earlier struggles. He'd fed so urgently, he'd nearly killed the woman. And then he'd nearly taken her sexually before she was ready.

No doubt about it—Marek had been powerless to stop himself.

Dayne was about to lose control himself. His erection strained against the confines of his clothes, testing the seams of his athletic boxers and cotton pants. His cock burned. His balls felt like heavy, hard boulders. He needed relief, however he could get it.

He unzipped his pants, shoved his hands down his shorts and made another adjustment. His cock throbbed hot and hard in his hand. Could he ease the burn himself?

He tried. Slow strokes, fast, gentle and hard. Nothing reduced the agonizing need. He needed a tight ass. Marek's hard body. Unfortunately, he'd left. To see that bastard brother of his.

Hmmm. Earlier, as Dayne had fed from Brea, he'd sensed a latent need in her. A suppressed longing. He briefly thought of stripping nude and paying her an impromptu visit but quickly dismissed the thought. Without the benefit of his venom coursing through her veins, making her soft and willing and compliant, she'd resist.

How glorious it would be to introduce Brea to her true nature. To liberate her from the invisible shackles holding her captive to her fears. The vision of her lying on the bed—arms and legs bound, her face flushed, her hair a golden-brown tangled halo around her head—flashed in his mind. He grimaced as another surge of lust ripped through his body.

Fuck it. Marek had received his relief. Dayne had denied himself. He couldn't wait any longer. Didn't matter how she fought. He would have her. He would seduce her. And he would make certain she'd be ready and willing the next time he needed her.

He found her in the bedroom, drowning in a pair of his sweatpants and t-shirt. She looked small and vulnerable, with the exception of the determined glare in her eyes.

Hunger pulsed through him, spiking in painful bursts, the intensity aggravated by the overwhelming impulse to hunt, subdue and conquer racing through his system. His muscles were tight knots. His heart pounding an erratic rhythm. His senses focused and intensifying.

She rushed past him toward the door. But he slammed it closed and locked it seconds before she reached it. He had to admit his speed put him at a distinct advantage. He didn't feel guilty for it.

Although she seemed nonplussed, the fire in her eyes didn't dim. A stubborn temptress, she narrowed them at him in challenge. "I need to go home. Now."

He knew words were useless. He had no interest in arguing with the woman. Body language was much more effective. He intentionally crowded her, forcing her to back away from the door.

"This isn't going to work," she blustered as she shuffled backward. "You aren't going to rape me again."

"I have no reason to rape you." He continued to drive her back toward the bed, like a shepherd guiding a lost lamb.

"Good. Then you'll do the right thing and let me go home." Her backside struck the bed and she flinched.

He stepped forward until the tip of her nose brushed the center of his chest. Her sweet scent, masked somewhat by the cloying scents of soap and shampoo, teased his nostrils. He inhaled, drawing it deeper.

"Helloooo! I'm talking to you." Her lips pursed, she waved a dainty hand in his face.

He resisted the urge to chuckle, knowing it would make it that much harder to break down her barriers. But she was so strong and sassy. Adorable. Sexy. Hot. The perfect package. Marek had chosen well, no doubt better than he would have.

"I heard what you said but I figured you didn't want to hear my answer."

"Yeah, well, doesn't matter. Because I'm not going to fall for your nonsense again. I have a job to do, and I'm going to do it. I have to do it."

"Or?"

"Or I'll have no job. Not that I expect you to care."

It was unfortunate to hear this. It didn't make him feel particularly guilty for what he was about to do, but then again, he'd never been the kind to let something like remorse get in the way of important matters. Nor people.

No scrap of a woman was going to stop him, that was for sure.

He'd make it worth her while in one way, even if it meant she'd be out of a job by the time he was ready to let her go. She'd get another job. He had no idea what was involved in finding a job but already he could see she was an intelligent, capable young woman. How difficult could it be?

She lifted her chin a fraction higher and narrowed her eyes a little more. "Like I said, I don't expect you to care about my problems. I just expect you to let me go."

"It's not that I don't care," he assured, reaching for her hand.

She knocked it away. "Don't fucking touch me." Her bottom lip quivered as she narrowed her watery gaze at him.

"I'm not going to hurt you. I only wish to give you pleasure."

"Then let me go." Her unsteady voice, a low, breathy husk, raked his frayed nerves. "Please. You want to give me pleasure? That would give me heaps of pleasure."

He reached for her hand again. This time she flinched when his fingers twined between hers but she didn't snatch it away. "Did Marek give you the clue he promised?"

"Yes." A deep inhalation pushed her breasts out, the fullness pressing against the white cotton t-shirt she wore. For the briefest of moments as he stared down, he could make out the delicate pattern of her lace bra underneath. She heaved a sigh, sweet-scented and sexy, and licked her lips before answering. "But it makes no sense."

"Is that so?" he asked, his gaze fixed on her ruby lips, plump and tempting. Did she know what she did to him? How much he wanted her right now?

"Yes. So couldn't you at least give me something useful to go on?" After pulling her hand from his, she flattened both palms on his chest and pushed gently. "And back off, would you? Both you guys are way too pushy and it's pissing me off. Haven't you two heard of a girl's personal space bubble? Or are you from Europe? I hear European people aren't as aware of those kinds of things as Americans are."

"Europe? Could be." He didn't budge. He liked the effect his nearness was having on her. Whether she would admit it or not, he knew she was getting aroused. The proof was everywhere. In the air around them. In her eyes. In the slight waver of her voice. And the way her fingertips moved over his chest.

She blinked. "You're not moving."

"No."

She stood mute for a moment, her gaze down around his bellybutton region, or maybe lower. "I'll move then." She started shimmying sideways, wiggling out from the cozy spot he'd backed her into.

He stopped her progress by gripping her hips. Feral hunger racked him, tightening his chest, his throat. "No."

"Oh no. Not again." A blaze flashed in her eyes. She hissed, "Dammit, let me go."

His fingertips digging into the soft swell of her hips, he tipped his head and lowered it to claim the kiss she was offering with those luscious pursed lips.

She struggled for no more than a second before relinquishing with a quiver. His tongue traced the seam of her mouth and she parted them, inviting him to taste, take, plunder.

His body trembled, the need building so quickly he fought to maintain even the slightest trace of the humanity that remained within him. He could easily succumb to the temptation to become the hunter, the beast.

His tongue stroked hers while his hands pulled her flush to him. She softened, molding her curves against his hard angles, and whimpered.

When he broke the kiss, her eyes were glassy, her eyelids droopy, her cheeks rosy.

"I...I..." she stammered. "Not again. Please. Don't rape me. I just want to go home."

"No one has raped you. No one is going to rape you. This way." He gently pushed her back. She resisted, kicking, pounding her little fists against his chest. Her fingers closed around his wrists as he forced her onto her back.

"No," she murmured while scooting away from him. "Don't. Please. Why don't you find Marek? You're gay, bi, whatever. You can take it either way. Just let me go."

"I'm sorry, I can't." He crawled over her on his hands and knees. His mouth watered at the sight of the slender column of her neck. Couldn't he take a small taste? Just a little? What he'd had earlier was no more than a tease. How could he wait even a single hour?

"Oh God." When she reached the opposite edge of the bed, something flashed in her eyes. "Why can't I think? What kind of drugs are you giving me?"

"We haven't drugged you." He had her trapped now, beneath him. He straightened, dropping his lower body on top of hers and pinning her down with his weight.

"You have to be." Her lips rounded into a delicate O.

"No, no drugs. We would poison ourselves if we did something that foolish." Bending his elbows, he lowered his upper body until his chest hovered within a fraction of an inch from her breasts and his mouth almost touched hers. "It's the blood-bind. You can't resist and neither can I."

"Blood-bind?" she whispered. "I don't understand."

"No need to understand. Just accept it. That's all we can do." He kissed her again, the intimate dance of their tongues unleashing the pent-up desire coursing through his body. His hips rocked back and forth, rubbing the length of his erection against her legs. His hands twisted, freeing his wrists from her grip. While his tongue stroked and thrust her into willful surrender, his hands caught hers and forced them out to the sides.

He could feel her relinquishing control, her resistance fading away. Her quivering submission stoked the blaze raging within him. She moaned into their joined mouths.

He broke the kiss, but only long enough to free himself from the confines of his clothes. To his surprise and pleasure, she sat up and eagerly grappled for the garments as he struggled to shed them, clawing, pulling, ripping. The sound of tearing fabric, punctuated by Brea's gasps, filled the room.

Next it was her turn. But he forced himself to undress her slowly, kissing every inch of skin as it was exposed to him. Stomach, breasts, neck, face, then he forced her onto her back and worked his way down, hips, legs, knees, feet.

She lurched and shrieked when he forced her legs apart, hooked his finger inside the crotch of her sodden panties and pulled, tearing the dainty garment away. "Oh God," she murmured over and over. Head rocking from side to side, full lips parted, eyes closed.

"Yes, that's it." He slid a finger into her slick depths, bending it at the knuckle to increase her torment. Meanwhile, his mouth ravaged her breasts, taut nipples, pink and perfect and delightfully sensitive. She arched her back, thrusting them higher in the air.

What a beautiful sight. He'd never seen anything as glorious. Her slick folds were swollen, wet with her fragrant juices, ready for him. Her body was trembling and tight, ready for the release he wasn't prepared to give her yet. He reclaimed his hand from between her legs and sat back, just drinking in the vision before him for a moment, relishing the moment as if it would be his last.

Her eyelashes fluttered as she lifted her eyelids. She made a sweet mewling sound and replaced his hand with her own. Her slender index finger traced slow circles over her clit.

Damn.

He nearly shoved her hand away and buried himself inside her.

No, he wanted this to be for her pleasure. He would get what he needed soon enough. He had to give her what she needed first.

He would help her overcome the uncertainties he'd sensed earlier. It might bring them closer, not just strengthen their physical bond but the emotional one as well. He ached to not only possess her but to know her, to be a part of her.

"That's it, baby," he encouraged. He lifted her knees and pushed them back, until her pussy was wide open to his feasting eyes. "Damn, you're perfect."

"I want you inside me," she pleaded. Her other hand smoothed down her flat stomach, over her trimmed mound to join the other one. She pushed two fingers inside, shivering as she pulled them out.

He ached to lick away the juices coating her delicate fingers, to feast on her sodden pussy until she'd come a dozen times.

But first, he knew what he needed to do. "Trust me."

A deep red flush crept up over her chest to her face. Her legs were trembling, her hips rocking back and forth. She was about to come. She was lost in her pleasure.

He pulled her hands away and forced them back out to her sides. "No. There's not a more beautiful sight than you like this, Brea. Touching yourself for me. But it's too soon."

"I'm dying."

"Trust me."

She snapped her knees together and steadied her swimmy gaze on his face. "You've got to be kidding me."

"No. I don't want this to be like any other time." He eased her knees apart again. Her leg muscles tightened, resisting his efforts to position her. "Like it's been with any other man." His own words surprised him. Not because he was attracted to Brea and wanted to have sex with her. But because he'd allowed himself to become so hardened by the hatred he'd carried for so many years, he was shocked by how much he cared for Brea. How he wanted to reach her, touch her heart.

"But—"

"I can give you more pleasure than you've ever dreamed of. But only if you're brave enough to let go. Fully. Do you have the courage to do that?"

Her eyes widened. Her face went pale. He braced himself for the answer he feared she would give him, instead of the answer he wished for. The one that would set her free from whatever fears were shackling her. He didn't know what they were, but he could sense them.

Chapter Four

ℬ

"Our plan is working, Your Highness. However, I haven't been able to locate the Sacred Triad yet." Marek knelt before his king, bending until his forehead rested on the polished stone floor.

"Rise, Marek," his brother said irritably. "You know I can't stand it when you kneel before me like some peasant. You're blood, for the goddess' sake."

That was true. But respect and humility was the king's due, and it was Marek's obligation — not to mention pleasure — as his younger sibling, to show the man respect who'd raised him from infancy. Not to mention gratitude. Since taking their father's place, His Sovereign had given Marek a great deal over the many years. As he had all his loyal followers.

Which was why the Rebellion made so little sense.

If there was anything Marek had learned, being the second in line to a royal dynasty, it was that politics was rarely about justice, who deserved to serve.

No, more often it was about greed. Deceit. Selfishness.

He'd never admit it but he'd gladly surrender his life for his brother. After all, Kaden had saved his life on more than one occasion.

Besides, he wanted Kaden to stay in power. He would rather face an eternity of suffering than reign as king. But if fate saw to put him in power someday, he would lead his people as his brother had — justly, and with heart.

"If I don't show my respect for you, how can you expect the rest of your people to?" he reminded Kaden, "especially with the Rebellion — "

"Fine. You've done enough groveling at my feet." His brother patted the empty throne beside him, the one that would soon be inhabited by the new queen. Although Kaden had yet to marry, he had chosen a bride. His chosen, Lena, would spend the next moon's cycle preparing for her nuptials as most women did—by emptying her betrothed's pockets. "Come, sit and tell me about your first blood-bind."

Marek slumped into the queen's throne. "It's nothing like I imagined."

His brother's expression soured almost imperceptibly. "How so?"

"No one told me about the hunger."

Kaden's eyes brightened. "Oh yes. The hunger. I'd like to say I'd forgotten about that minor issue but I'd be lying."

"So why not warn a guy? You love me, remember? It would've been nice to know...so I could prepare."

"Yeah, I love you, but that's beside the point." Kaden shrugged. "But really, there's no way to prepare for the hunger. Besides, it's kind of a tradition, let the newly bound mates find out for themselves."

"Some tradition." Marek rose to his feet and raised his fists in mock threat. "Speaking of traditions, are you in the mood for a little sport? I recall a tradition where a certain younger brother kicks his big brother's ass. It's been awhile. Come on, you're itching for a beatin'—"

Voice unsteady with laughter, Kaden caught Marek square in the chest, sending him staggering backward. "Hey, what happened to respect?"

"I'll still respect you after I kick your ass. I owe you a pounding or two...or ten." Marek led with a right jab that hit nothing but air next to Kaden's ear and then followed up with a left hook that almost caught him in the belly.

"For what?" Nearly doubled over with laughter, Kaden shook his head. "Look at you. I haven't seen you like this in centuries. It's the bloodlust talking. Want me to call your mates to you so you can release some of that excess energy before you hurt someone? Like yourself."

Sobering, Marek grumbled, "Don't bother. I'll be heading home soon…well, I will as soon as you tell me why you called me here."

"Just wanted to check on you, see how you're doing."

A lie?

Kaden was never too busy to see Marek when he came to ask for advice, but he never summoned him. "How kind of you. Now tell me the truth."

"Honest. That's it."

So Kaden wasn't going to level with him? That was a first. Kaden had never lied to Marek, at least not that he'd known. Why now?

"Is something wrong?" Marek asked, probing for some clue.

"Nothing that you don't already know about. There's talk the rebels have the Triad. But I think that's a rumor. If they did, why haven't they used it yet?"

"Because they're spreading false rumors for some reason."

"Why?"

"I don't know. Maybe to gain more supporters?" Marek narrowed his eyes, focusing on the center of Kaden's forehead. What was that? A red smudge spoiled his brother's otherwise picture-perfect face. "What happened there? Get some of your lunch on yourself? Really, ever hear of a napkin?"

"What are you talking about?"

Marek motioned at the spot on Kaden's face. "There's something red…" He touched the spot and a bolt of searing heat blazed up his arm. Without thinking, he jerked backward, nearly throwing himself off balance. "What the fuck?"

The color instantly washed out of Kaden's face. "It's begun."

"What's begun?"

Kaden raised a trembling hand to his forehead, his fingertips exploring the red mark, which seemed to be growing before Marek's eyes. "We have our answer now. The rebels aren't spreading false rumors. They have the Triad. Which means we have until the new moon to get it from them."

Only six nights? The heart that had only recently begun beating, thanks to the blood-bond with Brea and Dayne, dropped to Marek's toes. He was staring his worst fear in the eyes. His brother would suffer an agonizing death, just as their father had so many centuries ago. Their only hope, Kaden's only hope—the Triad. "No."

Gone was the laughter. Kaden's voice was low, husky and heavy with fear. "It's up to you. No one else has been able to find it."

"I won't let you down." Marek charged from the throne room. "I'll get it. If it kills me."

* * * * *

Brea's insides were tangled into painful knots of agonizing need. Her head was foggy, like her brain had soaked in a vat of Absolut for a week.

Gone was the rage, the anger, the guilt, the frustration. In their place—desperate lust.

So what if Marek had all but raped her earlier? So what if both Dayne and Marek had kidnapped her? So what if she was about to lose her job?

She wanted Dayne to fuck her. She wanted him so bad her whole body ached, even her teeth.

Made it mighty tough to say "no" to his question. Did she have the courage to let go of her fears? At this point, with her pussy burning to be filled, her nipples hardened points and her skin practically blistering under Dayne's fierce, nuclear-fusion-hot gaze, she was almost willing to do something crazy, like dance upon the shards of a broken mirror while holding a black cat.

"You've been waiting for a long time," he mumbled, his face buried in the crook of her neck. The tickle of his breath produced a coat of gooseflesh over one side of her upper body. His teeth grazed her skin.

Hot and cold at the same time, and shivering from both the emotions and sensations pummeling her insides, she sucked in a gulp of air. "You have no idea what you're talking about."

His response was not spoken, yet it drove his point home and silenced any arguments she might have thought to raise within the next few hours.

He smoothed a flattened hand down her torso and cupped her sodden labia. His fingers left a trail of musk-scented dampness up her abdomen as he drew a line up to her bellybutton. Lifting his head and drilling her with a gaze that left her insides as soft as marshmallows sitting in the desert sun at high noon, he placed those very same fingers on her lips. "I could eat you all day you taste so good." His tongue slicked a damp trail over his adorable lower lip.

She mirrored him, tasting his fingers and the lingering flavor of her arousal. She parted her lips, pulling his fingertip into her mouth and swirling her tongue around its tip.

His mouth lifted into a seductive smile. "There's no crime in being a sensual woman, in knowing what you want and asking your lovers to give it to you."

Made sense to her, in her current pseudo-intoxicated state. Never before had she been basically rendered brain dead by sexual overload, but there she was. Dead in the brain, oh yes. Her neurons were withering by the millions.

"Don't you agree?" he prodded when she didn't respond to his last statement. He punctuated his question with a little pinch of her nipple.

It hurt but in a good way, a very good way. Her back tensed, thrusting her breasts high in the air.

His eyes glittering, he smiled at her and pinched again. "I'll take that as a 'yes'."

She was incapable of correcting him, since her tongue was sort of glued to the roof of her mouth. No sense in trying anyway. It was complicated. He was right in a sense—there was nothing wrong with a woman knowing what she wanted and asking for it. But—and this was a big but—there was something wrong with a woman doing so with a virtual stranger who'd kidnapped her and was holding her hostage.

Now if only her body would get with the program and quit reacting to his every look, touch and word!

Lust was surging through her body in relentless waves, the crests growing closer and closer like the waters of a storm-tossed Pacific. The man was just so freaking gorgeous! It wasn't fair! Why oh why did things have to be like this? Why couldn't they have bumped into each other at the library or Blockbuster Movies? Strike up a conversation about the second *Pirates of the Caribbean* and then head over to Starbucks to stare into each other's eyes and stumble through awkward first-date type of conversation over mocha lattes?

She'd known everything about her former lovers before they'd seen her naked. That was, until today. Until Marek had taken advantage of her altered state and seduced her out of her clothes somehow.

She wouldn't be able to live with herself if she let Dayne do the same thing. Two new lovers? In the span of a few hours? Ack!

She rooted around deep inside herself, desperate to find a morsel of her self-control. Gathering her strength and willpower, she started squirming beneath him again. Unfortunately, her efforts failed to produce the effect she'd expected.

Dayne's heavy breathing gusted her face. His neck, ears, cheeks turned a deep raspberry color. It would have been kind of cute, if she hadn't been painfully aware of the reason for his color change.

The reason was the suddenly hard, thick bump resting against her thigh.

As if she needed a clue, he blinked and growled.

The growl thing was also sexy. Was there anything the man did that wasn't sexy? He blinked sexy. He smiled super-sexy. He moved sexy, muscles bulging and stretching.

She decided closing her eyes was a good idea. "Please get off me."

"I will if you can make me," he taunted playfully.

Ugh. He sounded like a silly schoolboy who'd just tackled her on the playground. Charming and mischievous.

Her insides melted even more. It was official now, she was going to get him off her or she was going to die trying. She ignored the fact that her insides were the consistency of soup and her willpower was almost completely pulverized as she struggled to worm out from under the two hundred plus pounds of drool-worthy male positioned above her.

Her breasts rubbed against his chest as she moved. The friction was delicious and decadent and sensual. The sensation produced some interesting effects between her legs.

A deep rumble vibrated from Dayne's chest. She felt it inside. In her stomach. Her empty pussy.

Would he just let her up?

Time for desperate measures, unfortunately.

She really did not relish what she was about to do.

She jerked, bending her knee so she'd catch him in the delicates. No man could take a direct shot in the testicles without being incapacitated for at least a few seconds. A well-placed kick could send even three hundred pounds of pure muscle to the ground for even longer.

As it turned out, Dayne was no exception.

The second her knee made contact, the air from his lungs gusted her face. He yelped then curled to the side, rolling off her.

Freedom. She did a log roll to the edge of the bed, but just as she was about to leap to the floor, a steely grip caught her wrist. He yanked her back roughly then positioned himself so she couldn't get a second shot, pinning her on the bed again.

"That. Wasn't. Nice."

"Neither is kidnapping someone, holding them hostage and forcing yourself on them with some kind of crazy mojo—"

"I wasn't forcing anything on you. And as far as Marek goes, he didn't either."

"I said 'no'. I said 'wait, stop'. Which makes what happened force in my book."

"What book is that?"

"The Brea Maguire book of law."

"Well then how about telling me what crime this qualifies for in the Brea Maguire book of law?" Still holding her to the bed with his knee, he bent down and whispered, "You said 'yes' after you said 'no'. And then you said a lot of other things. Would you like me to repeat them?"

Cool air caressed her skin but it did nothing to chill the lust and the rage welling up inside her.

How dare he throw her own words back in her face! Clearly, they were doing something to her to make her react this way, and he knew it. If it wasn't drugs they were using, it was something else—hypnotism? Subliminal messages? Mind control? This wasn't like her. Period.

"Bastard!" She fought with every bit of her strength, but he dodged her strikes so easily, she felt like she was a furious toddler attacking a world champ boxer. Within seconds she was worn out, not to mention so friggin' turned on she was tempted to spread her legs and beg him to quit playing and end her suffering.

A girl under the influence of hypnotism/mind control/whatever could only take so much teasing.

Yet the cautious side of her would never let her actually give in. No way!

"I have the perfect punishment. You won't be able to move a muscle when I'm through with you. Not even to blink an eye." He gathered her wrists in one of his fists and lifted his weight off her, moving carefully to restrict her range of movement while positioning her as he wanted—flat on her stomach, arms positioned in a wide vee, legs stretched apart. He produced black straps from somewhere and secured her wrists to the two massive posts at the head of the bed without breaking a sweat. And, despite her kicking, did the same with her ankles.

Oh God, her lumpy, cottage-cheesy ass was out there front and center in a fully illuminated room! Could she just die now?

She tried to see what the bastard was about to do next, but since he'd left the room, she could only guess. She supposed it would be stupid to think he was going to perhaps get himself a snack, maybe take a nap...or drop dead. Yeah, that was stupid all right.

She heard his footfalls within seconds as he stomped back into the room.

Every muscle in her body tensed. Her heart thumped against her breastbone so hard it hurt.

He stopped at the foot of the bed. "It's a shame you can't see what you're doing to yourself."

What the heck was he talking about?

Something landed on her head, blocking out all traces of light. Dark. Smothering. Terrifying.

Something else touched the sole of her foot. She tried to jerk it away but she couldn't. Tears of frustration and confusion burned her eyes. Not since that night with Steve had she felt so out of control. Sure, she could breathe okay. She could speak. But otherwise, he had her under his complete control. She couldn't scratch her nose if she wanted to.

Anger quickly morphed to irrational panic. In her head, she knew she was in no immediate physical danger. But that didn't stop her heart rate from kicking into supersonic speed, and her stomach from roiling like Mt. Vesuvius on a bad day. "Let me loose. Now."

"You're in no position to make any demands," he pointed out coolly.

Argh! She tossed her head back, trying to knock away the cover, and clamped her eyes closed. Bile burned her throat. Hot tears seeped from her eyes, running in salty rivulets down the sides of her nose. Damn it, she was through being tough. She was scared. Fucking terrified.

Why were these guys doing this to her? She didn't ask for it this time. She didn't deserve this!

"Please."

He walked around the side of the bed and inched the blanket down, uncovering her head.

Light. Air. She gulped several deep breaths.

"What are you feeling? Does the danger thrill you like I thought it would?"

She turned her head, letting him see with his own eyes what her answer was.

His expression remained firm, yet his eyes softened a tiny bit.

Did he feel guilty?

"What are you feeling?" he repeated gently.

She narrowed her eyes at him. He knew the answer. Why ask? What kind of game was he playing? "What is this?" Her voice wavered, punctuating the effect of her watery eyes and sniffly nose.

Tawny Taylor

His brows drew together. "What do you mean?"

She sniffled and rubbed away a fat teardrop hanging on the tip of her nose on the bed. "You know exactly what I'm feeling. Why are you pushing me for an answer?"

"Because I think you need to hear the answer."

That made no sense. "If I answer will you let me loose?"

"Perhaps."

Awkward, heavy silence hung in the air between them. Her heartbeat slammed in her ears, easing the silence but not the tension. For some reason, she didn't want to answer him. Maybe he'd use her fears against her somehow. Who knew? But the need to escape the awful, unrelenting panic crashing through her body overruled her fear of the unknown. "I'm scared."

"Scared? Why? Have I done anything to hurt you?"

"No."

"You could breathe, right?"

"Y-Yes."

"Then what are you scared of?"

"I don't know. It's hard to explain."

The mattress sank a bit as he sat beside her. He rested one of his hands on her back. It was warm, and the touch was undemanding. Reassuring. "I'd like to know."

"What do you care? Why do you and your pal need to play games with me? What do you expect to gain from this? Do you think I'm easy? That I want this?"

He shook his head. "You're not getting any answers from me until you answer my question first."

She bit back a scream of frustration. She hated head games! She hated people dissecting her thoughts and feelings. They were hers. Private. Off limits. Even sometimes to her stupid shrink. But this guy wasn't going to let her get away with sidestepping his questions. That was clear. Her stomach

66

convulsed again and she swallowed the steak and potatoes she'd eaten earlier for the second time.

Oh God, she just needed to be let loose! To be able to move around freely.

"I'm just scared. That's all."

"That's not good enough."

Frustrated and in the iron grip of nauseating panic, she screamed, "Why the fuck not? This isn't funny. It isn't a game. You're fucking with my head, and damn it, I don't like it!"

"Why not?" he asked in a tone so smooth and calm, she'd swear they were chitchatting about the weather.

His calmness acted like gasoline on a bonfire. She could see herself going berserk but she couldn't stop it. She was at her limit. Only one thing mattered—freedom. She yanked at the bindings, kicked, thrashed. Tears ran unchecked from her eyes.

To hell with trying to guess what this fucker was up to.

To hell with trying to talk him into letting her go.

To hell with everything but escape.

Her wrists hurt like hell. The bindings bit into her skin and ground into her bones but she didn't stop trying to break loose.

"I need out."

"Why?"

"Fuck you!"

He sandwiched her face between his hands and drilled her with his gaze. "I'm not hurting you. Do you hear me? I'm not going to hurt you."

"But I can't move. I can't want...you have control. Just like Steve, you're going to think..." She couldn't breathe. It was like an invisible elephant was sitting on her back, pressing her into the mattress. She gulped frantically at the thin air.

"Yes, I do have control, but that's not a bad thing."

"It's always a bad thing. I can't deal with it." A sob burst from her throat. "I didn't ask for this."

"Yet you crave a lover who will take control."

"No, I don't. You're wrong. Bondage games aren't for people like me."

He sighed heavily, stood and walked to the foot of the bed. "You would be happier if you could learn to deal with these issues." He released one ankle and she nearly wept in gratitude. When he unfastened the second restraint and went around to the head of the bed to free her wrists, her heartbeat slowed.

As soon as he had the second wrist was loose, she curled her body into a tight ball, wrapped her arms around her legs and clenched her chattering teeth.

"Brea." He stood beside the bed, looking confused. "I thought...I sensed you needed..."

"I needed you to let me loose. That's all. And I made that perfectly clear. So don't talk about what you thought I needed."

Chapter Five

ᔕᏱ

"What happened?" Marek stormed into the room, dragging a gust of crisp, fresh air with him. His mouth pulled into a taut line, and his eyebrows drawn together, he rushed to the bed. "What's wrong?" His gaze hopped back and forth between Dayne and Brea, who was still struggling to get a grip on herself and the bastard who'd caused her to lose it in the first place.

"She's a little shaken," Dayne offered the lame explanation.

"A little?"

"He tied me up," she added, in a teeth-chattering, wavering, watery voice.

"I'm sorry. I had no idea she'd react this way. I thought..." His voice low, Dayne let the rest of his words trail off.

No way was she going to let him get off with some lame excuse and a mumbled apology. "He sat there while I was freaking out and refused to let me loose. Fucking bastard!"

Marek sent Dayne some death daggers with his eyes. He sat beside her on the bed, pulled the blanket up around her still-shaking form. "I'm very sorry about this."

"Yeah, so let me go home," she demanded. "This has gone on long enough."

"I can't."

"Why the fuck not? You have each other. What the hell do you need me for? I don't understand what's happening to me. You practically raped me..."

"Rape? I didn't rape you."

"Yeah, yeah. I asked for it. Don't remind me. I don't care what you say, I'm not to blame. I'm not thinking straight. And this asshole scared the shit out of me by tying me up and somehow messing with my mind. I can't take any m-m-m-m-more." She started bawling again, which only pissed her off more.

"But we do need you." He pulled her against him, wrapping strong arms around her body and enveloping her in his scent and strength. "More than you know."

She was too worn out to fight her way out of his hug. She closed her eyes and relaxed into his embrace, letting his warmth, the slow, steady sound of his breathing and heartbeat slowly soothe her. After an eon, maybe two, the sobs stopped. The river of tears stopped. And she settled into a weird sort of peace, like the quiet after a wicked summer storm.

"It's more than needing you," Dayne said, dragging a chair across the room. He positioned it directly in front of her and sat. "We aren't just after cheap thrills. Or a lost statue. Or a piece of ass. We want to get closer to you. Know you. Understand you. Help you. There's something holding you back. I can sense it. And that was why — "

"Why you what?" she spat. "You guys kidnapped me for some reason I have yet to understand. And now you want to understand me? Help me? Like a friend? Please. I'm not that stupid. Or gullible. You tied me up like one of those chicks on the 'net. I'm not like them."

"Do you hear what you're saying? Women who like to be tied up aren't 'chicks'. They're women who know what they want, what they need. And they've accepted themselves." Dayne captured her face between his flattened hands and stared into her eyes. "I want to help you. Can't you sense the truth? Don't you feel it, the connection between us? I realize it's hard to believe but I genuinely care about you."

That was just it. She did sense a connection between them. Which made this whole thing that much more confusing. She pulled on his fingers, easing his hands from her face. "I...I...don't like that stuff."

"Dayne's telling the truth. We both care about you. And there's nothing we won't do to make things right between us." Marek used an index finger under her chin to force her to meet his gaze. "What happened between you and Dayne?"

"I didn't hurt her."

"I was scared, that's all."

"Of what?" Marek prodded. He tucked a lock of her hair behind her ear. Such a gentle, sweet gesture.

Of myself?

"You feel it too, don't you, Marek? She craves a little excitement and danger in the bedroom, a dominant lover who'll test her boundaries."

"Yeah. I do." Marek nodded. "What were you scared of, Brea?"

"Sense how? You two talk like you can read my mind or something." Her eyes still burning and nose still sniffly, she sat, conflicted over the compulsion to keep her secrets to herself and the urge to finally deal with the fallout from that night with her former best friend, the confusion, guilt and frustration that had basically left sex as little more than an empty physical exercise. But why did it have to be these guys? What kind of future could she expect to have with a couple of guys who kidnapped women to supposedly make friends? "You don't know me."

"Maybe we're pushing too hard, too fast?" Dayne asked.

Marek looked askance. "Brea?"

"Yeah, like he said, it's happening too fast. That's all. Especially the bondage stuff." That was partially true. True enough. "And the head games."

"We'll slow down then." Dayne cradled one of her hands in his. "I'm sorry, Brea. I swear I'll do anything to make things right between us."

Strange, but a part of her believed him.

"Feel better now?" Marek asked as he ran a hand down her back in slow, repetitive strokes.

"A little."

"Good. Because I need to ask you for something else."

Her shoulders tensed. "Ask me what?"

"Have you had any luck solving the first clue?" Marek asked, trying hard not to let on both how much he hoped to hear good news and how urgently he hungered for a taste of the delightful spitfire of a woman sitting before him. Pounding heat pulsed through his body, sent to all parts by the heart she had kick-started. His cock, however, got the bulk of it.

Narrowing her eyes, she spat, "You want to talk about that? Now?"

"Well…"

"That worthless bit of nonsense you left for me?"

Not the answer he had been hoping for. "I take that as a 'no'?" He'd hoped to leave the second clue for later, to buy him another taste of the sweet blood coursing through her veins, but with his brother's illness progressing so quickly, could he afford to wait? Could he afford to think about his needs? Or even hers? "I have another clue."

She leaned closer, her position making the blanket gape. He had a clear view of the tempting swell of two firm breasts. Two perfect, pink-tipped, firm breasts. "Fork it over, pal. That first one wasn't even close to helpful." As if to add to his already monumental agony, she thrust those breasts forward, an unintentional invitation, no doubt.

Rendered dumbstruck, he handed her the scrap of paper and waited, his breath caught in his throat. Between the worry about his brother and the unwelcome heat of the hunger, he felt like he might literally implode.

She read the clue then planted her hands on her delightfully curvy hips and glowered. "What kind of game are you playing?"

"It's no game," he said to her breasts. He tried to lift his gaze but darn it all, what guy in the grips of the hunger could resist staring at those?

Still completely unaware of how much skin was showing, she shifted, making the cover slide even farther down. Oh the agony.

She waved her arms in the air. "If you're serious, and not trying to mess with me, why dole out little bits of worthless information? What are you hoping to gain from all this?"

A whole lot! "Then you don't know what either clue means?"

"No. How could I?" She dropped her gaze to the paper, still in her fist and read, "It's critical to walk in the Secrets?" She shook it in front of his face. "How can you walk in secrets? It makes no sense. Where'd you get this? From a fortune cookie?"

She was so charming when she was frustrated. "Not exactly."

Shaking her head, she dropped the paper on the bed. "It's meaningless, just like the first one."

"But it's all I have. Whoever sent them must expect me to solve them...or find someone who can solve them for me."

"Or maybe not?" she asked, her expression softening a little. "Maybe they don't want me to figure them out at all?"

"Then why bother giving them to me in the first place?" he asked. Perhaps someone was feeding his brother these clues to keep him from locating the Triad.

Was he being sent on a wild-goose chase? Or maybe just being distracted. He hadn't thought of either of those possibilities until now. It was entirely possible.

Yet the optimist in him refused to believe it.

"Who's giving you the clues?" She scowled. "I'm getting the vibe you're after the Triad for yourself. Do you want it for something?"

"No. I just want to help you."

"Hmmm... Why do I get the impression you're keeping something important from me?"

"Let me see," Dayne offered, hand outstretched. "Maybe I can help?"

"You'd be willing to help me too?" she asked, still sounding skeptical. Her expression was a mixture of wariness and gratitude.

"Sure." Dayne encouraged her to give him the paper by curling the fingers of his outstretched hand.

"Then maybe—just maybe!—you're no worse a man than Mr. Tight-lipped," she said, punctuating her statement with an audible harrumph. She motioned at Marek. "He's messing with me, and if you ask me, he owes me better than this." She glowered at Dayne, shaking a finger at him. "But I'm still not letting you off the hook yet. Terrifying a girl like that. It's inexcusable, apology or not. You're both on my shit list right now. I don't get what you two are up to, but I know there's something going on." She rolled off the bed, taking the blanket with her and wrapping it around her body.

Such a shame, to have all those delectable curves hidden.

Her hair was tousled, giving her the delicious post-sex, rumpled look he adored. As she scurried across the room, one slender leg cut through a gap in the blanket, giving both Dayne and him a glimpse of one shapely thigh and calf.

They swapped hungry glances.

His cock stirred to life once again, letting him know how neglected it was feeling.

She plucked the first clue from the table, shuffled back across the room and thrust it at Dayne. One side of the blanket drooped, exposing her left shoulder and the top of her breast. "Here. Maybe you can make sense of this. If your friend here isn't playing with me, then these are two of the most impossible, ambiguous clues ever."

"Where did they come from?"

"The first was found at the sight of the theft," Marek explained, again forcing his gaze from the perfection that was her breast.

"Really?" Dayne asked, sounding genuinely shocked.

"Really?" echoed Brea, also sounding surprised. "Let me see them again," she demanded, motioning to Dayne. "There was no mention of anything like this in the police report."

"Yeah, well that's because the police didn't see them," Marek admitted.

"How'd you get this?" Brea challenged, eyebrows lowered.

"I—I'm not at liberty to explain right now."

Dayne handed them back and cleared his throat. "I think they're meaningless. Planted. Someone's trying to steer you wrong."

Brea studied both papers carefully before speaking. "Dayne could be right. But together they do seem to make a little more sense. See here?" She spread them both on the bed then pointed at the second clue. "One of my favorite movies ever was *National Treasure*. Either of you seen it?" She gave them each a questioning glance and at their shaking heads, continued, "Great movie but that's not the point. The hero has to follow a series of clues to find the treasure. One of them was a rhyme. In that rhyme, a word was capitalized to indicate it was a proper name. So if we apply that to this clue, that means Secrets is a proper name. Does it mean anything to you guys?"

"No," Dayne said. "I don't know anyone nicknamed Secret or Secrets. Nor do I know of a place called Secret. Do you?" he asked, looking at Marek.

"What about the Book of Secrets?" Marek suggested, still trying to get a grip on the lust churning through his system.

Dayne's jaw dropped. "Shit, I hadn't thought of that. The Book of Secrets. Sure. But what's it mean?"

"What's this Book of Secrets?" Brea asked, her gaze ping-ponging back and forth between them.

"It's our people's sacred text," Marek explained, inching closer to Brea. Her shoulder was so lovely. Smooth. Soft.

"Your people's?" she echoed, turning her body toward him. Once again the blanket around her started sliding south. She caught it and tugged it up. "Are you in some kind of cult or something?"

"Not exactly," Marek answered, his mouth flooded with saliva. "It contains our laws, beliefs and — of course — secrets." His cock was hard as concrete and his balls heavy as lead. He moved another few inches closer. The scent of her skin teased his nostrils.

"Yes, that has to be it." Her eyes widened. "Where is it? Is there more than one copy? Is it far away? We need to take a look immediately." She spat the questions machine-gun style, in quick succession as she rushed across the room toward the closet.

"It isn't far." Marek dogged her. "It's kept in the *Zal Halirgi*, our most sacred place. But we can't just walk in there uninvited. We're going to need to make some calls first. And–"

"Fine. You make the calls and I'll try to figure out the rest of these clues." Brea waved him away with one hand while snatching up the first clue. She chewed on her lower lip while studying the piece of paper, flipping it over in her hands. Powerless to stop himself, he stared at her plump lip, wishing he could nibble it. "The end. The beginning. Maybe we need to read the book backward?" When she finally realized he hadn't left yet, she sent him a questioning glance. "What?" She dragged an impatient hand through her silken hair and the blanket dropped another inch, hovering just above a pert nipple.

A frantic wave of desire blasted through his body, nearly knocking him to his knees.

"There won't be anyone to take our call until sundown," Dayne said, answering her before Marek could find his tongue. "We have to wait."

"Oh, phoo!" she cursed, pursing her lips. She plopped on the mattress. "Are you sure?"

Dayne nodded. "Absolutely positive."

She glanced at the clock. "That's hours from now. It's barely morning. I need to find the Triad right away."

So do I.

Marek sat next to her and rested a reassuring hand on her shoulder. Her eyes widened as she lifted them to his face. "We'll go as soon as we can. In the meantime…" He swapped a second hungry look with Dayne. "There are some other issues we need to address."

"I-Issues?" she stuttered. An attractive pink flush spread over her face and upper chest. She fumbled with the blanket as her gaze dropped to his lap. "What issues might those be?" She sucked in an audible gasp.

His fangs lengthened with the all-too-familiar burn. "We're hungry. I kept my end of the bargain. Now it's your turn to keep yours."

She visibly swallowed then whimpered. "Oh. No."

* * * * *

Brea could not believe what she was seeing. Both Marek and Dayne had fangs! *A la* Dracula. What was up with that?

The scariest part was that those chompers could not be the fakes people donned at Halloween. One second they hadn't been there. The next they were. Neither guy had fiddled with his mouth. Their hands had been nowhere near their heads.

So she had to believe one of two things. Either she was hallucinating or vampires really did exist.

She couldn't say which she preferred. She jumped to her feet and made a beeline for the bathroom.

"Look at me," Marek demanded in a firm voice.

Damn if she could resist obeying the command. She stopped in her tracks and slowly turned to face him. Her gaze shifted to the right. It landed on his neck then climbed up over an adorably clefted chin to a set of tempting lips. Then it inched farther north, following the line of his narrow, straight nose to his eyes.

Dark eyes glittering with erotic promise.

She remembered to breathe just before she keeled over.

"You don't remember yesterday, do you?" he asked, stalking closer.

"Yesterday?" she echoed, struggling to remember what had happened thirty seconds ago.

"I'll take that as a no. Don't worry." At her side now, Marek swept aside the strands of hair tumbling over her shoulder. "We'll be gentle."

She stood frozen, suddenly overcome by desperate desire. Marek tipped his head to graze the side of her neck with his teeth. At the same moment, Dayne approached her from the other side. His body so close she could feel the heat radiating from it, he laved her shoulder with his tongue.

A thick coat of goose bumps covered her entire torso. Shivering, she clutched the blanket still loosely wrapped around her body in a fist and let her head drop back.

Firm but gentle hands guided her toward the bed. She plopped on the mattress, aware of little but the feel of Dayne's tongue blazing a slick trail of liquid fire over one shoulder, and Marek's lips, tongue and teeth doing equal damage to the right side of her neck.

Her breathing deepened to meet the increasingly desperate demand of her body, which was slowly heating up from the inside out.

And then the first shocking bolt of pain blasted up her neck. Out of reflex, she jerked to one side, only to have a second hit her on the opposite shoulder.

Sharp pain morphed into pounding agony...and then desperate desire.

Afraid to move and break whatever magical connections were responsible for the pulsing heat surging up and down her spine, she dropped the blanket and blindly reached out. She clawed at the first body her hands came into contact with.

Need, so urgent it made the soles of her feet cramp, overwhelmed her senses. She could no longer hear, touch or see. All she could do was let the mounting passion carry her away, like a wild, thrashing river.

Sometime later, she realized she was on her back. Two sets of tormenting hands were stroking her to oblivion. One was inching up her thigh, promising to reach her heated center in no time. The other was heading north from her bellybutton. She was pretty certain one of those devious limbs was about to reach her breast in one, two, threeeeee...

Ahhhhhhh.

A fingertip traced the seam of her nether lips, dragging hot juices up and down from clit to anus. Another tormented her nipple, stroking it into a tight, hard pebble.

Her buttocks clenched, the burn adding to the ecstasy whooshing through her body in intensifying waves. She couldn't remember another time when she'd been so aroused, so desperate for release.

These guys had magic hands. Magic!

She finally accepted the fact that all that pulsing heat and instant lust she read in romance novels could actually be for real. Until now, she'd always assumed it was a fantasy.

Her shrink was going to get an earful whenever she went back to him. If she went back to him. The idea of sticking with her two magicians had its merits.

She wanted to see them, to watch their glorious bodies, corded muscles and tight sinew, as they stroked and kissed her to heaven. Two of them! She was going to be with two men at the same time. If someone had told her this would happen a couple days ago, she would've called them insane.

Now she was the one about to go insane—though not in a bad way. The gorgeous guys, one dragging his tongue over her nipple, the other weaving a trail of kisses and nips up her inner thigh, were about to drive her completely crazy.

Hot. Tight. Trembling. Desperate.

"Mmmm…" Dayne purred, his voice thick with male satisfaction. "I love the way you taste."

She loved the way he tasted her!

Both men were nude, one kneeling on the bed beside her, the other standing between her parted thighs. Marek lifted one of her ankles and planted a tickly kiss on the inside. Dayne pinched her nipple between his thumb and forefinger, rolling it to increase her pleasure.

Her head sloshing around in a deepening pool of desire, she admired the way the roped muscles of Dayne's shoulders bulged and stretched as he moved. He smiled when her gaze met his. "It's so hard to wait. You make it hard." He lowered the hand not busy tormenting her breast to his cock. Circling his fingers around the thick shaft, he pumped up and back. A droplet of moisture glistened on the tip.

She wanted to taste it. More than she wanted her next breath. "Dayne," she said on a sigh. Her arms felt heavy, like she'd overdosed on downers. She lifted one and pointed at his rod. "Please."

He growled, the sound feral and wicked and thoroughly erotic. "You want this?"

"Not yet." Marek flickered his tongue over the sensitive spot on the back of her knees, and a delicious tension wound up her leg to the base of her spine. She arched her back and gasped. Her pussy was burning to be filled.

Of course, being the heartless bastard that he was, Dayne decided that while she was about ready to die, he'd add to her misery by pinching both nipples until the biting pleasure-pain made her whimper and plead for mercy.

And then, not to be outdone, Marek sped up his progress on his way north to her pussy. She both sighed with relief and cried out in agony the instant his hot mouth closed over her slick folds, sending searing bolts of heat up her back.

Relief! She needed it now.

While she thrashed her head from side to side, Dayne straddled her head and bent over, offering a delectable view of his round, muscular ass, smooth-shaven balls and cock.

She licked her lips and opened her mouth to take him in. Salty-sweet. That's how he tasted. Unable to do anything but, she sucked him hard, lifting her hands and using one to cup his balls and the other to stroke up and down his shaft.

He trembled over top of her, his outstretched thigh muscles tensing into sexy, roped bulges.

She tensed when Marek parted her labia to expose her uber-sensitive clit. She knew the first swipe would likely steal her breath.

And did it ever!

"Ohhhhhh," she murmured around a mouthful of delicious man. Could it get any better than this? Seriously? Two men who looked like gods were touching her, looking at her like she was the most desirable woman on earth.

"That's it. Suck my cock, baby. Oh yeah," Dayne mumbled as he slowly pushed his hips forward and back, fucking her mouth.

Between hard sucks and light flickers of his tongue, Marek chanted, "Yes, let me taste your cream. Damn you're sweet. Give me all of it."

"Oooohh." She could feel climax prowling ever closer, like a wild animal creeping up on its prey. She both ached for release and burned to hold it off. Why couldn't this last forever? The bliss.

"You will come for us." As if to ensure his demand be met, regardless of her wishes, he thrust two fingers inside her pussy, bending them to stroke the special place inside.

She tightened her grip on Dayne's cock and sucked him deep into her mouth while consciously gripping Marek's fingers with her inner muscles.

Dayne withdrew from her, turning around to close his mouth over a nipple. His touch branded her skin as Marek's intimate strokes pushed her over the edge. Sanity fled as the first of a million pounding contractions blasted through her body in what was the most amazing climax of her life. It was beyond words. Beyond everything. And the second it was over, she hungered for another.

Marek lapped at the juices seeping from her pussy, murmuring words she couldn't quite comprehend. Then, as she felt the heat of a second orgasm gather in her stomach, he stopped. "Can we both take you?"

She blinked open her eyes, briefly wondering when she'd closed them. "Both? Is that possible?" She really hoped it was. Then she realized the only way it could possibly happen. One was going to have to fuck her ass. A quiver of anxiety shimmied up her spine. "Ohhhh. I don't know." She looked at Marek's cock. It was long and thick. She looked at Dayne's. It was at least as large as Marek's. Both were well hung.

Her untried anus puckered.

"That's gotta hurt like hell," she said with a shudder. *What am I thinking?*

"Not so much that you won't enjoy it." Marek lifted his index finger to his mouth and then, his eyes focused on hers, sucked the digit into his mouth. He withdrew it with a pop and glancing down, pressed gently at the orifice. The skin burned. She sucked in a gasp and tightened her legs, stomach and buttocks.

Dayne rolled off the bed. As she was in the midst of a fairly uncomfortable—albeit surprisingly sexy—experience, she lost track of him. He reappeared next to Marek a few seconds later, produced a bottle of lube and when Marek lifted his hand, flipped the lid and squirted the clear substance on Marek's fingers.

Marek smoothed the cool liquid on her burning perineum, concentrating his gentle touches to the area surrounding her anus. "Relax, baby. We want to make it good for you." Dayne left Marek to return to her side on the bed. He lifted her shoulders and slid underneath her. While Marek slowly breached her anus, he worked his hips under her bottom, moving inch by inch. His sweat-slicked torso glided against her back.

She tipped her hips down and clawed at the bed. More. She wanted to feel their cocks driving into her, stroking her into another orgasm. Her ass easily accommodated Marek's finger. The slow, gentle thrusts stoked the blaze building in her belly.

She cried out when he withdrew it, leaving her painfully empty.

She wasn't left to suffer long.

She felt him smooth more lube over her ass and pussy then felt the invasion of two cocks—one in her ass, one in her pussy.

Oh, good God almighty! The two men synchronized their motions. Innnn. Outtttt. Innnn. Outttt.

She was going to die.

Marek added perfectly applied circles to her clit to the other incredible sensations and she quickly relinquished, letting the pulsing heat of another climax shimmy through her body.

Both men groaned as her pussy and ass rhythmically sucked them to release. On the wake of their guttural cries, they spilled their scorching seed into her pussy and ass, slowly thrusting in and out to drive it farther inside.

And when they'd all stopped twitching and pulsing and quaking and shaking, they slid out from inside her, gently positioned her between them on the bed and encircled her in their arms.

Her fanny rested against Marek's groin. His breath heated her nape. And Dayne's knee was wedged between her legs, one arm under her head, the other resting protectively on her hip.

This was heaven.

How'd she get so lucky, to end up with two to-die-for Chippendales?

Chapter Six

ಓ

"What do you mean I can't go with you?" Brea demanded, sure they were once again pulling a quick one on her. Two-timing, scheming, lying kidnappers! She'd been such a fool. Of course they weren't going to help her. Why would they?

The clues had been a ruse to delay her. And she'd bought their lies.

"Not just anyone can storm into our most sacred place and start riffling through the pages of the Book of Secrets," Dayne reasoned.

"That's right," Marek piped in as he worked his bod into a snug black t-shirt and pair of worn jeans. The soft blue cotton did wonders for the man's backside, she noted begrudgingly. "No outsider has stepped foot inside the *Zal Halirgi*. Ever. It's simply forbidden."

"But I need to see the book. How do I know if you two will look for the right thing?" *Or if you'll lie and claim you found nothing?*

"You don't." Dressed in a white ribbed pullover and black pants, Dayne looked like he'd stepped out of a magazine spread. His GQ-ish hunk-next-door good looks were nearly the mirror opposite of Marek's more rough and raw, bad-boy qualities.

They both suited her just fine, despite the fact that they were both a couple of lying wieners.

"I give my word," Marek vowed, "we'll do whatever you tell us to. With these," he added, handing her a cell phone, "we can keep in contact the entire time we're there."

"It's hardly the same. How am I going to know what to look for if I can't see anything?"

Marek shrugged. "It's the best we can do." He dragged a familiar duffle bag from the closet and tossed in some supplies. Then he gathered the clues, tucked them into an envelope. "Guess we're ready to go."

"I had a thought." Brea pointed at the envelope. "We didn't check those clues for invisible ink. What good is the Book of Secrets if we don't know yet what message we're decoding?"

Dayne nodded. "Hmmm. She has a point."

"Invisible ink?" Marek sounded skeptical. "I thought we were looking for the code in the Book of Secrets."

"See?" Brea shook her head and tsked. "You are going to be worthless to me until you get your hands on a copy of *National Treasure*."

"Worthless?" Dayne asked, an evil grin splitting his face and making her nether regions warm.

She plucked the envelope from Marek's hand and pulled the papers from it. "You guys have any lemon juice?"

"Lemon juice?" they repeated in unison.

She heaved a sigh of the weary. "Yes, of course. It was in the movie. I'll need some lemons, a hair drier and some Q-tips."

"I'll see what I can find," Marek grumbled, heading for the door.

"Thank you." She turned to Dayne. "And a laptop with internet access would come in mighty handy right now."

"That won't be a problem."

As Dayne brushed past Marek at the doorway, Marek mumbled, "Sure, you get the easy one."

Dayne simply grinned and shrugged. He returned long before Marek did, set a snazzy laptop with more bells and whistles than Dell's latest offering on the table and sat in a nearby chair to watch.

She set to work right away, Googling every keyword she could think of that might relate to the Triad, including the former owner's name, the Book of Secrets and the *Zal Halirgi*. The former, she found. The latter two, nothing, outside of a couple websites dedicated to online fantasy games and some obscure religious cult.

Interesting.

Both Chippendales had talked about the *Zal Halirgi* and book as if they were real. Were they members of that bizarre underground cult? Did they believe Christ would make his second coming in a spaceship and beam them aboard for a millennium of bliss, while rocketing through the universe?

As she surfed the 'net, she rubbed a couple of sore spots on her neck and shoulder. They were tender, achy and bruised but she couldn't remember having hurt herself.

As soon as Marek returned, a bowl of lemons in one hand, a box of Q-Tips in the other, and a hair drier wedged between one thick bicep and his rib cage, she attacked the first clue. She flipped the scrap of paper over, rubbed lemon juice all over it and then dried it to a crisp.

Nothing. No code. No secret message. No map.

She flipped it over and did the same to the front.

Again, nothing.

Frustrated and feeling time slipping away, she did a rush job on the second clue.

Nothing.

Now what? Were the clues fake? Was she using the wrong stuff to read the invisible ink? Or was the secret code somewhere else?

The tangy scent of lemons clinging to her fingers, she went back to the computer and typed *invisible ink* into the search field. She clicked on the first site, an online encyclopedia.

What was this? The writers of *National Treasure* had it wrong? Lemon juice didn't work as a reagent? She could hardly believe it! Didn't those movie scriptwriters research stuff?

"UV light?" She went to the fluorescent desk lamp and held the paper in front of the bulb. A series of dim, shadowed figures appeared on the back of the paper. "A-ha! There it is. Black light. I bet that'll work." A smile of relief pulling at her cheeks, she turned to Dayne. "I don't suppose you have one of those funky black lights sitting around?"

"Uh...?" Dayne said.

She glanced at the clock. It was a little after seven. "You can buy one just about anywhere, K-Mart, Meijers, Radio Shack. Do you know where one of those stores are?"

"Yes," Marek said when Dayne gave her a blank stare. "If you had any doubt I was willing to help, you shouldn't anymore. I'll be back in a bit."

She caught his wrist as he turned toward the door, and tugged. When he glanced over his shoulder, she said, "Thank you."

A gentle smile warmed his features. "You're welcome."

While he was gone, Dayne kept her from climbing the walls by chitchatting about his family, the history between him and Marek—she sensed he hadn't given her the whole story there—and his computer programming company. She intentionally kept her distance from him, since it seemed that the minute he got within five feet of her, her hormones started surging through her body and thoughts of a carnal nature flooded her brain. At least if she kept a good seven to ten feet between them, she could think about more than how adorable his butt looked in his pants or how the pure white of his shirt complimented his tanned complexion.

The internet was all but useless, so her hands were figuratively tied. When there was a lull in the conversation, she set a course around the room. Bed, door, bathroom, desk then back to the bed again. "How much longer do you think he'll be?"

"Hard saying. If he doesn't get back here soon, we'll be waiting until tomorrow to go to the *Zal Halirgi*."

"Why's that?"

"They'll be closed."

"Closed? That's worse than banker's hours. I thought you said they were opening at about six. What is this place anyway? *Zal Halirgi*? Is it like...a church of some kind?"

"A church? Not hardly," he said around a rumbling chuckle. Little quivers of sensual awareness rippled through her body. "The most sacred place doesn't have a lot of traffic, since its only purpose is to hold our most treasured documents. For that reason, it's only open to visitors for an hour a day."

"So how much time, exactly, do we have?"

He studied the clock. "About twenty minutes."

"Shit!"

* * * * *

Marek stared at the green glowing numbers on the van's digital clock. Time was running out and he was stuck cooling his heels in gridlock, thanks to a multi-car pile-up.

Stupid humans who didn't know how to drive on wet roads. You'd think they'd be more careful, since they were mortal.

He finally broke clear of the snarl and lead-footed his way home. The *Zal Halirgi* would be closed in twelve minutes.

If the light didn't work, they would lose a whole night. If only they'd thought to tackle this earlier. Then again, he wouldn't have been able to go to the store until after twilight anyway. The Sons of the Twilight received only one dose of the medication that allowed them to walk in sunlight each year. It was carefully controlled by the Council to avoid the kind of abuses they'd seen in centuries past.

Of course, since he'd known he'd have to find a blood-mate this year, he'd chosen to reserve that precious dose for that day.

Home. At last. With no time to waste.

The black-light bulb in a white plastic bag, he raced inside, ran up the stairs and rushed into the room.

This had to work.

"Here you are," he said, breathless from running, from worry and from the erotic hunger that blasted him in the gut like a well-placed sucker-punch. Would the hunger ever ease?

Brea snatched the bag and, hesitating for a moment, turned and dashed toward the nearest table lamp, simultaneously unwrapping the bulb.

Clearly Dayne had warned her time was short.

She unscrewed the bulb and replaced it with the black light, switched on the light then instructed Dayne to cut all the other lights in the room. Instantly, they were enveloped in an eerie blue glow.

Dayne's white shirt shone brightly, as did his teeth when he opened his mouth to speak, "How's this supposed to do anything?"

Brea lifted the first scrap of paper up to the light and even from a distance, Marek could read the series of numbers scrawled over the entire surface. She'd done it, figured out how to read the code. He had to admire her sharp mind. "There we go! I can read them. Pen! I need a pen and paper. Anything."

"Desk drawer," Marek said.

"Of course." The drawer opened with a scrape of wood against wood. The sound of pencils and pens clattered in the plastic tray as she sifted through them. "Got it. God, I hope you can read this. I'm writing so fast," she said as she alternated between reading numbers and recording them on a fresh piece of paper. Finally, she jumped to her feet, thrust the paper at him and shooed them both toward the door, "Go, go, go!"

"We'll be back soon," Marek said over his shoulder. He held his cell phone and the code in one hand, fished for the van's keys in the other. Dayne loped along behind him, silent.

* * * * *

Brea fingered Marek's spare cell phone as she stared at the door, shut behind the guys after they'd left. Her nerves were tied into tight knots. Anxiety rushed up and down her spine. She couldn't sit still. Couldn't stand still either.

Ack! Waiting was agony.

She beat a permanent path from the bed to the door as she paced. Back and forth. Back and forth. After some two hundred round-trips, she decided to try the door, just for kicks. No doubt it would be locked.

Unlocked.

Unlocked? Hot damn!

She tossed the cell phone on the bed, threw open the door and dashed into the hallway. Down the stairs. Through a foyer to the front door.

Was this some kind of trap? Did they have the front door rigged to keep her inside? That was stupid. Of course not. They hadn't had time.

Whoo hoo! They'd forgotten to lock her door. She was free! Freeeeee!

She yanked open the front door and dashed outside. The crisp night air felt wonderful. It smelled wonderful too, of wet grass and flowers and nature. Freedom!

Ahhhhhh.

She stood in the middle of the huge, immaculately manicured front lawn. Her Chippendales either spent *beaucoup* hours working on their lawn or paid a service to handle it for them. Not a twig was out of place on the shrubs, the lawn was so lush and thick it looked like a carpet and the flower beds, lit with a row of adorable copper lanterns, were overflowing with gorgeous blooms. The crabapple tree standing sentry at the driveway's end was covered with white blossoms that seemed to glow in the moonlight.

Enough admiring the landscaping. Now that she was free, how was she going to get home? She had no idea where she was. Plans whirring through her mind, she hiked about halfway down the loooong gravel driveway before she stopped.

Was she making a big mistake by leaving now? If Marek wasn't pulling a quick one on her, and there really was a *Zal Halirgi*, and they really were following a bona fide clue, she'd be an idiot to walk away now.

What to do?

She wandered slowly down the rest of the drive, which opened up onto a rural road cutting through thick forest. Looked pretty remote. She could be walking for miles before she ran across a neighbor.

Better head back.

She did a one-eighty and trudged back to the house. Luckily, she realized as she tromped across the porch, she hadn't locked herself out. She let herself in the building but refused to head back up to her room. She'd spent way too many hours cooped up in there already. Besides, her new freedom provided the perfect opportunity to snoop.

After walking around the living room, opening the drapes and windows to let some of that wonderful fresh air inside, she started inspecting her surroundings more closely. If she couldn't leave then she'd keep herself occupied. Maybe she'd learn something handy about her captors, even discover some information she could use later.

She headed for the dark walnut bookcases lining the living room wall first. There were a few books—James Rollins, Dan Brown...Anne Rice?

Her Chippendales liked vampire novels?

A hazy image flashed through her mind—of eyes dark with hunger. White teeth, sharp and elongated, like a dog's canines glittering in dim light.

Weird.

The achy spots on her neck and shoulder throbbed. Wincing, she rubbed at the pain. A shiver snaked up her spine.

Was that image some kind of memory? From a dream maybe? Or a movie she'd watched a long time ago?

Cold. She wrapped her arms around herself and hurried to the window. The chilly, damp air wafting through the windows, stirring the drapes wasn't helping. Window closed, she headed back to the bookshelf.

Further over were some more books, nonfiction. Again, the subject matter was vampires. Ick. Vampire movies seriously creeped her out. She'd barely managed to sit through *Interview with a Vampire* the one and only time she'd tried to watch it.

Another chill charged up her spine. The hairs on her nape stood on end. She scrunched up her shoulders and tightened her arms around herself. She was getting a serious case of the willies. Time to move on.

The kitchen. That had to be a vampire-free zone.

As it turned out, it was not only a vampire-free zone but also a food-free zone.

And then she remembered what they'd said immediately after kidnapping her—talking about her need to "feed" as if it was a foreign thing to them.

Maybe eating wasn't entirely strange to the Chippendales, but storing and preparing food at home most certainly was. She searched the fridge and every cupboard and didn't find so much as a breadcrumb or bottle of beer. Her old college boyfriend hadn't been anywhere close to Mr. Betty Crocker but he usually had a bag of chips and some Budweisers on hand. This was bizarre.

The hairs on her arms decided to stand on end too.

Rubbing a shudder away, she headed toward the foyer, passing though a dark-paneled office housing a gorgeous desk and more matching bookcases. She poked around the uber-tidy room. There wasn't a scrap of paper to be found, not a utility bill or even piece of forgotten junk mail. The trash bin was empty. The desktop, polished to a gloss, was empty. She didn't find a single photograph or family memento. It was completely devoid of life.

Who were these guys? And where'd they come from? She climbed the stairs, her hand tracing the top of the mahogany stair rail. Time to check out their bedrooms.

People didn't just materialize out of nowhere. They had pasts, families, parents, siblings, jobs and childhoods. Somewhere in this house there had to be some hints into who her captors were. And she was determined to ferret them out.

For some reason, it mattered to her.

But just as she shuffled into the first room, flipped on the light switch and swept up the one and only photograph she'd found thus far in the house, the shrill ring of the cell phone caught her ear.

Marek? Had to be.

Did he have news? Had they solved the code?

The mystery of her abductors forgotten, she raced back to her room, eager to catch the call.

Chapter Seven

ඬ

It couldn't be!

It was impossible.

She was dead.

Long dead. Slaughtered decades ago.

Dayne's eyes tracked the Watcher as the robed, hooded figure trotted down the corridor in the opposite direction from where they were headed. Her galloping gait was eerily familiar, an unsettling reminder of his sister.

It was the lively bounce in her step, so unusual a trait in a Watcher, even a young one.

But Rane couldn't be a Watcher. Life-long servants of The Keeper, they were chosen before birth, raised from infancy in seclusion and taught the sacred rituals before they could speak. Before they could know life outside of the *Zal Halirgi*.

Up until her death, Rane had enjoyed a normal life as the pampered second child, the youngest of two.

"This way," their guide, The Keeper, murmured, pushing a heavy door open and motioning with his hand for Dayne to pass through the portal ahead of him.

Dayne stepped past with care, fearful of stepping on The Keeper's golden garment. Resembling a medieval robe, complete with the huge sleeves that dragged on the floor as he walked, it conveyed the importance of the man's station far more clearly than his withered and wasting form did.

"We're sorry for coming so late," Marek said, following behind. "We were held up—"

"No need to apologize." The Keeper waved a heavily wrinkled hand, motioning Marek past before following them.

Pulling the door closed behind them, he stopped a mere footstep inside the inner sanctum, the room where the Book of Secrets was displayed. "It isn't the first time. I will remain with you until your task is complete." The Keeper urged them forward, toward the crystal pedestal sitting in the middle of the room. A single shaft of pure white light from some unseen lamp overhead cut a blade through the oppressive darkness. The floor, ceiling and walls, black as pitch, seemed to vanish into endless shadows.

Dayne's heart raced as he watched Marek gently lift the gilt cover off the Book of Secrets, revealing the black and red tome underneath.

What were these clues? How had Marek found them? And who was sending them?

Was there a traitor within the Rebellion or was this treasure hunt a ruse? While Marek was preoccupied upon their arrival, explaining the nature of their visit to a Watcher, Dayne had stepped away to contact his most trusted allies. None had claimed responsibility for the cryptic messages. Nor did they know who might have sent them.

If by some chance the clues were real and did lead Marek to the Triad, his allies—his dearest friends—might be discovered. They could be sentenced to death.

That was one risk he couldn't live with.

With thoughts of his sister clouding his mind, and Marek beside him, searching the Book of Secrets for the key to the Rebellion's failure, he planned his next move.

* * * * *

Nothing. He could find nothing tying the Book of Secrets to the numeric code Brea had transcribed for him. Not in the beginning. Nor at the end.

Was she mistaken? Were they looking in the wrong place? The book was too heavy to lift so searching the platform it lay upon was impossible. His hope faltering, he looked at Dayne, who looked as puzzled as he felt.

There was nothing to be seen on the walls. At least, not without perhaps that special light.

He hadn't thought to bring it along.

He tried the cell phone again. He'd tried to contact Brea just after they'd arrived, but she hadn't answered.

It rang once, twice, three times. She wasn't going to catch it before it switched over to voice mail.

Where was she?

He punched the button, cutting off the call and handed the phone to Dayne.

"I'll keep trying," he promised.

"Thanks." He stared at the numbers, written in looping, feminine handwriting. She'd seemed so sure about this. Seemed so sure he'd be able to solve it.

She'd looked at him like he was her savior.

He didn't want to fail her. But hell, what did she expect? He was no one's savior. Case in point—he was about to let Kaden down too.

"Still no answer. Perhaps she's in the bathroom. I'll try again in a few minutes." Dayne pocketed the phone and tipped his head, indicating the paper with the code. "Maybe it was just a prank?"

He refused to believe that. No one but he and Kaden knew the Triad's curse had been activated. He and Kaden...and of course, whoever was responsible for the curse.

Could Dayne be the culprit?

A huge weight landed in his gut.

There'd never been any question about Dayne's feelings for Marek's family. It started so many years ago, during the raid. Dayne's parents had been involved with a fringe political group who'd wanted to expose the Sons of the Twilight to the human political powers, thinking they'd gain financially.

It had been a terrible day. A day no Son of the Twilight would ever forget, now that it had been recorded in the Book of Secrets. No doubt Dayne hadn't forgotten either. Or forgiven.

But surely he knew what a catastrophe it would be for Kaden to die.

Marek narrowed his gaze to the paper. They were columns of numbers, three numbers in each series, separated by dashes.

Could they be page numbers?

The first one was one thousand forty-three. He gently turned the pages, stopping on the designated page. He searched the page for a sign, a symbol, a clue.

Just lots of words.

He skimmed the page. It was a chapter about the laws of the humans. Nothing about the Triad or the curse.

He closed the book and shook his head. To think he was this close—inches from the answer—and yet he lacked the brainpower to see it. He had never felt so helpless.

He looked at the column again. If the first was a page number, what could the second one be? He looked down at the book, willing it to declare its secrets.

There were page numbers. Paragraphs. Lines. Letters.

The second number was twenty-eight. He counted down to the twenty-eighth line then over.

Shoot! Not enough letters in the line.

He went backwards. Last number as the page. Second number as the line. Third number as the letter.

The result—B.

He did the same with the second line of numbers. Then the third.

B. T. R.

Wasn't making much sense yet. He tried a few more.

H. U. P.

Damn.

He kept going, hoping if he took it back to Brea, she'd be able to figure out what it meant.

T. W. E. I. N. B. C. P. Y. I...

No use trying to read it. Obviously the letters were shuffled. Or he'd done something wrong.

Dayne was standing next to The Keeper, by the door. Their conversation, carried out in hushed whispers, didn't quite reach his ears. Dayne was nodding, his expression dark, his eyes cast down. His hands were balled into fists and tucked behind his back.

A trickle of concern wormed its way through Marek's insides. Could he trust Dayne?

Seeming to sense Marek's gaze on him, Dayne looked his way. Their gazes tangled and held, and an invisible current of energy charged between them. Dayne's lips parted then the corners lifted into a semi-smile. "Are we finished here?"

"I guess." Marek crossed the room, headed for the door. He wasn't convinced he'd solved the code but what else could the numbers mean? "I'm sorry to keep you so late," he said to The Keeper who stood sentry, bent and brittle as a dried twig, a notable contrast to Dayne's youthful strength and vitality.

"It was no trouble." The Keeper's eyes, the shade of morning fog, met his. "You found your answer?"

"I hope so."

"As I said, you may stay as long as you need."

Marek stopped walking. Why was he in such a hurry to leave? If the Keeper was in no hurry to chase them out, he needed to take his time. This was his only chance to solve the clue. The paper crackled as he unfolded it again to take one last look at the code. What else could the numbers mean?

The end is just the beginning.

Unless...

Could it be?

"I think I'll go back and take one last look." Marek rushed back to the book and, starting at the last page instead of the first, looked up the first letter. The second. The third, fourth and fifth.

T. O. T. H. E.

Tothe? To the? Words! They'd made words. Relief rushed through his body in soothing waves, sweeping his sagging spirits up from the murky depths they'd sunk to.

He'd done it! He'd found the answer. Maybe his brother wouldn't suffer the same end as their father.

If only the Triad had been destroyed as it was supposed to have been. He'd learned only days before Kaden was struck ill that the Triad had not only survived the last attempt to destroy it but had been tracked down by the Rebellion and stolen.

"I'll be just a few minutes more," he said over his shoulder.

The Keeper nodded, his lined face brightening. "Time is nothing to me. It has far greater value to you, Son of the Twilight."

* * * * *

Brea checked the cell phone for the hundredth time in the last hour. The phone had rung only once and when she'd tried to call the number back, her call was switched immediately to voice mail. Either Marek was on his phone or it was turned off.

Left to fret and worry and suffer, she'd gone back to snooping. She'd discovered the house was Dayne's and that Marek was only a guest, not a resident as she'd first assumed. She'd found only one photograph in the entire house, the picture of a beautiful woman, enclosed in a beautiful carved frame and sitting in the place of honor in Dayne's bedroom — on top of his dresser.

Every girl knew that spot was reserved for only one woman—the one he loved, girlfriend, wife, ex-whatever.

Niggling jealousy skittered through her nerves, warming her cheeks.

Who cared if Dayne loved another woman?

Who cared if she was fricking perfect, with the cutest nose and the most amazing eyes...and lips that had to have seen more than their share of collagen injections.

It was so easy to hate a woman who looked that good. Probably not a hint of cellulite on her butt either. Some women were so lucky.

God, to think he'd seen that woman naked, and then her. He most likely had compared their bodies, that woman's smooth perfection to her own lumpy, bumpy imperfection. Was enough to make a girl sick. Or give her a whopping headache.

She went to the bathroom in search of pain relief.

Outside of a couple toothbrushes and a tube of toothpaste, the medicine cabinet was as empty as the refrigerator. No shaving cream or razors. No hair products or clippers or tweezers or combs. No cold medicines or Q-tips.

And no pain relief.

What was with these guys?

Her head was going to explode. She got a headache after having sex with these guys? Weird. Her pounding cranium squeezed between her palms, she dragged her stressed and weary body down the hall to her room. But just as she turned the corner, she heard the rattle of the front door's lock, followed by the wonderful sound of two Chippendale's voices.

Her head be damned, she had to hear what happened!

Chapter Eight

ഇ

Hours later, spent scouring the web for sites on ciphers and codes, then huddled over scrambled strings of numbers and letters, they had the code decoded and the riddle solved. Well, Marek said he thought he might have the riddle solved. Brea, who still suffered from a wicked migraine despite the Excedrin Dayne had so sweetly volunteered to buy, had no idea what the riddle meant. Where the heck did the sun always shine?

It was the wee hours by the time they'd wrapped up the night's work. The wannabe private investigator in her screamed to head out immediately to find the next clue but her body refused to budge. She was beyond exhausted. Her eyes felt like they'd been sandblasted—dry and itchy. Her eyelids refused to lift fully between loooong blinks. She could swear lead weights were tied to her arms. And her back was tight and stiff.

Yet when she finally allowed herself to go to bed, her mind refused to shut down. Thoughts of the past couple of days kept the gears whirring along at top speed. The fact that she was sandwiched between two stunning, naked men made it that much more difficult for her to apply the brakes.

Two men who had kept their word. Thanks to them, she was one enormous step closer to finding the Triad.

With a sigh, she flopped onto her back.

Dayne—either trying to make nice since that little tying-up fiasco or genuinely a sensitive man—rolled onto his side and smiled at her. He stroked her arm, light touches, soothing. Sweet. "What's wrong?" He lifted her hand and flattened it between his. Then, twining their fingers, lifted it to place a kiss on each fingertip.

His eyes never left hers.

"Can't fall asleep."

"Really?"

She knew what was happening. It was in the way he pursed his lips and the way his eyes glittered.

She was all for it. Fuck her into a coma. She wouldn't complain. In fact, she might thank him in the morning after enjoying several hours of sound sleep.

"I can think of a way to help you fall asleep," Dayne offered, smoothing a hand up her arm.

"Sleeping pills?" she asked, letting her eyelids shutter out the distraction of sight so she could focus on the simple pleasure found in his slow, sensual touches.

"Something better," he whispered in her ear. His breath tickled the sensitive skin under her earlobe, making her shudder and sigh.

"Uh…" It was so hard to be cute and clever when her brain was melting like ice cream in a blast furnace.

She whimpered as a second set of hands got into the action. The guys undressed her then eased her onto her stomach. One performed magic on her neck and shoulders, rubbing out the kinks with the skill of a professional masseur while the other rubbed the soles of her feet.

It didn't take long before she was feeling soft and girly and oh-so hot. She shuddered at the memory of both of them fucking her, one powerful body beneath her, the other over top. Never in a million years had she ever imagined herself wanting to be with two men, now she was wondering if it would be a downer going back to having only one lover.

There were definite benefits to an extra set of hands…and a second mouth…and other extra parts.

Marek eased her knees apart and teased her slit with fingers and tongue while Dayne tormented her breasts. Together, the sensations, the pleasure, the heat, the tension coiling in her belly, nearly drove her to madness. She was too worn out to be patient. She just wanted release and she wanted it now.

"Fuck me," she demanded. "Fuck me now."

Marek pushed her legs back, spreading them wide, and claimed her with one stroke. Strong hands squeezed, pushed, dominated. Hips pistoned his thick cock in and out.

A moan of pure bliss broke through her pursed lips.

Now positioned somewhere at the foot of the bed — watching? — Dayne echoed her, with a deep, rumbling groan.

Marek's intimate strokes settled into a perfectly delicious pace, neither too slow nor too fast. She blinked open her eyes to watch his beautiful body work, knowing what a glorious sight those flexing muscles would make.

Then she realized what she was seeing and gasped, shocked into a powerful orgasm. For an instant, the image of Dayne's hands cupping Marek's shoulders as he drove into him from behind seemed burned into her mind like a photograph on film. It seemed to feed the heat pulsing through her body in wild waves. She opened her eyes again. She had to see. She had to watch. She'd never seen anything like it. Marek's cock was still gliding in and out of her, slowly, lubricated by the juices scenting the air musky sweet. Behind him, Dayne knelt on one knee, the other knee bent so his thigh pressed against the side of Marek's hip. From her vantage, she couldn't see Dayne's cock as it fucked Marek's ass, but she could hear the slap, slap of skin striking skin.

And she could plainly see the rapture on both their faces. That was one vision she never wanted to forget. And luckily for her — after all, how many girls saw such things? — the sight of two male faces lost in erotic bliss was the last thing she saw that night before she finally fell into a deep slumber.

* * * * *

It was hard to be mad at her Chippendales the next morning, given the activities of the night before, but she was pretty close to furious. Furious and tingly. Furious and giddy.

"I am so tired of you two telling me how I can't do anything." She stood in the middle of the bedroom, totally naked—she was past the point of caring about her cottage-cheese thighs—hands on hips, eyes narrowed to little slits and a menacing glare focused on Marek's ear. It was the only part of his anatomy she could look at without softening.

She was so damn weak!

They were still lying in bed. Marek's leg was thrown over Dayne's hip. The rumpled sheet barely covered Marek's adorable ass then wound in a twisted bunch between their bodies and up over Dayne's torso.

Eye. Candy. Yum.

"Would you two wake up?" she shouted, annoyed by their tired act. She was up and ready to go—well, not exactly ready to go—but she was vertical. It was almost eleven. Time was a-wastin'. They had clues to find. And unlike her nocturnal Chippendales, she worked better in daylight.

When they continued to ignore her, she stomped into the bathroom. She'd give them another twenty minutes. Then they were getting up or she was going to physically remove them from the bed.

How the hell would she do that?

She cranked on the shower. A bath in cold water. That would do the trick.

As long as she didn't mind sleeping in a wet bed tonight. *If* she was still there tonight.

What if she found the Triad today? Then what? She'd be able to leave, return to her safe and peaceful former life.

She'd have to take the Triad back to its owner. And then she'd go to her apartment. She had plants to water. Dust bunnies to slay.

Wow. Her life seemed so...lame.

Suddenly less enthusiastic about the day's possibilities, she showered then toweled dry. The temptation to climb back into that warm and cozy spot between her Chippendales was almost too much for her. But she resisted. She went to the closet and found herself yet another pair of huge sweatpants that almost fell off. She inhaled Marek's scent as she pulled on a Detroit Lions t-shirt.

Would he miss this old shirt? Wasn't like the Lions were good or anything.

She plopped onto the bed to pull on some socks, taking a second to rub away the ache in her neck and the knot in her left calf. Must be lack of sleep. She'd had the weirdest aches and pains the last few days.

"Guys. I'm hungry. I need to eat." Understatement. She was starved.

Two low growling rumbles came from the bed. One of them said something like, "Should have bought more last night..." and the other came back with, "It was your turn. I was trying to solve that damn clue."

"I checked the kitchen. There's not so much as a Pop-Tart in this joint. What do you two eat?" Come to think of it, she had yet to see either of them consume anything, not even a glass of water or a protein bar. "Is someone going to go buy me an Egg McMuffin or something? Dayne?"

His head poked up from under the sheet and he looked at her with tired, blood-shot eyes. "Can't, babe. Sorry. But I'll call in an order frooooooom..." A yawn dragged out the last part of the word before he continued, "The restaurant down the street. They deliver." And then his head fell back down, dead weight.

Good grief. If the guy was that worn out, then she could go get her own food. She'd lived alone for years. She could take care of herself.

She searched both their pants pockets for car keys and money. Feeling optimistic, she took the clue with her. Then, not exactly thrilled with the prospect of being seen in public dressed as she was, she scurried around, hunting down her own clothing and shoes. She found everything but her shirt in Dayne's bedroom closet.

Really. Had it been necessary to hide the rest of her stuff all this time? She wasn't so vain that some poorly fitting sweats would've stopped her from escaping if she'd had the chance. Grumbling about kidnappers who underestimated their captives, she gave up the sweats, opting for her jeans, pulled on her shoes and headed out to the garage.

It felt so good to be out among the real world again. She drove the enormous white van to Big Boy's for some breakfast. While she scarfed down an absolutely scrumptious omelet, she studied the clue, every word.

What did it mean?

To the place go thee where the sun never sets,

Past worlds that guard a rival's darkest secrets.

A twist to the left brings thine treasure in sight.

But a wrong turn and darkness defeats Twilight.

There was obviously a theme of astronomy — the sun, worlds or planets. She could think of at least two places where there might be some kind of model of the solar system, both of them science museums that were open to the public. But why would anyone risk hiding something that valuable where it might be found by anyone — a fifth-grader on a school field trip, a tourist from Timbuktu, a group of suburban moms dragging hyperactive toddlers through the museum to gain a few moments of peace.

But if it wasn't a public place, something the average girl would know about, how could the person who'd supplied the clue think she'd solve it? She couldn't possibly know if somebody had a solar system painted on a bedroom wall in some subdivision off Canton Center Road. It was feasible. But impossible for her to know about. She had to assume the clue's writer knew this.

After paying her check, she drove to the closest science museum, about twenty minutes away. She parked down the street in the public parking structure, tromped the block and a half to the museum, forked over the eight-dollar entry fee and wound through rooms full of themed science exhibits. Weather. Machines. Chemistry. The space exhibit was on the third floor, housed in a room with glow-in-the-dark stars painted on black walls. A huge model of the solar system hung about ten feet over her head, suspended several feet below the ceiling by cables.

Okay. So if this was the place, where was she supposed to look? A twist to the left? From what point?

She did a three-sixty, looking for a hint, a symbol, a sign. The walls were full of hands-on exhibits, meant to be manipulated by children with sticky fingers. No one in their right mind would hide a valuable treasure in one of those.

Besides the door through which she'd entered, there was only one other door. Depending upon which direction she was facing when she stood under the planets, the door could be on her left.

It was worth a try.

Locked.

Why did that not surprise her?

She had no tools. No credit cards, not that the old card-in-the-crack trick worked for her anyway. She hadn't been able to get herself in her own front door when she'd accidentally locked herself out last winter. She'd have to use her brain.

She had an idea.

She went back down to the information desk and informed the elderly woman posted there she'd accidentally lost her wedding ring under the door.

The woman was all too happy to call the manager to open the door.

Success!

Brea followed the manager back up to the solar system room, filling every moment they were together with profuse apologies and stories of the last time she'd lost her non-existent wedding ring.

Politely listening, he nodded, pushed the key into the door's lock and opened the door.

It led to the tiniest closet that had ever existed. Tiny and most definitely empty.

Still not ready to give up, she dropped on hands and knees — lost-treasure hunting was not for the vain or easily embarrassed — and searched the floor with her hands. Was there a loose floorboard? A trap door? "I can't believe it isn't in here. It must've fallen in a crack or rolled further back," she explained, as she ran her hands over every inch of the floor. "I'm so sorry. Am I keeping you from something important?" She forced a tear to her eye before looking over her shoulder. A little sympathy could come in handy.

He twisted his mouth into a semi-snarl. "If you'll kindly close the door when you're through, I'll come back later to lock it."

Yes! That was exactly what she'd hoped he do. Didn't want to look too happy though. Her eyes stinging as she forced more tears, she nodded, "Absolutely. Thank you."

As soon as she was alone, she set about searching every inch of the closet's walls, floor and sloping ceiling.

Nothing. Shoot!

Was she at the wrong place? The wrong room? The wrong building? Thankfully, the museum wasn't hosting any school groups and the solar system room, being at the very top of the building, was empty except for her. It gave her plenty of time to search the room.

Over an hour later, defeated and frustrated, she left.

Where to next? Back to the house? Back to her place? The clue playing through her head like a stuck song, she walked back to the car. The multi-storied, concrete and steel garage was quiet and dark, save the murky yellow light oozing from the fixtures dotting the cement walls at regular intervals, and the occasional distant squeal of tires or blast of a horn from the nearby road. Her senses alert, she hurried down the narrow alley toward the stairs, housed in a closed section in one corner. She clambered up the metal staircase then pushed through the door marked with a huge three. Third level above ground.

She never felt safe in these garages. They were creepy. Dark. She was alone. Surrounded by thick concrete walls and thousands of empty cars. How easy would it be for someone to knock her in the head and have their way with her?

Jittery and chilled from both nerves and the cool, damp air, she rushed toward the van. Had to be parked on the far end, opposite the stairs, of course.

She had a funny tingly feeling between her shoulder blades. Was someone following her? She whipped around and listened, figuring if someone were following she'd either see or hear them try to duck behind a car.

Nothing. Okay, she was just being paranoid.

A little less petrified, she continued walking. A heavy sigh of relief slipped through her lips when she reached the van and hooked her fingers under the door's handle.

Something flew past her ear, something tiny and fast. She ducked out of instinct. An instant later, when a hole the size of a bullet punched through the windshield, she knew what that something had been.

Someone was shooting a gun? At her? Why?

In full panic mode, she dragged open the door and hurried into the vehicle. Staying low, and praying like she had never prayed before, she fumbled with the keys, stuffing them into the ignition. The passenger side window exploded, the pebbled safety glass showering down on her. Another bullet whirred through the air and hit the windshield from the rear, creating a second ring of shattered glass next to the first.

She couldn't move.

She couldn't breathe.

It was over. She was dead meat.

Was this how it was going to end for her? Had she spent all those years hiding in her apartment to be shot and killed in a parking garage?

Hell no!

Her chest on the passenger seat, she scooted toward the driver's side, working her legs down under the dash. The second she found the pedals, she hit the gas and jammed the vehicle into reverse. The vehicle jolted backward, striking something hard that went thump.

Ha! Had she hit the son-of-a-bitch? Knocked him out? She hoped so! She changed positions, allowing herself to sit up so she could steer as she continued backing out of the parking spot. Using the driver's side mirror as a guide, she cranked the wheel to the left, turning the vehicle to the right and punched the gas. The right side of the van raised then fell, first the rear then the front. Bump, bump.

Her insides surged up her throat. She stomped on the brakes. The van wasn't traveling fast, so it lurched to a sudden stop. "Please tell me I didn't just run over a human being." Sure, she hadn't been sorry for knocking the would-be killer out, but killing them…oh no. She was not a killer.

She sat very still, eyes straight ahead, fingers gripping the steering wheel so tightly her hands were numb. She listened, not sure whether she wanted to hear someone moving outside or not. For sure, she didn't want to hear any more gunfire.

What to do? Drive away, saving her hide but possibly leaving a human being lying near death on the ground? Or check and see if she'd indeed run over someone?

God, she didn't want to get out. Either way, she figured she wasn't going to like what she saw. If she were watching this scene on television right now, she'd be screaming at the stupid heroine, calling her too stupid to live for even thinking about getting out of the vehicle. In the movies, the chick who did that got the ax. Quite literally.

But in real life, it was different. She wasn't an animal. If she hurt someone, the human being in her demanded she at least call for help.

She took a few deep breaths and twisted around in her seat, sneaking a glance at the passenger-side mirror. She saw nothing but the reflected image of a bank of parked cars and a concrete wall. No crazy murderer with a hockey mask and a weapon in each hand.

She inched higher, trying to see a few more inches of the ground in the mirror. Nothing. She lifted her foot off the brake, shifted into drive and let the vehicle roll forward a few feet, her gaze bouncing back and forth between the view out the shot-out windshield and the reflection in the mirror.

There was something on the ground. Something dark. That looked a lot like a person.

Oh God.

She turned around in her seat, adjusted the angle of the mirror, and while staring at the form lying sprawled on the ground, hit the horn. It, he, whatever, didn't move. Didn't twitch. Didn't jump. No human being was that good at playing dead.

She fumbled for the phone in her pocket, checked to make sure it was powered up. She even dialed 9-1-1, although she didn't put the call through yet. She wanted to make sure she hadn't just run over a bag of clothes or something first. She shifted the vehicle into park.

The phone at ready, she inched open the driver's side door, stepped out onto the running board and dropped her head, looking under the vehicle for feet.

It appeared no one was hiding around the back of the van. She placed one foot then the other on the ground and slowly, cautiously, left the safety of the vehicle.

"I-I have a gun," she lied, knowing it was probably pointless. "Don't move or I'll shoot." She took one, two, three steps forward and stopped.

It was a woman.

Still holding the gun. Sort of.

Her face was ashen.

Her eyes were staring straight ahead. Sightless. One pupil huge, the other a pinpoint.

Dead.

The air thinned. The world whirled around her head, making her feel like she was on a runaway carnival ride. For some reason, all she could think to do was snap a picture of the dead killer with the phone's digital camera. Then, sitting in the van, she called the police, "Hello, I'd like to report an accident," she told the dispatcher with a shaking voice. "I h-hit someone. I think she's dead."

Chapter Nine

හ

"It can't be her." Marek stared blindly at the wall, the phone resting in his palm. "W-Why?"

"Who is it?" Dayne asked, first looking at Marek and then at Brea when he didn't respond.

Brea shrugged. "I don't know. The police wouldn't tell me anything. They just asked me the same questions over and over, and left me sitting there for ages, wondering if they were going to arrest me for vehicular manslaughter or something. All I know is that she is dead. I ran her over, but thankfully the authorities decided it wasn't intentional. I've never had an accident before. I've never killed someone before either." She placed her hand on Marek's arm. He was still looking dazed. Confused. "Marek?"

Staring straight ahead, he slowly shook his head and extended his arm toward Dayne. "It makes no sense."

Dayne took the phone and lifted it to view the photograph captured on the tiny screen. "Ohhhh..."

"What makes no sense? Who is she?" Brea urged. "She shot at me. No one has ever shot at me before. She almost killed me. Why?"

Her words seemed to finally jolt Marek out of the spell he'd fallen under. His expression cleared, the confusion lifting. "My brother's fiancée Lena. Our future queen."

"Queen?" Brea repeated. There were no queens in the United States. Were her Chippendales legal citizens of some other country? "Queen of what?"

"Sons of the Twilight," Dayne explained, handing the phone back to Marek. "I agree. This makes no sense—"

"Sons of what?"

"The Twilight," Marek repeated, nodding to Dayne. "Must be some mistake. Maybe she picked up the gun when the real shooter dropped it."

"Sons of the Twilight," Brea echoed over the guys' conversation. "Is that some kind of secret society? Like the Masons?"

"Kind of," Marek said.

"Not really," Dayne said, nodding. "Yes. Now that makes sense. She must have picked up the gun after the shooter ran. And of course, Brea wouldn't know that since she was ducking low to avoid being shot."

"Yeah," Marek agreed distantly. He picked up the phone again and studied the grainy photograph. "Maybe if we printed a copy, we could see the detail a little better."

"Doubt it. These old phones don't take the best quality pictures. They're less than one megapixel."

"Damn. I'd like to know for sure. I should tell Kaden about this."

Suddenly feeling like a third wheel, Brea watched the guys talk about the photograph, the woman, what they should do next.

"Are you sure you weren't hurt?" Marek asked, his gaze sweeping up and down her body. "You shouldn't have left by yourself. You have no idea how dangerous that was."

"I tried to wake you two up but you wouldn't budge. It was late. Broad daylight. And you two were dead to the world. What are you? Nocturnal or something?"

The two guys swapped sidelong glances.

"What?"

They both shook their heads.

"I was starving but neither of you could be bothered with getting me some food." She continued, her rant gaining momentum, "What did you expect? And why the hell don't you have anything to eat in this place?"

Frowning, Dayne crossed his arms over his chest. "I told you to order some carry-out—"

"Correction," she interrupted. "You said you'd order carry-out. Besides, I'm tired of that place. That's all I've had since you brought me here. A girl likes a little variety, you know. And while you two were getting some beauty sleep, I thought I'd solve the clue. I didn't expect anyone to chase after me with guns blazing."

Marek sighed. "We should've told her everything sooner," he said to Dayne.

Dayne shrugged his shoulders and murmured, "I think you're making a mistake."

"Everything? What everything?"

"It's a little complicated." Marek looked down at the phone in his hand then set it on the table and stood.

"Complicated? Imagine that. So what's the big secret? There's something really strange going on here. I'm not stupid." She poked an index finger at Dayne. "You never eat." Then she pointed her other index finger at Marek. "You sleep during the day. You both are obviously hiding things from me. People are chasing me. Are you two government agents or something?"

"No," Dayne answered, positioning himself beside Marek. "We're...vampires."

She started to laugh but the guys' serious-as-death expressions made her guffaw lodge itself in her throat. However, her constricting windpipe didn't stop a chuckle from escaping her lips. "Vampires?"

They both nodded.

"Real-life, blood-sucking vampires?"

They nodded again.

"Can't-go-out-in-the-sunlight vampires?"

116

They nodded a third time.

"Ha! I got you there. You kidnapped me in the middle of the afternoon. Explain that one to me."

"We are given a special pill once a year," Marek reasoned coolly, "to enable us to go out in the sunlight. It only lasts for a few hours though."

"A pill? Uh…" Wow, what's a girl to say when her lovers drop a bomb like that on her? "Are you two trying to scare me off with this crazy story? 'Cause I'll gladly leave on my own. I'm not in love with you or anything." Not in love, but up until now, she'd been mighty close to falling in serious like with her Chippendales. "I mean, you guys kidnapped me. Not the other way around."

Marek stepped forward. "We needed you. We still do."

"Why? For the Triad?"

Marek's gaze shifted to Dayne.

"That's it? You kidnapped me to help you find the Triad? You weren't going to help me? I was right all along?"

To think she'd started to believe they were working together. The three musketeers.

How stupid was she?

A million emotions blasted through her all at one time. Anger and hurt were the biggest. She felt used. Worthless. Manipulated. Once again, she'd trusted the wrong male — males.

"I'm so out of here." She rushed to the door but Marek caught her arm. "Let me go, dammit. I'm not going to help you."

"We still need you."

"Fuck off and die."

This time it was Dayne who spoke, "If you leave before sunset tomorrow night, that's exactly what will happen. To both of us."

"Did you know about this too? About the Triad?" she asked him, hot tears blurring her vision, even as wild, wicked desire pulsed through her body. Now was so not the time to get horny.

"No. I swear I didn't know."

"I don't believe you. I don't believe either of you. Not a word you say. You're both a couple of lying creeps. Then again, why would I even consider trusting a couple of guys who stoop to kidnapping women? Hello?" She yanked her arm free from Marek's grasp and knocked on her skull. "Is anybody home? I'm such an idiot." She wrapped her fist around the doorknob and pulled but Marek slammed the door shut and blocked her path. "Move out of my way," she growled.

"Not until you hear everything."

"I've heard enough."

"My brother is dying."

"So sad for you."

"I need the Triad to cure him. The Rebellion stole it from your client, to use it against my brother. It activates an ancient curse."

"This sounds like the plot from some low-budget movie." She shoved him, using her weight to try to knock him out of her way. Of course, he didn't even twitch. It really pissed her off that she was so weak.

Marek gripped her upper arms in his fists. "I need your help."

"I'm already on a case. Hire your own private detective."

He shook her, not exactly gently but not hard enough to cause brain damage either. It was enough to make her meet his gaze. His eyes were teary and red, full of genuine pain, desperation. "Have you ever lost someone you loved?"

She tipped her head to leer at him. "Yes. I have."

"Could you have stopped it?"

"No. But if I could have, I would've done anything—"

"That's just it. I can do something. With your help." A single tear slipped from the inner corner of his eye and ran along the side of his nose. "Only with your help."

That little droplet of water doused her anger. She'd never been able to resist a man who was vulnerable. "You're not lying?"

"No."

"You're really a vampire?"

"We've both bitten you several times but you don't remember. Our venom acts as an amnesiac."

That explained some things. "Is that why I hurt here...why my body reacts the way it does?"

"It's the blood-bond. It causes what we call the hunger."

"The hunger?" she echoed, trying to wrap her brain around the fact that vampires really existed.

"The hunger is the byproduct of a chemical change in your body. It makes you desire us. And vice versa, us desire you. And each other."

Then her desire for them was...artificial? At least she didn't have to feel guilty for falling in instant lust with them.

She looked to Dayne for reassurance. It came in the form of a simple nod...and a fangy sneer.

"I knew there was something weird about you two." She shrugged away from Marek, shuffling back a couple of steps to get a long look at her Chippendales. "It's pretty creepy, you know. You guys have been snacking on me all this time and I don't remember a thing. Anything else I've forgotten?"

"Oh, I don't think so," Marek answered, chuckling. "We've done our best to make sure everything else has been quite memorable."

"Ohmygosh! Oh. My. Effing. God! Am I a vampire too? Did you turn me? Am I going to have to drink blood? Oh, I hate blood."

Laughter glittering in his eyes, Dayne took a single step closer. "Humans can't be 'turned'. The movies have that all wrong. They have a lot of things wrong."

She huffed a huge sigh of relief. "Is that so? What else do they have wrong?"

They sandwiched her between them, fangs bared.

The air thinned and heated. Her skin started tingling, first at her nape then her chest, stomach, lower. "Is this how it goes?" Being carried away by the erotic heat swirling through her body, she closed her eyes and tipped her head back, baring her throat. Crazy impulses flashed through her mind. She wanted to explore the dark side of her desire, to experience firsthand what it felt like to submit, to be conquered and controlled. "You use me and abuse me?"

"I don't know," Marek said, laving her shoulder with his tongue. "I kind of think you'll come to like that part." When his fangs pierced her skin, a powerful orgasm pulsed through her body. She surrendered on a moan.

"Are you ready now? Ready to give this another try?" Dayne held a set of restraints in his fists. "No one is forcing you. It's your choice. Your decision, yes or no. We'll do as you wish."

She looked at her Chippendales, the two men who'd proven to be a whole lot more than a couple of sexy, manipulative kidnappers. They hadn't always done what she'd wanted. But in the end she had to be grateful for that fact. Because by pushing her, stripping away her defenses, they'd helped her see how she'd allowed her fears to hold her prisoner. Issues with trust, of taking risks — with her life, body, secrets and heart.

She wanted to be freed. From all her fears. Her Chippendales hadn't raped her. She'd seen it as rape because of her feelings about bondage, or more specifically accepting her desires as a woman. What had happened with Steven had been terrible, but a combination of things had contributed to that night, some her fault, some his, and some nobody's. To say that night didn't matter anymore wasn't fair. Because the experience had left her scarred, unable to accept herself. To say that those scars had completely and miraculously healed wasn't realistic either.

But thanks to Dayne and Marek, she was ready to take the first step. She slowly peeled away her clothes then, standing before them completely undressed, said, "Yes, I think I'm ready now." This time, when Dayne secured the restraints around her wrists, she trembled with nervous anticipation instead of cold terror.

"Will you tell us what happened?" Marek sat on the bed and pulled her onto his lap. "What secret have you been hiding?"

Her gaze swept over his face before settling on his eyes. Kind eyes, full of genuine concern. She started slowly. Each word stuck in her throat. It took effort to pry them loose, one at a time. "I had a friend. A dear friend. I trusted him. I needed him. I was away from home. Unsure. Maybe I was foolish when I let him tie me up. But he'd never done anything, said anything, that made me feel it wouldn't be okay. We were playing, just experimenting." Hot tears ran from her eyes, blurring her vision. She did a lot of blinking, sniffling, as the memories of that night swept through her mind. Marek thumbed away a droplet dribbling over her cheek and for a short time, she just sat there, letting his gentle touches and watery eyes touch her heart. A soothing peace spread through her, giving her strength to continue, "And then it went wrong, and I couldn't stop him. And afterward I blamed myself. I felt guilty, since I'd been the one to suggest he tie me up. It couldn't be normal, my obsession with bondage. Only prostitutes liked that kind of thing, right? Prostitutes and mentally ill people. So I shut it all out, my sex life, my desires. They were dirty and abnormal. Wrong."

"They're not dirty or wrong. Hell, the psychologists dropped S-and-M from their list of mental illnesses." Her face caught between his hands, Marek kissed her cheeks, her nose, her forehead. "You're not obsessed. You're curious. That's completely okay. Your friend was wrong. Very wrong. You know that now, right?"

"I'm starting to see that."

Marek nodded. "Then you're ready."

"With us, you have all the power, Brea, regardless of the restraints," Dayne said as he eased her onto her back and slid his hand between her thighs. "I promise, if you say the word, we'll stop."

"What word?"

Standing and unzipping his pants, Marek donned a fangy grin. "How about Van Helsing?"

"How very appropriate." She couldn't help smiling. Yes, this was what she had always craved, what she'd been missing in her physical relationships in the past. Sex would never again simply be a physical exercise. The joining of male parts to female parts. It was as much mental as physical. She wasn't abnormal or sick just because she was curious about domination and submission. She wasn't asking to be raped. She wasn't dirty. There was no reason to feel guilty for asking for certain things. No longer would sex be just about reaching the finish line, the Big O. It would be about power, submission. Surrender. Discovery. Experimentation. She had her Chippendales to thank for that.

* * * * *

Marek's words wouldn't leave Dayne's head. They played through his mind, over and over, in that trembly voice. Neither would the image of his blood-mate's pain-filled eyes.

Was it the blood-bind? Did it make his heart soften to his enemy's pain? Or was it something else? Did it matter?

He wasn't sure he could go through with his plan anymore. Not when he looked into Marek's eyes. He felt Marek's pain. Deep in his gut. It took the form of a cold, hard weight that sapped his strength and left him feeling empty and lost. How could he destroy Marek? Sure, he no longer sought to kill him. But he knew now what Kaden's death would do to him. Marek would never be the same man.

But what about his commitment to the Rebellion? To the friends who had backed him all these years? They'd sacrificed so much. How could he just turn his back on them now?

He was between hell and Hades. He had to make a choice. But which one? Who would he betray?

* * * * *

"I only checked one science museum before she stopped me." Brea was dressed, but Marek could barely resist the urge to strip her clothes and make sweet love to her all over again. The more he had of her, the more he wanted her. He could still taste her honey on his lips. Could still smell her special scent clinging to his fingertips.

He watched her pull a brush through her hair. How he ached to run his fingers through the satin strands again, to pull. And taste. Skin, juices, kiss.

It was the hunger. The fucking hunger!

Angry and frustrated, he forced himself to move farther away. Her scent followed him. And the memory of her cries of pleasure played through his head. He went to his weapons closet. What to take with him? Gun? Dagger? Sword?

He lifted the saber off its mount and weighed the weapon in his hands. Guns were effective enough for humans. But he would need a silver blade. Sons of the Twilight could only be killed with a blade forged from silver.

How fitting, he thought wryly. He'd use a gift from his father to defend his brother's claim to the throne, and his life.

"Can you think of another place with a model of the solar system? Or a sun and planets?" Brea asked.

Marek's addled mind slowly caught up with the conversation. Brea was sitting on the bed, looking up at him with expectation.

"Honestly no," he answered. "That's where I thought we'd search first."

She stood, her jaw set. "Okay. Well, you two can't go outside until after dark. That's hours from now. It's up to me. I'll hit the science center in Bloomfield Hills next—"

Dayne interrupted, "No, you can't leave. It's too risky."

"I'll be extra careful."

Dayne wasn't going to give in. He posture reflected his attitude. "No. Absolutely not. We'll wait until dark and go together."

Brea tossed her hands in the air. "But if the museums are closed, how will we get in? If we have to break in somehow, we'll run out of time. What if the first couple of places are the wrong places?"

Marek traced the swirling engravings in his sword's hilt, his mind lost in his worries and doubts. "We just have to make sure we're going to the right place first."

"How will we do that?"

"I don't know."

Was there any hope that they could save his brother's life? He looked at the clock on the nightstand. The second hand measured Kaden's final hours with racing tick-tocks. Yet they were still no closer to finding the Triad than they were this morning.

He needed a miracle. Just one little miracle.

His heart heavy, he set down his sword, crossed back to the desk and hit the power button on the computer. Until sundown, the only searching they could do was on the web.

Chapter Ten

ॐ

Brea set the stack of maps printed off the computer on the car's dashboard and slid into the passenger seat. Dayne had kindly volunteered his car for this road trip, since Marek's van was not exactly roadworthy with two shot-out windows and a shattered windshield.

Beside her, in the driver's seat, Dayne started the car and shifted it into gear.

"If we follow the route I mapped out," Marek said from the backseat, "we should have enough time to search at least two of the museums before sunrise. Unless we're caught trying to break into one of them."

Silent, Dayne steered the vehicle onto the winding dirt road.

Brea pulled the first map off the dash and studied it. "We need to head north on I-275."

"Okay," Dayne responded distantly.

Brea stiffened, again wondering what was up with Dayne. All afternoon, while Marek and she had been scouring the internet for clues, he'd been withdrawn, quiet, detached. She'd asked him several times what was wrong, but being a man, he simply said "nothing".

But his eyes couldn't lie. Not to her. He was struggling with something. A very difficult decision of some kind. She couldn't help wondering if it had something to do with the Triad.

Ten minutes later, she learned her suspicions weren't silly paranoid thoughts to be shrugged off.

They were at the entry of the freeway…rolling past the ramp to northbound I-275.

"Uh, you missed the turn," she said as she pointed out the window. "Dayne?"

He didn't respond.

She twisted in her seat and glanced back at Marek. They traded worried looks. Obviously, Marek was as surprised as she was.

He shifted forward on the seat. "Hey, Dayne? What's up? Change of plans?"

"Yeah," Dayne snapped, looking over his shoulder. "What's wrong? Don't trust me?"

Marek and Brea traded a second worried look.

And then everything went blurry and Brea lurched forward. She caught herself on outstretched arms less than a second before her head struck the dash. "Dayne!" she shrieked, when her brain registered the red brake lights ahead.

"Dammit!" Dayne shouted, counter-steering the car out of a skid.

"Wha—?!" Marek barked from the back.

The car's tires gained traction on the asphalt none too soon. The car screeched to a stop so close to the Ford in front of them Brea could see the driver's panicked gaze in the rearview mirror.

Arms still out, palms pressed against the dash, Brea dragged in a lungful of air. She could hear both Marek and Dayne doing the same. She looked to her left, studying Dayne's profile.

His face had gone white. His knuckles too. "Everyone okay?" he mumbled.

"Yeah," she answered, her voice shaky.

"I'm okay too," Marek muttered.

"Good." Dayne didn't say another word. He didn't turn his head. He didn't loosen his grip on the steering wheel. And neither Brea nor Marek dared ask him any more questions. Brea figured they'd have their answers soon enough— assuming they made it to their destination alive.

About forty minutes after their close call, the car rolled to a smooth stop behind a building that looked like some kind of church. Dayne shifted the vehicle into park, motioned to Brea to stay put then twisted in his seat to talk to Marek. "I don't know if there'll be anyone here waiting for us or not. But I'm almost positive this is the right place."

"What is it?" Brea asked. It didn't look like the kind of place one would expect to find a model of the solar system.

"Holy Redeemer Presbyterian Church. Better take some weapons," Dayne warned.

The two men gave her a warning glance before getting out of the car.

Marek opened her door and poked his head inside. "Stay here. And keep your eyes open," he whispered. "If things get bad, drive away. Save yourself."

She hoped it wouldn't come to that. "Wouldn't it be safer for me to come with you?" She scooted into the driver's seat and opened the window.

The two guys traded questioning looks over the car then said, "No," in unison.

Of course not. Why did she know they'd say that? "Be careful. Please."

Marek ducked down again and whispered, "There's a dagger in the trunk. As soon as we're inside, get it. Keep it with you. Stay safe. I'm not sure what's going on here. Something isn't right."

"I'm scared."

"I love you." He palmed her cheek gently.

She pressed her hand to the back of his. "Marek."

Slowly he moved away, his eyes heavy with worry. "Stay safe," he repeated.

Her heart doing its best to bust through her rib cage, she watched her Chippendales head inside then popped the trunk and snatched the leather-sheathed dagger. Shaking, she returned to the relative safety of the car, locked the doors and stared at the building's entry.

She doubted she'd be able to take another breath until both her Chippendales were back with her, safe. Ironic, but she couldn't care less anymore about the stupid Triad. Her case, her job simply didn't matter.

* * * * *

Marek held his sword drawn. There wasn't a muscle in his body not tensed, ready. His senses were alert—sight, hearing, smell. His nerves jangled. He stopped in the center of what had probably been the church's sanctuary, a massive room, empty now, topped with a glass dome. The walls were covered in painted tiles, the mural a clear representation of the solar system.

"The clue?" Dayne, standing at the opposite end of the room, pointed at a section of the wall next to him. "What did it say again?"

Marek switched his sword to his left hand and stuffed his right into his pocket. He retrieved the folded piece of paper and smoothed it against his chest. "To the place go thee where the sun never sets, past worlds that guard a rival's darkest secrets." Shifting his sword back to his dominant hand, he hurried across the empty space. His footsteps echoed off the walls, ceiling and floor. "What do you see?"

He followed the direction of Dayne's pointed index finger to a swirling symbol stamped in one of the clay tiles. The identical symbol graced the base of his sword's polished blade. "The symbol of the Sons of Twilight?" He traced the curling lines with his fingertip. "This has to be it. How'd you know to come here?" He used his fingers to search the lumpy surface of the tiles for some kind of button, switch or knob.

"I...had a suspicion."

Clearly Dayne wasn't telling him everything. Should he press for more? Or trust his former enemy? "The rest of the clue reads, 'A twist to the left brings thine treasure in sight. But a wrong turn and darkness defeats Twilight'. See anything that turns or twists?"

Dayne stood beside him, mirroring his position, one fist gripping a silver-bladed sword, the other hand flattened against the wall, skimming over its surface. "Not yet. But there is an interesting hole here...shit!"

Marek swung around just in time to see Dayne lift his sword high over his head. Operating on pure reflex, he ducked and lunged out of the path of Dayne's blade, curling into a ball. He somersaulted on the floor and leapt to his feet, spinning on one foot at the clang of metal striking metal.

He scooped his dropped sword up and stood frozen in shock. Dayne shuffled backward, just escaping a blow to his shoulder. His assailant's small, compact body, clothed head-to-toe in black, moved quickly, taking advantage of Dayne's position. He'd backed himself against the wall but he was doing okay defending himself.

Marek was about to come to his aid when Dayne glanced Marek's way and shouted, "Look out!"

Marek simultaneously lifted his weapon and turned, swinging it in a wide arc. The blade sliced into the assailant behind him, dragging a red gaping wound across his torso. The masked attacker staggered backward then stumbled and crumpled to the ground.

A rush of similarly dressed men fell upon him. The deafening clang of silver striking silver filled the room. Marek didn't have time to think, only act. And react. Attack. Defend. Parry. Block. Over time, the blows came less frequently as the number of his attackers decreased.

And then it was done. He stood in the middle of the carnage. Mangled black-clothed bodies strewn about his feet.

Dayne was about twenty feet away, also standing. His clothes were stained red, splattered with their enemy's blood.

Marek looked down at the closest body. They were all so small. He ripped the knit mask away, finding the face of...a woman. "What is this?" he murmured, not expecting an answer.

Stepping up beside him, Dayne answered, "It's really quite clever. Since the Sons of Twilight cannot be exposed to sunlight, having all female warriors means they have a tactical advantage."

"Did you know?"

"What? That they were women?" At Marek's nod, he whispered, "Yes."

Marek dropped on one knee. "I've never slain a woman. Women shouldn't be warriors. They shouldn't be facing this kind of danger. What made them want to do such a thing? And what about their husbands? Their fathers? Their brothers? Did they know?"

Dayne offered a hand of support on Marek's shoulder. A simple touch, yet it spoke volumes. Marek brushed a golden lock of hair from the dead woman's face and gently forced her eyelids closed. From the neck up, she looked like she was napping. The ugly gouge across her stomach ruined the façade.

Dayne gave Marek's shoulder a couple of pats. "We should get going. Before they send in another unit."

"There are more?"

"Plenty. They'll be here in about," Dayne glanced down at his watch, "four minutes."

"Was this a trap?"

"Not exactly." Dayne rushed toward the wall they'd been inspecting before the attack and extended an arm back to Marek. "Let me see your sword."

Marek felt his forehead wrinkle in confusion. He hesitated, not sure if he could trust Dayne or not. He'd more or less confessed to knowingly leading them into an ambush. What was next? For all he knew, his sword might be the only thing keeping him alive. Who was his enemy? His ally?

As if he sensed Marek's suspicion, Dayne turned to face him fully. "We're running out of time."

"You say," Marek shot back.

"Yes, I say we're running out of time. What are *you* trying to say?"

"For all I know, you brought me here to have me slaughtered. And now that Plan A has failed, you're going to disarm me so you can kill me yourself."

"Why would I bother warning you before that first blow if that was the case?"

"Maybe you decided you wanted the satisfaction of killing me yourself?"

"And kill myself in the process?"

"Maybe revenge is worth it to you. After all, there was a time when you would've done just about anything to be in this position. I know that."

"You're right. I did want revenge, and I had planned on killing you. But not anymore." Dayne looked past Marek to the dead bodies strewn about the floor. "Nothing's worth all this."

His suspicions easing, Marek moved closer to his bound mate. "I want to believe you. But you spent so many years hating me. My brother. Blaming us."

"Let's just say I've been enlightened." He thrust his hand forward and yanked Marek's sword from his loose grasp. Instinctively, Marek turned and leaped, landing in a roll about ten feet away.

Dayne spun around and, holding the sword by the blade, thrust the handle of Marek's weapon into the hole carved into the tile. "The engraving. Your sword is the key." He twisted it ninety degrees to the left. There was a groan of stone grinding against stone. An opening appeared in the wall.

Illuminated from a single shaft of light from above and, about fifteen feet within the otherwise pitch-black room, sat a single crystal pedestal not unlike the one holding the Book of Secrets. Atop the pedestal was the Triad.

"We have less than two minutes," Dayne reminded him. "Trust me now?" Turning, he rushed into the dark room.

"Wait!" Marek called after him. "Remember the rest of the clue?"

Dayne slammed into something invisible and stumbled backward.

"We take a wrong turn and we're done." Hurrying to Dayne's side, Marek felt the surface in front of them then looked down. It seemed that the walls were made of some kind of transparent substance, a lot like glass. "It's a maze." He looked down at the floor.

The darkness beneath their feet was strange. It had depth, rather than looking flat, like tile. He stomped a foot. The answering sound was hollow. "I get it. We take a wrong turn and we'll fall down there."

"No pressure," Dayne said dryly. "We don't even know where the corners are."

The pounding of dozens of running feet made them both look back. A crush of warriors were headed their way, swords raised.

"Shit!" Using one hand on the slick wall as a guide, Marek led the way at a fast jog. He dragged his sword out of the scabbard and the blade caught a shaft of light from somewhere. Pinpoints of light glittered off the reflective surface of the walls. "This way!" he shouted, recognizing a black area to the right as a doorway. Similarly, black gaps large enough for a grown man to fall through on the floor indicated wrong turns.

Dayne dogged his heels as he ran, also tipping his sword to flash stars on the floors and walls, a celestial guide through the blackness.

The screams of their pursuers as they took wrong turns and tumbled into the abyss chilled Marek's blood and caused him to falter twice. He wanted to stop, to beg them to turn back, but he knew they would no sooner believe his warning than he'd trusted Dayne.

Both of them reached the Triad at the same time. Dayne looked askance before reaching for it.

Marek nodded. "I trust you."

Dayne cradled the relic that would save their king's life in his arms as if his own life depended upon it. "Wonder if there's another way out?" He pointed behind Marek, to the handful of warriors who had managed to make their way safely through the maze.

"I really don't want to kill another woman."

Dayne took a long look around them then nodded his head, as if he'd made a decision. "Do you trust me?"

"Yes."

Dayne moved around the side of the pedestal, to the last gap in the floor that they'd avoided. He held the Triad over the hole. "Stop!"

Marek's heart climbed up his throat.

"You will throw down your weapons and retreat or the Triad will be destroyed."

The warriors halted, set down their swords and started shuffling backward.

Dayne motioned for Marek to go ahead. "I'll follow but not until you're safe."

It was one of the most difficult tests of trust Marek had ever faced but he did as Dayne said. Even after he was safely outside the maze, he didn't take his eyes off Dayne. He couldn't. Not until he too had passed the final gap in the floor.

The warriors retreated, seeming to accept the defeat too easily. It made him edgy as they walked out of the building, the Triad in hand.

When they reached their car, he realized why the warriors hadn't attacked.

Two warriors dragged Brea around the side of a black van, the silver blade of her dagger pressed to her throat.

"The Triad," one of them demanded, releasing Brea's arm to thrust an upturned palm toward Dayne.

They'd gotten this close, only to lose it? Marek could see Brea was pleading for them not to hand the relic to the warrior. But he had to. He knew that neither he nor Dayne could stand by and watch the warriors kill her.

Even if it meant the death of his brother.

Unless...what if they destroyed it before the curse was lifted? What would happen? Would the curse be broken? Or would Kaden die?

Damn it. He faced an impossible decision.

At least in death, Kaden would be spared the agony of the curse. But that was an extremely small comfort. He was Marek's only remaining family.

"There's no hope of escape." The warrior holding Brea jerked the dagger, causing the blade to bite into the skin of her neck. A rivulet of blood dribbled down from the wound, yet Brea remained silent, defiant.

Fuck! There was precious little time to decide. What would Kaden wish? For him to hand over the Triad and save their own butts, thereby sealing his doom? Or to possibly assure no king after him would endure the agony of the curse?

He took another look around. They were grossly outnumbered, and since a half dozen warriors surrounded their car, even if he was able to get Brea free from the one holding her, they'd have to escape on foot. How likely was that?

"Let her go, and you can have it," Dayne demanded, pulling the relic tucked in his jacket out into view.

Marek's body tensed. He'd have to time it just right, push Brea clear of the warriors' reach and then kick the Triad out of their hands. He hoped the impact as it fell would destroy it. History dictated the ancient artifact was not easily damaged.

But if he were successful, and the Triad destroyed, the warriors would leave. They'd no longer have any reason to pursue them.

And his brother...he only hoped he'd be given the chance to explain. And say goodbye. At least his suffering would be over.

Dayne stepped in front of Marek, the Triad held at arm's length in front of him. One of the warriors pushed Brea forward, using her as a shield.

Marek moved silently and slowly.

"Release her," Dayne demanded again.

"Not until we have the Triad."

"You won't get it until she's released."

"Then we can kill her." The warrior pushed the dagger's tip deeper into Brea's neck. Another crimson droplet formed at the wound. Brea gasped but she didn't speak, didn't beg, didn't cry. "Once she's dead, her blood-mates will die. Then we will have the Triad."

Dayne lifted his hand higher and lunged forward.

Now!

Time slowed to a tenth its normal speed as Marek threw himself forward, knocking Brea to the ground. He leapt to his feet and, spinning, kicked the Triad out of Dayne's hand. It flew about twenty feet and landed with a heavy crunch on the pavement.

There was a moment of shocked silence before Dayne and the two warriors dashed for the fallen relic. Marek turned to Brea and helped her back to her feet.

"Are you okay?" He gave her a quick up-and-down as she staggered to her feet.

"I think so." Grimacing, Brea rubbed her backside. "Those were chicks. Women bad-guys. Did you know that? Bitches!"

"Yeah." Marek swallowed a chuckle at Brea's expression. "We found out inside."

"You wouldn't believe how much I wanted to kick their asses. But they took my knife. I'm glad you didn't give them the Triad. They were going to kill us all anyway." A strand of hair fluttered across her face, carried by the breeze.

He gently tucked it behind her ear and pulled her trembling body against his for warmth and support. "I figured as much. Let's get you back to the car. You're looking a little shaky."

"I'm fine…okay, not really," she admitted, tucking herself under his arm. "I've spent the past nine years hiding from danger and the last few days facing more risks than Indiana Jones."

"It's destroyed," Dayne said, running up to them. He handed the broken pieces to Brea then they both looked at Marek.

Brea was the one to ask what they all three wanted to know, "What's this mean for your brother?"

Marek pulled open the passenger side door for her. "I guess I'll find out soon. If the gods are with us, the curse will be broken. If not…"

Chapter Eleven

ဢ

"You destroyed the Triad?" Kaden said by way of a greeting.

Marek's mood darkened instantly, all traces of hope completely obliterated. Eyes burning, heart heavy, he dropped to his knee, setting the relic's fractured pieces on the floor. "We had no choice. I'm sorry we failed you. I failed you. After everything you've been through lately, Lena's death...if I could take your place and suffer the curse myself, I would."

"I know." His brother pushed himself up from his chair, the strain of his exertion etched into his features. The curse had progressed quickly. His body was visibly frail, withered like The Keeper's. "You did well, my brother. As well as I could hope." Kaden reached a hand down. "Stand."

Marek refused to accept his brother's aid as he stood. He was, after all, well and strong. His brother was dying. Who should be helping whom?

Kaden swept him into a tight embrace and smacked him on the back heartily. "I owe you my life, baby brother. And you," he said, releasing Marek and pulling a stiff-limbed Dayne into an equally enthusiastic hug, "I owe you even more."

"Your life?" Marek asked, bewildered. "What does this mean?"

"I—I—" Dayne stuttered as Kaden released him to turn toward the wall behind his throne.

Kaden patted Marek's cheek as he shuffled past him, scooping up the shattered relic. "It means, little brother, that the curse can still be lifted. I will recover. You made the right choice." To Dayne, he said, "I asked Marek if he would agree to the blood-bond with you, Dayne, both of us knowing what you felt about our family. You have some powerful allies among the Rebellion. I didn't expect you to turn your back on them. I'd only hoped you might come to believe that your family's tragic death had not been ordered by this crown."

"I...don't really know yet what happened. I only learned what price some pay for revenge and felt it was too great."

Kaden gripped the curved armrest of his throne in one hand. "Every man makes his decisions by his own heart and mind. Whatever the reason, I'm grateful to you for your help. Perhaps someday, the mystery of your family's death will be solved."

"I hope so."

The groan of rusted hinges accompanied the sight of a hidden door swinging open behind the throne.

"We are both searching for answers, you and me. Perhaps we'll find them together?" Turning, Kaden lifted his hand to indicate they should follow him through the opening. "I have something for both of you. You must accept my apologies though. There will be no pageantry, no ceremony. Just the three of us. But I have good reason for keeping this a secret." He turned, a pair of identical swords in his fists. He handed one to Dayne, the second to Marek. Then he nodded and planted his hands on his hips. "Congratulations, men. You are the first two Cytherean Guards, an elite team of men. Chosen by me. And for a very special purpose." He set the Triad on the floor, at the center of an intricate triangular design in the floor's tilework. "At the center of our world is the sacred number — three. Just as it takes three — two of our kind and one human — to renew our lives, it takes three to mend the Triad." Dropping to his knee, he placed his palm over the relic's pieces and indicated with a nod that Marek and Dayne should do the same. The moment they had positioned their hands over top of Kaden's, a jolt of power blasted through their bodies. Bolts of electricity shot from their fingertips, the energy gathering into a ball of cracking, snapping brilliance in the air, like a miniature star. Humming, it hovered over their stacked hands for several seconds before dropping to the floor and consuming the Triad.

The white flame extinguished as quickly as it had appeared, leaving a fully restored Triad smoking on the floor. Kaden cleared his throat, lifted the Triad and stood. "The Rebellion is far from over. Dark times are ahead. As Cytherean Guards, it is now your duty to protect the secrets of the Sons of the Twilight."

Marek stared down at his fist, still tingling from the powerful magic, his fingers curled around the sword's hilt. "Then you've learned what the Rebellion's plans are for the future?"

"No, I've lost my most reliable source of intelligence, my future bride."

Dayne's startled gasp echoed in the small space. "Then you knew she was—"

"The clues?" Marek interrupted. "That's why you were so sure they were for real."

"Yes, the clues came from Lena." Kaden shrugged. "And I knew she was with the Rebellion. I had my reasons for sleeping with the enemy."

"Damn, I'm sorry." Dayne murmured.

Kaden gave both Marek and Dayne an empty smile. "Nothing for you to be sorry for. Being king is both an honor and an obligation. I had to make some hard decisions. But they were mine to make. Not yours."

* * * * *

Brea paced the living room. Could there be any worse punishment? What had she done to deserve such treatment? Marek had insisted she could not go with them to check on his brother. He'd never given her a reasonable excuse. Yet she hadn't felt right arguing with him. Everyone faced pain in their own way.

Including her.

Truth was, she needed the time to herself. She needed to figure some stuff out. Some important stuff. Not exactly life-or-death but pretty damn close to it.

The three of them had completed the final night of the blood-bond. Her Chippendales had done things to and with her that she never in a million years would have dreamed of trying. And then they'd held her tenderly. She'd fallen asleep nestled between their hulking bodies, warm and satisfied and content.

Her contentment was short-lived, however. Just before her Chippendales had left, Marek had told her she was free to leave, to stay, whatever she wanted to do — at sunrise.

The Triad was history, destroyed, worthless. So she didn't need to stick around for that anymore.

She could go home. Soon. Within a few hours.

She knew she should be glad to leave. This had always been a temporary situation, even though Marek had confessed his love for her. And even if she secretly loved both him and Dayne back.

It wasn't like the emotions were genuine. They were the byproduct of some bizarre hormonal state, driven by physical changes in her body. Once she was out of range of her Chippendales' pheromones, she'd realize she didn't really love them...right?

And what about the woman in the picture? Who was she? And where was she?

Her insides ached like they'd been yanked out, run over by a Hummer and then crammed back inside the empty shell of her body. This hunger as they called it sucked big time. It hurt worse than any heartache she'd ever suffered through.

Even though she was miserable beyond words, her heart did a happy little hop in her chest when she heard the guys' voices at the front door. They were home.

It was time to say goodbye.

Ack.

She pulled in not one but two deep breaths, scooped up her purse as well as Dayne's Lions shirt—and headed toward them.

Marek was the first one to speak, "I see you're ready to go."

"Yes," she said, trying not to sigh. "I-I'm ready."

Dayne stepped forward, his piercing eyes drilling into hers. "This is harder than I thought it would be." His statement echoed her own thoughts.

"I figure it'll get easier when I'm farther away."

"Why's that?" Marek, standing behind her, snaked an arm around her waist and pulled her flush against him. She felt the rigid length of his cock, hot and hard against her derriere. Unwanted desire pulsed through her body.

She stiffened, unwilling to allow the baser needs of her body to dictate her actions any longer. This was an unnatural response. She didn't really love these men like she thought. Like she wanted to. Her mind and body were tricking her.

"Why's what?" she asked, concentrating on not rubbing against him like a cat in heat. It was so tempting. Her back was already arching, lifting her bottom up.

"Why will it be easier when you're farther away?" he whispered.

Dayne knelt in front of her and ran his hands down her legs. He gripped her ankles, using pressure to force her to widen her stance. "We want you to be happy, Brea. More than anything, that's all that matters."

She dropped her head back, letting it rest against Marek's chest. "Then stop. Please. Don't put me through this any longer. It's not real. Your feelings. My feelings."

Marek's fingers slid under her top and mapped her rib cage. Teasing. Tormenting. "What makes you believe that?"

"What you said earlier. About the hunger," she murmured, already losing her ability to think.

"Ah. The hunger." Dayne's hands smoothed up her blue-jeans-clad legs to cup the heated juncture of her thighs. He applied delightful pressure to her throbbing parts. "We just learned the hunger ends at sunrise."

"It does?" Her heart started thumping heavily in her chest.

"Did," Marek corrected.

"What time is it?"

Dayne moved aside, letting Marek guide her toward the heavily draped living-room window. "Come and see."

Brea pulled one side of the curtain up to peer outside.

"Whatever emotions you feel now," Marek said, back-stepping away from the light spilling into the room, "are yours. They aren't the effect of any kind of chemical reaction or unnatural urge. Not anymore."

"And what we feel is just as genuine," Dayne added.

Tears gathering in her eyes, Brea let the drapery fall back over the window and turned to her Chippendales. "Then I..." The words sat in her chest, refusing to come out.

Here she'd spent the last couple of days taking the kind of risks she'd spent years avoiding. She'd basically closed herself out of life, denied herself all the joys and pain that made life worth living.

No more. She wouldn't hide any longer. Life was a wonderful gift and it was meant to be lumpy and sometimes painful. Those rough parts made the good ones all the sweeter.

It had taken a couple of undead Chippendales and the Friday the thirteenth from hell to help her learn how to live again.

How ironic.

The words she'd started to speak slipped easily through her lips now. "I'm falling in love with you. But what about the woman in the picture?" she asked Dayne.

"Picture?" He looked quizzically toward the stairs then smiled. "Oh, that picture." She found herself in the middle of a Chippendale sandwich. "She doesn't hold a candle to you, Brea. Besides, there's something very unnatural about mating with my cousin."

"Cousin?" she repeated, a giggle bubbling up from her stomach. "So does this mean you wouldn't mind making this a permanent arrangement?"

"Nothing would make us happier," her Chippendales said in unison.

"Terrific. I'll move in tomorrow. But I have a couple conditions."

Her Chippendales slanted wary looks her way.

"First, I have to park my car in the garage. It was my father's, you know. And second, you both must sit down and watch *National Treasure* with me. Tonight. Just in case we end up in another treasure hunt in the future."

Her Chippendales exchanged guilty looks and nervous chuckles.

And here she'd thought she'd been joking about the treasure hunt thing. "Wwwwwhat?"

They proceeded to erase every worry from her mind, doing what they did so well—using and abusing her, in the most wonderful way.

The End

CARNAL HUNGER

જી

Trademarks Acknowledgement

ೠ

Chapter One

ɛɔ

Jasmyne Vaughn hadn't realized her mother was a drug addict until the day Maria Vaughn came home sober.

It had been many years since Jasmyne first became acquainted with the sweet, attentive woman her mother became when she wasn't stoned, and Jasmyne could count on one hand the number of times she'd seen that woman since then.

Once again, the other—moody, irresponsible, unstable—Maria was back.

Jasmyne swallowed a few choice words and thanked the lady on the phone who was most definitely not to blame for the terrible news she'd just heard. No, it was never fair to shoot the messenger, regardless how horrible the message. The blame fell entirely on the shoulders of one stubborn, infuriating woman.

Ironically, Jasmyne loved her mother. Very much. Too much, in fact. Which was why she was tempted to do just about anything—legal or otherwise—to get the woman to stay in rehab long enough to get clean for good. It was also why she'd unwisely let her mother stay at her house the night before.

If only she could rewind time.

Never mind the fact that this made five failed attempts to get her addicted mother to complete a rehab program. Five. In the last two years. All but the last had been completely funded by Jasmyne's very tired and nearly depleted bank account. She'd finally gotten wise and given up after the fourth time Maria had gone AWOL.

How many times had she heard the old saying—until an addict was ready to change for themselves, they would continue their self-destructive ways?

But despite the fact that Maria had evidently been an addict since Jasmyne had been in diapers, she just couldn't get herself to give up hope. Nor could she turn her back on her mom. Maybe it was a genetic thing, this lack of common sense. Maria had surely proven she suffered a serious case of common-sense-itis, and that was even before she'd become hooked on drugs.

No doubt, it had been that foolhardy hope, wishful thinking that had inspired Jasmyne to open her door and welcome her mother in last night.

Maria had sounded so sincere when she said she was ready to turn her life around. And then, while Jasmyne was sleeping, she'd practically cleaned her out. Money. Jewelry. DVDs. She took everything that could be sold on the street, and left the state.

Yes, Jasmyne cared about the money and jewelry. Money didn't come easily, not by any stretch. But what bothered her the most was the box her mother had stolen, the one that shouldn't have been in her house in the first place.

Her boss was going to kill her. And for good reason.

Anyone who'd worked as long as Jasmyne had at her job knew it wasn't safe taking undelivered packages home. A courier for a company that specialized in the discreet delivery of valuable, sensitive or rare items and documents, she never took undeliverable items home—at least not if she could help it. Last night, she'd had no choice.

Jasmyne checked the clock for the third time. Almost 2:00 a.m. A noise had woken her over an hour ago, and she'd spent every minute since then taking inventory of what was missing and making phone calls, searching for her thieving, conniving mother. Cussing, she yanked her suitcase out from beneath her bed.

Thanks to the frequent impromptu trips — between her job and her mother, she'd racked up thousands of frequent flier miles — it had been quite some time since her trusty Samsonite had been in storage. She tossed the luggage onto her bed, unzipped it and started gathering the essentials she'd need for the next few days. As she lobbed socks, sweats and t-shirts onto her bed, she mentally ticked off the short list of things she'd have to take care of before leaving for Detroit. Of course, the first item on that list was a call into work.

Work. Oh shit. What was she going to do?

The last time she'd called in "sick" — about four months ago — her boss, Carol Stick-Up-Her-Ass Swanson had warned her that if she called in again, she'd be fired.

And she could hardly tell her the truth about the stolen package. Could she? If she did, her mother might be facing criminal charges.

This was bad.

A job was hardly something she could go without. A regular paycheck afforded her a home. Food. And possibly her mother's next treatment — if she ever decided she was ready.

Or her legal bills.

Shit.

She slumped onto the bed.

What a dilemma. Stay home, find a legit way to deal with the stolen package, possibly keep her job...and watch her mother get hauled off to jail.

Or lie to her boss, run down her druggie mother and try to get the stolen package on her own.

Ack!

Neither was without its risks, or consequences. She weighed both and in the end decided to delay her visit to Detroit temporarily and do things the right way...kind of.

She had a reasonable explanation for why she hadn't brought the package back last night. Her boss would be pissed when she claimed she'd forgotten it this morning, but Carol had no grounds for firing her—until she learned the package was missing.

She'd have to pretend to make repeated attempts at delivering the package to buy them both some time. Then she'd put in for some vacation days and as soon as it was cleared, she'd be on a plane, headed to the Motor City.

There were two facts that would never change—her mother's addiction to methamphetamine would not go away on its own. And the addict always went home when she wanted to get high, where all her druggie friends lived.

A few days. She'd have to wait just a few short days until she could get the time off. God, she hoped her mother would hang on to that box until she got there! Jasmyne had no idea what was in it. Experience had taught her it was hard enough tracking down personal possessions sold on the streets. It would be impossible to hunt down the unknown.

She needed to find out what was in that box. To do that, she needed to get her hands on the paperwork in Carol's office. She shoved the half-loaded suitcase into the closet and reluctantly headed back to bed.

* * * * *

The phone's shrill ring woke Jasmyne up sometime later, cutting short a freakish nightmare starring her mother and a couple of her junkie friends. Her eyes slitted, she glanced at the glaring red numbers on her clock and fumbled for the phone.

Good news never came at 5:07 in the morning.

"Hello?" she croaked in her raspy middle-of-the-night voice.

"Jas."

"Mom? Where are you?" Jasmyne's stomach twisted in her gut. Her mother was calling her? Good God! The devil was skiing in hell. "Where are you?"

"I…I don't know. Some men," her mother stuttered, her voice barely above a whisper, "they've taken me somewhere."

"Oh God." Now fully awake, Jasmyne threw off the blanket and jumped to her feet. "Call 9-1-1! Do it now. Right now. Hang up with me and call for help. I can't do anything–"

"Jas," her mother interrupted. "I'm sorry about taking those things from your house—"

"We'll talk about that later. Call for help."

"Can you come help me? You'll find me, right?"

"Whose phone are you using?"

"One of theirs…they…I…went…dark…" Loud noise muffled the rest of her mother's explanation.

Frustrated, angry, terrified, Jasmyne pressed her phone tighter to her ear, desperate to make out what her mother was saying. "Louder, Mom. Who's there with you?" She heard voices. Male voices. Shouting. A woman's scream. A lot of scuffling…

And then the line cut off.

Jasmyne's hand trembled as she slowly lowered the phone to read the number on the caller ID display. It was a Michigan area code. No surprise there.

Knowing her mother probably couldn't, she dialed 9-1-1, tucked her phone between her chin and shoulder and headed back to the closet for her half-packed suitcase.

Having a job was highly overrated.

Her mother needed her. She'd actually called. That was a first. Maybe she had finally hit bottom. If she had, how could Jasmyne ignore her plea for help?

* * * * *

"I heard some of them have resorted to kidnapping." Asher Pryce swept the closest thing he could reach into his fist and hurled it across the room. The signed Galle vase struck the brick wall with a satisfying crack and showered the floor with fractured bits of clay. "Kidnapping!"

His closest friend, Draven Falk, didn't look particularly shocked by Asher's uncharacteristic outburst. If anything, Asher realized, after taking a second to study his expression, he looked relieved. Draven eased himself into the nearby leather chair, rested an ankle on his knee and tucked a fist under his cleft chin. "It isn't like kidnapping is foreign to the Sons of the Twilight. We all hunt."

"Yes we do. But we all release our prey when we're through. That's different. That's survival. An unfortunate necessity. The Binding lasts only one week. And the women aren't harmed. We just feed from them and then, if we don't take them as our long-term mate, our *Uxor*, spouse, we release them. They return to their lives a little low of blood but with some fond recollections of a vacation, visit with a relative, whatever memory we decide to give them." Asher resisted the urge to hurl a second piece of pottery across the room and instead paced the full length of the Savonnerie rug.

Draven was being his usual cool, silent self. Generally, his think-first-talk-later brand of support was exactly what Asher needed. But not today. No, he was too frustrated, pissed, desperate for Draven's quiet approach to be any comfort. He wanted his friend to cuss like a sailor and vow eternal damnation to the wrongdoers who'd more or less taken Asher's creation, an organization created for the purpose of protecting specific political interests of its members through legal and moral means, and turned it into something he didn't recognize anymore. Something he was ashamed of.

Stopping to toe the remains of the vase he'd thrown, Asher added, "The women being kidnapped by the White Hawk Alliance are being infected with some fucking virus, brainwashed and trained to fight our battles. Women. Human women. They're being injured. Killed. That's wrong. It's all wrong."

"I agree." Draven stood and offered Asher a silent show of support, a hand on his shoulder. "I'm here now. We'll make this right." A tense silence hung between them. Draven patted Asher's back then motioned to the bar. "I think you need a drink."

"I need more than that." Asher nodded at Draven's offer of a glass of sherry. After several swallows, the anger and frustration hadn't eased, but a soothing warmth had taken root in his belly. "Thank God you agreed to help me, Draven. I can't do this alone. There are too many of them now, too many who are willing to do anything to reach their goals. Even attack our king with an army of innocent humans. Even kill me if I try to stop them. I don't know what the hell we're going to do."

"Neither do I." Draven slanted him a worried look over the top of his glass. "But like you said, we've got no choice."

"No, I have no choice. You do." Asher gripped the glass in his hand so hard it shattered. Shards pierced his skin, a trace of alcohol stinging as it seeped into the cuts in his palm. He threw the broken pieces into the fireplace and looked down at his hand. No blood spilled from the gashes.

Yet another sign.

Asher slumped into a nearby chair. "And you know I hated having to drag you into this, don't you?" The effects of the Hunger had made his sinking spirits plummet even further the past few days.

He didn't have much longer. He'd been through it before and could read the signs. At his age, it came about once a year unfortunately. The Binding was a distraction he didn't need right now. The physical hunger. And the carnal. The temporary but desperate, overwhelming need to possess both his mates sexually. Human and immortal. Male and female. Again and again and again.

Not only did he have roughly two hundred pissed off vampires to turn around, but he had a personal matter to take care of. One that would cost him his life if he ignored it for another night. But to do that, he had to find a Son of the Twilight who also suffered from the Hunger. He had to take the Binding.

* * * * *

Draven hid his guilty conscience behind a calm front — the mask he'd worn for so long for everyone but his best friend that he almost felt naked without it. If not for the fact that he was now forced to lie to the only person he'd never deceived before, he'd be proud of how well he was hiding his true feelings.

Asher needed his help.

The members of the White Hawk Alliance demanded his help.

The bastard — his enemy — expected his help. Or else.

He was being pulled in so many different directions, he didn't know what to do next. Forced to make impossible decisions. Agonizing sacrifices. Or face painful consequences.

And he had no choice but to do what he could for all of them.

Unfortunately, there was yet one more snag in this already complicated situation. One mistake that could never be taken back would make it impossible for him to help anyone.

He poured Asher a second glass of the Pedro Ximenez and handed it to him. His friend's condition had him worried. Taking a closer look, he saw the signs. Not only was Asher weak from the Hunger, but he was on edge.

Asher wasn't the kind to blow up over nothing. And Draven had firsthand knowledge that things were even worse than Asher knew. That was just the problem — if Asher found out the truth, he'd refuse to take the time to hunt, to take a blood-bond. He was always thinking of the Hawks first. Everything else came second.

If he had to, he'd take the Binding with Asher. At least then his friend would get the blood he was going to need. Asher didn't know it yet, but he'd already lost the Hawks to the ones who'd muscled and lied their ways into positions of power.

The king was as good as dead.

The Hawks' last attempt at assassinating King Kaden had failed, but Draven knew their next plan was as foolproof as it was underhanded. Brutally inspired. Effective. And so devious he had to wonder what kind of men possessed the minds to not only plot such a strategy but have the courage to carry it out.

Draven drained his glass and set it on the bar. He turned to his friend. "Take the blood-bond with me."

Asher's pale lips started trembling. He blinked once, twice, three times, raked his fingers through his thick ebony waves, tousling them. "Thank you."

Draven smiled, his fangs extending at the anticipation of the blood they would soon share. "No thanks necessary. Let's go find our prey."

Chapter Two

ᔕ

Jasmyne hated Detroit Metro Airport. It was ugly, old, lacked access to adequate ground transportation — taxis and buses — and it reminded her of past visits, trips she'd just as soon forget.

Not to mention, she wasn't particularly happy with the response she'd received from Detroit's police department when she'd called. Her mother was not officially a missing person at this point, let alone a kidnapping victim. In other words, Detroit's finest weren't going to do a damn thing.

Dragging her wheeled carryon behind her, Jasmyne headed toward the main corridor leading to the exit. Her flight from Chicago hadn't taken more than forty-five minutes, but she'd spent almost twelve tedious hours in O'Hare, trying to catch a flight. She'd finally snagged herself a seat on the last flight of the night, arriving a few minutes before midnight.

Bone-weary and bleary-eyed, she headed outside. A blast of chilly air sliced through her spring jacket like a knife through Jell-O. She hugged herself and cursed her lack of planning. Unlike past trips, she'd spent absolutely no time checking the local weather forecast before packing. Of course, it was like winter here. That was just her luck.

Just like it was her luck that there was this huge conference in town and there wasn't a rental car to be found this side of Lake Michigan.

Teeth chattering, she quickly decided she'd catch the first hotel shuttle that showed up. Who cared what the room would cost? She had a brand spanking new Visa in her pocket, with a wide-open credit limit. She'd have to worry about the financial end of things later.

After roughly thirty minutes of freezing her ass off, she gave up. No shuttles had come. Obviously, they quit running after a certain hour of the night. And naturally, since she'd always flown into town during the day, she hadn't known that.

She stomped over to the huge display window emblazoned with the hotel photographs and phone numbers. Attached to the backlit display was a black circa 1960s telephone for calling the hotels for room information and shuttle service.

Marriot. Days Inn. Red Roof? She closed her eyes, picked one then lifted the phone to call.

No dial tone. No freaking way!

"Shit! I hate this stupid city."

Knowing it was pointless, she poked the little button on the phone until her knuckle cracked, simultaneously making promises to every deity she could think of if they'd summon up a dial tone for her. She thought about the cell phone tucked in her purse, wishing she had been able to afford the coast-to-coast service. It didn't work outside her zone. Worthless.

She did a quick scan for a pay phone. Nothing. Argh!

There had to be someone around with a cell phone she could use. Right? Airports were always full of people jabbering on wireless headsets. No problem.

She turned to survey the room behind her. Empty.

God, she was exhausted. Her feet were killing her. Her back hurt. Her head was pounding. And she was going to have to head back upstairs to the main concourse if she was going to find a phone.

But do it she would. She had no other choice.

A hotel bed was sounding better and better by the second.

She scribbled down a few phone numbers on the glossy back cover of the *Glamour* magazine she'd bought in O'Hare and headed back toward the escalator. As she stepped on, the door behind her opened with a whoosh and a cold draft swept into the room. Out of curiosity, she twisted to glimpse over her shoulder.

Ooooh.

She nearly stumbled off the lurching staircase.

Wow, was that man gor-gee-us. With a capital G.

The object of her instant case of lust took three measured steps into the room, lifted his chin and met her gaze.

The air she'd just inhaled wedged painfully in her throat. She spun around, swallowed and stumbled off the escalator when it reached the top.

Now what? Phone. Forget the hunk downstairs. He was down there, and she was up here. Besides, unless he worked for the local Marriot or had a cell phone she could use, he was no good to her.

Phone. Hotel. Sleep.

She did a one-eighty, searching the concourse for either a pay phone or a likely target. There was the man to the right, carrying a briefcase and dialing his phone with his free hand as he hurried toward the gates. Nah. He was moving too fast. Probably late for a flight. He wouldn't help her.

She looked in the opposite direction. There was that woman, the one with the stroller. And the shrieking kid. And the bulging blood vessel running up the center of her forehead.

Hmmm. She circled around and peered down the descending escalator. Maybe Mr. Gorgeous had a phone. He hadn't been walking like he was in a hurry and he didn't have a screaming kid in tow. She wondered if he'd left the building, since he hadn't come up after her. Chances were, since he was down on the lower level where the arrivals collected their checked luggage, he was waiting for someone. His wife?

Her stomach rolled.

Why did that thought give her a case of indigestion? The man was a perfect stranger. His marital status should be the

last thing on her mind. She was, after all, here for one reason —
to locate and drag her junkie mother to the nearest rehab
program that would accept Visa.

But she did need a phone, and a phone from one man
with a to-die-for face was as good as any.

She hurried down the descending escalator. He was still
there, standing with his back to her, feet planted wide, arms
crossed over his chest, apparently watching for someone to
enter through the glass doors.

Her gaze took a little tour of the back side of his body.
Broad   shoulders.   Nice   trim   waist.   And   that
butt...*mmmmrrrooooowwww*. The man knew how to fill out a
pair of snug jeans properly. Uh huh.

Quit staring at his butt.

Her cheeks warmed. A few other parts of her anatomy
heated too. She fanned her face, cleared her throat, smiled
brightly and said, "Excuse me."

He turned slowly, lifting an arm, as if he were moving in
slow-mo on purpose so she could catch every muscle bulge
and ripple. The inside of her mouth dried until her tongue felt
like old leather. It tasted like a pair of old boots.

What she wouldn't give for a handful of Altoids right
now.

Yes, she knew her lust was poorly timed and
inappropriate. She had much more important things to think
about than the way anyone filled out their jeans.

But she'd never been face-to-face with physical perfection
before. Dark-haired, dark-eyed, built-like-a-god perfection. It
was unnerving. She wasn't sure whether she wanted to just
stand there and stare at him forever or turn around and
pretend like she hadn't seen him.

He lifted an eyebrow and slanted a wicked smile at her.
"Yes?"

She actually heard herself gulp. Had she asked him something? Oh. Yeah. She giggled nervously, shuffled her feet and muttered, "Phone?"

He looked confused.

"Cell phone? Do you happen to have one?"

"Oh! Yes." He slipped his hand into his pocket and withdrew the tiniest cell phone she'd ever seen. He held it out for her, a silent offer. He had long, tapered fingers, neatly trimmed fingernails. She could almost imagine those hands lightly stroking her arm, her thigh, her stomach. "You needed this?"

"Thanks." Her fingers brushed his as she accepted the phone. The brief contact sent a rush of heat over her chest and stomach. She fumbled with the magazine. Her hands felt swollen. They were numb and her fingers didn't move the way she wanted. The magazine's slick paper slipped from her grasp. It hit the tile with a splat. Luckily, the phone didn't follow. "Oh shit."

As if her face wasn't already blistering hot.

Tightening her hold on the phone so she wouldn't drop it too, she bent over, flipped the magazine over and read the first number written on the back. She punched it into the keypad and hit the call button. Waiting for someone to answer, she lifted her gaze to the man.

He just stood there, looking cool and patient, nothing like a guy who was expecting someone to come dragging down the escalator with an armload of luggage at any moment. She gave him a strained smile while listening to a recorded greeting from the Days Inn. With her free hand, she plucked up the dropped magazine.

Finally, a human being answered the call. Yay!

Bad news. It would be another twenty minutes or so before the shuttle would be by to pick her up. Darn. But at least the night would soon be over and she'd be able to grab a few hours sleep before heading out to hunt down her mother.

After thanking the clerk, she ended the call and handed the man back his phone. "Thanks so much."

"You're welcome." He didn't head back to the door. Nor did he walk toward the escalator. He just stood there.

Talk about awkward.

He looked at her like he expected her to do or say something.

She shifted her weight from one foot to the other and rolled the magazine into a tight tube to keep her hands busy. "Um...are you waiting for someone?"

"Kind of."

She nodded and took a shuffling step toward the door. It was way too soon to be worried about watching for the shuttle, but the way Mr. Gorgeous was looking at her was making her nervous. In a not-so-good sort of way.

Time to send him the leave-me-alone vibe.

"Well, thanks again." This time she turned and took longer and more determined strides toward the door.

A spot between her shoulder blades started tingling, the one that always got that tickly feeling when someone was staring at her. She didn't know for certain whether he was still standing back there, ogling her, but she sensed it. She really wanted to turn around and see if her hunch was right.

Don't do it.

A puff of air caressed the side of her neck, making the skin of her arms and shoulders pucker with goose bumps. "I could give you a ride if you need one," he said directly behind her.

Instinct made her lurch forward.

Kick-started by a rush of adrenaline, her heart slammed into her breastbone. Her insides hammered against her ribcage. Heated blood rushed through her system, electrifying her nerves, intensifying her senses.

Something was wrong. He'd said he was waiting for someone. Why was he hanging around her?

Time to take a walk. Should she go outside or run upstairs, where there were more people? Not many, but a couple.

She hoped.

Her hand gripping the handle of her rolling suitcase, she whirled around and met his gaze.

He wasn't going to hurt her. No. She was just being paranoid. It was exhaustion. That was what was making her overreact. Right?

"Excuse me." Focused on the escalator about twenty feet away, she side-stepped around him and hurried across the room. She hated leaving the door, knowing she might miss her shuttle for no good reason. But if Mr. Gorgeous-but-creepy was up to no good, staying put or heading outside were both stupid. Better to play it safe.

"I'm sorry. I didn't mean to frighten you."

God, he was practically on top of her again!

She broke into a run, stumbling as she stepped onto the escalator. Something jerked her suitcase, wrenching the handle out of her hand, and nearly sending her toppling backward down the escalator's metal steps.

She caught the handrail with both hands and twisted, finding her suitcase lying on the bottom few steps, thumping against the stairs as they rolled up under it. The man was tugging on the handle, trying to pull it free from whatever had caught it, but he was struggling.

Her insides twisted into a painful knot.

What was going on? Was this guy dangerous or not? His jaw was set, his eyes narrowed as he yanked on her bag. Either he really wanted her stuff or he really wanted to help her.

That was silly. This man wouldn't want a suitcase full of women's clothes. Duh. First, they weren't even close to being the same size. Besides, it wasn't like he was hurting for money. His clothes, grooming, shoes all suggested he was living a good life.

Quit being such a moron.

She hit the top stair, circled around and, while checking the area for people, headed back toward the down escalator. She saw as she descended that he was still fighting to free her suitcase.

"The strap's caught on something," he said through clenched teeth. "I can cut it loose, but I didn't want to do that without asking you first."

"Sure. Go ahead."

He produced a tiny Swiss Army knife from his back pocket, flipped up the blade and started sawing at the caught strap. It took longer than she expected for him to cut through it. Finally, the strap snapped and the suitcase rolled backward, landing at her feet.

"Thanks." She grabbed the handle and lifted, pulling the luggage to her side. "I…uh…appreciate your help."

"Not a problem." His smile was blindingly brilliant, and the most adorable set of dimples appeared at both sides of his mouth. Instantly, her fears seemed as ludicrous and impossible as little green aliens taking over the country.

Really. This guy. Dangerous. Funny.

Their gazes tangled, and she found herself wanting to stand there and lose herself in his eyes for the next several hours. Sleep? Who needed sleep?

It was only the distant rumble of a vehicle outside that made her break the connection and hurry toward the door. "My shuttle!"

It was leaving. Leaving! It couldn't have been over twenty minutes since she'd called.

"Shit!" She stomped on the rubber mat, activating the automatic doors. They slid open and she raced outside, her free arm waving in the air as she raced after the rolling vehicle. "Stop! Please! Wait!"

The red brake lights didn't illuminate. The van continued around the corner, out of sight, and she slowed to a walk. "No. Fucking. Way!"

She wanted to kick something. To scream. To point her finger at Mr. Gorgeous and blame him. Of course it wasn't his fault she'd freaked out, assumed the worst and run like an idiot from him. It was her fault. Her problem.

She just had to go back in there, call the hotel again, apologize and ask them to send the van back. Or call a different hotel. Yeah. That was a good idea.

It wasn't a huge disaster. Just a minor setback.

Once again, she worked herself out of a meltdown.

She took a couple of calming breaths, did a one-eighty and headed back toward the terminal. There weren't any cars parked outside. It was eerily quiet. She half-walked, half-ran back inside, only to discover Mr. Gorgeous was gone.

The minor setback had just become slightly more significant.

"No biggie. I can just head upstairs. There are bound to be some other travelers on the main concourse still." She didn't want to think about the fact that the entire lower level—which also housed the luggage claim belts—had been empty for a long time now. No planes had arrived in at least a half hour. Surely, there were planes departing at this time of night.

She headed back up to the main concourse and quickly realized the semi-more significant setback might qualify as serious. There wasn't a single person in sight. Not a one. No flight personnel or airport employees. No frenzied business travelers racing toward their gates. No women pushing screaming toddlers in strollers. No one.

Where were the effing pay phones?

She wandered down the low-ceilinged maze of corridors, peering into one dark store after another, closed off behind metal roll-down gates. After she reached a dead end, she turned around and headed back.

Well, she supposed if she spent the rest of the night in the airport, she'd save herself the cost of the hotel. But a big bed piled with soft down pillows had sounded so good.

Disappointed, she went back to the luggage claim area and plopped down in a shadowed corner, her back up against the wall. She snugged her suitcase close to her side, draping one arm over it, and closed her eyes.

Within seconds, she sensed someone was watching her. She lifted her heavy-as-lead eyelids.

"Come with me. I insist."

Ah, so Mr. Gorgeous hadn't left yet. A few bits of her anatomy decided they were glad. But her more intelligent parts reminded her that taking a ride from a stranger was a bad idea. Very bad. Stupid. Insane. Especially a stranger who'd given her a weird vibe. "No thanks. I'm fine. Honest."

"You're exhausted, and it isn't safe for you to sleep here."

"Yeah, well, I wasn't going to sleep," she joked, finding his attempt at playing the protective stranger kind of charming. "I was just resting my eyes for a minute."

"Resting your eyes? I've heard that one before." He offered one hand to her, and reached for her suitcase with the other. "Come with me."

"What are you doing?" Once again suspicious, she knocked his hand aside and looped her arm through the suitcase's telescoping handle. "What do you care about my safety? Are you a policeman or something?"

"No."

Darn. That would have been convenient. "Then what gives? Why are you hanging around an empty airport terminal? You have to admit, it's a little bizarre."

"Yes, well, it's not like I come here and stalk pretty women every night for kicks. I was here for another reason…"

His half-spoken admission made her feel a smidge better. No, he hadn't told her what the other reason was, and it seemed he wasn't going to. But just the fact that he wasn't following her, waiting for just the right moment to do...something...eased her worries a bit.

Had he really called her pretty?

He nodded toward his extended hand. "I just want to give you a ride. Honestly, it's safer accepting a ride from me than the local cab drivers. Half of them have rap sheets a mile long."

She had never considered that possibility. Was he playing her? She had to admit, she'd ridden in a few cabs in Detroit. It was entirely possible he was telling the truth. "No way."

"You think I'd lie to you?"

"Seriously? You expect me to answer that?"

He responded with a single raised eyebrow.

She had to admit the more she sat there talking to him, the more at ease she felt. And the more tempted she was to just get up and accept his offer of a ride with the grace it probably warranted.

But there was still this little voice in her head, like a pesky mosquito that buzzed around her head at night. It was just loud enough to be annoying. Don't go! That's what it kept saying to her. Over and over.

Maybe they could just stay there and talk a while longer. He could keep her company while she waited for another hotel shuttle. Chat about his job, why he hung out in airports in the middle of the night, what he did to get those picture perfect arms...

Okay, that was a stupid idea. Was she really thinking about sitting here, shooting the breeze with Mr. Gorgeous like she'd bumped into him at her fave nightspot? Why would she bother with this now? She was here for a couple of days, tops...at least she hoped her mission wouldn't take longer than that. Bottom line—there was absolutely no chance this was going anywhere.

"Gotta say, this is a first," she confessed, building up for the Big Letdown. "I'm really flattered and grateful for your offer. But I'd rather just borrow your phone again and call for the shuttle."

"Fair enough." He handed her the phone, swinging around as the door slid open behind him.

Good. Someone else was coming in. Her gaze hip-hopping from the phone's color screen to the open door, Jasmyne started punching in the hotel's number.

She stopped dialing for a split second, caught dumbstruck by the god who was sauntering through the doors.

Another one. What were the chances of that?

Two absolutely stunning men were the only two human beings in the whole freaking place. Maybe there was some kind of conference for male models going on close by. She could only be so lucky.

Hunkilicious sauntered inside, his sharp-eyed gaze sweeping the room until it halted when it reached Gorgeous. His expression darkened. "Hey, what's taking so long?" Hunkilicious looked as strong and intimidating as Gorgeous, but he moved more slowly, like he was tired or something.

Gorgeous stepped away, flagging Hunkilicious to follow him.

Obviously the two knew each other. Hmmm.

She watched their exchange as she talked on the phone with the Holiday Inn's desk clerk.

"Things aren't exactly going the way I thought they would," she heard Gorgeous say.

Hunkilicious gave Jasmyne a once-over then walked toward the door, motioning to Gorgeous to follow him.

Those two were going to have a powwow? Obviously, they knew each other.

I smell fish. Time to make like Dorie and just keep swimming.

She thanked the clerk and ended the call. The two guys were still conferring in the corner next to the door, and it seemed, by their postures, that they were disagreeing about something.

"Excuse me," she said, regretting the fact that she couldn't just drop the phone and leave. She stood up, and with her suitcase handle gripped tightly in her hand, she extended her arm, palm up, phone resting in her hand. "The shuttle's on its way back. Thanks for letting me use the phone."

The two guys gave each other a look she didn't much care for. Then Gorgeous, another one of those stunning smiles in place, stepped forward and plucked the phone from her hand. He stared at her, his gaze sharp and unwavering. "Glad to help." He slipped the phone into his pocket and took a second step forward. "Safe travels, beautiful."

"Sure," she mumbled, unable to wrest her gaze from his. Awkward moment. "Thanks again for letting me use the phone." She nodded, a silent dismissal, or so she hoped. She then somehow managed to free herself from that steel trap of a gaze and turn around.

Hunkilicious had, sometime when she'd been busy staring into Gorgeous' eyes, positioned himself behind her. He stood mere inches away, an enormous human blockade between her and the door.

"'Scuse me," she muttered. Inside her head, she kept hearing Dorie's obnoxiously upbeat voice, *Just keep swimming, swimming, swimming.* She shouldered her way past the man, toward the door.

The fish odor was definitely getting stinkier.

A shiver snaked up her spine. Something told her to run. Run now. Run as fast as she could. She listened, bolting through the door, her suitcase dragging behind her. But, as it had been a long, long time since she'd done the fifty-yard dash, they caught her before she'd gotten far. Someone knocked into her from behind, sending her stumbling forward. Her knees slammed into the concrete sidewalk, but she caught herself on outstretched arms before doing a belly flop into a puddle. Tiny pebbles and shards of broken glass cut into her palms, and sharp pain radiated from her knees up her thighs. Adrenaline pushed her on.

Up. Run. Now.

Leaving her suitcase behind, she scrambled to her feet, her gaze focused on the distant set of headlights approaching. She belted out a single, "Helpppp!" before whoever wrapped an arm around her waist turned, hauling her back in the opposite direction.

Despite fighting like a cat in a room full of Doberman Pincers, she quickly lost the battle. Moments later, she found herself in the backseat of a car, gagged, blindfolded, hogtied, breathless and petrified.

Chapter Three

ຄ

Draven couldn't stop puzzling over his reaction to the woman in the airport, the one who was now in the backseat, struggling and terrified. He glanced over his shoulder again. The tang of her fear burned his nostrils. The scent had its expected effect — driving his physical hunger to agonizing levels. Yet it produced an entirely different kind of result as well.

He'd taken the blood-bond many times. Hunting had always been a matter of survival to him, nothing more. Never had he felt anything for his prey other than the expected — hunger, desire, the need to possess.

But this time it was different. So different it was unsettling. Tonight he'd walked away — several times — before he'd taken her.

Problem was he couldn't stay away. That was the strangest thing. He'd tried to leave more than once. But he'd gotten no farther than outside the door before he was driven back inside. Each time he prayed as he ran that she hadn't left.

And yet he'd struggled to claim her.

How long had he waited to take her? A half-hour. No, longer. If Asher hadn't come in, reminding him of how desperate his situation was, he might have sat there for several hours, just watching her.

His index finger traced the front seam on her purse.

Who was she, this woman who had somehow gotten to him?

He caught the bag's zipper and tugged. Her wallet was tucked between a glasses case and cellular phone. A phone.

Why hadn't she used her own? He pulled out her wallet and flipped it open.

Jasmyne Vaughn. From Rockford, Illinois.

He wondered what had brought her to Detroit. Business? Visiting family or friends?

He studied her picture. Her hair was a different color now, a deep mahogany with gold highlights framing her heart-shaped face. In the photograph it was a flat dark brown color that made her look sad and tired. The new shade suited her golden skin tone, and the gorgeous color of her eyes—the brilliant green of a spring leaf.

She had a birthday coming this week, her thirtieth. Ironic. He knew he looked like he might be in his early thirties, but he'd celebrated his thirtieth a long time ago.

Hundreds of years ago.

He returned her ID to her wallet, turning his attention to the array of cards in the other pockets. Credit cards. A frequent-flier card. Triple-A membership. A collection of business cards from assorted hospitals. Interesting, they were all from doctors at substance abuse facilities.

Suddenly uncomfortable for snooping, he tucked all the cards back in their places and returned her wallet to her purse. Soon, very soon, he would know some of her most intimate secrets, yet he felt like a prying bastard for digging through her purse. Did that make any sense to anyone but him? Probably not.

He twisted in his seat, turning back to check on her again. She'd stopped struggling, and the scent of her fear had dissipated. She had relaxed. That was good. It might allow him to go slowly with her, something he'd never wanted to do before. Normally, he went fast, the predator within him unleashed by his mate's fright. But this time he ached to take his time, savor every moment.

His gaze wandered over her form. She was on her stomach, bound at the wrists and knees, arms behind her back, legs bent at the knees and ankles secured to her wrists. She'd fought them so violently, they'd had to hogtie her to prevent her from injuring herself. Her face was turned away from him. She was a slight woman, slim, even a little bony with the exception of her derriere. That was most definitely round. Her jeans did a very nice job emphasizing its shape.

He suddenly noticed her breathing. Her back rose and fell in a slow, steady rhythm.

She was sleeping. How very...unexpected.

He had taken the blood-bond many times. Never had his prey fallen asleep after capture. This woman, Jasmyne, she fascinated him. Not just because of her seeming acquiescence to her situation now but because of the things he'd seen earlier. She was sensitive, beautiful.

For some reason, two words kept coming to mind as he looked back at her.

Mine. Forever.

* * * * *

Jasmyne's mind did a lot of mental gymnastics as she lay in the vehicle's backseat, bound and gagged, blindfolded, powerless and at her captors' mercy. At first, her thoughts were along the *ohmigod-I've-been-kidnapped-and-I'm-gonna-dieeee!* variety, but they later shifted toward the *could-they-be-the-same-guys-who-kidnapped-my-mother?* direction. Whether it was by dumb luck or design, she just might have caught herself a lucky break.

Assuming her kidnappers didn't have some absolutely heinous plan for her, of course.

At this point, she was hoping she'd caught a lucky break. If there was one thing she could say about herself for certain, it was that she was not a fan of pain. If those two men were thinking of torturing her for some reason, she could only hope they'd show some mercy and put her out of her misery with a single gunshot to the head. Fast and painless. That was the only way to go.

As morbid as it was, this was not the first time she'd thought about how she'd die. But it had been a long while since she'd set her heart on one particular method.

Slowly, despite her best efforts to stay alert, her exhaustion overcame her. Her body became heavy. Her breathing slowed. And her dreams carried her away to a place where her mother was safe and well.

She awoke when the car stopped. The two front doors opened with a metallic creak then slammed. The back door next to her head opened, and a soft gust of cold air, smelling like gasoline and grass, brushed her face. She tensed.

Two sets of hands caught her arms, still bound together behind her back. They lifted her gently from the car, face down, supporting her under her chest and hips. Their feet shuffled across a hard floor and then up a short set of stairs and inside someplace warm and silent that smelled clean and fresh, slightly piney. She heard the crackle of a fire somewhere as they carried her around a corner or two.

Finally, they set her down on something soft.

Would they tell her now what was going to happen? She'd be mighty grateful if they'd untie her. Or at least take the blindfold off and awful gag out of her mouth. Her tongue, lips and throat were dry as parchment. A big glass of water sure would be appreciated.

Someone started tugging on the ties of her blindfold and it fell away.

Her gaze darted around the room.

Okay. Um…this wasn't what she'd expected. She'd been taken to a Better Homes showplace. Why? If it weren't for the fact that she'd been carted in bound and gagged, she'd swear she'd been escorted to a private luxury condo.

Wow.

This was the most gorgeous bedroom she'd ever seen. Decorated in masculine but subdued colors — tans, creams and browns. The bedding looked expensive. The furniture looked expensive. The window coverings looked expensive. And was that a real animal fur on the floor?

Surely these men wouldn't murder a woman in this room. The blood would make such a mess. No. Surely not. Gorgeous and Hunkilicious couldn't be planning on killing her.

But if they weren't up to something bad, why snatch a woman from the airport in the first place?

Someone, positioned behind her, unhooked her arms from her ankles, allowing her to straighten her legs. Her cramped muscles let their resentment at being bound for so long be known. She tried to twist her upper body to see who was behind her. If she could see his eyes, she'd have some idea of what she might expect next.

Unfortunately, her position didn't allow her to see much of anything. Yet. She started wriggling, but then a set of strong hands clamped down on the backs of her thighs.

He wasn't holding her butt, but the position of his hands had the same result. Out of instinct, she stilled.

As it turned out, that was a good thing. The gag was the next restraint to come off. Her jaw ached as she worked the kinks out, but she didn't let the pain stop her from asking questions. "What's going on?" she snapped. "Who are you?" A zillion other questions lingered on the tip of her tongue — like, what the fuck? — but she decided becoming outwardly hostile at the moment was probably not the way to go. Not yet.

But she promised to keep an open mind if she didn't get the answers she deserved in an appropriate timeframe. Like immediately.

"You are in my home," one of her abductors answered calmly.

His home. Either these guys were the worst kidnappers ever, or they didn't give a damn about the law. Were they above the law? Politicians? Policemen? Ambassadors from another country? Who kidnapped someone and took them *home*?

Unless they figured she wouldn't live to report the crime.

Ack!

Then again, she'd seen enough episodes of *CSI* to know that it was virtually impossible to hide all traces of blood, hair and so on in a crime scene. Maybe if she had an opportunity, she'd even help the investigators a smidge by intentionally leaving behind a few strands of hair in some strategic places.

Time to make a plan. Hmmm...

Normally, with the exception of her mother, she was a don't-rock-the-boat kind of girl. She placated people rather than stir things up. It was her upbringing. She blamed it on her grandmother, who didn't leave anywhere—even a grocery store—without making a handful of new friends. Smile. Be friendly.

But this situation hardly called for some polite small talk. Or did it? She vaguely remembered reading in a magazine somewhere that it was smart talking about yourself if you're ever abducted. Then again, maybe it was the other way around. Huh.

Maybe it would throw these guys off if she suddenly pulled a one-eighty and acted like they were her best pals. They might underestimate her. That could work to her advantage. Then again, if she gave them a tough-girl act, they might decide she wasn't worth the grief and let her go.

Did she have it in her to be rude with anyone but her mother?

Time to test herself. "There are other ways for men to score a date, you know," she snapped at whoever was behind her.

"Yes, but we were running out of time."

What the hell? Running out of time? It must have taken her a full ten seconds to puzzle out that one. Then it hit her like a smack upside the head. "Ohhhh. Ya got it wrong. Cinderella's coach turns into a pumpkin after midnight. Not the prince's."

A warm chuckle sounded behind her. Directly behind her. Like so close to her shoulders that a coat of goose bumps instantly sprang up all over her upper body. The sound of that low rumble tickled her insides and somehow made her want to smile, despite the bizarre and scary situation.

A shudder skipped up her spine, starting at the small of her back and racing to the base of her skull. She pretended she hadn't shaken like some lame romance novel heroine on the verge of a lust-driven mania by demanding, "Okay. Fun's over. Time to let the tied-up girl go."

"No, not quite yet," one of them responded from farther away.

That wasn't the answer she was looking for, though it wasn't like she was about to die of shock. Clearly, these two had brought her here for a reason—a reason they had yet to share with her. Of course they weren't going to let her go now.

But at least it gave her the opportunity to test a theory.

"What about my mother?" she asked.

"Mother?"

"Yes, the other woman you kidnapped? You remember her, don't you? Kind of looks like me but with brown hair. Older. Name's Maria."

"We haven't kidnapped any other women...hmmm."

She didn't like the sound of that hmmm. Nor did she like the rest of the response. So much for hoping these two were the same guys who'd taken her mother. Not that she hadn't realized it was a long shot. "When can I go home?"

"Soon." The word was whispered in her ear.

She jerked, slamming her head into something hard. A sharp pain shot through her skull and she yelped. "Ouch!

Dammit. Now look what you did. I'm hurt. What the hell do you want from me?"

Soon was not good enough. If these guys didn't have her mother, someone else did. It was still a strange coincidence that they'd both been abducted in Detroit. Within days of each other.

Then again, if these men had been waiting for her at the airport, how could they have known when she was flying in? She hadn't told anyone.

"I didn't mean to startle you." Fingers gently probed her still-throbbing skull. "I feel no lump," the kidnapper behind her murmured. "I think you'll be okay."

Hmmm. This seeming concern for her wellbeing gave her an idea.

She sensed by her captors' gentle treatment that they didn't want to see her hurt, let alone dead. Even so, this was still a desperate situation, which called for some swift thinking. "No, that's just it. I won't be okay," she said, trying to sound as grave as she could. "I have a very serious medical condition, and I need to take my medicine. Seizures," she blurted, naming the first life-or-death medical condition she could think of. "The way I'm feeling right now, I'm thinking it's time to take my medicine."

"That's okay. We brought your bags. I can get it for you."

A cool sensation passed over the exposed skin of her hands, and the tiny patch of skin at the small of her back, exposed when the back of her t-shirt slid up a smidge.

"I don't see any medication in your purse."

Of course you didn't. Because there isn't any, except for the Midol I carry for an emergency. "Oh no. I must have forgotten it! What'll I do? If I don't take it on time, I'll start having seizures, and they won't stop. This is serious."

She got a set of hmmm's as a response. Then she heard some whispering. Had they bought her lie? God, she hoped so. Even though she'd always considered herself the world's worst liar, maybe she'd finally found someone even she could deceive.

A moment later, the remaining restraints were removed.

Hot damn! If she played this right, she could find herself free within moments. She hurried to sit up and face her kidnappers, hoping some sad puppy eyes would seal the deal.

"Strip," Hunkilicious demanded.

Jasmyne gasped. After their reaction to her seizure story, that had been the last thing she'd hoped to hear. *Goodbye. Sorry for scaring the shit out of you. Here's a little cash for your trouble,* yes. Not, *strip.* It took at least three seconds for her to find her voice. "What the hell?"

"I said strip." Hunkilicious was standing on the opposite side of the room, his arms braced against the back of a wing chair. His shoulders were stooped, his head flopped forward. He looked like he was either drunk or sick. "Let's have a look at you."

That was what her family doctor always said.

Hmm...maybe Hunkilicious was a doctor, and he was going to give her a physical exam, to see if she was lying. "Uh...I don't need to be examined. I just need my medicine."

She watched him struggle to work his way around the chair. This wasn't making sense. He could barely stand. From the looks of things, he was the one who needed a doctor.

Then again, doctors were human. They drank. They took drugs. Maybe he was having a bad day. And maybe she was an idiot for wanting to believe that.

"What medication are you taking?"

"It's uh..." What drugs were prescribed for seizures? She, of course, had no idea. "My doctor just changed my prescription. I think it was called...Ibutitrophitan. Or something like that."

"You're lying." He took a couple of staggering steps toward her. His gaze narrowed until she felt like a big, juicy steak on display at a soup kitchen.

Shit, of course he's not going to examine me. At least not like a doctor would.

Not that that shocked her. She'd been kidnapped. Kidnapped women were sometimes sexually assaulted. And this kidnapper was obviously loaded. A drunk man, kidnapper or not, could have an overwhelming sex drive, even if he lacked the ability to do anything about it.

Just great. What a night. Kidnapped. Hogtied. And now she was going to be raped by a guy who could barely stand upright.

She searched the room for the other guy, the one who'd helped her with her suitcase. He'd seemed a little more...normal.

Drunk guy smacked his hip into the side of the armoire as he took another couple of sloppy steps toward her.

Maybe if she delayed him, he'd go crawl into the nearest bed to sleep it off. Or better yet, perhaps if she could get him to lie down—ideally without her—he'd just fall asleep on his own. She dashed around the side of the bed, putting the enormous piece of furniture between them. She patted the mattress. "You look tired."

"You have no idea." He half walked, half dragged himself around the end of the bed.

Really, he looked pathetic. Pale, sweat coating his face. Shaky. She actually felt a little sorry for him. She pulled the coverlet down and fluffed a pillow. "Look, I'm not sure what you're thinking, but what you need to do is to lie down before you either fall over or throw up."

Darn it, where'd the other guy go? She so wanted to talk to someone who wasn't giving her I'm-going-to-eat-you-up looks. She needed to get out of there, find herself a rental car and a safe place to rest for a few hours so she'd have the energy she'd need to track down her mother before who knew what happened to her and that package.

Slumped forward, drunk guy slurred, "If I lie down, I'll die."

Nodding, she motioned to the bed. "I hear you. Bed spins are the pits. My mother —"

"No. I'm serious. I'm running out of time. If I don't take the blood-bond right now, I'll die."

Blood-bond? What the heck was that? Not that she needed to know the gory details. Anything involving the word "blood" couldn't be good.

"I'm what you mortals call a vampire. I need to drink your blood," he slurred.

"A vampire?" Looked like Hunkilicious was a hardcore drunk. He was delusional. His brain was pickled. So sad since he couldn't be older than his mid-thirties.

Her attention focused on his hands, she dodged his attempts to grab her. She shuffled along the wall, past a dresser and window. The minute she was beyond his reach, she broke into a hard run, heading straight for the closed door.

She hit it at a full run, the impact sending a jolt of pain blazing up her outstretched arms. Her teeth clacked in her mouth as the shockwave rippled through her body. Afraid to look back, she grabbed the doorknob and twisted. It turned. She pulled. And was stopped dead in her tracks by Gorgeous.

"There's something wrong with him," she said, thumbing over her shoulder. "He's sick, I think."

She supposed it would be too much to hope Gorgeous was too worried about his friend to care whether she walked out.

His brows furrowed. "I know." He closed his enormous — uber-strong! — hands around her upper arms and forced her back into the bedroom. Then, one hand still wrapped around her arm, he produced a key from his pocket, pushed it into the lock and turned it before tucking it safely back in his pocket.

She was locked in.

"Let me go," she demanded. She was the world's worst pickpocket, but she'd get that key, dammit. Somehow.

"I'm afraid I can't." He headed toward the bed, dragging her behind him. "It's too late."

"It's never too late to do the right thing." Stumbling over her feet, she struggled against him, trying to pry her arm free. But he had a hold like an anaconda.

This was wrong. This was all wrong. Why would these guys treat her so carefully and then hurt her? Their actions were so strange. At the airport. When they'd abducted her. And now.

Conflicting. Strange. Terrifying.

And then there was that whole vampire story thing.

Panic coiled in her belly. Tight. Hard. It felt like a steaming hot chunk of volcanic rock had landed in her gut. The heat spread up and out. Into her chest, her face.

The bed was getting closer.

Ohmigod.

This wasn't happening. No. No one was going to drink her blood. Or rape her. Or hurt her. She was just confused. Panicking for no reason. Yeah...

The drunk kidnapper climbed onto the bed. On his knees, he scooted toward her. His dark eyes glittered. His tongue swept over his lower lip. Then he smiled and she realized that a certain unlikely story had to be true.

He had fangs.

Exactly what kind of hell had she just been dragged into?

Chapter Four

෨

They had him over a barrel, to borrow a tired cliché. Fuck. How could he come out of this with his hide intact?

Asher needed one thing from him—correction, two. Unfortunately, Draven knew there'd be hell to pay if he gave his friend both—the blood-bond he needed to save his life and the help he needed to save the White Hawk Alliance.

No time to think about that now.

Draven tried not to look at Jasmyne. Her eyes did something to him. It was as if they delved deep inside, reaching into the shadows, searching out his secrets. He didn't want to be vulnerable. He couldn't afford to be vulnerable.

She was crying now. Her soft sobs echoed in his head. He wanted to tell her to stop. He wanted to plead with her to stop. The beast within him was stirring, wakened by the scent of her fear. The hunger was intensifying. His upper jaw ached as his fangs extended into position. He'd taste her soon and his pain would end. The burning in his belly amplified. Agony.

Asher lunged forward, propelled by what Draven knew was desperate, blinding need.

Jasmyne screamed and dropped to the floor.

A part of him despised the hunt. But there was no other way. It was the blood-bond that extended his life. Sometimes he wished he could resist the urge to hunt. But when he was gripped by the burning hunger, the bit of humanity that remained within him slipped into the shadows. And the predator took over.

Like now.

He inhaled deeply, drinking in the aroma of his prey's terror. He wanted her.

He stooped, swept her into his arms and lowered her to the bed. As expected, she fought him, but he wasn't as weak from the hunger as Asher. He easily overpowered her, pinning her on her back. He held her hands over her head. Her breasts rose and fell with each rapid gasp. Lust swelled within him. His cock hardened. His balls tightened.

"Now," he said on a grunt, indicating with his head to Asher. He held her wrists tightly although he knew the instant one of them bit the woman, the resistance would cease. Cold terror would be replaced by burning desire. Their terrified victim would become a willing participant.

Asher's hand trembled as he struggled to unfasten her pants. He was going for her femoral artery, a wise choice. But not without its risks. Draven shifted, balancing himself above her torso to keep her still enough for Asher to remove the rest of her clothing from the waist down. Shoes. Socks. Jeans. Cotton panties.

Oh, her scent. A bouquet of woman and soap.

Shrill screams echoed through the room. Between the sounds and smells, he became instantly dizzy, nearly blind with need. "Hurry," he pleaded as he repositioned himself. He used his arms to secure their quarry but angled his upper body so that he could bend down and taste her skin. More intoxicating scents swept into his nostrils as he nuzzled the crook between her shoulder and the slender column of her neck.

She shrieked again and then went dead still.

Asher had bitten her. His venom was pulsing through her blood vessels. It would take less than ten seconds.

Nine, eight, seven...

He ran his tongue along her jugular. Her heartbeat fluttered beneath her skin, a staccato tempo that beat within him.

Six, five, four...

He ached to sink his teeth into her sweet skin, to drink her essence and then give back the pleasure she deserved. But he had to wait a few more agonizing seconds until Asher had taken what he needed.

Three, two, one...

He forced himself to turn his head from the temptation that pulsed before his eyes. He watched as Asher suckled the tender flesh at the crook of her thigh. He knew the second Asher's venom had reached her brain.

She stiffened beneath him, cried out one last time. Her scream of terror morphed into a groan of pleasure and then she shuddered and went soft.

It was safe to release her hands now.

The instant he let them go, she reached for him, raked her fingernails down his chest and clenched the bottom of his knit shirt in her fists. His gaze wandered over her writhing body, up to her shoulders, her neck, face. Her eyes told him what her mouth could not. The loneliness, worry and pain he saw within their depths nearly brought him to tears.

How could he sense so much already? He hadn't even bitten her yet.

He tried to look away, to break the invisible tether that had bound him to her somehow. But he couldn't. She was holding him. Pulling him into her.

No. He didn't want to feel her pain, her frustration, her agony. He didn't want to feel her joy either. But dammit, there was nothing he could do.

This wasn't happening. Nonono.

The connection forming between them was so overwhelming, he literally pulled away, shifting his weight back until he was seated on the mattress beside her. He guessed by her expression that Asher had stopped feeding at the same time.

"No," she whispered.

The separation was shredding his insides to pulp. Why?

Confused, his body inflamed by desperate hunger, he scooted backward. He had to complete the blood-bond. He had to feed from her, to consume Asher's venom, now pulsing through her veins. But he hesitated, unsure what the connection would be like then. Would it be much more intense? He didn't want to know.

"Draven?" Asher whispered behind him. He smoothed a hand down Draven's back, a reassuring touch. "Feed."

What was it about this woman? Nothing had been normal, not since he'd first seen her in the airport.

"I need you." Asher's touch became firmer, more erotic. He sat up and slipped his hands beneath Draven's shirt, exploring Draven's lower back.

Jasmyne did the same, running her flattened palms up his stomach. Her fingertips teased his nipples, causing the hunger to flare white-hot again. He shuddered, swept her hair aside and bit her.

Sweet blood flooded his mouth and instantly a blaze ignited in his body. He felt his heartbeat speed up, pushing the life-sustaining heat through his chest, up his neck, down to his cock.

Asher pressed against his back, Jasmyne against his front. Heaven. Hell. Strange thoughts and images swept through his mind. Somewhere deep inside, a light flickered in the shadows, illuminating all the demons he kept hidden there. He was afraid of what he might see next, feel next, but he kept swallowing. He was powerless to stop.

"She will die," Asher said.

The words were like shards of glass being ground into his heart. But goddess help him, he couldn't stop. He needed more of her essence, more of the light, even if it would unleash the demons.

"Draven." Asher yanked on his arm, but he still did not release her. He couldn't. He pulled in another mouthful, and a burst of stars ignited behind his closed eyelids.

He felt Asher struggling to protect their mate, but the last thing he could endure was to be separated from her. Somehow, the darkness he saw within her healed him, chased away the heavy cloak of blackness inside him. He finally saw his secrets, the ones he'd hidden even from himself. He wasn't afraid anymore.

"Draven!"

A sharp pain blasted through his head. Instinctively, Draven loosened his bite, and then before he realized what had happened, he was lying on the floor, Asher standing over him, breathless and wild eyed.

"What the fuck, Draven? You almost killed her."

"I...don't know." Stunned by both the shock of having nearly lost control and the blow to his head, Draven slowly sat up. The world spun for a second or two before stilling. "Is she okay?" He couldn't see her. He needed to check, make sure he hadn't hurt her. If he had...

"She'll be okay. She's just weak." Asher offered him a hand up. "You took too much. I've never seen you do that before."

"There's something about her. I've never felt anything...seen anything..."

"Yeah. I felt it too." Asher pulled Draven into an embrace. "Dammit, I'm sorry, but that scared me. I had to stop you."

"Yeah. It scared me too." As it always did in the Binding, an urgent, agonizing carnal hunger swept through his body for his bound mates. Jasmyne. And Asher. Yes, Asher.

He kissed Asher with all the tenderness he had within him. They undressed each other, shared gentle touches until the sweet caresses had evolved into passionate strokes, demanding, taking.

And then, together, they roused a dozing Jasmyne.

It was time. To give back. And give back he would. For the many gifts he knew she would give them both.

* * * * *

Jasmyne woke to the sight of two naked men standing at the foot of the bed. Chests puffed, arms tensed, abs taut, other parts...erect...they were a study in male perfection. She felt funny—jittery, bleary eyed, foggy headed and really, really aroused. More than ever before, even a little while ago.

This made no sense!

She had been kidnapped. She was being held against her will. She shouldn't be feeling excited. No, most definitely not.

Wow, did they have the world's most amazing bodies, or what?

At the moment, she didn't want to believe these men were bad. God help her, she just didn't. It wasn't only the raw beauty of their bodies that was messing with her head. Or their picture-perfect faces. No, there was something else there, something she couldn't see or touch.

She remembered that moment, no more than a heartbeat ago, when she'd been pinned to the bed under one man while the other stripped her jeans and panties off. She'd been terrified, shocked, enraged. They were going to rape her!

And then there'd been pain. Excruciating. Blinding. Blessedly brief. Desire followed. Not just a mild, simmering passion but erotic hunger so intense it was painful. Her blood felt like acid burning in her veins. Her skin was scorching. Her breasts tender. Her pussy spasmed with an instant orgasm so powerful it stole her breath away.

But even that wasn't the strange part.

Just as she'd been swept into bliss, she'd felt something strange. The only way to describe it was some kind of bizarre psychic connection. It was like someone had climbed inside her body, her head. Or maybe she was inside him. She felt everything he did and vice versa. She thought his thoughts, as if they were her own. His voice echoed in her head, blending with her own inner voice. Memories she had never possessed suddenly swept through her mind. And the most amazing sense of completion filled her soul.

It was magical.

But then it ended and she hungered to feel it again, even if it would last only a few seconds. It was him, the one who'd loaned her his phone. She had no idea why or how he'd gotten inside her head, but she had all the proof she needed.

"Draven," she whispered, speaking his name for the first time. She loved the way the word felt in her mouth as it swept over her tongue and through her lips. "Oh God, Draven."

A spark flashed in his eyes but it quickly extinguished. She had no idea what that flicker was, whether it was something good or bad. But she wanted to know. Everything. She wanted to understand Draven, to belong to him. In all ways.

It was in-freaking-sane.

Although she knew it was, she simply could not find the strength to deny herself the pleasure he offered in that strong, silent way of his. She sat up and extended her arms, desperate to feel closer to him and to the other man, the one she knew was Draven's best friend Asher.

They crawled onto the bed, moving toward her as one. They reached her at the same time. Draven settled on her right side, Asher on her left.

She leaned into Draven, eager to reconnect with him. There was this empty void inside her now. She wasn't sure if it had been there all her life and she hadn't realized it or if he'd taken a part of her with him when that strange psychic connection had been broken. All she knew was that she ached to be complete again, and she knew he was the only one who could do that for her.

He wrapped his arms around her and she tucked her head into the crook of his neck. He smelled wonderful, like home. She felt Asher move behind her, felt the heat of his body on her back even before he touched her. His hands slipped beneath her shirt and at first she flinched. But then a wake of tingles swept up her spine, and she was caught in a wave of blistering heat. Like the shock of stepping out of an air-conditioned room into the stifling heat of an August afternoon, the effect was instantaneous and overwhelming. She whimpered, threw her head back and sucked in mouthfuls of cool air. Still her body burned.

Relief. Now. Please.

She felt the rest of her clothes being removed. She was eased back until she was reclining against Asher and her legs were stretched out in front of her. She blinked open her eyes.

Draven was kneeling beside her. His intense gaze raked over her nude body, her breasts, her stomach, lower. "Open for me, Jasmyne. Open now."

A quiver of anticipation shimmied up her spine. She slowly bent her knees until they were tucked under her chin. Then her gaze fixed on his, she let him ease them apart with his hands until she was open and vulnerable.

Her heart was banging against her breastbone so hard it hurt. She couldn't catch her breath. It felt like she'd just raced around the block at top speed. Her head was spinning.

She wanted the sensations to stop. And yet she didn't. Right now, at this moment, she had absolutely no control over anything. The man behind her was supporting her. The one in front of her was controlling her every movement with his words. Together, their strokes on her shoulders, neck, stomach, breasts were driving her to a point of complete surrender.

"I'm going to taste you now," Draven said. He then bent down, parted her labia with his fingers, and swirled his tongue over her clit.

Asher's hands slipped around her sides. "Accept what's yours." He pinched her nipples.

Every nerve in her body charged with thousands of volts of electricity. Her muscles clenched into agonizing cramps. She heard herself beg for mercy, but she didn't feel the words vibrate in her throat.

Draven and Asher increased the torment, adding finger thrusts in her pussy, and whispered demands for her submission. She wanted to submit to these men—oh yes she did. In every way. To relinquish her every thought and action. Her body. Mind.

Why?

She did know. Three-hundred sixty-five days a year, she had to stay in control, both for herself and for her mother. For just the briefest moment, giving herself up to another human being, a powerful one, sounded like heaven.

"Yes," she murmured, as the first spark of orgasm flared through her. She pulled her legs back, clenched her stomach and pressed into Asher. Her pussy convulsed around Draven's fingers. He stroked her gently until the sensations eased and the intense pulses cooled to pleasant twitches.

As the heavy cloud of desire surrounding her lifted, she became increasingly confused.

She glanced down and realized she was wearing no pants. No underwear. No shirt. And she couldn't remember when or how they'd been removed. Nor could she figure out why she was in bed with two men she barely knew. It was like she'd lost a block of time. Or like she'd just woken from anesthesia.

What the hell? She jerked upright.

"You have given us a great gift," Draven murmured, sitting up and smoothing one hand up her arm.

What was he talking about? "Me? A gift? I haven't done anything." Had she?

"Now we will show you our gratitude." Asher reached for her shoulder.

She knocked his hand aside. Funny, he'd been drunk a few minutes ago. Now he looked so intense, strong. Sober. Not to mention naked. "Gratitude for what? I don't understand." Why couldn't she remember anything? Panicking, she scooted on her rump, fighting for any distance she could put between the two strong men and her much weaker self.

"It's okay," Draven reassured her, lifting his hands. "We don't want to hurt you."

Draven. His name was Draven. When had he told her?

Something wasn't right. Could be she fainted and missed an important conversation. That was entirely possible. She was a little lightheaded, woozy. Sure. Right. Wrong. If she'd fainted, she would still remember passing out. Or falling. Something.

She didn't want to believe they'd slipped her some kind of drug, but that was the only thing that made much sense.

They had better not!

She checked her wrists for needle marks. Nothing. Maybe they'd given her a pill. Oh, this was too scary for words! Ever since reading on the internet that drug addiction was passed from generation to generation, she'd avoided taking over-the-counter painkillers for fear of developing a habit. What if they'd given her something super-addictive? Shit!

"Stay away." On hands and knees, she headed for the relative safety of the opposite side of the bed.

The two guys didn't follow her.

She inhaled a couple of deep breaths before hopping from the bed.

This was the most terrifying situation she'd ever faced.

Clothes?

There! On the floor. Thank God. Hands positioned to hide her delicate bits, she watched the men closely as she shuffled closer to her rumpled garments. Her left leg hurt, or rather, a spot between her pubic bone and thigh. Oh God, maybe they'd raped her. No, her other parts didn't hurt, although they were warm and wet. She didn't want to think about why that might be.

Maybe they'd bruised her when they'd undressed her. She scooped up her panties, stumbled into them and yanked them up. Much better.

The guys just sat on the bed, patiently watching her, like it was not at all unusual for her to be there. Like they weren't surprised that she was freaking out right now.

Some people lived very strange lifestyles.

Asher. The other one's name was Asher. How did she know that?

It was hard to believe that she'd once read a sexy story in a swinger's ezine and had brought herself to a swift orgasm daydreaming about being with two men at once. Jasmyne Vaughn. The girl who hadn't lost her virginity until she was twenty-three. And who hadn't done anything more adventurous than giving her ex-boyfriend a little oral sex in a car. And now she was sitting naked with two guys. Two!

Ironically, the subjects of her daydreams didn't hold a candle to these two, either.

Rather than ponder those mysteries any longer, she bent over, grabbed her shirt and jeans, and tugged, hopped and wiggled her way back into them. When she had her shirt on and her pants buttoned and zipped, she crossed her arms over her chest. "Which one of you is going to drive me to the nearest hotel?"

They looked at each other, shrugged then turned their gazes back to her.

Grrrr! The strong, silent thing was getting a smidge old.

Draven stood. Asher stood. They had erections that seemingly didn't quit, even when the object of their lust was heading for the door. But that wasn't going to stop her from leaving. Draven caught her just as she'd wrapped her fingers around the doorknob. He forced her to turn and face him with a nudge to her shoulder.

"We don't want you to leave."

Too funny. Like she was going to stay just because he wanted her to. "I have to."

"But there are some things you don't understand — "

"There are some things you don't understand either." Before Draven interrupted her again, she added, "My mother needs my help. And I need to find her before she sells my package to some drug dealer for a few ounces of crystal meth — "

"You can't go," Draven said, as if she hadn't just explained why she had to leave immediately. He then continued to explain in vague terms why he would not let her leave. "we...need you...Asher and me...it's life or death...blahblahblah..."

He was wasting his breath. And her time. She turned from him, grabbed the doorknob and...remembered the door was locked.

Dammit.

Key. Pocket. Where were his clothes?

She did a one-eighty, searching the room for his discarded clothing, spotting it lying in a pile next to the bed.

Of course she had approximately two hundred pounds of determined male between her and her target. Perhaps if she pretended to agree to hang out for a few days like he wanted, she'd catch him by surprise.

Did she have any other options?

Chapter Five

ဢ

Asher sensed there was something strange going on between the woman and his best friend. He'd hunted with Draven before, and Draven had never hesitated to claim his prey like he had this time. Nor did he lose control when he fed, like he had with this woman.

And now Draven had intentionally let enough time pass for the effects of their venom to wear off and their quarry's thinking to clear. The woman was confused, scared and ready to leave. Little did she know that wasn't going to happen. When she found out, things were going to get ugly.

Why'd Draven do something so stupid?

Every Son of the Twilight knew it was easier to persuade their prey to stay the full week if they sated their hunger fully before the venom wore off.

For the first time in centuries, he actually wondered if there was something he didn't know about Draven. His best friend. The one man he'd always known he could turn to. And a fellow member of the Hawks.

Then again, he had to wonder if this trouble with the White Hawk Alliance was making him paranoid. No two hunts were ever the same. Yet he wanted to read something into every little deviation.

He was letting this shit get to him. It didn't help that he'd received more troubling news about his enemies.

He hated to see the woman struggle. It was so unnecessary. The best thing to do was to get it over with swiftly. Draven knew that.

They needed to sate their hunger before the woman suffered anymore. Only after that was done could they move forward with their plans to take back the Hawks. Time was running out. If they waited much longer, they stood absolutely no chance of reclaiming the Hawks before it was too late.

Jasmyne put on her game face. Of course she was the world's worst poker player, so she figured her expression was probably as transparent as glass. But that was okay. All she needed was to get her hands on that key. Then she'd wait for the right moment. Sooner or later the guys would go to the bathroom, fall asleep or get hungry. She'd just have to be ready to act when the opportunity presented itself. Once she escaped the bedroom, she'd figure out what to do next.

Only a little bit more...

"How long would I need to stay here with you?" She kept her gaze up, focused on Asher's face, as she inched closer to Draven's clothes. Finally her unshod foot nudged the pants. Yay! Her heart did a little flip flop in her chest.

Now, how to get the key...

"One week," Draven said, stepping up to the bed. He stood opposite her, the bed between them, his arms crossed over his chest.

Ha, more like one hour. "Just one week? That's all?"

Asher nodded, standing to mirror Draven's pose. "I know it sounds cliché, but you won't be sorry."

Yeah. Rightttt. Did these guys have the world's biggest egos or what? "And what am I supposed to do during this week? Be wined and dined and waited upon hand and foot?"

"If that's what you want, sure."

As if! "There's no such thing as a free lunch. What's the hitch?" She curled her toes around the pants and slowly swung her leg to the side, dragging the garment under the bed. With an enormous mattress stretching out between her and the two guys, would they see what she was up to? God, she hoped not!

Draven and Asher gave each other one of those do-we-tell-her looks and then turned their gazes back to her again. "There's a small hitch. We just ask you to keep a very open mind."

"Why does it not surprise me—a pair of men are standing naked telling me I need to keep an open mind? You want to have crazy sex, don't you? Like with animals or something."

Asher was the first to respond, "Animals? Hell no. But crazy would be good, depending upon how you define it."

Draven gave her a look she couldn't quite read. His gaze shifted, and for the briefest of moments, she read uncertainty in his expression. Finally he spoke. "This is all very complicated, Jasmyne, but I intentionally waited until now to talk about this because I wanted you to make the decision freely."

"Freely? Waited for what? You kidnapped me. Drugged me—"

"No, we didn't give you any drugs," Draven said, sounding defensive. "I'm telling you the truth."

"Let's be real. Why would I believe anything you say? None of this makes sense. If you didn't drug me, why can't I remember getting undressed? What's going on?"

"We did kidnap you—that's true," Draven admitted without a hint of guilt. "But we could have claimed you earlier. You wouldn't have been able to resist."

Claimed? What the hell was he talking about? She was so exhausted she could hardly keep her eyes open. They felt like they'd been plucked from her head, ground into crushed concrete and then crammed back in her skull. It hurt to blink. To think. To do everything.

She was too fired up to relax, yet she was too exhausted to remain standing up. Maybe if she sat down for a minute. Just a short rest. Yes.

She more or less collapsed onto the bed and took a bleary-eyed visual tour of the room, searching for a clock. She found none.

What kind of person had no alarm clock in their bedroom?

The kind who didn't have to wake up at a certain hour. Duh.

God, she felt so weak. She slumped to the side. This was it. Her body had had it. She couldn't stay awake another minute. God help her, she was about to be under their complete control again. They'd be in a position to do anything they wanted, even give her more drugs. She simply lacked the strength to fight any longer.

"You need to rest."

Yes, I do. "I can't," she mumbled, struggling to sit back up. "It must be getting late. I need to find my mother." She was trying to talk herself into waking up, but dammit, her dull brain and sore muscles just weren't listening. Yeah, like they hadn't drugged her! Liar.

"Why don't you rest, and we'll look for her?"

Rest sounded so goooood. "Why would you do that? Help me?" She inspected Draven's face through her slitted eyes. Her eyelids weighed as much as sand bags.

"Because I want to." Draven walked around the bed and sat beside her. "Do you have any idea where we should look?"

Would he actually...? Hell, if he was serious, she'd be a fool to blow him off. "I have some addresses. In my purse. Most of the time she's with one of her friends," she mumbled, letting her eyelids fall closed. "Take the photograph."

"We'll do our best." He pressed a kiss to her forehead, and she smiled.

"Thank you," she whispered. Sure, she felt awful, sleeping when she should be searching for her mom. And the doubting-Jasmyne part of her didn't believe her kidnappers would put in even a small effort to find the missing Maria

197

Vaughn. But the head-in-the-clouds part believed Draven would do his best. In her heart, she knew he was a man of his word.

She also knew he was hiding some very serious secrets from his friend. But that was for them to work out. She had enough troubles of her own.

* * * * *

"What are we doing?" Asher caught Draven's arm and gave it a sharp tug. "We have some other issues to deal with — a group of murderous bastards to stop, for one. Why are we trolling the ghetto looking for Jasmyne's mother?"

"Because I said we would. I need to do this." He shrugged away from Asher's touch. How could he make Asher understand? Hell, if roles were reversed, he wouldn't.

"Why? Why would you give a damn about a woman we barely know? Dammit, Draven. Lives are on the line here. If we don't stop those bastards, who's to say what'll happen next? They're kidnapping innocent mortals and using them to do their dirty work —"

"I'm not going to let you down. We will deal with the Hawks. It's late. We don't have much time left tonight." Draven pointed at the clock on the car's dashboard. "Sunrise is in less than an hour. We couldn't do anything tonight anyway. When we get home, we'll sit down and lay down a plan to deal with the situation. I promise."

Asher sighed heavily, giving the expression his trademark weight. "Fine. Okay."

"Good. Now help me find this first address. We've been down this block twice, but I haven't seen the address. This neighborhood is a shit hole."

"Maybe that's because the house is gone." Asher motioned to a weedy lot housing a dented, rusty old van missing all four tires, hip-high grass, and no doubt hundreds of vermin.

"Shit. I should've known this wouldn't be easy. What's the next address on the list?" Draven turned a corner, driving toward the nearest main street. Even though the mortals posed little danger to him, these old residential neighborhoods full of torched houses, impoverished and neglected children and filth were not his favorite places to spend the evening.

"It's on the thirty-six thousand block of Oakwood."

"Look it up on GPS." Draven started thinking about the van in the empty lot. No one would actually live in a piece of shit like that. Then again…

"Will do." Asher typed in the address on the GPS unit. "Hmmm…hey, where we headed? Oakwood's back the other way."

"Just want to check something first."

"You're not thinking —"

"That someone's living in that van? Maybe." Draven took a couple of rights, bringing them back to the rusted vehicle. He put the car in park but left the engine running. "Be right back."

Asher nodded.

Draven's superior night vision allowed him to avoid the many obstacles hidden in the overgrown grass as he made his way up to the parked van. It was a cloudy night. There was little light, and since there were no streetlights, the slight flicker he caught in a window was like a blinding beacon.

It looked like whoever was inside had covered the windows, but a small tear in one of the makeshift curtains had let a tiny beam escape. He heard no one stirring inside as he approached, no movement. He guessed the inhabitant was either asleep or not home. His knock on the rear door produced nothing, no response except the scurry of several animals from under a nearby shrub. Caught in the reflection of the car's headlight, an opossum's eyes glowed silver as it paused in the street to glare back at him.

He knocked again, harder.

This time, the van rocked as someone moved inside. A corner of the curtain lifted then dropped. All motion stilled.

He waited. And waited some more.

Had he really thought a person who lived in a van, in Hell-on-Earth, would throw open his doors and greet him with a smile? There was always hope. He knocked again.

This time, a male shouted, "Fuck off. I have a gun."

Yeah. And he was a vampire. No big surprise there. In Detroit even the toddlers carried guns.

"I'm not a cop. I'm just looking for someone, a...friend."

"Yeah, well I'm not a social worker, so fuck off."

At least he had a dialogue going. He decided to forge ahead. He pressed the photograph up to the scummy window. "Her name is Maria. Maria Vaughn."

The corner of the curtain lifted, revealing the heavily lined face of a man. His lips sank in, the effect of missing front teeth, and his wispy-thin white hair floated about his filthy head like a cloud. "I haven't seen that bitch in months," he spat. "She owes me money. She's not going to show her face around here, not if she knows what's good for her." The curtain dropped.

End of conversation.

Off to the next address.

As they pulled away, another car rolled past theirs. The windows were tinted, hiding the driver from view.

They paid a visit to every address on Jasmyne's list. Over and over, they heard the same story. Clearly, Maria Vaughn had burned some bridges and had, perhaps, run out of so-called friends to turn to. No one knew where she was. And it seemed that no one cared whether she lived or died, outside of wanting the money she owed them.

He dreaded telling Jasmyne the bad news because he knew how much she cared for her mother and how this would devastate her.

He turned to Asher. His friend. Who'd waited patiently for him to complete this task when they could have been dealing with the White Hawk Alliance problem. It was Asher's turn. "Let's head home and figure out what we'll do about our situation now."

"Sounds like a plan. But what about Jasmyne's mother?"

"Can't do anything more tonight. We'll talk to Jasmyne when she wakes up and see if she has any idea where to search next." He patted Asher's knee. "Thanks. For being patient. I don't know how to explain what's going on with Jasmyne, but something's different with this blood-bond. I don't understand it. I can't describe exactly why it's different or what it means. It just is."

"I...know. Kind of." Asher stared straight ahead as he spoke. "I could tell right away at the airport, something was different." He combed his fingers through his hair. "I just hope it's not going to hurt you. Us. You're not yourself."

"I think you're probably overreacting. Jasmyne isn't going to hurt me. But as far as me not being myself, that I won't deny."

"You're an intelligent guy. Realistic. A damn good friend. I'd hate to see anything bad happen to you, which is why I'm kind of having second thoughts now about dragging you into the shit with the Hawks."

"No. I've always been here for you as your friend. I'm not going to walk away now, especially after taking the blood-bond. We're in this together. Period."

That sounded damn good to his ears. If only it were true.

"Just tell me one thing," Asher said, finally turning to face him. "We're going to claim Jasmyne soon. Because this is hell."

"Yeah. I'm in bad shape too. Sorry about that. This fucking hunger is killing me too. I don't think I'll be able to wait much longer either."

Chapter Six

ဢ

The things I do for love.

For the third time, Jasmine swallowed the bile rushing up her throat. "Yes, I promise to go to dinner with you. But not tonight."

"Tomorrow," her coworker demanded on the phone.

"No, not tomorrow. I told you, I'm out of town."

There was a stretch of silence that made Jasmyne squirm, but she resisted the urge to fill it with promises she'd regret— or rather more promises she'd regret. As it was now, she'd already vowed to go to dinner with Ken in exchange for some vital information.

She needed him on her side, at least for now.

Ken had access to the file room. He could find out what was in the package her mother had stolen. He was desperate enough to get in her pants to do just about anything. And she was desperate enough to use his lust to her advantage.

"Fine. I'll wait. You have an email address I can reach you at?"

Great, she'd have to delete her Gmail account after this. She reluctantly gave it to him.

"Got it."

"Are you going to email me the information or call me back?"

"I'll scan the ticket and email it."

"Great."

"You owe me big time."

Great. "You agreed to the terms," she reminded him, worried he'd start tacking on additional conditions. She hated being dependent upon anyone for anything. Her life had taught her to avoid it at all costs.

"Yeah, yeah. So what do you think of Spanky's?"

Her stomach dropped to her toes. "Spanky's is a stripper bar," she stated flatly.

"I know. But they have the best burgers and sandwiches in town."

Sure. It's all about the patty melt. She knew she'd regret going to Ken. He was a first-rate creep. But darn it, if she'd been able to get the information another way, she'd gladly have done it.

"You're a class act, Ken."

"I do my best."

"Just get me that manifest in the next hour, or you'll be chomping on...burgers...at Spanky's by yourself."

"I love it when you get all bossy with me."

She didn't bother stifling the groan. The image of Ken dressed in drag, on his knees, pleading for mercy from a leather-wielding mistress flashed through her mind. It was so not a pretty sight, but it did make her smile. If she had a whip, she just might use it to keep the man in line.

At the rattle of the doorknob, she murmured a swift "Bye" and hit the button, cutting off the call. She handed the cell phone back to Asher as soon as he entered the room. "He's going to email it to me."

Asher's smile was blindingly bright and she secretly decided she liked it. A lot. "Excellent. Can you trust him?"

That's questionable. "Do I have a choice?"

Her captor's smile faded. "Sorry. We did the best we could."

"I'm not blaming you. Even if I had been free to search for her on my own, I wouldn't have gotten any further than you did. In fact..." She wasn't sure if she should admit this to Draven and Asher. It wasn't something she was fully ready to admit to herself. But for some reason, she felt compelled to confess anyway. "I'm kind of grateful to have someone working with me on this. I've hunted down my mother on my own so many times." She blinked at the burn in her eyes and nose.

No, she wasn't going to cry. No no no. Oh hell, yes she was. She was tired. Yes, that was it. Exhausted.

A tear slipped from each eye and trickled down her cheeks.

Asher's expression got all soft and teddy-bear sweet.

What about that. She'd seen every part of Draven, from the dark and brooding man he tended to pretend to be, to the very devoted, vulnerable friend he tried not to be. But Asher was still very much a mystery to her. During that brief connection with Draven, she'd seen the memories Draven cherished of his friend. She knew enough about Asher to trust him and even admire him. However, she didn't know him like she did Draven. She'd never known anyone like she did Draven, even her own mother. Or herself.

She still didn't understand it.

Asher gathered her into his arms and she slowly relaxed into his embrace. She couldn't remember the last time she'd been held like this. Cuddled and comforted. Cared for and cherished.

Was that why she hadn't taken the phone Asher had offered and called the police for help?

How easy it would have been. He'd even left the room. Yet she'd done exactly as she had said she would do—called Ken to get the information about the missing package. If she'd called the police, she'd be free. And then she'd be able to search for her mother without distractions, and if she was lucky might find her mom before she'd sold the contents of the box.

God, she hoped whatever was in the box was worthless.

She managed to hold the rest of the tears welling in her eyes at bay as she sat cocooned in Asher's strong arms. A part of her wanted to stay there with Asher, safe, protected. Yes, this whole thing had started out as a kidnapping. She wasn't denying that. But she sensed the power had shifted somewhat. Asher and Draven were still strong, domineering men, but she wasn't afraid of them. Nor did she resent them for kidnapping her.

For the first time in her life, she'd have someone at her side as she dealt with her mother. To prop her up when she was tired. To encourage her when she was discouraged. In a way, she never wanted that part to end.

That was it. She was crazy.

She stiffened, leaned away from Asher and wiped the lingering wetness in her eyes with her sleeve. If nothing else, life had taught her one thing—she couldn't count on anyone. Not her mother. Not a couple of men she'd only met last night. What was wrong with her? She'd never been so foolish. Gullible. So easily duped.

No one did anything for nothing. There were strings attached to every kind deed in life. She simply hadn't seen the strings Draven and Asher had tied to theirs. Yet.

"I'm okay," she mumbled, turning her head so she didn't feel so vulnerable. She sniffled, blinked a few times then scooted farther from him. "Do you have a computer I can use?"

"We have a laptop." He stood. She didn't see him, but she felt the bed bounce as his weight lifted off the mattress. "I'll get it."

"Thanks." That familiar restlessness returned when Asher left the room. The tickly, jittery sensation she always felt whenever she didn't know where her mother was. For some reason it seemed to ease when Asher or Draven were near, but the moment they left the room, it came back.

She started pacing the room. She didn't doubt Asher would bring the computer like he'd said, but she did wonder how long he'd take. Or whether he'd make some kind of demand in return. She wasn't nearly as comfortable with Asher as she was with Draven.

And speaking of Draven, where was he? He hadn't come back to see her since very early this morning, when the two of them had told her they hadn't been able to find her mother.

She missed him.

She was standing next to the door when it opened. Draven. Her heart did a little hop in her chest.

"Jasmyne." He stood framed in the doorway, a laptop case gripped in one fist. He closed the door behind him as he entered, but unlike Asher, he didn't lock the door.

He set the case on the table in the room's corner, unzipped it, flipped it open and hit the power button. "We have wireless internet, so you can sign on to your email from here." He lifted his gaze to her face, and she read something in his dark eyes. An emotion she couldn't name. His entire mien was different than before, kind of stiff. He was nervous. No, upset. Or angry.

Why did it matter what he was feeling?

All too aware of how close he was, she slipped into the chair and opened the internet browser. He stood there, a silent, powerful force, beside her. She could feel the tension between them. It was like a series of invisible wires with electricity zapping and snapping back and forth.

Thanks to her jittery nerves and uncooperative fingers, she had to type her email password three times before she got it right. The first message was from Ken, and it had an attachment. "Good. It looks like he found it." She clicked on the message, skimmed the contents of the email—a reminder about the terms of their agreement—and then double-clicked on the attachment.

Draven gave a disgusted grunt.

"Diana's Star?" she read aloud, ignoring the flare of heat that had charged up her spine. "Wonder what that is." She glanced up, catching Draven's quirked eyebrow. "Do you know?"

"I've heard of Diana's Star, but I didn't think the artifact really existed. Not literally."

She typed the so-called relic's name into Google. Nothing useful came up. She tried Diana, Star, Relic. Still nothing. She huffed a loud sigh. "I'm getting nowhere on the 'net. Will you tell me what you know?"

He settled his butt on the edge of the table. His firm thighs stretched out in front of him, he crossed his ankles and arms. One of his knees brushed against hers. "I've never seen a picture of the Star, but I read about it years ago. Like I said, it's more a legend than anything, sort of like the infamous Holy Grail, Cup of Christ. No one actually believes it exists, but people are always drawn to stories about it."

"Well, evidently the box my mother stole contained something the owner was calling Diana's Star."

He nodded. "If the legend is true, the Star is a special piece of jewelry, a ring or charm, fashioned from silver. It bears Diana's mark, the star."

"Then I suppose it's valuable." She skimmed the figures on the scanned document. She didn't like the fact that there was no assessed value on the paperwork.

"If the artifact in that package was authentic, even if it isn't the legendary Diana's Star, then it would be priceless. Simply because of its age. We're talking almost three thousand years old."

"Hmmm. I wonder if someone on the street would know what they were looking at?" She set the manifest aside and turned her attention back to the computer.

"It's possible they wouldn't. Silver tarnishes, and of course, these days silver jewelry isn't the most precious."

It was hopeless. A waste of time. She closed the search box and shut off the computer. "I guess there's some hope then. Although I still don't know exactly what I'm looking for. The box was fairly small but still a lot larger than what I'd expect for a single piece of jewelry."

"Maybe it was enclosed in a vessel of some kind."

"Yeah. But why wouldn't the vessel be listed on the manifest too?"

"Because it's not valuable?" Draven suggested.

"Maybe." She pushed back from the table and stood. Her leg brushed against his thick, denim-encased thigh. He caught her hand in his and lifted it to his chest, where he sandwiched it between his breastbone and palm.

Oh, uh, wow.

He was so close she could smell the fresh scent of his soap. The aroma tickled the inside of her nose, and a little fluttery sensation quivered inside her tummy. Happy little butterflies. That had OD'd on high-octane nectar.

She'd fully intended to ask him to drive her down to her mother's old stomping grounds, but for some reason she couldn't speak. Her throat had collapsed like a garden hose run over by a Hummer. No sound would come out. Not even a little squeak.

She heard the door open behind her, but she couldn't turn to look. She didn't need to. Asher had just entered the room. She felt his presence. The nerves at her nape buzzed with sensual awareness.

Images flashed through her mind. At first bizarre, frightening—blood, dark eyes. Then tender—a woman, infant. And finally unexpected—wildly erotic images. Of Asher and Draven. Kissing. Tongues thrusting in and out of each other's mouths. Their hands exploring each other's bodies. Fists gliding up and down erect cocks.

She'd never fantasized about two men fucking. Oh God, it was naughty, fascinating, intoxicating.

Stars shut out her vision, like she'd stood up too fast. Her knees buckled and Asher caught her from behind, hands on her hips. Draven pulled on her hands, coaxing her toward the bed. "I...we can't wait any longer. The hunger is too much. You feel it too, don't you?"

"Feel?" she mumbled, letting the two men lead her toward the bed. Did she know what she was feeling right now? Did she care? Her body was demanding something. Her muscles. Blood. Entire being. It was like she no longer controlled her body or mind. She was caught up in a wild, thrashing river of wanting. She was helpless, powerless.

The guys whispered erotic promises as they stripped off her clothes and positioned her on the bed. She lay on her back, arms up and out, hands fisted, legs spread-eagled. Right now, the vulnerability of being in such a submissive position thrilled her beyond words, beyond logic. She wanted to be powerless. She wanted these two men to take over, to push her to a new place where she'd never been.

"That's it, sweet Jasmyne," Draven murmured. "You see now. You've wanted this for a long time, to let a man take control."

Yes, oh yes, she had.

"We only want to give you pleasure, to free you to explore and discover and experiment," Asher added as he knelt between her spread legs. While she watched, Draven and Asher undressed each other. And just as they had in those brief visions, they kissed, they touched, they stroked. Two powerful men, beautiful men. It was mind-blowing to watch.

Neither seemed to dominate the other as they explored each other's bodies. They both maintained equal power. One man to another. Both very much in control of both themselves and each other. Only she would be submissive to them. And that made her feel oh so good. Special.

She hadn't moved a muscle since they'd positioned her, not even a finger. She hadn't wanted to distract them. But more than that, she wanted them to be pleased with her obedience.

Finally, muscles taut, mouths drawn into tight lines, eyes fierce, they turned their attention to her. A rush of heat flared in her stomach. Another between her legs.

A fever burned in her veins.

She silently begged for their touch, for the relief every cell in her body demanded. Would they do it before she died?

"Do you like to watch us?" Draven asked, just before he dragged his tongue down Asher's arm.

Jasmyne licked her lips, tasting salt. "Yes."

"You have been so good. So patient and obedient." Asher lifted her ankle and kissed the sole of her foot. His soft lips tickled the sensitive skin on her inner sole. His fingers teased her ankle, calf. It was a struggle to keep from wriggling. "You deserve a reward. No, two."

She liked the sound of that! Bring 'em on.

Draven left Asher's side, crawled on hands and knees toward her. His intense gaze, paired with Asher's climbing strokes and kisses, made her shudder. By the time Draven had settled beside her shoulder, Asher had reached the top of her thigh. Her leg was straight up in the air and he was bent over, nibbling, licking and kissing his way to heaven.

Draven kissed her mouth. His flavor was a blend of him and Asher. Delicious. Spicy-sweet. His tongue swept along the seam of her lips and she parted them to welcome it inside. It didn't approach shyly but charged in and took over, getting all bossy and domineering. It tasted. It thrust in and out. It mated with hers, while demanding hers remain as submissive as the rest of her body. He nipped her neck then moved lower, pulling her nipple into his mouth. He tormented the other one with his fingers.

And while Draven took charge of her breasts, Asher took charge of her body from the waist down. He forced her legs wide apart, tormented her labia with his fingers, and then did magical, wondrous things to her clit with his tongue, lips and teeth.

Within seconds, she was ready to come. Her entire body was one huge trembling knot of erotic tension. She was being swept away into a colorful world of intense sensations that made her head spin. Scents, sounds, flavors.

And then they stopped.

She wanted to scream. She'd been right there. On the edge. Her pussy twitched. Empty. Burning. Aching to be filled. And so wet, her juices were running down her bottom.

Draven scooted behind her, lifting her upper body off the bed and supporting her weight with his hands as he slipped beneath her. Coming up on her knees, she leaned forward, letting him slide down so that his erect cock was positioned directly underneath her pussy. She was upright on her knees, facing away from Draven, looking down at his long, muscular legs.

Asher held her waist. The muscles of his arms bulged as he lifted. "Squat," he said. "I'll help support you." Legs spread, he knelt in front of her, straddling Draven's thighs. "We both want you. We'll both have you." He pressed his upper body to hers, wrapped his steely arms around her and eased her onto Draven's cock, until it was deep inside.

She gasped.

Draven's cock was thick and hard and just the right size to fill her completely. He groaned, the sound blending with her stifled moan.

She let Asher set the pace of her up-and-down motions, thankful for his support. At first, she moved slowly, moving her hips in slow circles as she descended to increase their pleasure. Then Asher started lifting her faster until she was rising and falling so quickly her ass smacked Draven's skin, creating a delightful slapping sound and Draven's gasping breaths echoed in her head.

Oh, the pleasure. She didn't want it to end, and yet she did. She ached for completion, and for the connection with Draven she knew it would bring. Already, as he fucked her, she felt something strange. The sensation of her hot pussy gripping a cock she didn't have. The heat of her ass when it smacked against a stomach she didn't possess. The sounds and tastes that weren't from her ears and mouth. She even smelled her own desire, and the scent was driving her wild.

Just as she was about to come, Asher pulled her up, completely off Draven's cock.

"We both want you. At the same time."

"Oh..."

She'd had anal sex once. It had been okay but not great. And although she knew—thanks to the occasional visit to online porn sites—that it was entirely possible to take one man in the rear and another in the vagina, she was not sure it was going to be all that great. At the moment though, being so close to orgasm that she'd do practically anything to get to the finish line, she was more than willing to give it a try.

For one thing, it turned her on to think she'd be possessed by both of these amazing, strong, sexy men at the same time. Imagination alone was taking her to some very happy places.

Asher left for a moment, returning with a tube of KY. He dispensed some on his fingers and spread it over her clit, vagina and anus. Then he held her as she lay back and slowly accepted Draven's thick cock in her ass. Her skin burned but as the muscles opened, the pain eased.

Oh, so full.

She lay very still, resting on Draven's upper body, her head thrown back, spine arched. Asher gently urged her legs farther apart, his penis gripped in his fist. Slowly, he worked inside her. She felt both men moving. Innnnn. Outtttt. Friction. Ohhhh. Supporting one of her knees, Asher used his free hand to play with her clit, drawing slow, lazy circles over it. Heat gathered deep inside her, swelling, building until it rippled out to her limbs and face.

And then he was there again, Draven. His thoughts, memories, pain, joy, hopes, fears, she experienced them all. She cried out as her pussy and ass pulsed around their cocks, milking them. She felt their cum, simmering hot, filling her pussy and ass. Driven by some primal urge, she started rocking her hips, increasing the friction. Increasing the pleasure and torment, and delaying the inevitable separation from Draven she knew was coming.

God help her, she didn't want him to leave her. He was as much a part of her as she was. And now that she'd had him like this, fully, she knew she'd be driven to have him again. And again. And again.

How was this happening?

She had to find out. She needed to know.

Chapter Seven

ജ

This could not be a coincidence. Their new mate had a personal tie to the very artifact the Hawks were after. As if he wasn't already in a tight spot.

Draven had made a commitment to Asher to help him. He'd made a commitment to Jasmyne to help her...and he'd been forced to make a commitment to a certain individual in the Hawks. Draven was damned, any way he looked at it.

Fuck.

Once the bastard who was holding his secret over his head found out what he was up to, a chain of events would be set in motion that he would be powerless to stop. And one of the people he cared for the most would suffer, the child no one knew about but him and the little girl's mother.

Fuck.

If he didn't help Asher, he wasn't sure he'd ever be able to face himself in the mirror again.

Fuck.

If he didn't help Jasmyne, he'd let down a woman he already cared a hell of a lot about.

Fuckfuckfuck.

How could he possibly make a choice between the best friend he'd always loved and trusted, a woman who had somehow found her way into his heart when no woman had done so before, and the innocent child who'd done nothing to deserve any of this?

Weary, he slumped into the closest chair. After returning from the search for Jasmyne's mother, he'd spent the

214

remaining hours before sunrise hunting down his daughter's mother and strategizing with Asher.

He sensed Asher was frustrated by his lack of helpful suggestions on how to stop the blood-lusting bastards who'd taken over the White Hawk Alliance. But he had no choice.

It all started over control of a drug the Sons of the Twilight had become dependent upon—Eclipse. It was manufactured in a plant owned by a couple of high-ranking members of the White Hawk Alliance. Once, not so long ago, there'd been enough Eclipse in the marketplace for any Son who wished to live like a mortal to spend nearly every day out in the sunlight. But that had changed recently. The underground government of the Sons of the Twilight had slowly started taking over distribution of the drug. The White Hawks were fighting for the drug's deregulation, but the king had instead tightened control, taking all but a small percentage of the drug and hording it in some undisclosed location. It seemed he believed the raw ingredients of the drug were in short supply. The owners of the plant knew otherwise.

Eclipse allowed the Sons of the Twilight to walk in daylight. Now, thanks to the shortage, some Sons didn't even have a single dose to allow them to hunt for their blood-bond. They had to hunt at night, which was not so much a problem as it was an inconvenience. However, there were a small number of Sons who suffered because of the lack of Eclipse. The Sons who had to hunt in Alaska and other northern locations during the summer, for instance. And the ones whose livelihood depended upon their ability to work during the daylight hours.

It all seemed so unnecessary, but he didn't know all the technical details. Perhaps the king was right in stockpiling the drug. Maybe there was the possibility of exhausting an ingredient in the drug. He had no idea what it was made from. All he knew was that things were getting ugly, and they weren't going to improve until something changed.

He was exhausted. A few hours' sleep would be good right now. If only he wasn't expected to catch a runaway mortal, plan a takeover and...save the freakin' world.

"She's insisting on leaving," Asher said as he rushed into the room.

"Let her go." Draven waved his concern away.

"But we need her for another six nights."

"She'll come back."

"How can you be sure?" Asher challenged, sounding skeptical. "I've never let a mate leave."

"She needs us as much as we need her."

"I don't know about that." Asher settled on the overstuffed arm of the chair. He handed Draven a stack of paper. "I wasn't going to say anything more, but I want to know more...what exactly is the deal with you two? Have you figured it out yet?"

"No." Draven skimmed the papers, personal information about a handful of key White Hawk members. He knew he wouldn't find anything useful there, but at least his request had kept Asher busy for a little while. "Hmmm..."

"Did you find anything?"

"No, not yet. But I'm looking. The White Hawk Alliance is such a huge organization. There are a lot of people to check out."

"I've been thinking. We need to find out exactly how the Hawks are going to assassinate King Kaden. We already know who they're prepared to put in his place. But I'm completely shut out. You're not. You're still talking to a few of the Hawks in positions to know at least a little, aren't you?"

"Not so much anymore," he lied, hiding the guilt he knew Asher would see in his eyes by pretending to read the papers in his hands. "I think they all know whose side I'm on."

"Dammit. We need someone on the inside. We need information. What do you think about Dayne Garrott?"

"What about him?"

"I've heard he's been kind of backing off from the Hawks lately. Maybe he can tell us something."

"I don't know. If the inner circle is aware of his shifting loyalty, he won't know any more than us."

"It's worth a try. He tends to start the night with a drink or two at Vibes. I think I'll head over there after sundown."

"Sounds good. Want me to go with you?"

Asher scrubbed his face with his flattened hands and blinked at him with heavy-lidded eyes. "Not if you have another lead to follow up on. Or someone else inside you can talk to."

"I'll see what I can do. In the meantime, I think we should both get some sleep."

"Yeah, I'm beat. Morning." Asher shuffled toward the door, stretching his arms as he walked.

"Morning." Draven set the papers on the table and dragged his weary body to the bed. Sleep first. Then he'd figure out how to avoid hurting the only three people on earth he cared about.

To his surprise, it was Jasmyne's face he saw in his mind's eye as he drifted off to sleep.

* * * * *

By dusk, Jasmyne had become thoroughly frustrated and was all too happy to return the car she had borrowed from Asher by nightfall, as she'd promised. She'd spent hours searching for her mother. She'd gone to her mom's every hangout, every drug den she knew about—those were always terrifying—and every shelter. She'd checked all the local pawnshops, searching for a silver ring that looked old enough to be an ancient Greek artifact. And she checked the local jails and hospitals.

Nothing.

She made a missing person's report, now that adequate time had passed since she'd last been in touch, stopped for a quick burger and headed back to Asher and Draven's house.

Pride dictated she'd have to offer to move to a hotel. Forget about the fact that she'd been kidnapped—she still was kind of clueless why they'd done that and then turned around and let her loose. Now she was free to leave, and that made her a houseguest, not a victim. But because she'd grown comfortable with the guys—okay, a little more than comfortable—she honestly didn't want to go sleep in some dumpy hotel by herself. But she didn't want to be a pesky guest who stayed past her welcome. If she sensed they didn't want her around anymore, she would leave.

She parked the car in the driveway, gave herself a mental boost as she prepared to give the "I should be going" speech, and headed inside with her dinner-in-a-paper-bag gripped in one hand, her super-sized fountain drink in the other.

All doubts about whether she was welcome to stay were eliminated before she'd muttered the first word.

Draven and Asher were standing just inside the door, looking like two kids who'd just welcomed the best friend they hadn't seen in months. They rushed forward, crushing her—and her dinner—between them.

Draven gently relieved her of the bag of food, and Asher did the same with the paper cup. They scooped her off her feet, using their arms to cradle her bottom, and away they went, up the stairs.

For the briefest of moments, as she was carted down the hallway, there was excruciating pain on the sides of her neck. And then thoughts of her empty stomach and painful neck immediately scattered from her mind, like pigeons chased away by a tom cat. Gone. A very different kind of hunger took over, one that was much more urgent and agonizing.

She wanted Asher and Draven, and she wanted them right now.

She threw her head back and enjoyed the ride, clueless where they were taking her, and basically not giving a damn. As long as they fucked her, she'd be perfectly content.

A few seconds later, the guys stopped walking and gently lowered her to her feet. She blinked open her eyes. They were in Draven's bedroom. That was as good a place as any.

Asher held her as she struggled to steady herself on her wobbly legs. Then both men stepped backward, crossed their thick arms over their yummy chests and in unison demanded, "Take off your clothes."

As if her legs weren't already about to buckle! Oh yes, she was all too happy to oblige.

She performed a little striptease for her hunky twins, gyrating her hips and seductively stroking her stomach and upper thighs as she removed one garment after another. When she was in her panties and bra, she stopped. Her breathing was way faster than that little bit of physical exertion should have called for, and her body temperature had spiked to near lethal levels.

They just stood there, looking at her like they could gobble her up in a single bite.

Hmmm, a bite or two might be nice. Or at least a touch. A word. Something.

Draven stepped forward and extended a hand to her. "This way."

She placed her hand in his and let him lead her toward the bathroom. The sunken tub had been filled with steamy hot water and scented oils. Asher gently removed her bra and panties. Together, they helped her into the bath.

A week ago, who would have ever thought she'd be in Detroit tonight, soaking in a bathtub while two absolutely stunning men lathered her hair and shoulders with the most gloriously scented shampoo this side of heaven? Certainly, she never would have imagined such a thing. Heck, a week ago, she wouldn't have even imagined herself soaking in her own tub with one man running his hands over her shoulders.

To think this would have to end soon.

To think this had started out so crazy.

"Sit up, baby, and tip your head back," Asher whispered. He used the handheld shower to rinse her hair. Hot water massaged her scalp, leaving her skin tingly. When he'd finished rinsing her hair, he lowered the showerhead, directing the pulsing stream to the back of her neck.

She let her head fall forward, stretching her muscles. Draven, positioned at the opposite end of the sunken tub, cradled her foot in one hand and smoothed soap over the top. He drew little circles on her skin, his soapy fingertips gliding down to the sole.

Sweet Jesus, she was in heaven.

There was a splash behind her, then the sensation of a bulky male sliding into the tub behind her. Asher smoothed his hands around her sides, simultaneously stretching his legs out on either side of hers. Then, palms flattened against her breasts, he eased her back until she was resting against him.

Draven lifted her leg higher, allowing him to gently caress away the tension in her calf. Thigh. Then, when his upward progress was inhibited by the soapy water, he lowered himself into the water too.

The tub was just big enough to accommodate two big guys and one smaller girl. It was slightly crowded although cozy. Legs and arms became tangled as the guys worked together to wash every inch of her body, both above the water's surface and below it. Before long, she had not one but two hands between her legs, exploring, stroking, possessing.

Awash in liquid heat, both inside her body and out, she closed her eyes and just let the sensations pulsing through her body carry her away. Soothing scents of lavender and candles swept into her nose. Sounds of water splashing and her own gasping breaths echoed in her head. The feeling of four hands, strong and dominant, moving over her body as if they owned her.

She had no idea how thrilling sex could be. Not that she was anywhere close to being a virgin. She'd had her share of lovers. But sex had always been just...okay. Never the exploding, pulsing, throbbing, ohmigod experience she'd read about in her favorite romance novels. In fact, she'd recently decided she'd be okay if she spent the rest of her life celibate.

After being with her guys, the idea of never having sex again depressed her.

This was beyond words. It wasn't just about anatomical parts rubbing together. It was about three people being vulnerable, taking risks, giving as well as receiving.

It was about finding the kind of connection with another human being that made her complete. Letting go of her inhibitions. And learning about herself.

The guys helped her out of the tub. Draven left the bathroom, a towel slung low on his hips, while Asher dried her off with the world's largest bath towel. He insisted on doing everything. She simply stood there like a queen, being patted dry by her servant. Then he took a bottle from a basket sitting next to the sink, poured a bit into his palm and beginning at her shoulders, rubbed the jasmine-scented oil over her entire body.

Now she really did feel like a queen.

Asher looked at her like she was the world's most beautiful woman, making her feel that way for the first time in her life. She'd always been so self conscious about how she looked. Unlike the average woman, she was bony. No curves. Anywhere.

Oddly, Asher and Draven didn't seem to mind. She'd had some guys—young, ignorant, cruel—tell her she was built like a little boy. Those comments had taken their toll, shaped her opinion of herself despite her efforts to dismiss them.

But Asher's heated looks were going a long way to reshaping that opinion.

The bathroom door opened, revealing Draven, who'd rid himself of the towel. His cock was, as she'd come to expect, at full staff. So was Asher's.

She noticed the swing suspended from the ceiling in the bedroom's corner the instant she left the bathroom.

A sex swing!

She'd never had sex on one of those. Heck, she'd never had sex anywhere but in a bed. Not even on the floor. But she'd seen pictures. She'd read about it. She'd even fantasized about it. Would the reality live up to the fantasy?

Her guys helped position her in the swing. Draven secured her hands up over her head. Asher cuffed her thighs in the padded supports.

Talk about being completely under their control. Her legs were spread wide. Her arms were straight up, over her head. And she was at their mercy. What a wonderful place to be. They had barely touched her and she was already on fire.

Draven knelt between her legs, his gaze devouring every inch of her body. Rushes of erotic heat pounded through her as she sat there, waiting, wondering what he'd do next.

He might taste her. Or fuck her with his fingers. His tongue.

When, oh when would he give her that thick cock?

She trembled as a ripple of wanting coursed through her body and chills spread over her skin.

Goose bumps puckered the skin of her arms, stomach, chest.

"Are you cold, Jasmyne?" Asher asked as he prowled around her, like a hungry jungle cat preparing to pounce.

"No."

Draven audibly inhaled. "You smell so sweet. Dammit, I don't want to wait anymore."

"Don't." It was a plea, not a demand, though she doubted they'd know it.

"We won't make you wait much longer," Asher whispered into her ear. Behind her now, he smoothed a hand down the center of her chest then over to cover her right breast. He nibbled on her neck and collarbone, which added goose bumps on top of the goose bumps that had already been there.

Meanwhile, Draven tormented her by licking, nipping and stroking every part of her from the waist down.

Except the parts she wanted him to lick and stroke.

This was a cruel game. One she knew she couldn't tolerate for long. Her body demanded swift completion. Every muscle and nerve. Within minutes, she was so desperate for the agony to end, she was begging. Over and over, she murmured, "Please" to her tormentors. But they continued. Asher suckling her breasts, Draven her clit.

Finally, as if they sensed she was about to find the relief she so desperately sought, they stopped.

Every inch of her body tingled.

Draven stood up.

A tube of lube in his fist, Asher circled behind Draven. His expression was a mask of fierce erotic hunger as he pushed on Draven's shoulders, forcing him forward until he was bent over Jasmyne. Asher dispensed some of the clear jelly into his palm and spread it over his cock.

"Have you ever watched two men fuck?"

"N-no," she stammered.

Were they going to…? Oh God, that was hot!

Asher tossed the tube on the ground, gripped Draven's hips in his hands and slowly forced his thick cock into Draven's ass. Draven shuddered as he entered, tossed his head back and met Jasmyne's gaze. His eyes were glassy, as if he was looking at her but not seeing her. His mouth had thinned to a tense line, and every muscle in his upper body clenched into sinewy ropes.

There was a flash and then a million disjointed images rushed through her mind again. Women. Men. Loneliness and solitude. A child. Regrets.

Swept up in the tidal wave of emotions, she closed her eyes and submitted to them, letting them carry her wherever they would. She found herself in a place where she didn't want to leave. Ever.

A magical place.

Her insides alternated between frigid coldness and fiery heat. She felt the friction of Asher's cock as it slowly eased out of Draven's anus, as if Asher were fucking her instead. And slowly, as Draven's mind joined with hers, her body melded with his. The orgasm they shared was the most powerful, bizarre, wonderful one she'd ever experienced. She simultaneously felt Asher's cock thicken inside Draven's ass, and Draven's hand gliding up and down his own cock. She felt his come rush to the tip and burst out, as well as her own vagina pulsing and muscles trembling.

She heard herself gasping.

And then Asher pulled out. Straightening up, Draven plunged his cock into her clenching pussy. He drove into her at the frenzied pace she silently demanded. She wrapped her hands around the straps securing her arms to the bar overhead. Yes, oh yes, she was going to come again. And so was he. Once more, she let him carry her away to that magical place, where they were one and they were whole and nothing else existed.

What is this place? she heard herself ask. Her words echoed, like she was speaking into a cave.

I don't know, Draven answered.

A few stuttering heartbeats later, she felt herself being pulled away from him. She wanted to cry. She tried to resist, but it was like the tug of a strong current, pulling her farther and farther away.

She opened her eyes. Draven and Asher were now kneeling side-by-side, facing her, their expressions dark. They looked at each other then at her again.

Something was wrong.

"What happened?" she asked.

"I don't know." Draven glanced nervously at Asher again. "I don't know why this is happening." He stood, gave her a sweet, lingering kiss and then unbuckled the straps holding her wrists.

Asher unfastened her legs and together they helped her to the bed.

"You need some rest," Draven whispered before pressing a kiss to her forehead.

"Yes," she agreed, feeling her body getting heavier by the millisecond. "Restttttt." She let the darkness carry her away, hoping it would take her back to the magic place she shared with Draven.

Chapter Eight

ॐ

"Start from the beginning," Asher encouraged as he set a tray with fruit, yogurt and a muffin on the table in front of Jasmyne. "Maybe you've missed something."

"Okay." She swallowed a couple of bites of melon before continuing, "My mother has a drug problem. Methamphetamine. She's run away from home before, but this time it's different. She stole a package from me that contains something called Diana's Star, and then she took a bus to Detroit, her favorite hangout when she's bingeing. But unlike all the other times she's run away, this time she called me, claiming she's been kidnapped and held hostage."

Asher's eyebrows dropped at least an inch. "Okayyyy."

She dug into the yogurt, delivering a couple mouthfuls before adding, "That's why I thought you and Draven had kidnapped her. It's hard to believe it's a coincidence that she was kidnapped, and then the night I arrive in Detroit, I was too."

"True but..."

"That's all you have to say?" she asked between mouthfuls. "I was hoping you'd be more help than this."

"I'm trying." He plucked her cell phone off the table. "May I?"

"Sure."

He flipped the phone open and pushed the power button. "I was just wondering, don't take this wrong, but can you believe what your mother said about being kidnapped? Or do the drugs make her delusional?"

"I've thought about that. She's never been delusional before. Do you think that's what it was? That she was having some kind of psychotic episode or something?"

His eyes widened and at least ten seconds of silence stretched between them. "I would, except one thing."

She inched forward, eager to hear whatever he was about to say. "What's that?"

"Did you happen to keep the phone number she called from?"

"It's on my cell. I didn't erase it."

He handed her the phone, and she clicked down to the unfamiliar number with the Michigan area code. She handed it back to Asher. "That's the one."

"Hmmm. She said the phone she was using to call you belonged to one of her kidnappers?"

"Yes."

"And you're sure this is the number that displayed when she called?"

"Yes. Why? What are you getting at?"

"This is Draven's phone number."

It suddenly felt like the room's temperature had dropped a hundred degrees. And then heated two hundred. "What? That would mean...no. You're kidding, right? Tell me you're joking."

Draven was involved in her mother's abduction? No. She couldn't believe it.

"What were you doing with Diana's Star?" Asher set the phone on the table.

"I'm a courier. I work for a company that specializes in delivering valuable or sensitive packages. I was supposed to deliver it to an address in Chicago. But there was no answer. I held the package overnight, planning on returning the next day—"

"And your mother stole it and disappeared." He nodded.

"You're not thinking..." Draven kidnapped her mother? For some old chunk of metal? No no no! He wouldn't do such a thing.

There had to be a misunderstanding. During those wonderful moments, she'd bonded with Draven in a magical, psychic way. She'd never seen anything about her mother. He couldn't have kept any secrets from her, especially none that significant.

But that still left her with one sticky question—how had her mother gotten her hands on Draven's phone?

Asher could be mistaken about the number.

It took her several minutes to find her tongue and free it from the roof of her mouth. "I've never taken an undeliverable package home, dammit. I never expected this to happen. If I don't find it, I'll lose my job. Then I'll have no way to pay for my mother's rehab. And God only knows what'll happen to my boss, who owns the company. She's a bitch most of the time, but I still don't want to be the one to put her out of business."

"That'll be the least of our problems."

She stared at the number displayed on her phone's screen. She needed to confirm the number. "Why do you say that? Can I use your phone again?"

"Sure. Here." He handed her the cell. "I talked to a friend of mine, a former White Hawk. Diana's Star is what they're using."

She double-checked the date of the call first. Then she slowly punched in the number, making sure she made no mistakes. "Who or what are the White Hawks? And what do they want with some crusty old silver ring?" She lifted the phone to her ear.

It was ringing.

"They're a group of very powerful Sons of the Twilight. And evidently, they're going to use it to kill our king."

Two rings, three rings...

Ah, one of those secret societies, like the Masons. "What king?" she asked, distracted. "The United States doesn't have a king."

Four rings, five. There was a click and then she heard a familiar voice, one that had said intimate things to her. "Hello, I'm not able to take your call right now—"

Eyes blurring, she snapped the phone shut, cutting off the call.

"The United States doesn't have a king, but the Sons of the Twilight do."

Blinking, hands shaking, she dropped Asher's phone into his hand. "And who are the Sons of the Twilight?"

Asher hesitated for at least ten heartbeats before meeting her gaze. "What do you know about vampires?"

"You and Draven are vampires," Jasmyne repeated, swallowing a sob. This was a cruel joke. It had to be. Now seated on the bed, she covered her face with her hands and closed her eyes. When would he give her the punch line? She was more than ready for it.

"Yes," Asher responded, serious as death. "We're vampires."

Oh my God. This isn't a joke. "Real bloodsucking vampires? A la *Interview with a Vampire* and *Dracula*?"

"Well, we'd prefer not to be compared to fictional vamps because those characters are a little stereotypical. Sort of like comparing your typical suburban housewife to Stepford wives. You okay?"

"Yes. No. No, I don't think I'm okay." Could her head spin any faster? Asher couldn't expect her to believe this pile of bullshit. Right? She took a good long look at his face. This funny little nervous twitch hit her in the stomach. He could be telling her a bunch of lies. About Draven. And himself. But why? "I don't understand."

He sat down and reached for her. As much as she ached to be comforted, she couldn't let him touch her. She scooted away.

"I know this is a lot to take in all at once. I'm as shocked about Draven as you are. But maybe it'll help to know we don't kill the people we feed from."

The twitch in her stomach amplified to a full-blown cramp. "That's gooooood. I suppose."

"We've fed from you," he admitted sheepishly.

"Then it's really good you don't kill them," she snapped as she swallowed the bile rushing up her throat.

Okay, there was no way either of her guys had bitten her. She would remember that. So, what did this all mean? That Asher was lying? About Draven being involved in her mother's disappearance. And about them being vampires. Why would he lie? Especially about such bizarre things.

Or maybe he wasn't trying to be deceitful at all. He could be the delusional one, not her mom.

She didn't believe either possibility. She didn't want to believe either. She'd spent a fair amount of time with Asher since arriving in Detroit. Until now, he'd showed no outward signs of mental illness. He was smart and sensitive and utterly sane.

The truth was, she liked Asher. A lot. And still reeling from Draven's seeming betrayal, she was feeling especially vulnerable. She hadn't felt the intense connection with Asher in the beginning like she had with Draven. Maybe that was good. Because she'd let that powerful chemistry with Draven kind of take over. But now she knew that an initial nuclear-reactor response didn't necessarily mean anything. It certainly didn't guarantee safety.

In the past few hours Asher had become her rock. He was quiet, powerful, intense and attentive. Not to mention extremely intelligent. Would she have to add "insane" to the list of traits he possessed? God, she prayed not!

Maybe they were vampire wannabes, like the ones she'd read about on the internet. Those people called themselves vampires, but in reality they were just normal human beings — with a bit of a blood-and-latex fetish. Not that she'd seen either of her guys wearing black latex — yet.

Darn it! Now what?

She figured she had three choices. Cut her losses now and leave. Head out on her own. Or stick around and try to sort out this huge mess, with the hope that Asher would lead her to her mom like she'd originally hoped.

If what he said about Draven was true, Asher could be an even greater ally in her search for her mother. Maybe it was totally foolish of her to think this way, but she needed his help. Time was ticking and she was getting desperate. Even a long shot was worth gambling on now.

For this reason alone, when Asher asked if she'd like to go with him as he checked on a couple of things, she agreed. For now she'd play along and see if she could determine what was truly going on. As she settled into the passenger seat of his car, she said, "I'm still trying to wrap my brain around all this. You're a vampire. How did you become a vampire?"

"We were born that way." He twisted at the waist to look over his shoulder and backed the car down the driveway. "Just the way you were born as a mortal."

This sounds so crazy! "Your mom and dad were vampires?"

"My mother was mortal, my father a vampire."

"Then your mother fed you blood when you were an infant?"

"Yes, she did."

"That's just wrong." She closed her eyes and rested her head against the headrest. "You're really a vampire? Honestly?"

"I've got the fangs to prove it if you want to see."

For some reason, even though she didn't want to believe him, she almost did. "No. That's okay."

Maybe there was a way to know for sure if he was an honest-to-god vampire, thanks to her weird mental connection with Draven. Bits of memories fed into her mind during those bizarre connections still remained in her head. Maybe the answers she sought were already there. Inside her. She concentrated, searching through the hundreds of blurry, faded images she'd acquired.

What she saw, and tasted, made her gag.

Blood.

Oh God, if he wasn't lying, vampires did exist. He was one.

So was Draven.

And she'd slept with both of them. Shit!

Did that mean she could end up pregnant with a vampire baby? She wasn't ready to think about it, but she sure needed to. "Not that I'm one hundred percent convinced about all this stuff yet, but uh, how's that vampire baby thing work? I—I mean, I'm a mortal. You're a vampire…"

"The exchange of venom during the Binding prevents pregnancy."

"Oh, thank God." That was a huge relief. Enormous. Gigantic. "Where are we headed?" she asked, deciding an immediate change in topic was in order. She didn't want to hear more about the vampire thing right now. Or think about it either. It was too much to deal with all at once. Too bizarre, shocking. Maybe over time, she'd get used to the idea.

"Tailing Draven. His car's up ahead. I had a feeling I knew where he was headed."

"Guess we got lucky." She sat taller, trying to spot Draven's taillights. "I've said it before, but I feel like I need to say it again. Thank you. For helping me."

"Sure." Asher glanced in the rearview mirror before returning his gaze to the windshield. He grimaced.

"What's wrong?" She twisted in her seat to check behind their vehicle.

"Nothing."

"Who's behind us? Is someone following us too?"

"I'm not sure."

She tugged her seatbelt tighter, just in case, and desperate to distract herself from her racing heart and sweaty palms, asked, "Do you have family close by?"

"No."

"No one? What about your mother?"

"She died years ago."

"Oh. Sorry." Long, agonizing pause. Another strange memory surfaced. This one took the form of an image of a woman, her head thrown back, neck bared. Jasmyne shook her head, desperate to escape the memory. "Were you an only child then?"

"I had a sister, but she's gone too."

Her attempt at small talk wasn't going very well, nor was it distracting her from thoughts of double-crossing wannabe vampires. "What about your father?"

"I think he's still alive, but I don't talk to him."

"Me neither. Actually, I never knew my dad. I don't even think my mom knows who my father is. I asked her. Lots of times, especially when I was a kid, but she never gave me an answer."

Asher said nothing, just kept driving, his expression unreadable.

"I think that messes with a kid's head—not knowing where you come from."

"Yeah?"

"Sure. When I was little, I'd never invite my friends over. They all had a mom and a dad, even if they didn't live together anymore. I had a mom, and a very disturbed one at that."

"It was very painful for you." Asher steered the car around a corner boasting a dilapidated gas station-slash-party-store. "Where's he going?" He glanced in the rearview mirror again and scowled.

Jasmyne turned to look out the back window again. "Where's who going? Is the car still following us?"

"It's back there. I can't afford to try to shake him right now. I'll lose Draven. And since I have no idea what Draven's doing down here, I don't want to take that chance."

"Is there anything I can do? I feel so helpless, just sitting here."

"At this point, all you can do is keep your eyes on the car behind us, and if he makes a move, let me know. I've got to keep my eyes on Draven."

"Fair enough." Thankful for the distraction, she situated herself so that she was both strapped in securely and able to watch out the back. "What car are we watching?" They were on a six-lane road, and there were several vehicles behind them. She didn't remember seeing any of them when she'd looked back before.

"It's the black sedan behind the delivery van. You can see it when we turn a corner."

"Okay." Gripping the back of her seat and staring out the window, she asked, "What reason would Draven have to become involved in my mom's disappearance and that star thingy? You said it was going to be used to kill your king?"

"It has to do with an organization called the White Hawk Alliance. We were both members, though I'm not exactly on good terms with most of the members right now."

"Why's that?"

"Because they're doing some things I'm not happy with. And they're not happy with me either."

"Why?"

"Hang on. I think Draven's seen us." He steered the car into a sharp right turn. "Damned if I'm going to walk away from the organization I founded just because a couple of bastards have decided to bully the rest of the members. I owe it to all the Hawks to stay and fight for them."

"I can respect that. But what kind of club is it? And how is a crusty old artifact going to be used against a king?"

"I'm not sure how they're going to use Diana's Star to assassinate him. Dammit!" He threw an arm across Jasmyne's back, a protective gesture, and slammed on the brake. Then, before she'd turned herself around—she was tangled in her seatbelt—Asher had exited the car.

"Stay in the car," he barked before slamming the door shut.

Scrambling to free herself from the belt, she watched the exchange outside.

Draven and Asher were arguing—shouting, arms flailing, expressions fierce. Because the vehicle's window was closed and the guys were a good fifty yards away, she couldn't make out what they were saying. Didn't matter. She caught the gist.

There could be no question. Asher believed Draven was doing something wrong.

Heart banging against her ribcage, she opened her door and stepped out. As she ran around the rear of the car, she caught sight of the black sedan parked down the road. Her stomach did a little flip inside her belly.

Asher needed to know they were being watched.

She knew he'd be mad at her for leaving the car, but dammit, he was too wrapped up in his argument with Draven to notice a 747, let alone a midsized car parked behind an overgrown hedge the size of a bus. She figured it was at least a fifty-fifty shot the person in there had a gun. And if that was the case, he or she was probably waiting for the perfect time to shoot.

God, what would she do if anything happened to Asher? To either of her guys?

Driven by raw terror, she pumped her arms and legs until her muscles burned. She didn't bother trying to get their attention from a distance. They were now throwing punches. And insults. And some very colorful curse words.

She waited until she was well within earshot before shouting, "You're being watched."

"I don't give a damn," Asher spat at Draven through gritted teeth. "You've been my friend forever. How could you do this to me?"

"Like I said, I figured one of us had to stay on good terms with the Hawks if we were going to find out what their plans were."

"Not buying it."

"Then that's your problem. Not mine," Draven shouted back.

Jasmyne waved her arms. "Guys, the black car is parked back there. Asher!"

"Where's Jasmyne's mother?" Asher demanded, ignoring Jasmyne's frantic waving.

"I can't tell you."

"Like I said, you're full of shit, you double-crossing fucker. You know how important it was for me to turn the Hawks around."

"Yeah, I know. But the truth is, you can't take the Hawks back." Draven huffed a sigh, raked his fingers through his hair and kicked at the ground. "You've lost. It's done. I can't help you. But that's not to say I didn't try. I did."

Breathless, Jasmyne stumbled to a stop next to Asher. "The black car."

Asher shoved Draven backward. "To think we're stuck in this fucking blood-bond for another three nights. I don't want to even look at your face, let alone your ass."

"You've always liked my ass," Draven quipped.

"Fuck you."

Still struggling to catch her breath, Jasmyne glanced down the road. The car was pulling away from the curb, heading their direction. She yanked on Asher's hand as hard as she could. "Car!"

Asher finally looked at her, then at the car rolling slowly toward them. "Get down." He pushed her toward Draven's parked car, forcing her to her knees behind it. He stooped beside her, and Draven shuffled around the opposite end of the vehicle, stopping on her right side.

"Who's that?" Draven whispered.

"Why don't you tell me?" Asher grumbled.

"I don't know. Fuck. They're stopping."

Both guys ducked down, throwing their arms over Jasmyne's shoulders, shielding her back with their bodies.

She squeezed her eyes shut and braced herself.

At least twenty racing heartbeats passed before she inhaled. No bullets whirred past. She took another breath. Several bazillion heartbeats later, the guys inched up to peer over the car's trunk.

"Isn't that King Kaden's brother, Marek?" Asher whispered.

"Yeah," Draven answered. "What's he doing out here, following you?"

"Maybe he's following you, since you're part of the conspiracy to kill his brother."

"Draven and Asher," the man her guys had called Marek called out. "I'm unarmed."

"Then again," Jasmyne whispered, "maybe he's following both of you."

Her guys looked at her as if she'd just revealed some awesome secret.

Draven silently motioned for her to stay hidden as he stood. "Kind of a strange place for a social call, wouldn't you say?"

"Yeah, well you two picked the venue," Marek said. "I had a feeling you wouldn't accept a formal invitation to my brother's place."

"It's hard to say." Asher stood up. He held his arms crossed over his chest, his back ramrod straight. Jasmyne guessed from the tone of their voices and body language that neither of her guys trusted this man.

"I have a proposal for you," Marek said, stepping closer.

"Yeah?" Asher asked, sounding leery. "What kind of proposal?"

Draven didn't respond.

"I've come at my brother's request. Accompany me back to his house and I'll explain all the details."

Asher's body remained tense, his tone guarded. "Since when is your brother interested in talking to a couple of nobodies like us?"

"He's always had an open-door policy to the Sons of the Twilight."

"Yeah. Right," Draven scoffed. "But how many of the Sons who've met with him have either disappeared or dropped dead afterward?"

"I don't know what you're talking about. No one has. That's a lie, spread by the White Hawks, and you know it."

"Then you're in the dark. In a lot of ways." Draven mirrored Asher's pose. "Thanks, but I think I'm going to politely refuse."

"Me too."

Jasmyne inched up so she could get a better look at the man named Marek. He was every bit as handsome as her two guys. His razor-sharp gaze met hers. "Who is this human? I hadn't realized..."

Asher scowled at her.

She mouthed *sorry* but refused to duck down again. There wasn't any point. He'd seen her now.

Marek motioned to the car behind him. In the next blink, she was dragged against someone, held by two steely arms while in horror she watched Draven and Asher fight for their lives.

Her scream echoed through the night.

Chapter Nine

ဢ

Draven sighed. He stood leaning against the wall opposite Asher, arms crossed, face flushed, jaw tense. One of his feet was propped up on a leather footstool. "You aren't going to win back the Hawks just by killing two men. They're in power for a reason. Because the other three hundred Hawks believe what they do. They all want change so damn bad they're willing to do whatever it takes to get it. Even close their eyes to the truth."

Glaring, Asher pushed off the opposite wall and walked to the door, closing a fist around the doorknob. "I can't believe a word you say anymore. What'd you do? Promise to help me just so you could run back to those bastards and tell them what I'm doing?"

"No. It wasn't like that."

"Then why?" Asher raised his hand before Draven could answer. "No, never mind. I don't want to hear your excuses. You're an ass. It doesn't matter anyway. I know now where your loyalties lie. That's all that I care about." Asher put an end to the discussion by leaving the room and slamming the door bridging Draven's bedroom from the rest of their suite.

Draven dropped his face in his hands. His heart felt like a lead weight in his chest, so heavy it hurt. He hadn't wanted things to go this way. He had never wanted to hurt Asher. But what he'd said was true. The men now at the helm of the White Hawk Alliance were there because the other members wanted them there. Even if Asher was able to kill them, two other like-minded members would step into their places—after Asher was killed first, of course.

His friend had to accept one simple fact. The White Hawk Alliance was no longer his. It had changed from a vehicle for positive change. It had a new focus. Its members had a new agenda — vengeance, power. Nothing would bring back the organization Asher had originally founded.

Draven slumped onto the bed. If only he hadn't been forced into the position of delivering the terrible news to his dearest friend. The truth would no doubt cost him their friendship. At least for now. He could only hope that someday Asher would understand and forgive him.

Only one benefit had come out of this. He was finally able to stop the guise of helping Asher and do what was necessary to protect his daughter. With the new information Marek had given them during their so-called friendly conversation, he'd be able to buy her safety once and for all.

Now he not only knew where Diana's Star was, but he also had a vague idea of where the king's stock of Eclipse had been hidden. It was ironic, that the woman he'd been searching for, Jasmyne's mother, had the one thing his enemy wanted most. All he had to do was get himself out of this fortress somehow, steal the ring and turn it, along with the location of the Eclipse, over to the bastard.

Then, Draven vowed, he'd walk away from all the bullshit. For good.

The first thing he'd do, given the chance, would be hold his daughter and tell her how much he loved her. It would be the first time he'd spoken those words to anyone.

There was only one tiny problem. Tomorrow night, after taking care of those important tasks, he'd have to sneak back into the palace in order to feed. The blood-bond wasn't something a Son of the Twilight could walk away from. At least not without killing himself...and the other members of the triad.

* * * * *

Jasmyne watched Asher storm from the room. She didn't approach Draven right away. It took her a while to build up the courage. She was so confused and hurt. She had so many questions but doubted he'd give her answers. Would he tell the truth or lie? Would she know the difference?

What he'd said to Asher had made sense to her, but she knew he was still holding something back. He hadn't told Asher everything.

Standing about five feet away from him, she asked, "Why are you keeping your daughter a secret?"

His elbows on his knees and his head in his hands, Draven sighed. "To protect her."

"From what?"

From everything. From the bastard. From...me. "It's a long story, and I don't want to get into it right now," he said to the floor.

She wasn't backing down. She had to know the truth. He was going to tell her everything, what he knew about her mom and why he'd kept it a secret from her. She would get it all out of him, whatever it took. The strange connection they shared and what knowledge it had given her would be a handy tool. "I know a lot of things."

"I'm getting that."

To meet him eye-to-eye, she dropped to a squat in front of him. "Why do you suppose that is? Do you feel the same things I do? Do you see my memories? My secrets?"

Silence.

"It seems," he answered, still avoiding making eye contact.

Annoyed, she stood. He sure wasn't making it easy on her. She wanted to believe he wasn't out to hurt her and Asher. But the evidence was mounting, and he wasn't exactly defending himself. Did he want her to believe the worst? "I've never experienced anything like this."

"Me neither."

She hurt. All over. Her head. Her heart. "I want to believe that. But it's hard. With everything...my mom. This thing with Asher."

He finally met her gaze. Once he did, he didn't withdraw again. "I'm not lying. Then again, you know I'm not. What else do you know?"

"Nothing about me or my mom. But I sense you're keeping other secrets from Asher. I don't really understand why though. He's your best friend. You've always been able to trust him. What does it have to do with your daughter?"

"It's too complicated to get into."

"In other words, it's none of my business," she snapped, hurt turning to anger again. "You've been lonely for a very long time, Draven. Why do you think that is? Or are you denying it?" Her insides churning and simmering, she swiped at the tears collecting in her eyes. "You probably don't want to hear my opinion, but that's too bad. You don't know how to follow your heart. Or how to trust people or let them in."

"I think you got some wires crossed." His body language said "don't go there" but she wasn't about to back off. There was too much at stake. He stood, arms crossed, and turned his back to her, pretending to be checking out the window.

He was on the run.

"No, I'm sure about this. Why didn't you marry the mother of your baby? You loved her, didn't you?"

He simply shook his head. "There were a lot of reasons."

"I've thought about this, a lot. What's happened with Asher and how you could have been involved with my mother...lied to me—" The sob wedged in her throat cut off the rest of her sentence. She had to swallow several times before she could speak again. "All I can figure is that you believe you need to stick with the plan, whatever the plan is. That it's all about what you think in your head needs to happen. Love has no part of any decisions—"

"Maybe you're channeling another man because you're way off base there. I never loved anyone."

"Never loved anyone. Not a single person? I don't believe that." Truth was, she didn't want to believe it. If she could be objective, she might. After all, look at what he'd done to two people he should have loved, the child he hadn't seen in years and the friend he'd lied to. "You might actually be happy if you let yourself love."

He stood and charged forward, crowding her until she staggered backward in an effort to steal a little personal space. "What do you know about love? Hmmm?" he demanded. "Who taught you how to love?"

Hands shaking, she took a step backward. "That was a low blow."

His expression dark, fire in his eyes, he wrapped his hands around her upper arms and squeezed. A muscle in his jaw ticked under his stubbled skin. "You're not exactly dealing love taps either."

She fought to free her arms, but instead of getting loose, she found herself being pulled closer. "Yeah. But for some reason, I feel like I need to help you," she shouted, rage building inside her like steam in a pressure cooker. "It's fucking insane after what you've done to me and my mom. But for some stupid reason, I'm driven to say something. You've missed out on so much happiness in life—"

"Yeah, and so have you."

"What are you talking about? I'm not like you. At all. I don't lie to the people who mean the most to me. I don't push people out of my life—"

"You're hiding from life too."

He was so full of shit. "You're talking out of your ass."

"Really? So you're going to deny the fact that you're so wrapped up in solving your mother's problems that you can't be bothered to look at your own? Baby, your mother's troubles aren't yours. She's an adult. It's about time you let her live the way she wants to, even if it's not the life you'd like her to have. She's entitled to make her own decisions."

She wanted to tell him he was full of shit again. But she couldn't. If anything, this little adventure had revealed a few truths she'd long denied.

She did go beyond the realm of helping when it came to her mother. She'd had that fact thrown up in her face long ago. But what she had never bothered to do before was take a look at why. Problem was, she didn't really have the strength to do that now. In a way, it was so much more comfortable to just live with things as they were. For one thing, who was to say what she would be left with if she changed. "Maybe you're right. I have let my mother take over my life. But if I don't stop her from hurting herself, sooner or later she's going to end up dead."

"Maybe she wants to die."

No. "You think?"

"I don't know." He pulled her into an awkward embrace. "The thing is, maybe you think I've made some mistakes. I know I have. But you have too. Your mother's been the center of your life for years. That's not the way you should be living. It's holding you back, denying you the happiness you deserve too."

She couldn't relax in his arms. Not with the pain of his suspected betrayal still festering inside and the sting of his words only adding to it. "How can I be happy when my mother's lying in a ditch somewhere stoned out of her mind?"

"So as long as she's using drugs, you don't deserve to live? To be happy? To love?"

"Yes...maybe. I don't know."

He gently stroked her hair, and she felt a little of the tension easing from her shoulders.

"She's like a concrete block tied around your waist. She's dragging you down."

"I'm all she has. I can't turn my back on her."

"I'm not suggesting you do that. I'm suggesting you quit chasing after her. When she needs you and she's ready to accept your help, you can be there for her. I'm sure her doctors have told you before, she won't change until she's ready to do it for herself."

Jasmyne closed her eyes and just stood there, silent, struggling with frustration, rage, hate, love. Behind her closed eyelids, tears gathered. Inside her chest, darkness swirled and thickened like storm clouds.

She wasn't sure how long it took for her to speak again. "I hate the drugs, the people who sell them to her, the so-called friends who drag her back into that hell over and over again."

"I know, baby, but nobody makes her do anything. She goes to buy the drugs because she wants them. And she seeks out those friends because she shares something in common with them."

"They're lowlifes."

"No, they're someone else's mother, brother, sister, father. And they're as lost in their pain as your mother. But none of them will drag themselves out of it until they want to."

More silence.

"I know."

"You say that, but you still act like you don't." Draven hooked his index finger under her chin and lifted it until her watery gaze met his. "I care about you, dammit. And I don't want to see you giving up on your life for someone who doesn't appreciate the sacrifices you're making."

He cared. About her. Did she believe that? She wanted to. "She's all I have."

He shook his head. "Not anymore."

"What are you saying, Draven?"

"I'm saying…" He looked away.

Her breath caught in her throat. The darkness in her stomach swirled round and round. "What are you trying to tell me?"

He blinked several times, audibly swallowed and then, when she was sure he was going to walk away, looked down at her. He dragged his thumb down the side of her face. "I want to be the reason you get out of bed in the morning. God help me, you were right about Allegra's mother. It was my choice. I'd decided it wasn't right, and I didn't love her. I wasn't capable of loving anyone. I sent her away. I sent my daughter away. And I've been fooling myself for so long, telling myself I did it to protect them. I did it to protect myself."

Jasmyne sat stunned. She knew how hard it had been for Draven to say those words. They put him in the vulnerable position he'd avoided his entire life. "Draven...?"

"I love you, Jasmyne. I can't make myself not love you."

Draven swallowed. Once, twice, three times. A cold sweat broke out on his brow and palms. He hadn't just spoken those words. The three he'd never muttered before to another person — male, female, adult or child. No.

What had made him do such a thing?

Never had he wanted to take back words before. The regret burned in his gut so fierce he felt sick. He never felt sick. He wasn't capable of feeling sick.

Just like he wasn't capable of loving someone.

What was happening to him?

All he knew was if Jasmyne turned her back on him now and rejected him, he'd be tempted to do something crazy like go sunbathing.

The silence between them was deafening.

He stared straight ahead, afraid to look at her face. He could just imagine what her expression was right now.

Shocked. Appalled. She believed he had played a part in her mother's disappearance. Of course she was hurt and stunned.

"W-Wow, Draven."

Eager to stop her from speaking, from saying the words that would surely destroy him, he crushed her mouth with his. He kissed away any words lingering on her lips. He kissed away the doubts and fears burning through his veins like acid. He kissed her with all the desperation he felt.

And she matched his passion and fire. This wasn't the kind of kiss she'd given him before. It was bolder and more demanding. Her tongue thrust into his mouth, gliding along his own in a possessive stroke. The authority she communicated through her lips and tongue thrilled him. Ripples of wanting gathered deep in his belly. His testicles tightened. His groin warmed.

Kissing him like no woman had ever dared before, she clawed at his clothes. One hand slid beneath his shirt and the other went south, to cup the growing bulge between his legs.

Fuck. If only he had the time to take her now. There wasn't a cell in his body that wasn't demanding release.

Willpower.

He gently broke the kiss and eased her away from him. To keep from grabbing her and thrusting his tongue back into that sweet depth, he stepped aside.

Her gaze dropped to his groin region.

Dammit, he needed to make an adjustment. His face burned. He turned around, unbuttoned his pants and made an attempt at diminishing the tent effect his erection had produced.

"That wasn't very nice," she grumbled, her tone wavering. "Didn't anyone ever tell you that you shouldn't start something you can't finish?"

"Sorry."

"I'm confused. Why'd you stop? I mean, you said that...those words. And now...?"

"I know I'm sending mixed signals. But I need to do something important."

"Does it have to do with your conversation with the king's brother? Or my mom? Will you tell me what's going on now? I need to know."

"I sorry, I can't. Not yet."

She turned away. Her shoulders tightened. "It's not fair for you to to keep me in the dark like this. Especially if it has to do with my mother."

"I am going to find her. I need you to trust me." He knew she would read the guilt in his eyes. He turned to face the opposite direction, determined to avoid telling her the truth, how he'd learned her mother was deeply involved in this whole thing. It would only put them both in danger. He could protect Maria from the White Hawks, as long as Jasmyne stayed out of the way.

First, he had to find Maria. He already had some idea where to start. Then he had to get the Star from her and take her somewhere safe. And only then would he tell Jasmyne what was going on.

Once again he found his loyalties at odds. Yes, he'd set things straight with Asher, but Jasmyne still believed to a certain degree that he was helping her find her mother. And the package she'd stolen.

How would he make her understand? He loved her. He'd do almost anything for her—with the exception of putting his daughter in danger.

Until the artifact was in the hands of his enemy, nobody he cared about was safe. Not his daughter, Jasmyne, her mother, Asher. He had to protect them all.

He was so fucking sick of being manipulated by the bastard, always fearing the consequences if he did the wrong thing. It had to end. He hoped the Star would buy his freedom. Finally.

"You're keeping secrets from me too," she whispered.

"I'll tell you everything when it's safe."

"Is it your daughter?"

"I can't talk about it yet." He tried the door. Unlocked. That surprised him. Then again, Marek knew they had just taken the blood-bond and that they had several more nights left. No doubt, he didn't expect any of them to leave unless they left together. Asher was Marek's insurance policy. He wasn't going anywhere. That was obvious after their meeting.

"Where are you going?" Jasmyne asked.

"Like I said, I have something to do. I'll be back before morning. I know it's hard, that I don't really deserve it, but I need you to trust me."

"You have no idea what you're asking. You won't tell me anything. How am I supposed to trust you?" She rushed through the open doorway. "I'm going with you."

He didn't need this right now. He caught her arm and pulled her back into the room. "No you're not. It's too dangerous. You need to stay here with Asher."

"If it's dangerous, then you shouldn't go alone."

"I'm not taking you."

She lifted her chin, pulled her mouth into a narrow line and glared through slitted eyes. "You don't have to take me. I'm an adult. I can walk on my own feet, thank you."

"Yes, I'm well aware of that fact." Feeling every second tick away, he shut the door and headed toward the connecting door to Asher's room. Rather than let himself in, he knocked.

"What are you doing?" Jasmyne asked, sounding leery.

"Making sure you stay safe."

"As soon as Asher learns you're leaving, he'll insist on going too."

"No he won't."

There was one sure way to keep Jasmyne and Asher from chasing after him. He caught her shirt in his hand and yanked, tearing it down the center.

Jasmyne's mouth formed an O of surprise. Her face turned pink, then red. Her eyes widened, but she didn't move to cover her exposed torso. Only a lace bra stood between his mouth and her delectable nipples. It was agony.

He rapped on the door again, harder this time, and with his free hand, reached for one of those glorious breasts. Desperate to cling to his willpower, he shut his eyes while his fingers traced one lace cup. Jasmyne's whimper echoed in his head and the intoxicating scent of her arousal filled his nostrils. He was nearly knocked to his knees by the powerful need charging through his system.

The door swung open. Asher's mouth opened, but before he'd so much as uttered a single word, it snapped shut. His gaze went right to Jasmyne's back, and then he caught one of her hands in his and pulled. She twirled around, halting abruptly when Asher's mouth claimed hers.

Draven used his body to force Asher and Jasmyne back into Asher's room. Asher took over from there, lowering her onto the bed. One of his hands glided up her leg. The other went to work on her bra strap.

While Draven staggered backward, battling every instinct within him, her bra fell away, revealing two golden-skinned globes. He didn't inhale on a regular basis, and he rarely inhaled deeply, but damn if he could help it now. His head was spinning, he wanted her so much.

Not now.

Asher pushed Jasmyne's pants down her smooth-skinned thighs.

Damn.

Draven took a single step forward then two steps back. He'd started this knowing he'd have to find the strength to walk away. If he was weak, if he couldn't leave, he wouldn't find Maria Vaughn in time, and his daughter would suffer the consequences.

His gaze fixed on Jasmyne and Asher, he slowly backed toward the door. The last image he saw before leaving the room was of Asher parting Jasmyne's legs and bending his head to taste her.

Her cries of pleasure followed him into the adjoining room.

Chapter Ten

ΕΟ

The voice in Jasmyne's head was screaming all kinds of colorful expletives but her body was completely ignoring them. Just moments ago, she'd been determined to head out to find her mother with Draven. Now she was lying on the bed naked, a willing participant in some wild monkey sex.

The guilt was not dampening the mood a bit. God, these guys turned her into a sex addict or something. Sex was now more important that saving her job and rescuing her mom.

Was there a switch somewhere to turn off the heat blazing through her body? And the tingles?

She supposed not.

But as she lay there, her eyes closed, her legs spread, and Asher's tongue doing a merry little dance over her clit, she had to question what it was about these two that had turned her into such a nympho. She'd never had this kind of appetite for sex. She hadn't enjoyed the few experiences she'd had. Okay, maybe a little bit. But now…holy smokes!

Liquid heat pulsed through her body in waves. With each heartbeat, the crests rose higher, the distance between them drew closer. Her breathing grew increasingly ragged. And the colors swirling behind her closed eyelids became more and more vibrant.

She inhaled through her nose, drawing in Asher's masculine scent. He smelled wonderful, of man and nighttime. He'd been outside. She could smell it on his skin when he lifted a hand to her chest and she'd kissed the tip of his index finger.

He was such a giving lover, much like Draven. He took such care with her. He worshipped her body like she was a

253

goddess. The reverence he displayed as he touched, explored, tasted. It made her want to give the same kind of respect and adoration to him in return.

If only he'd let her.

Up until this point, her guys had been in complete control during their lovemaking. They'd even secured her hands the last time, physically restricting her ability to caress, touch, explore. She enjoyed turning over control to them like that, more than she ever would have guessed, but this time she wanted it to be different.

She needed him to stop tormenting her. Before she succumbed to the orgasm that was slowly, steadily building deep inside. "Asher," she whispered. "Stop. Please."

He did as she asked. Still dressed, he levered himself up until he was sitting between her spread thighs.

Instinctively, she tried to scoot up and draw her legs together. It was one thing to be open and vulnerable when she was out of her mind with desire. It was another when she was more aware. While her blood still simmered and her heart thumped so heavily she could count each heartbeat, her head had cleared just enough to be a little self-conscious.

Of course Asher didn't understand her embarrassment. He had the world's most perfect body.

Scowling, he grumbled, "Don't."

"It's not easy to hold a conversation with you when I'm like this."

"I don't care to talk. I want to go back to doing...other stuff."

"But you're not even undressed yet."

"That's not a problem. I was getting to it." He caught the hem of his shirt in his fists and pulled.

"But that's just it." She sat up, catching his hands in hers. "I don't want to just lie here and watch you do everything. I want to give as well as receive."

For that, she was the recipient of a stunning smile.

"You have been. You've given Draven and me both plenty. That's why we serve you. It's our pleasure. We don't mind. At all." On hands and knees, he crawled forward until his knees rested on either side of her hips and his chest was inches from hers. His nose was nearly touching hers, but she didn't feel crowded, not in a bad way. This time, his proximity was welcome, no, more than that. She wanted him close. She needed him close. "What do you want, baby?"

She licked her lips. "To undress you."

"Very well. You may remove my clothes." He lifted his bottom off the bed, kneeling tall, arms at his sides. "You can start with my shirt."

She gathered a handful of fabric in each hand and pulled, but he didn't lift his arms. "What are you doing?"

"Playing." A glint of mischief flashed in his eyes.

"Ah. I get it now." She repositioned herself, kneeling to give herself more range of motion and then, the shirt lifted as high as possible with one hand, she leaned forward and ran her tongue across the smooth, flat plane of his stomach.

The sharp intake of breath was all the encouragement she needed. If he wanted to play, then she was game. She traced the ridge running down the center of his abdomen, from his belly button to the waist of his pants then skimmed her flattened hand up under his shirt.

His skin was smooth like satin, warm, and he smelled fresh, like he'd just come in from a walk in the woods.

She found one hard nipple with her fingertip and teased it until Asher's eyelids dropped down to cover those darkly intense eyes of his. She pulled on his shirt again. This time he raised his arms, allowing her to raise it higher.

As she lifted it over his head, she stood up. Shirtless, he captured her wrists in his hands and pulled until she returned to her knees. He tilted his head and lowered it until his breath feathered over her mouth.

Yes, kiss me.

Tense from head to toe, she closed her eyes and moistened her lips with her tongue.

"It's all about the power for you, isn't it? That's why you've never felt this way with another man. They didn't know. They couldn't know."

"I-I didn't know."

"But we do. And that's why it's this way with us." He pulled her arms out to the sides and twined his fingers between hers. Holding her hands out as far as her arms allowed, he kissed her mouth roughly. His tongue pushed past her lips, mating and stroking, possessing. After kissing her to oblivion, he licked and nipped a trail to that sensitive spot on her neck between her collarbone and ear.

The muscles of her right side pulled into tight knots and gooseflesh erupted over her arm, chest and back.

"There's so much yet you haven't experienced. We've just started," he said against her neck.

"Yes."

"What do you long for, Jasmyne?" He inched lower, kissing her collarbone.

She let her head fall back, content to just soak up all the attention he lavished on her. "This."

"This?" he echoed, swiping her nipple.

"Ohhh."

"Or this?" He covered that same nipple with his hot mouth and teased the aching tip with his flicking tongue.

Little bursts of hot pleasure flared along her nerves. And little gasps slipped past her lips.

"Hold still." He released one of her hands and dragged his fingertips along the inside of her outstretched arm. They tickled the sensitive skin all the way up to her armpit then ran along the side of her body, skimming the side of her left breast.

She struggled to stay perfectly still. It was close to impossible, with him touching her in all those places, the ones that had been sensitive for as long as she could remember. He even found a few she hadn't known about. There was a spot in the center of her upper back. And another just to the right of her armpit. And another where her jaw met her neck, by her ear.

"Sex is about exploration, discovery," Asher murmured, straightening up again. "It's about finding out what sensations excite you. Tastes. Textures. Smells. What fantasies drive you wild." His tongue swept along his lower lip. "I fantasize about you submitting to me, giving yourself over to me. Mmmm. And I love the way you taste."

A pleasant tingle swept down her body.

"Taste me." He unfastened his pants and pushed them down over his hips. His snug black underwear followed. His cock was hard, a pearly droplet of pre-come clinging to the tip. After working himself out of his pants, he closed his fist around the base. His gaze never left her face. Even though hers did tend to hover around his groin region, she felt him watching her.

Developed chest. Tight stomach. Thick, ropy thighs. Large arms that looked strong enough to haul her off her feet and carry her away to someplace she'd only dreamed of. Somewhere that was safe, where she could trust, where she didn't have to be in control.

Her arms were trembling, the muscles unused to the strain of holding them out for so long without support.

Asher pulled her arms behind her back, holding them in one of his hands. His hard body pressed against her soft one, making her feel small and vulnerable, feminine. He lifted her chin and whispered against her lips, "Take me with only your mouth."

"Okay."

When he released her, he fluffed the pillows and reclined into them. His rigid cock lay up against his body, the head resting just below his belly button. She was tempted to cup her hand around the base and lift it away from his body, but she resisted the urge. Instead, she bent over and traced the bulging vein along its underside with her tongue.

Yummy. Saliva flooded her mouth.

"That's it," Asher murmured. He pushed on her hip, easing her around until her fanny was facing him as she bent low to take the head of his cock into her mouth.

She'd given head before. It was one of those things she didn't care to do much. Her face got sore. She gagged if the guy pushed his cock in too deep. And thus when she was giving oral sex, whatever passion had built up inside her tended to cool off pretty quickly.

This was not the case with Asher.

He didn't thrust too deep or demand she suck him too hard. He groaned and moaned like a guy who was ready to melt. He tormented her with those wonderful hands of his. One finger stimulated her clit with the perfect pressure while another one stroked her intimately inside.

Before long, she was fucking him with her mouth in time to the spasming muscles rocking her hips forward and backward. She moaned around a mouthful of Asher.

His fingers weren't enough.

She wanted him on top of her, his cock gliding in and out of her wet pussy, reaching those places his finger couldn't.

Growing more desperate with each passing second, she released his cock and turned her head, resting her cheek against his thigh. She arched her back, a silent plea for more.

Deeper. Thicker. Harder.

"Are you ready for me, baby?"

"Yes."

"Ask me."

"Please, Asher," she begged, between gasps.

"Please what?"

"Take me."

"I will, but only if you show me how much you want me."

Oh God, what did he expect now? Hands still fisted behind her back, she focused on his cock, figuring he wanted her to go back to her previous activities. But he stopped her with gentle hands.

"No. Not like that."

"How?" What man played games like this in the bedroom? A cruel one. She wanted to smack him upside the head, she was getting so frustrated. Instead, she decided she'd make him want her as much as she wanted him. She started with her face, schooling her expression into her best I'm-going-to-attack-you look. Pouty lips, heavy-lidded eyes. Then she slowly leaned back until she was lying flat on her back, legs bent at the knees, thighs apart.

She'd never acted the part of the peep show whore before now, but she was quickly realizing there was a rush to touching herself in front of a man. It wasn't like this new bad girl act was coming naturally, but the longer she stayed with it, the more heat she saw in Asher's eyes, and the more fun she had.

"Do you see how wet I am?" she asked in her best bedroom voice. She reached between her legs and swirled her fingertips over her clit. A wicked thrill charged through her system.

Asher fisted his cock and gave it a couple of up and down pumps. "Yes, that's it, baby. I love it when you're bad. Show me more."

"I want that thick cock inside me," she murmured, pushing two fingers inside her slit. Her inner muscles gripped them, increasing her pleasure. The flame flickering in Asher's eyes intensified it even more.

He growled, literally, and after she plunged them in and out a couple of times, knocked her hand aside and caught her knees in his hands. "Enough."

She wasn't going to argue with that.

He entered her slowly, inch by glorious inch. She closed her eyes and focused on the pleasure he was so generously lavishing on her body. He not only thrust in and out of her at the perfect pace but also positioned himself so that he could stimulate her clit with his hand at the same time. It wasn't long before she was swept up in a brain-melting orgasm. Asher followed within a couple of heartbeats. He fucked her hard, driving into her with all the force she ached for until they were both breathless and spent and tingly.

Smiling and giddy, she opened her eyes. What she saw instantly put a damper on her mood. Asher was sporting fangs. Like Dracula. What was even weirder, she wasn't scared out of her wits. She was shocked. Taken a bit by surprise. But also curious, intrigued, fascinated.

He'd tried to prepare her. But how could a girl be ready for this? There was no denying it anymore. Those fangs were real. Asher was a vampire. And so was Draven.

"I won't bite you because my venom will erase your memory again. I wanted you to see for yourself, to know I was telling the truth."

"I-I see." She reached for her neck, half expecting to feel something there, blood, marks, something.

"Every time you've seen us like this, we've fed from you, wiping out your memory. This is why you've become so confused at times. Our venom is an amnesiac."

Still fingering her neck, she whispered, "You have to bite me? Why?"

"We have to take a blood-bond with another vampire and a mortal woman. The frequency required depends upon our age. The older we are, the more often we have to take the bond. It extends our lives by years, decades, even centuries.

Most of us take different mates each time. But to protect our kind, we are able to erase the mortal woman's memory of the week and replace it with other images."

Oh my God! "What is a blood-bond?" Her fingers walked down one side of her neck, stopping at a tender spot on her shoulder. It felt like a deep bruise.

"Two vampires feed from the same human for seven consecutive nights. The human's body reacts to the venom we inject in a chemical way, and it's that chemical that helps extend our lives."

This is weird. Too strange for words. And real. "Does it hurt? When you bite me?" One hand still exploring the tender spot on her shoulder, she dropped the other one to her inner thigh.

"A little. But our venom has a couple of effects on our mate. It's also an aphrodisiac. So you become so aroused, you forget the pain. It has similar effects on us as well. We're driven to possess each other and you. Our carnal hunger grows so intense it's nearly painful."

That whole carnal hunger thing was something, but she still couldn't get over the fact that they'd noshed on her and she couldn't remember. "And that's why I've been sore? On my shoulder? And here, on my leg?"

"Yes."

"Is the blood-bond what's making me see stuff with Draven?"

"See what?"

"I see his thoughts, his memories. I know things."

"I've never heard of anyone having that sort of reaction, but I suppose it's possible." When he smiled, his fangs were gone. "What kinds of things do you know?"

"I knew your names without your telling me. I knew you were friends. That reminds me. He was leaving, and he didn't want me to go with him."

"So that's why he started this with you and then left?"

"He knew I wouldn't be able to leave if you…if we… That sneaky bastard."

"It's a fucking miracle he could. Where was he heading? Did he say?"

"He wouldn't tell me, but I think it had something to do with my mother."

"We'll find him. And we'll locate your mother too. Can you trust me?"

"Yes, Asher. I trust you." That was no lie.

Chapter Eleven

∞

"He's gone," Asher announced as he entered the king's private office. "Draven escaped, and I have no idea where he's headed." Despite the fact that it felt unnatural after having plotted to have Kaden dethroned over the past several years, he dropped on one knee in a show of fealty.

"Please rise." Kaden, king of the Sons, sat behind an enormous desk, papers scattered across the polished surface. His brother Marek stood in one corner of the room, arms crossed, expression dark. "Draven will return. He must. The blood-bond."

"Only after securing the Star and handing it over to your enemies first," Marek spat.

Kaden gave his brother a sharp glare. A muscle in his jaw twitched. "Not now, Marek."

"Why not? You've determined we're keeping no secrets from this man."

His eyes slitted, Kaden planted his hands on the desktop and stood. "That's right," he enunciated in a near-whisper. "I believe we can trust him. Do you dare challenge my decision?"

Marek tipped his chin up and took a single step forward. "Yes. I think he knows more than he's telling."

If there was anything that made Asher feel awkward, it was when people argued about him while he was standing in the fucking room. He felt like he was invisible.

More than that, he was confused, even ashamed. Kaden, the man he'd conspired against for years, the one who had the power to do basically anything he wanted, had decided to not only spare him from vengeance but to welcome him into his inner circle of trusted allies. Marek, whom Asher had directly committed no crime against, viewed him as the enemy.

How ironic. How extraordinary.

His respect for his king had never been greater, regardless of the still unresolved issue with Eclipse.

He cleared his throat. "I don't know where Draven's gone, but I do know that he believes Maria Vaughn has Diana's Star. I also know Draven played some part in her disappearance, although I don't have any details."

"Diana's Star cannot be used against me." Kaden shrugged. "I'm unwed. I merely have to keep women at a safe distance and I'll be safe."

Marek shook his head. "Maybe we should just tell the truth about the Eclipse. Maybe then they'd stop blaming you. If it isn't the White Hawk Alliance, it's some other fringe group—"

"They will never stop blaming me. I'm their leader. It's my duty to take the blame. I knew that when I accepted the crown."

Marek charged across the room, fists at his sides. "Dammit, how am I going to keep you safe when you're doing everything but sticking your head in a fucking noose? Next you'll probably say you should go meet with the bastards face-to-face on their turf. Make it easy for them to slaughter you."

"Hmmm," Kaden said, tapping his chin. "That's not a bad idea."

"Tell me you're joking or I'm going to have to lock you in your own damn prison."

"Ha!" Kaden scoffed, brushing past his younger, visibly flustered brother. To Asher, he said, "I get no respect from my brother, you see? But it doesn't matter. All I care about getting this situation settled for once and for all. Have a seat." He motioned toward the leather sofa positioned between a pair of towering bookcases. "Maybe you'll go back to the White Hawk Alliance with this information. Do what you must. I won't stop you. In fact, I welcome you to do just that. I think it's time for all the Sons to know the truth about Eclipse." He sighed as he settled into the wing chair next to the couch. "All our lives are about to change, and there's nothing anyone can do about it right now. Not even me. But with your help, we might be able to stop some good people from making a very terrible mistake."

* * * * *

Jasmyne's head hadn't done so much spinning in her life, not even when she'd gone on a high school field trip to a local amusement park and spent the day on whirling, racing carnival rides. In a way, it was all so overwhelming she couldn't really absorb the facts. Like a victim of a terrible tragedy, she felt a certain detachment from everything, like these things weren't really happening. Her mother was just on a binge, like every other time. She hadn't become involved in some conspiracy involving vampires and magical Greek artifacts.

Now riding in the back seat of Asher's car, Marek in the front passenger seat, she flip-flopped between wanting to curl up in a ball and sleep for a month and needing to get a grip on what was going on. At this precise moment, she was all about getting a grip. "So let me get this straight. Kaden is king of the vampires—correction, Sons of the Twilight." She made quote marks in the air with her fingers. "Marek, you're the king's brother, and you're going to help me find my mother? Why?"

"She has a very valuable relic."

"So you've said." Her glance bounced back and forth between Asher and Marek. Both facing forward, they were looking all serious and let's-save-the-earth-ish. Their expressions compelled her to admit the guilt she'd been harboring since the morning she'd learned her mom had disappeared. "I'm kind of embarrassed that I'm putting so many people out since it's my fault my mother stole the package in the first place. I knew how she was." Jasmyne sighed and slumped back in her seat, staring out the window. "If only I hadn't left the package sitting out where it was so easy for her to steal."

"It's not your fault," Asher said, keeping his gaze focused on the road. "You had no idea what was in the box or what it could potentially be used for."

"True. But I knew my mother. And I knew she has fingers stickier than Super Glue."

"No one is blaming you." Marek twisted to look back at her from the front passenger seat. "Actually, the fact that our enemies haven't gotten the Star yet tells me that your mother's been protecting it. I have a feeling if you'd made your delivery a few days ago, according to schedule, it would already be in their hands by now."

She couldn't be understanding Marek correctly. "Then you're saying it's a good thing my mother stole it?"

Marek nodded. "Very."

She wasn't convinced. From her point of view, her mother's actions had caused plenty of bad. Her job was in jeopardy. Her mother's life was in danger. Maybe from the viewpoint of a vampire king, it was a good thing. But not so much from hers. "I guess I shouldn't feel so bad that you're involved. You would be anyway."

"Exactly." Marek paused, glancing forward then back again before continuing. "But we recognize the danger your mother is in. Even if they don't have it yet, if our enemy knows what your mother has, they'll stop at nothing to get it from her," Marek warned. "We need to find her before they learn what she's hiding. Any help you can give us?"

Was it possible she'd missed some small but significant detail, something that might lead them to her mother? "I've told Asher everything. My mom's a drug addict. Methamphetamine is her drug of choice, but I think she does other stuff too. Cocaine, prescription painkillers, marijuana. Every time she's been on a binge, she's ended up coming to

Detroit. That's why I started my search for her here. That and the phone call I got the night she disappeared. She called me with Draven's cell phone and claimed she'd been kidnapped."

Marek did a lot of head nodding but said nothing.

"It was that phone number that made the connection between Jasmyne's mother and Draven," Asher said, steering the car around a corner. "I've known Draven my whole life, not to mention I have more than a passing knowledge of the Hawks. But damned if I can guess where they've taken her. We've checked with all of Maria's past local connections. No one has seen her."

"I think I know where she might be," Marek said. "It's hard to see from the road, it's isolated and it's extremely secure. And they have the perfect cover, running a drug and alcohol rehabilitation center on the property." Marek reached into the black bag at his feet and handed a folded up newspaper to Asher.

"Isolated? Around here?" Jasmyne asked, watching Asher skim the paper as he drove.

"Well, damn!" Asher met Jasmyne's gaze in the rearview mirror. "It's perfect. I wish we'd known."

Jasmyne inched forward. "What? Where is she?"

"You hadn't heard?" Marek asked Asher.

"No. I guess I've been out of the loop longer than I realized. Even when I was still a member, I didn't hear about things." Asher raked his fingers through his hair and huffed a weary sigh. "It's obvious I lost control of the Hawks a lot earlier than I thought. Maybe what Draven said is true — that it's too late for me to save the White Hawk Alliance."

The disappointment and frustration Jasmyne heard in Asher's voice made her insides twist into agonizing knots. The White Hawk Alliance meant so much to him, as much as a friend, a parent. She wished she could help him somehow. All she could do was offer support and comfort from someone who'd been there. Frustration, anger, hurt, those were staples in her life. She knew the pain of wishing she could change something she had no control over—like another person's life.

Yes, she and Asher had a lot in common.

She leaned forward and rested a hand on his shoulder. He patted it, curled his fingers around hers and pulled, forcing her forward. He pressed a sweet kiss to her palm.

"Thank you, baby."

Before her heart rate had returned to normal, he released her hand again and returned his to the steering wheel.

She spent the rest of the ride sitting in the backseat trying to make sense of what Marek and Asher were discussing. A part of her felt like a third wheel, shoved in the back of the vehicle and more or less left out of the conversation, but another part was glad to have two very powerful and capable men helping her search for her mother.

At this point, she wasn't sure what she'd do about the relic when—if—they found it. If she didn't return it to her boss, she'd surely lose her job. Yes, there were other jobs to be found, but not many. And not well paying, with health insurance, paid vacation, and sick leave. She'd have to bus a lot of tables to take home the kind of paycheck her current job earned her.

The reduced income meant, of course, she'd have to sacrifice even more if she was going to pay for yet another trip to rehab for her mom.

If she didn't pay, no one would, and any chance of her mother getting over her addiction would be lost. She could see herself taking a second and third job just to pay for basic necessities. Again. Just the thought of going back to working two or three jobs made her tired.

Back when she'd had no choice but to do just that, she'd walked around in a haze of exhaustion so thick, she'd forgotten her phone number and address once. Locked her keys in the car. Left her cell phone in a grocery store bathroom.

She'd learned she wasn't the type who could function well on three hours of sleep a night.

She cut short her thoughts when the car rolled to a stop in front of a huge steel gate. This was like no gate she'd ever seen. It was enormous, tall and topped with razor wire. Looked a lot like she imagined a prison would. She'd never been to a prison.

"Where are we?" she asked.

"This was once a women's prison," Marek explained. "It was closed down about a year ago, the prisoners moved to other facilities, and the state auctioned off the property to the highest bidder."

"And you're saying my mom's in there?" Acid burned her throat and a huge lump of something wedged itself about halfway between her stomach and mouth. She swallowed. Hard. Several times. It didn't move.

"There's a good chance she's in there." Asher shifted the car into park and looked at Marek. "Okay, we're here. Now how are we going to get in? It isn't like we can call someone and ask them to let us in." He pointed at the camera positioned at the top of one metal pole. "I'm sure someone's watching."

"I can think of one surefire way to get us an invitation inside." At Asher's questioning glance, Marek tipped his head in Jasmyne's direction. "I'd be willing to bet they'd be very glad to see our passenger."

"Yes but I'm not real crazy about drawing their attention to her."

She waved. "Hello, I'm here. What did you think you were going to do? Make me sit in the car and wait?"

Asher didn't answer.

"It's the only way," Marek reasoned.

"I'm not using Jasmyne as bait," Asher growled. "No way."

That annoyed her more than it probably should have. Really. Did he think she'd sit there like a good little girl while they were the big brave men and did all the work? Not a chance. Granted, in the bedroom, she appreciated Asher's take-charge tendencies. And she'd even welcomed his help in searching for her mother. But this was different.

He wasn't going to allow her to help. That was bullshit.

Annoyed and a little nervous, she unclipped her seatbelt, opened the door, and while Marek and Asher were busy strategizing, stomped up to the gate, waved at the security camera and poked at the red call button on the little metal box fused to the pole.

A tinny voice responded, "How can I help you?"

Jasmyne ignored the sound of the car doors behind her opening and Asher's hushed order, "Get back in the car!"

Like hell she would. She'd not only taken care of herself for years but also her mom. And their lives had never been a bed of roses. Sure, there'd been times when she'd been frightened for both their lives. But she'd never been so scared she'd park herself in a car and let someone else handle everything for her.

The truth was, even if she wanted to, she couldn't allow herself that luxury. With an addict in the family, she had to be strong. That didn't mean she needed to take stupid chances. But it did mean she couldn't afford to let herself go soft, rely on someone else for everything.

She didn't want to think about the timing of this revelation.

She smiled at the security camera and waved. "I'm here to see my mother, Maria Vaughn. My name is Jasmyne. I believe she's a…patient."

"One moment please," the voice responded.

Asher caught her wrist in a steely grip and pulled, forcing her around. His eyes were dark slits, his face a mask of fury. "What the hell are you doing?"

"Saving my mom."

"That's not the way to save her. If you'd given Marek and me a few minutes, instead of rushing to do something stupid–"

"Marek suggested it!"

The metal gate started rolling to the right. And a Hummer raced toward them.

"Shit!" Asher said. "Car. Now!"

"Shit," she echoed.

"There's no way we're going to outrun that," Marek shouted, racing toward the passenger side. "They're just going to run us over like an ant on a highway.

"Shit," she repeated, scrambling to open the car door. Her fingers weren't cooperating! "Open, open, open!" she chanted. "Yes!" She yanked it open.

"We've got to at least try." Asher pushed Jasmyne into the backseat, slammed the door and dived into the driver's seat. He threw the gear shift into reverse and looked over his shoulder. "Dammit!" The car, which had just started careening backward, screeched to a halt.

"What?" Jasmyne slammed backward then bounced forward. She hadn't put on her seatbelt yet, so she turned around and poked her head up to peer out the rear window. "What's wrong? Oh...no!" A Hummer, identical to the one they'd seen roaring toward them, was blocking their escape route. "Oh no no!" She twisted forward, and saw the first Hummer was parked in front of them. Yes, they were the meat in a Hummer sandwich. Not a good place to be, especially when a girl was a passenger in a Honda.

A couple of men bounded from Hummer Number One, big guns aimed at the windshield. "Get out of the car," one of them shouted.

Shit.

Asher glanced over his shoulder, giving Jasmyne a worried grimace. "Please. Please stay in the car this time."

"Sure." As if she hadn't regretted what she'd done, now she felt beyond awful. Darn it, Marek had made it sound like such a good idea. And if these people were operating a so-called drug rehab center in this building, who would have guessed they'd greet visitors with Hummers and guns, treat them like invaders? Obviously, she wouldn't have had the guts to go up to that gate and ask to be let in if she had. Talk about a no-brainer.

Maybe. Then again, maybe not.

She couldn't say for sure one way or another. If she knew for a fact that her mother was inside that horrible place, she probably would. She could only imagine what kind of terrible secrets people like this locked behind all those security walls and gates and fences.

The only thing she might have done differently was make sure she had a Plan B, just in case she ran into trouble.

Not that any Plan B would prepare her for this.

She felt like a little scaredy-cat, sitting in the car while Marek and Asher faced the guys with guns unarmed. Here she'd been trying to make things better for everyone and she'd made them a whole lot worse by acting impulsively without thinking things through.

She'd reacted instead of being proactive. Why?

Because she was scared, terrified to let herself rely completely on another human being.

She wedged her upper body between the front seats and watched the scene outside. Marek and Asher hadn't been shot yet, but that was hardly any reason to expect things to be okay. The guys from the Hummer still had the guns pointed at them, but Asher and Marek's postures were relaxed as they talked. Finally, after what seemed like a million hours, the men lowered their guns and Asher motioned to Jasmyne.

Her gaze bouncing from bad guy to Asher to Marek to bad guy, Jasmyne climbed out of the car and slowly walked toward Asher and Marek. Knees as soft as marshmallow cream, she stopped between them and stood with clasped hands. "Are we facing the firing line?" she whispered.

"Not yet," Marek responded.

"Sorry. I'm…not sure why I did that."

"It's okay." Asher caught her hand in his and squeezed.

One of the bad guys barked, "In the truck," and within minutes, she was wedged between Asher and Marek in the Hummer of Death, bouncing toward the prison.

God, she hoped she'd find her mother inside. Alive. And they'd both live to see the outside of this building again. Very soon. And Asher and Marek would be safe too.

She made a few promises to every deity she could think of, hoping she'd buy a miracle or two. They definitely needed them.

The vehicle rolled into an enclosed garage. The enormous door sealing off the entry rolled into place, closing them inside. They were escorted out, across the empty garage, through a thick metal door and into a narrow hall.

Her head was spinning. Her stomach was in her throat. If it weren't for the fact that Jasmyne had Asher and Marek on either side of her, she was sure she'd either pass out or throw up. But she forced herself to keep moving. One foot in front of the other.

A pair of armed men were in front of them, leading the way, another followed behind, no doubt making sure they didn't turn tail and run. Not that she thought they could. About every twenty feet, they passed through a locked door. Of course, once they went through each one, the doors were locked behind them. By the time they stopped walking, they'd gone through at least three sets of those doors.

Trapped like a cat in a dog pound. Full of rabid pit bulls.

They were escorted to a tiny prison cell with concrete walls, a solid metal door, no windows and a single cot. Unable to stand, Jasmyne dropped onto the cot and covered her face with her trembling hands. She felt the thin mattress sink beside her as Asher sat. He wrapped an arm around her shoulders and pulled her against him.

She was all too grateful for the gesture.

"What is this place?" she asked, her voice as shaky as her hands. "Is it really a drug rehab—a hospital or a prison?" Her teeth literally clacked together, she was quaking so badly. "What do you think they've done with my mom?"

"I'm convinced it's not her they're after but what she has. I don't believe they want to hurt her. But even if they did, I have a feeling she's a strong woman. Look at the daughter she's raised. She'll be okay."

Despite her best efforts and Asher's encouraging words and gentle touches, the tears started flowing...and flowing...and flowing. The dam busted loose and the torrent swept her away. She didn't get her emotional feet back under her until the door swung open and a pair of very intimidating men stepped inside.

These two were scary in a whole different way than the other ones had been—the guys who'd escorted them inside at gunpoint. When she looked in their eyes, she saw only empty blackness.

"If you wish to see your mother alive, you'll do as we say," the first one said to her.

Shit, Mom. What kind of trouble did I get us both into this time?

Asher placed his bulk between her and the towering meanies. "What do you want from us?"

"Nothing." The one speaking extended his right arm, and the one who'd yet to even grunt charged at Asher and Marek, shoving them aside. Jasmyne jumped up but before she'd taken even one step away, the jerk behind her had an arm wrapped around her middle and was hauling her toward the door.

She screamed and clawed at the man's arm. The closer they got to the door, the more frantically she fought. Feet, hands, head even, she used everything she had to try to break free. But it wasn't good enough. Seconds later, Marek and Asher were unconscious on the floor, and she was at the mercy of two of the scariest-looking men she'd ever seen.

The one holding her clapped a hand over her mouth when she started screaming again and hauled her through a maze of halls to a larger open area. Two stories tall, cells lining all four walls. Up above, a balcony-like walkway provided access to the cells on the second level.

The mean guy dropped her right there in the middle of the enormous room, and she had to fight the temptation to kick him in the knee as she scrambled to her feet.

She had never been more pissed. Or terrified. But right now, she needed to use her head, not let her emotions get the better of her. Somewhere in this hellish place she believed her mother was being held prisoner. If she didn't act wisely, who knew what would happen. To both of them. And Asher.

Oh God, get it together, girl!

"What do you want from me?" she managed to say through chattering teeth.

"You're the bait."

She was pretty sure she didn't want to know who or what she was helping these two creeps catch. They already had Asher, and Draven was on their side, or at least that's what she thought. So it was possible her mother had escaped. And now they were going to use Jasmyne to recapture her.

No. That had better not be what they had in mind. She'd rather die than cause her mother to fall into the hands of these awful men.

One of them held up a camera phone. "When I motion to you, I want you to beg your mother to come back. I'm going to record your heartfelt plea and I won't send it until I'm happy with what I see. So it won't do you any good to do any improvising, if you get my drift. Look, I even prepared a cue card." He elbowed the other guy, who handed him a white erase board. Then Mr. No Talk pulled a gun from his hip holster and positioned himself beside her, the unfriendly end of the weapon pressed against her temple.

Now holding the white erase board in front of his chest with one hand and the phone with the other, the man nodded.

Eyes blurry, the contents of her stomach in her throat, she read, "Mom, it's Jasmyne. I'm here at Extreme Intervention. I came here to join you. Please come back. We'll be together at last. The way I've always wanted."

"Very good." The man set down the board and nodded to his partner.

The other one — thankfully — removed the gun from her head. She swallowed, hard, and took a shaky breath. But her relief was short lived. The one who didn't talk dragged her to one of the open cells and locked her in. And then they left.

All alone. What she wouldn't give to have Asher there with her. She hadn't realized how much she'd come to rely on him.

That fact scared her almost as much as the fact there was no chance she'd escape the prison cell.

Chapter Twelve

ഇ

He should have known they'd find a way. Draven stopped the video clip, placed a desperate call to the mother of his child, and after leaving an urgent message, dropped the phone into his passenger's upturned palm.

"I have to go back," Maria whispered, tucking the phone into the niche in the vehicle's dashboard. "My daughter. The people at Extreme Intervention are threatening to hurt Jasmyne."

"Dammit!" He stomped on the brakes and steered the skidding car toward the shoulder, then maneuvered it into a U-turn. "Those fucking bastards."

One arm braced against the dash, Maria leaned forward in her seat. "You have to trust your child's mother will know how to protect her. I'm sure everything will be okay. Although I don't understand what I have to do with your daughter."

"Susan has no idea what she's up against."

"That may be true, but she is a mother. Sometimes that's all it takes."

Draven peered at Maria for a moment before turning his attention back to the road. "I hope you're right. If anything happens, I don't know what I'll do. Allegra's just a kid. She doesn't deserve to be dragged into this."

"No child deserves to be dragged into her parent's shit." Maria rubbed at the tears seeping from the corners of her eyes. "I know how you feel. It's because of me that Jasmyne's being held hostage. I just couldn't take another minute of that place." The two shared an understanding look. "Maybe we've both made mistakes. It's time we make up for them."

Draven nodded and depressed the accelerator to the floor. The vehicle zoomed down the winding country road as they discussed exactly how they'd make up for decades of fuck ups.

* * * * *

Dozens of women dressed head-to-toe in black, rifles in their hands, marched by, single file, stiff, their faces lacking any expression whatsoever, like some kind of military special operations unit.

What was going on here?

Jasmyne stood up and watched them file past her barred door. "Help me, please," she whispered over and over again. Not a single one of them met her gaze. They simply stared forward. Expressions blank. As if they were in a trance.

Gave her a serious case of the creeps.

But she persisted, continuing to plead with the machinelike GI Janes marching by, hoping by some miracle one of them would hear her and respond.

Finally her persistence paid off. The last woman marching by turned her head and looked at Jasmyne. For only a split second. It wasn't exactly the response she was hoping for, but it was something.

The parade ended. The sound of footfalls grew more distant until they faded completely away. Jasmyne lost hope. No one was going to help her.

Defeated, she returned to the cot in the rear of her cell, sat, dropped her head in her hands and closed her eyes. Locked in a prison cell. Alone. Unarmed. Somehow she had to find a way out of this impossible situation. Somehow…

She wasn't sure how long she had sat there before she heard someone approach her cell. The frustrated and tired part of her didn't want to know who was there. The hopeful part did.

She looked up.

It was the woman who'd glanced at her.

Jasmyne ran to the locked door, rattling off in a hushed voice, "I'm being held prisoner. I think my mother's here somewhere too. And some...friends. They're in danger." She wrapped her hands around the cold bars and gripped them tightly. "If you could find a way to get me out of this cell, I think I could find them. Please, I need your help—"

"Who's your mother?"

"Maria Vaughn. Do you know her? Do you know where she is?"

The woman's eyes brightened with recognition. "Yes, I know Maria. Then you're...Jasmyne, right?"

"Thank God, yes! Is she okay?"

The woman smiled. "I'm Juliette. Of course she's fine. This place isn't as awful as you probably think. Your mom was my roommate for a while before she moved to the Diamond Block. She's doing really great."

Really great. Had she missed something here? Her mother had claimed she'd been kidnapped. She'd never said she was in rehab. So which was it? "Great. Wow. My mom. What's the Diamond Block?"

"That's the highest level. You start here, on the Pearl Block. It's not the nicest place, but if you do what the nurses say, you can move up pretty quickly."

She didn't know how to respond to what she was hearing. She had a funny suspicion this woman had no idea what kind of people were running this place. "Uh...did you come here on your own? Or were you kidnapped too?"

"Kidnapped? No one's brought here against their will. Extreme Intervention is a fabulous program. I heard about it from a friend of mine. I quit school to come here. Everything else had failed."

"Why? What kind of program is this Extreme Intervention?"

"It's an intense drug rehabilitation program, a combination of boot camp and traditional rehab. Not everyone thinks it's the best one out there. I've heard some criticisms about the extreme methods they employ, but you can't argue with their success rate."

"Drug rehabilitation. For real."

"Sure. What else did you think it was?" The woman tipped her head to one side and studied her for a handful of seconds. "I better get going. I'm going to get into big trouble if Sergeant Blackmoore discovers I'm missing." She turned away, waving over her shoulder. "Good luck!"

Drug rehabilitation.

Her ride over with Marek and Asher had prepared her to expect this place to be the hub of criminal activity under the cover of some drug rehab guise, not a place where women genuinely came to fight their battle with addiction. It couldn't be both...or could it?

Now she had to wonder if her mother had been kidnapped or had come here on her own. She never would have guessed a program as extreme as this one could do the job. When so many others had failed.

Jasmyne wanted to believe it could. Wow.

For the first time since discovering her mother had disappeared, she was actually kind of hopeful. For all of two or three minutes. And then confusion returned.

She didn't have to wonder why her mother had left prematurely, even after experiencing some measure of success. That had happened plenty of times. But no legitimate program would stoop to holding hostages to coerce runaway patients to return.

Something just wasn't adding up. As much as she wanted to buy that woman's rosy-hued picture of what was going on here, she just couldn't.

That left her back at square one, trying to find a way to get out of this cell.

She shook the door. Nope, wasn't going anywhere. She inspected the other three walls. Sure, it was a stretch to expect to find a loose panel hiding a secret exit, but what the hell?

Of course it didn't take long to realize there were no secret passages or trap doors. Slowly she succumbed to exhaustion and hunger. Her strength fading, she lay down on the cot and closed her eyes. She couldn't do anything for her mother right now. Maybe the best thing to do was get rested, so that if the opportunity arose later, she'd be ready for it.

Yes, that sounded like a good plan.

* * * * *

"Time for your medication," somebody sing-songed, intruding into Jasmyne's dreams.

Medication? Obviously this woman thought she was a patient. Jasmyne lifted her heavy lids. "I'm not—"

The nurse, dressed in your standard nurse uniform—tunic, baggy pants and a plain white jacket—thrust an arm through the bars. In her fist was a little clear plastic cup with a pill in it. In her other hand she held a bottle of water.

Jasmyne shook her head. "No, you don't understand. I'm not a patient here. I don't need—"

"Of course you need these. It'll make you feel better. Look at you, poor thing. You're suffering. She shook the cup, rattling the pill inside. "There's no reason to go it alone. Take it."

"No, I'm not withdrawing—"

"Of course you are. I read your chart. There's no way you could quit all those drugs cold turkey without hurting." She shook the cup again. "Take it," she demanded, her voice taking a sharp edge. "Or I'll have to report you. You read the rules in intake. You know what'll happen if I have to report you."

Actually, I didn't, but I can guess.

There was no way she was going to take that drug. That was out of the question. She wasn't a drug addict. There was no saying what it might do to her. Heck, she could get really sick.

Maybe that was someone's intention.

That just settled it. There was no way in hell she was going to take that pill. But maybe there was another way to get Miss Attitude off her back.

She put on an appropriately acquiescing expression. "You're right." Intentionally moving in a sloppy, uncoordinated fashion, like she'd often seen her mother walk, she went to the bars and accepted the proffered cup and bottle of water. She tucked the tablet under the tongue, gulped the water and then murmured, "Thanks." She turned her back to the nurse and carefully spit the medicine into her fist.

"Wait a minute. Turn around."

Busted. The medication in her fist, Jasmyne slowly turned.

"Open."

Damn.

"Your mouth," the nurse said, pointing at her face. "Open wide."

Semi-relieved but half-expecting the nurse to figure out what she'd done, Jasmyne eagerly opened, sweeping her tongue from side-to-side.

Evidently believing Jasmyne had swallowed the medicine, the nurse nodded, gave her a pleasant smile and said, "That's better. Now get some rest. You'll feel much better in a little while. You'll see."

Jasmyne wasn't nearly as convinced as Nurse Ratchet was.

To avoid calling attention to herself, she settled back on the cot. But this time she didn't let herself fall asleep. Now that she'd rested, it was time to do some serious brainstorming.

Somehow she had to get herself out of this situation. No one else was going to. After this much time had passed, she had to believe no one else could. Not even her rock, Asher.

* * * * *

"Honestly, I don't believe Draven's on the other team." Leaning against the wall, arms crossed, Marek shrugged.

"Despite the fact that we're locked in here and he's out there somewhere? Despite the fact that Jasmyne's mother called her on his phone? And he betrayed me?"

Marek waited several moments before responding. "My last blood-bond was with a man who was determined to murder me."

"Oh yeah?"

"Yes, and my brother Kaden knew it when he asked me to take the blood-bond with him. But he knew something else. He knew that the bond would force us to deal with things, work through them. Within the week, we were hunting down the Sacred Triad together and saved my brother's life. This could go the same way."

Was it just his imagination or had Marek's attitude taken a one-eighty? "Or Draven could be delivering Diana's Star to the man who's masterminding your brother's assassination."

"I don't believe he'll do it."

"Since when? I've known Draven my whole life, and I can't say I'm that confident. You're willing to leave your brother's life in his hands?"

"If my brother is, then I am."

"What's that mean? Why the change since we've come here? Back at your brother's place, you didn't even want to trust me."

Marek smiled and shrugged. He slipped his hand in his pocket. When he withdrew it, he turned it over, revealing a tiny cell phone.

"Did you call for help?"

"Nope."

"Why the hell not?"

"Because I'm waiting," Marek responded coolly.

"For what? To hear your brother's dead?"

"No, to see what Draven's going to do next." Marek tucked the phone back in his pocket.

"Why take the chance?"

"Because it's the right move. For now."

"What if you're wrong?"

"I'll worry about that if or when the time comes."

None of this made sense. No one he knew or respected would be willing to risk their brother's death. For what? Unless this was about more than Diana's Star. More than Eclipse and the White Hawk Alliance. What were Marek and his brother really up to?

Chapter Thirteen

ဆ

"What time is it?" Maria asked. She motioned to the car's dashboard clock. "That's got to be wrong."

Draven checked his phone. "It's two a.m."

"Oh! Good. Time for PT."

"Pee tea?"

"Physical Training. It's part of the program. All the patients have to participate in three sessions of PT every day. One of them is in the middle of the night."

"What program? You mentioned it before."

"Didn't you know? Extreme Intervention is a drug and alcohol rehabilitation program. Sort of like a drug boot camp. It works. First, it's free, which means even I could afford it. And even though it's extremely intense, it's not painful. The medicine they gave us for withdrawal worked like a dream. I've never felt better. Strong. Clearheaded. Young. It's the first program I haven't ditched within twenty-four hours... I actually stayed four days before I'd had enough." She sighed. "That was only because I didn't like the other medicine they started giving me in the second phase. Made me feel kind of foggy in the head. I'm still not sure why they've stooped to holding Jasmyne hostage to get me to come back. Even for Extreme Intervention, that's a little weird."

"I'd heard they were running some kind of business out of the building, but since I haven't been back there since they bought it, I had no idea they'd already started. So what does PT have to do with us now?"

"I'm not sure I understand what you mean by all that. But as far as PT goes, it's the only time we're allowed to go off property — during our middle-of-the-night runs."

"Which means?"

"The gate's unlocked. But unless I'm turning myself in, returning to the program, we can't drive in. The camera."

"I'm one step ahead of you." Draven steered the car down a dirt drive leading to a house set deep on a wooded lot. He found a safe place to hide the car, and then together they jogged the half-mile to the prison. The gate was closed, but moving carefully, silently, Maria opened it enough to allow them to slip inside.

As they hurried up the winding drive to the building, Draven fought a horde of doubts and fears. They didn't have much of a plan. He was relying on Maria's knowledge of the prison and what little she might know about its security systems to get them inside. And she had denied repeatedly having Diana's Star. Either she was lying or the bastard's source was wrong.

But what choice did he have other than to trust her? Since he'd heard from one guy in the White Hawks, who'd informed him he had no one to turn to, Draven knew he wasn't going to just walk into the building like he had a few months ago. None of the Hawks were going to help him. The only person he could trust was already inside, also being held hostage.

Dammit, he'd had it all figured out before he'd received that call. That's what a guy got for double-crossing the devil. Jasmyne, Asher and Marek were in there somewhere. How the hell would he get them out without handing over a relic he didn't have?

At least he'd placed a call to Susan and warned her the bastard knew she was in town. But he wasn't convinced that was enough to keep her and Allegra safe. He ached to wrap his arms around the little girl and protect her like a man.

And speaking of protecting, he was aching to wrap his arms around Jasmyne and protect her as well. How had the Hawks gotten their fucking hands on her? Had they found her outside somehow, or had she learned where her mother was and walked into a trap?

Much like he was walking into one now.

Maria led him around the rear of the building to a loading dock in the rear. He questioned how she'd learned so much about the enormous building in such a short time. According to Jasmyne, she'd been missing for less than a week. And if she'd truly been as bad off as Jasmyne had said, she'd have been laid up in bed, suffering from withdrawal for at least the first two.

Something wasn't adding up, regardless of what she'd said about the miracle medicine.

Perhaps she'd been here before. Then again, that wasn't likely, since the Hawks had owned the building for only a few short months.

"This way." Maria motioned toward a pedestrian entry next to the large loading dock doors. "My friends and I like to come out here to smoke. They always forget to lock the door when they go back inside." She opened the door and disappeared inside the inky blackness within.

Draven hesitated to follow her.

If Maria was leading him into a trap, would she be receiving her daughter in exchange? Ironic if that was the case, since he was in this shit because he'd decided to trade the Star for his daughter.

Oh hell, he had no other choice but to trust her. It would be stupid to sit outside and wait for them to find him. He glanced up, searching for cameras. Sure enough, there was one directed at the truck docking area.

If someone was watching him, it could already be too late.

Half expecting to be ambushed the second he entered, he inched inside. It was pitch black and silent. He blinked, waiting for his eyes to adjust to the thick darkness but he still remained blinded.

The Sons of the Twilight naturally possessed keen night vision, so it surprised him that he couldn't see a damn thing, not the hand he held in front of his face. Somehow, the Hawks had learned to produce such an impossible darkness. One that not even their vision could penetrate.

Something brushed against his hand. Instinctively, he flinched, a blade of unease slicing through his body. He'd never been completely blinded before. It gave him a new respect for how terrifying the night would be for humans. For Jasmyne.

"It's okay," Maria whispered. "It's just me. It looked like you were having some trouble. I thought I'd better help."

Draven nodded.

"What's wrong? You look like a blind guy who dropped his walking stick."

Maria could see him? That was an even bigger surprise. "I can't see anything. It's so dark in here."

"Really? How strange. I can see fine. The light's a little weird, kinda greenish. But it's not like I'm having trouble getting around or anything." She stopped tugging, and he nearly stumbled into her. "Watch your step here. We're going up three stairs."

Ingenious. They'd somehow found a way to blind only the Sons. "Okay. Thanks." He cautiously felt with his foot until he found the first step, second, third. A door opened and light spilled out from the hallway beyond.

Relief. He released Maria's hand while simultaneously scanning the area for guards, cameras, danger. It couldn't be this easy, breaking into this place. It was like a fucking fortress. If there was one thing he'd noticed the one and only time he'd been there, it had been the security cameras. They were everywhere. Hallways. Rooms. Bathrooms. Of course, he had never imagined he'd be trying to sneak in. Dammit.

"I can get us back inside to a point. After that, I'm not going to be much help, outside of knowing where they're holding my daughter." Maria pointed at the camera positioned just below the ceiling. "They don't usually turn this camera on. No one comes back here."

He hoped she was right or there'd be trouble. Not that he didn't expect trouble anyway. With that phone call tonight, he'd officially called his relationship with the Hawks over. Forever.

He still had the key card that had been issued to him. But he didn't expect it to work. As far as he knew, it was a simple matter to reprogram the many locks the key cards opened in the building, denying him access. They were all connected to a single central computer, like a hotel.

The issue arose when they reached a door at the end of the corridor.

Dead end.

A narrow window in the door provided a glimpse into the hallway beyond. Maria stood to one side. She motioned for him.

He nodded.

Leaning against the door, Maria slumped her shoulders. "This is it for me. I don't know what to do from here. I don't have a key to open this door. And the camera on the other side is on. I can see it. I don't think we're going to get past it without being seen."

"I have a key, but I doubt it'll work."

"Unless they're expecting us to come this way. They did send us that photograph for a reason. They know you're with me, and they want me back."

"Sure. Which means they're going to make it as easy as possible for us to get in."

"Right. But not out."

"Yes." How the hell would he get Jasmyne and Asher out of there alive? He had come rushing back in completely unprepared, no doubt exactly as the Hawks had wanted him to. Dammit, he might have made a mistake that would cost them all their lives.

"What the hell?" he muttered, reaching into his pocket for the key card. The card, which had a tiny chip in it, would alert the Hawk's security team of their location. Within minutes, he expected they'd be greeted by a horde of armed guards. If he was lucky, they'd let Jasmyne and Asher go, even though he didn't have the Star. But that wouldn't be the end of his problems. If they left this place alive, he'd be escorted to the bastard who had manipulated him, used him, more or less fucked him. And denied him the most important relationship of his life.

What did he have? What resource, information, tool that could be bartered for their lives, besides the one thing he didn't have—the one that would cost a king his life?

* * * * *

"He's back in the building," Marek stated, snapping his cell phone shut. "Draven brought Jasmyne's mother back."

Asher wasn't sure if that was good or bad. "How do you know? Who called? What's going on?"

"An associate works in the security office."

"If that's the case, what are we doing sitting here? Couldn't your associate get us out earlier?"

"Yes, but I wasn't ready yet. We couldn't get to Jasmyne, and I don't want him losing his job. It's mighty handy having a contact inside your enemy's lines. He has his orders. He'll be here once they make their move to take Draven into custody."

"Taken into custody?" Asher was confused. If Marek had a contact inside, had access to so much information, and had the capability to take care of this by himself, there was no need to get him and Jasmyne involved. Why would he wait so long to take action in the first place?

They were being jerked around.

"Draven double-crossed the Hawks. My source doesn't have access to all the details but I have a feeling you'll have your answers soon." At the rattle of the doorknob, Marek stood and motioned to Asher. "Ready?"

"I guess. We don't have any weapons. Nor do we know where they've taken Jasmyne."

"Taken care of."

I don't like the sound of this.

The door swung open, and a man Asher didn't recognize from the Hawks swung an arm inside, dropping a black backpack on the floor at Marek's feet. Then the door closed.

Marek swept up the bag, unzipped it and pulled out several articles of clothing, including a couple of security uniforms identical to the one their courier had been wearing. Then he sat down to scrutinize a piece of folded paper he pulled from the bag. "Make sure to avoid looking directly at the cameras. They're old and the images aren't the best. As long as they don't get a clear shot of our faces, no one will know who we are."

"Got it. Don't look at the cameras. This guy. Who is he?" Asher stepped into the uniform, watching Marek carefully.

"A valuable resource." Marek folded the paper and tucked it into his shirt pocket.

What the hell he was walking into?

Disguised, they opened the unlocked door and headed down a narrow corridor. The occasional armed guard rushed past them, headed in the opposite direction. Not one of them gave them a second look. They kept pressing forward.

"She's up ahead in a block of cells reserved for newcomers."

"She's safe?"

"Yes. They're treating her like a patient. She might be a little doped up, but she hasn't been harmed."

Asher actually inhaled a deep breath, releasing the tension that had pulled the muscles of his neck and shoulders into painful knots. The agonizing cramps in his gut didn't ease, though. Those wouldn't, not until he'd gotten Jasmyne and Draven out of the building.

At a locked door, Marek produced a key card from the pocket of his uniform and swiped it through the lock. The lock's indicator light flashed green. Unlocked. They hurried down a hall, around several corners, and through a couple more locked doors before stepping into a wide open area.

"There." Marek pointed at a barred cell door.

Asher followed the direction of Marek's gaze.

She was standing at the door, gripping the steel bars in her fists. Her expression shifted from relief to terror and back again. "Asher," she whispered. "Thank God. I tried to find a way out of here, but I just couldn't."

"Are you okay?" Asher's entire being ached to snatch Jasmyne to him and hold her. Never let her go. Ever. Not in a few minutes, hours, days, years.

Marek couldn't get the door open fast enough.

The moment she was free, Asher dragged her against him. Hands shaking, he grasped her tightly, cupping the back of her head with one of his hands, the other flattened on her back. He closed his eyes and inhaled, pulling her scent deep inside.

"Thank God you're okay."

She had her arms wrapped around his waist. He wanted to beg her not to let go, to never leave him. "Where's my mom? Did she come back? What's going on?"

"Your mother is back on the premises. Draven brought her back."

"What's happening? Is this place really a rehab center?"

"In a matter of speaking," Marek answered, nodding. "The patients do quit using drugs. But there's more than that going on here. Unfortunately, there's no time to talk now, not if we're going to get out before sunrise." He motioned for them to follow, and with Jasmyne tucked safely against his side, Asher hurried down the corridor. They stopped outside a locked door that looked identical to the many they'd already passed through.

Marek produced two guns. One he handed to Asher. The other he kept. His expression grave, he inserted the key card into the slot and threw open the door. "Ready?"

Asher nodded.

Chapter Fourteen

ဢ

It took a full ten heartbeats for Jasmyne to comprehend what she was seeing. Her mother stood between two men, a gun gripped in her fists, arms stretched straight in front of her. The business end of the weapon was pointed at Draven.

Before the scream of terror had made its way up her throat, all hell broke loose. Marek and Asher stormed past her, guns pointed at her mom and the two men on either side of her. Marek's weapon fired, and the guy on Maria's right dropped. A stunned Maria flinched a full three seconds later. She lunged to the left then rebounded to the right, just in the nick of time. Marek's gun fired again, and the man on the left was at her feet before Jasmyne had blinked.

Maria leveled the gun she'd been holding at Marek.

Jasmyne shrieked, "Mom! No!"

Maria swiveled, aimed at Jasmyne's shoulder, and fired.

Jasmyne threw her hands over her face and lurched to the side. Someone behind her went, "oof." There was a heavy thud.

"Run! This way," Maria shouted, gun still in her hand. She caught Draven's hand in hers and charged toward the door.

Asher forced Jasmyne to turn and propelled her around a dead woman dressed all in black, and out the door after Draven. With Maria leading the way, they dodged whirring bullets as they raced through a maze of white-walled corridors. They made it through the main exit and Jasmyne was about to take her first inhalation when her mom stumbled forward, seeming to have tripped over something. Her head fell back, her knees buckled and slowly she crumpled to the ground like a puppet cut from its strings.

Jasmyne leaped to the side, nearly tripping over the fallen woman. That was not her mother. Lying on the ground, eyes wide with fear. It couldn't be. No.

Somewhere in the distance, the pop-pop-pop of gunfire sounded. But Jasmyne ignored it, dropping to her knees and smoothing the woman's hair back, to uncover her eyes. Jasmyne's hands trembled. Her knees felt like they were made from molten marshmallows. Her stomach burned like she'd swallowed battery acid.

What the hell had just happened?

The woman was still breathing, although her chest rose and fell in jerky uneven, shuddering movements. A puddle of deep crimson was gathering underneath her head. A tiny rivulet was running downhill, toward Jasmyne's feet.

Jasmyne felt a hand on her shoulder but she couldn't drag her gaze away from the woman lying there, struggling for each breath. "Oh, God. Call for help. Someone! Help her!"

"I'm so sorry, Jasmyne," she heard Draven whisper behind her. "Your mother was trying to help me by pretending—"

Jasmyne squeezed her eyes shut, unable to accept what she saw. It was a nightmare. A hallucination. "Where the hell's the ambulance? This is not my mother. No no no!"

"Are you sure?"

"Yes." She sandwiched the woman's hand between hers. It was cold. Too cold. And limp. Agonizing pain tore through Jasmyne's insides. She slumped forward. "No. I don't want it to be her. If I say it is, then the nightmare's real."

"Oh, Jasmyne. I'm so, so sorry. This wasn't supposed to happen." Draven gently pulled her against him, palming her head until she had buried her face in the crook of his shoulder. The sobs escaped her body in angry, excruciating bursts. The tears stung her eyes. She wanted to stop. She wanted to be strong and help her mother breathe. She wanted to be swallowed up in darkness, to forever forget all of this.

Her mother. She was...dying.

Good God, what would she do without her mom? Maria needed her. And now, facing the possibility of losing the woman, Jasmyne knew how much she needed her mother.

Maybe it wasn't a healthy relationship, this thing between them. Her mother was the troubled child, and she was the loving parent. Things were definitely fucked up. But dammit, fucked up or not, her entire life had revolved around it. She'd lose herself if she lost the center of it all.

Pushing away, Jasmyne turned back toward her mom. "I need to help her. Mom, where does it hurt?"

Draven didn't release her although he loosened his hold. "Baby, there's nothing you can do. It looks like she's been shot in the neck."

"No!" Frantic now, Jasmyne fought out of Draven's embrace. "You don't know that. She's hurt bad. I can see that. But I can help her breathe until the ambulance gets here. Would somebody call the fucking police?"

"Look at her." Draven caught her shoulders in his fists. "There's nothing you can do. I'm no doctor, but I'm not sure there's anything a doctor could do."

"No."

"I know it's a lot to take in right now. Too much. But you have to—"

"I have to help her. That's what I have to do." She bent over and pressed her ear to her mother's chest. She could hear an odd bubbling sound, like air being blown through a straw into a glass of milk.

She cupped her mother's face in her hands and brought her face within inches of her mom's. "Just stay with me, Mom. Help is on the way." Her mother's eyelids fluttered. Her lips moved and the slightest gust of air brushed against Jasmyne's cheek. "What is it, Mom?"

"Let me go," the woman whispered so softly Jasmyne could barely hear her.

Jasmyne released her mother's face. "Is that better?"

Maria slowly moved her head from side to side. "No." She gasped, and Jasmyne was ready to scream from frustration. What was taking the ambulance so fucking long? "I mean let me go. You wouldn't let me live the way I wanted. But you're going to let me die the way I want."

Tears stung Jasmyne's eyes. "We don't need to talk about this now, Mom. Later. Okay? You're not going to die."

"No." Her mother's eyelids lifted, and she met Jasmyne's gaze though bloodshot eyes. "I love you. It's better this way. When I'm gone, you'll finally live."

"No."

"That piece of junk jewelry is hidden in my bra. They wanted it but I didn't give it to them. And your friend Draven too. Take it. I want you to have it. Only you."

"I'll get it later."

"No. Now." Her mother's right arm started to lift but dropped back down again. "I can't." She gave Jasmyne an encouraging nod when Jasmyne reached for the neck of her knit top.

She slipped her hand down the cleft of her mother's breasts, finding a small metal piece tucked in her bra. "Got it."

"Good." Her mother's eyes shut again. "I didn't sell it. I bet you thought I would."

"No, you didn't." Just as Jasmyne's fingers caught the ring, her mother sucked in one last rattly breath and then stopped.

The artifact her mom had died to protect in Jasmyne's fist, she sat by her mother's side and wept until the police and ambulance arrived and Draven and Asher coaxed her to a warm, safe place between them. She wept for all the years her mother had suffered, and the hope she'd always held that some day the suffering would be over.

It had ended. But not in the way she'd wanted.

And then the most awful thought struck her. She hadn't even told her mother she loved her.

She glared at Draven. "I hate you for this. Why'd you bring her back here?"

"To save you." Draven glanced at his cell phone, turned tail and ran down the driveway, leaving her there sitting on the ground with her dead mother. Alone.

Asher stooped beside her and took her hand in his. "I'm here, baby. You're not alone."

* * * * *

Draven knew how his hasty departure had looked to everyone—Asher, Marek, Jasmyne.

Jasmyne hadn't needed to say those five words for him to know who she felt was responsible for Maria's death. He couldn't blame her. It had looked bad. Unfortunately, there'd been no time to explain things.

Allegra was in danger, and he'd delayed going to her, having instead taken the risk to return Maria to the Hawks, hoping he could save Jasmyne. He might have saved Jasmyne's life but he'd failed her in another way. Damn.

And now, because he still didn't have Diana's Star, he feared he'd failed his baby girl too. He couldn't know yet if it was too late. He didn't want to think about the consequences if he was.

The bastard was an impatient man. When time was up, it was up.

The run back to the parked car was just long enough to give his imagination time to run wild. A half-dozen possibilities flashed through his mind, none of them good.

Once Draven knew the bastard had learned of Allegra's identity, her relationship to him and her location in Illinois, Draven had contacted her mother, wired her money and told her to get in the car immediately and drive to Michigan. No credit cards, he'd warned. No cell phones either. He didn't want them leaving a trail.

Draven's enemy would never expect them to come to Michigan. No doubt, the bastard had people monitoring airports, borders to Canada and Mexico, train stations, even bus depots.

Unfortunately, Susan had either forgotten about the cell phone or intentionally used it. When she'd been less than thirty miles away. His enemy knew where she was. That was when he'd gotten the call. That was when he'd lost his temper, refusing to help him anymore. Nobody who made a deal with the devil saved his soul.

The bastard wouldn't manipulate him anymore. He'd had enough of living this way, disowning own daughter, denying everything that mattered, fearing the people he loved would be used against him somehow.

Draven had taken a chance, called Susan's cell phone and warned her. A meeting place and time were agreed upon.

Now, less than two hours later, after that whole hellish scene at the prison, he drove to the location, keenly aware of all the vehicles around him. Despite the anxiety coiled in his gut, he forced himself to take wrong exits every now and then and drive in a circle to make sure no one was following. A half hour later, he pulled up in front of the building, a hotel on a crowded suburban thoroughfare.

He rushed inside, bypassing the front desk. His heart in his throat, he approached their room, located on the third floor at the far end of the corridor, and knocked.

Eventually, after peering through the peephole, Susan opened the door.

Allegra was sitting on the floor behind her, playing with some dolls.

"Thank God you're safe." He stepped inside and pushed the door shut. He didn't sit. Didn't speak. Didn't go to Allegra. Even though he felt awkward standing there, arms at his side, his daughter and her mother closer than they'd been in years.

His baby girl had grown. A lot. It killed him that he'd missed so much.

Five years, three months and sixteen days. That's how long it had been since he'd last seen Allegra face-to-face. She didn't know who her father was, his name, nothing. For all practical purposes he was a complete stranger to her.

What had he done?

He'd cheated her of what every child wanted. He didn't deserve the privilege of hugging her now. This was the way he'd insisted it be. He'd felt she'd be better off not knowing him rather than wondering when she'd see him next. It had been for her protection.

The beautiful little girl was looking up at him, wide-eyed and curious. But she didn't speak. And just the slightest hint of wariness darkened her eyes.

He gave Allegra one last smile and then turned his full attention on Susan, sitting at the round table in the room's corner. He motioned to the empty chair beside her. "Can we talk for a minute?"

"Sure," Susan snapped. She whispered something to Allegra and the little girl bounced away, headed for the pile of toys on the bed. He sat. "Why are we here?"

"I need to talk to you."

"You have my phone number."

Of course Susan wasn't going to be happy about this. From her perspective, it probably looked like he was just jerking her and Allegra around to be a prick. How could he help her understand this was for Allegra, not him?

"I told you why I couldn't call."

"I can think of a million safer places to hide than miles from the men you claim are out to get her."

"Mommy, what's in here?" Allegra pointed at a closed door next to the bed.

"Nothing, sweetie," Susan said to their curious little girl. "Just another hotel room. Some other people are staying in there. We have to leave the door closed."

She had his sister's nose and eyes. Staring at Allegra, Draven said, "There is that old saying about seeing what's under your nose. It worked. For a while. He still wouldn't have known if—"

"Yeah, yeah. If I hadn't used my phone. I know. But I have more than a sneaking suspicion this bullshit is not why you dragged us out here, instead of somewhere far away. Safer."

"That's just it. I don't think far away would be safer."

Susan sighed. She looked tired. Beneath her eyes, deep bruises darkened the skin. "What's going on? Is this how we'll have to live? Hiding, running? Always expecting someone to be tailing us? Afraid?"

"No. You won't. I'm going to make sure of it. That's why I wanted to talk today. In person."

"You're going to make sure of it? How?" Susan scrubbed her face with her palms. "I have a feeling I know where this is going. And if I'm right, it's a bad idea. Bad."

"We made a mistake—"

"Give us some money and we'll disappear."

"I made a mistake—"

"No." Elbows on the table, she flipped her hands around, palms facing him. "Don't tell me you've had a personal revelation."

"Well…that's kind of where I was going with this."

"God, I knew it. Don't. Just don't."

"He knows. We can't hide her anymore. He'll find her again."

Susan stood, arms wrapped around herself. She stared at their child playing on the bed. "Allegra's five years old. She was doing well. She was happy. You wanted it this way. And yes, I agreed it was better. It's not fair to—"

Not wanting to distract Allegra, Draven took Susan's hand in his and pulled, coaxing her to sit. He forced himself to speak slowly, calmly. So much was at stake. He wanted to shout he was so frustrated. To release the tension pulling his nerves into excruciating knots. "It's not fair to deny her a father. Someday she might resent us—me. She could feel abandoned. Unloved."

Susan inched forward, flattening her hands on the table. "Or she might resent you for dragging her into a situation that's confusing and terrifying."

"I told you. I'm taking care of my father. He won't bother you anymore."

Susan said nothing.

"I can set it up so that we never see each other if that's what's bothering you about this."

"That's not it. Kids need stability—"

"And two parents."

"Sure. Two parents who are on the same page and who are willing to make sacrifices for their kids."

"You think it hasn't been a sacrifice forcing myself to stay away from her this long?"

Susan narrowed her eyes at him. "I wonder, Draven. I really do. Has it?"

"Hell yes. That little girl's the only child I have. I don't even know what I've missed the past five years, but that's not why I want to make a change—"

"You want to know what you've missed? About two years of sleepless nights. Ear infections. Teething. Diaper rashes. Lots of stumbles. A few stitches. Potty training..."

Draven resisted the urge to slam his hands on the table. Susan was torturing him, and dammit he wasn't man enough to take it. "You're enjoying this, aren't you?"

"No. I'm just trying to paint a more realistic picture here. Being a father isn't just about trips to the park and birthday cakes. It's about middle-of-the-night trips to the emergency room and math homework."

"I want those things too. I want to help. To be another source of support and guidance. Not to undermine your authority. This whole thing made me realize I can't protect Allegra by pretending she doesn't exist. I'm just letting the bastard cheat us both."

Silence stretched for eons. Susan stood and walked to the window. She pulled the curtain a fraction of an inch to the side and peered through the narrow slit. "We live in Illinois. You're here in Michigan. Even if I agreed to this...whatever it is. How can it work, practically?"

"What if I told you I'd be willing to move to Illinois? Close enough to take Allegra to school. To pick her up."

"How are you going to do that? During the day?"

"I'll find a way. The bottom line is I made a mistake, Susan. I know that now, and I'm very sorry I left you to handle our daughter all by yourself for five years. But I'm here now. I'm Allegra's father. And I'm willing to do whatever it takes to be a part of her life. I'm doing this because I love her. I want to be a father. I want to try. I'm not afraid anymore."

Susan continued to stare out the window for several more minutes. He sensed her inner conflict between hope and disbelief, anger and gratitude.

He'd done none of them any favors by staying away for five years. He hoped Susan, and more importantly Allegra, would give him the chance to make it up to them.

Finally, Susan spoke. "Okay," she murmured on a sigh. "I can't tell you where you can live. And I won't tell you to stay away. But you can't expect everything to go smoothly right away. It's going to take some time."

"I'm more than willing to be patient. Thank you."

She finally looked at him. Her expression was softer now, the rage in her eyes cooled. "What happened to you? I never expected this."

"A lot. But mostly someone taught me how to follow my heart, not my head."

"That's a very special woman."

"Yes, she is."

"Don't send this one away."

"I have no intention of doing anything that stupid."

"Glad to hear it. For her sake."

"No, this one's probably going to send me away."

"Not if she's as intelligent as I expect she is."

Draven stood, gave Susan a quick smile and headed out the door.

It was time to face the bastard who'd threatened his daughter. No one would make that mistake again.

Chapter Fifteen

ഔ

He spied something suspicious outside in the parking lot before he'd even reached his car. The fucker hadn't taken long to find him.

He'd sent women. Dressed head-to-toe in black. The pair had just exited a car parked next to Susan's. Draven recognized the vehicle. It belonged to the Hawks.

Asher had been right about this. It was bullshit. The Hawks were using women. Mortals were doing their dirty work. And the bastard, Draven's father, wasn't above using those mortals for his purpose either.

Ha! If only the Hawks knew. The bastard wasn't a Hawk. He was using their resources for his purposes. Then, like everything else, everyone else, he'd destroy them.

The bastard deserved everything Draven was going to do to him.

But the women, who he suspected wouldn't remember what had happened the next day, did not. If possible, he needed to stop them from assassinating his daughter without harming them. How many more were on the way?

His rental car was parked about twenty feet away, toward the rear of the parking lot. Hoping the assassins were too busy to notice him, he zigged and zagged his way to it. Would it be too much to hope there'd be a weapon in the trunk? A rope, anything?

The interior was weapon-free. He found a wrench in the trunk and a bungee cord. His makeshift weapons in hand, he made his way back across the parking lot. A car rolled past him, lights off.

More assassins.

His attention divided between the women who were now approaching the hotel's side entry and the car that had just arrived, he ducked behind a parked car.

Two people exited the car—men. They were holding something in their hands and hurrying toward the women. When they passed beneath the one lamp illuminating the parking lot, Draven recognized one of them.

Asher.

Abandoning his hiding place, Draven ran toward them. Asher spun around, leveling a gun at Draven's chest. He lowered it. "Dammit, I almost shot you."

"How'd you find me?" Draven whispered, peering past Asher to see who was with him. "Where's Jasmyne? And what are you doing here?"

Marek stood about five feet behind him, a gun gripped in his fist as well.

"Helping you." Asher motioned toward the hotel. "We can talk about the other stuff later. Jasmyne's safe. The assassins are inside the building already." He broke into a run.

Draven followed.

"I'll go around to the front." Marek tucked his gun into the holster strapped beneath his jacket. He said over his shoulder, "The Hawks plant chips on all their members' cars."

"I should have known."

"Let's go, buddy." Asher pulled the door open. "We have a child to save. Your child."

"Sorry. I wanted to tell you—"

"Later," Asher interrupted, stepping into the silent hallway.

They took the stairs up to the third floor. There was no sound of footsteps up above them as they ascended. Either the women had taken the other staircase at the opposite end of the building, or the elevator. Draven inched open the door and peered into the hall. Susan's door was less than ten feet away. He saw no one near the room's door. Not the assassins. Nor Marek.

Then he heard a sound. The click of a lock engaging. The door next to Susan's.

The adjoining room.

He pointed. "I bet they're in there."

He wanted to pound on Susan's door, warn her. But he wondered if that would put them in more danger. He yanked his cell phone out of his pocket and hit redial, praying Susan would answer. If she kept the doors closed, they'd be safe. For now.

"What is it now?" Susan grumbled.

"Don't open the door, whatever you do."

"What? Why? Ally, no!" There was a clatter then the sounds of shuffling, a child's scream.

Marek rounded the corner, coming from the elevators, and the three of them kicked their way into the room through which the assassins had entered. Asher and Marek rushed into Susan's room ahead of Draven, guns leveled straight ahead. The faint poof of two shots, muted by silencers, echoed in his head.

Draven shoved his way past them to find Susan standing in the corner, Allegra behind her, and the two mortal women lying sprawled on the floor.

"I thought you said you'd take care of this," Susan said in a wavering voice.

"I am. Right now." He snatched the gun out of Marek's hand and headed toward the exit.

"I'll stay here," Asher volunteered.

Marek followed Draven outside.

* * * * *

Draven knew where to find him, the bastard who'd pushed him too far. What kind of sick sonofabitch hurt an innocent child? The kind who deserved to die a slow, agonizing death, that was what kind. Unfortunately, Draven wasn't prepared to deal that kind of justice tonight, only a swift and relatively painless death.

That would have to do. The bastard could not remain alive.

The heavy bass of dance music thrumming through his body, and the stench of sweat and cigarette smoke burning his nose, Draven forced himself through the gyrating bodies packed on the dance floor, heading toward the private room at the nightclub's rear. As expected, the man he was determined to kill was seated in his usual place on a black leather couch, a cigarette pinched between his lips, his arms draped over a pair of beautiful women flanking him, and a double scotch on the rocks in one hand.

"Draven Falk," his enemy said, smiling. He plucked the smoldering cigarette from his mouth and tossed it on the carpeted floor. "What a surprise." He smoothed his free hand up one shapely thigh and the owner of the slender leg smirked, her scarlet lips twisting into a wry smile.

Draven simply pulled the gun out and leveled it at his target. "Didn't anyone ever tell you smoking will kill you?"

"I don't inhale." The man's smile didn't fade. Clearly, he was either accustomed to threats on his life, or he didn't give a damn whether he died or not. "Do you honestly think this will solve anything? Leave us." He pushed the grappling women away from him, and they clambered to their feet and wobbled past Draven on stilettos, tugging their short skirts down to the middle of their thighs. "Where's my property? I spared your fucking life, expecting you to bring it to me."

"I don't have it."

The smile Draven had come to despise remained, reminding him of those many times the expression had been used to taunt him. It wouldn't work. Not anymore. "You aren't trying to fuck me, are you?"

"No. Me fuck my own father? Why would I do that?"

The man stood and took slow, sauntering steps toward Draven. "Why haven't you shot me yet, Son? Feeling a little torn?"

"You were going to have my daughter slaughtered. Your grandchild."

"She's nothing to me. Just like you. Don't you wish you could say the same? But you can't. Because even if you couldn't trust yourself to care about a woman, you've always had a soft spot for your dear old dad, the man you get your name from, Draven Falk, Senior."

"You're wrong. I guess you've rubbed that spot raw, Dad. Because I think it's finally calloused over."

"But don't you want to know your mother's secret? If I die, it dies with me."

"To hell with it." He squeezed the trigger and put a single bullet in the center of his father's forehead.

Maybe he had shared more with Jasmyne that he'd ever realized. They both had let their parents destroy their lives. No longer.

* * * * *

"It's true then?" Draven repeated for the third time. "All the Eclipse that has been manufactured in the past year is toxic? Every single batch?"

Standing next to an enormous metal security cage situated at the rear of the king's cavernous secret storage cellar, King Kaden handed both Draven and Asher a printed sheet of paper. "Yes. This is why I've had to quarantine it all. I can't risk anyone being exposed to it. They'll die."

"Why not tell the truth? Why let it get to this point, where the Sons are ready to kill you, where they're blaming you?" Asher asked, fingering the page.

Kaden turned toward a control panel mounted on a solid sheet of metal next to the cage's door. "I couldn't risk the wrong people getting the information. Not until we'd found the source of the poison."

While Kaden deactivated the security system protecting the contents of the cage, Draven skimmed the information on the paper. Some kind of lab results indicating a foreign substance discovered in several samples of Eclipse. "Why would any Son taint Eclipse? We all need it."

"That's the question we need to answer. If we can find the why, then we'll figure the who." Kaden pulled open the cage door and stepped to the side. "We've already eliminated your father, Draven. Unfortunately, he was our prime suspect."

"What else do you have?"

"Not much," Marek admitted, stepping forward. He'd been standing back, with another man at his side, a man Draven would never have expected to see in his company. Dayne was not only a fellow White Hawk member, but had also planned to assassinate Marek as vengeance for his family's death.

Rumor was he was now Marek's blood bound mate. Draven hadn't given the rumors any thought...until now.

Dayne hadn't been as active in the past few months with the Hawks as he had once been. He still attended general meetings, but he hadn't been a presence at some of the more intimate conversations with key members. And he was here. In the king's cellar. With his sworn enemies--the king and Marek, Kaden's brother.

Dayne's presence also explained a few other things, like why no other guards had followed them out of the rehab hospital when they'd escaped. And how Marek had been able to track him to the hotel.

"It's taken this much time to identify the substance and trace it back to the Eclipse." Dayne motioned to the open cage door. "We've tested every single bottle in here."

Draven's gaze slid from Dayne to Marek to Kaden. "How did you discover the Eclipse was tainted in the first place? And why did it take so long to find out what it was?"

Kaden shrugged. "We weren't looking for it, for one thing. At first I thought it was something else, a spell."

"What? Who?" Asher said, turning a questioning glance Draven's way. He folded the paper with the lab results and tucked it into his pocket.

Kaden swallowed, letting one, two, three beats of silence swallow them up before saying, "My parents—*our* parents—were the first two victims."

"Damn," Asher whispered.

"I'd believed it was the Sacred Triad that the Hawks had used to kill them. I'd believed that for years. It wasn't until Dayne brought some facts to my attention that I had their bodies exhumed. Luckily we don't have our bodies embalmed like mortals do. The time spent underground actually made the effects of the toxin more aggravated and somewhat easier to identify."

"It was still a bitch, though," Dayne stated. "We had to figure out how they'd ingested it."

"Do you think it's a Son? A White Hawk?"

Kaden motioned at the thousands of boxes stacked in the cage. "If it is, then it's someone who doesn't use Eclipse, who doesn't need it or who's stockpiled enough to supply himself for a long time. Who might that be?"

This made so little sense. Draven shook his head. "Someone who doesn't need to work during daylight hours, doesn't hunt very often. If he's young and doesn't need to hunt for years, he might risk tainting large amounts of Eclipse."

"Someone who has the capability to make his own?" Asher offered.

They all nodded.

"All the key members of the White Hawks have checked out," Marek said. "None of them have a motive, outside of trying to get rid of our king. But I can think of a lot of simpler ways to do that."

Obviously, Marek and Kaden had been working on this for a while. But still, Draven felt like they were missing something. "Why would this person continue to taint the Eclipse after seeing no one else was getting sick? He knows the Eclipse isn't being distributed. What's the point?"

Looking thoughtful, Marek suggested, "Does he think he can force the Sons of Twilight off Eclipse entirely for some reason? So he continues adding the toxin, expecting someone to test each batch?"

Asher leaned back against a stack of boxes. "The guy's got balls. With every batch, he'd risk being discovered."

"Yeah," Draven agreed as he continued to try to puzzle the mystery out. So far, the pieces just weren't fitting.

"With discovery comes certain death," Kaden stated, heading for the cage's exit.

Marek followed his brother through the exit. "Which means whatever his purpose, he feels it's worth risking his life."

Asher was the third one to leave the secured area. "What the hell is worth dying for? Risking innocent lives?"

Draven knew of only one thing worth dying for. "The life of someone you love?" he offered.

Kaden's eyebrows lifted with surprise. "Interesting. How would Sons taking Eclipse risk someone's life? Maybe he doesn't want us walking in the sunlight."

That was a question he couldn't answer. "I don't know. Maybe."

"Will we ever know?" Asher asked.

"Yes. Hopefully soon. That's why you're here." Kaden waited for Draven and Dayne to exit the cage before securing it. "I want to ask you two a question."

"What question?" Asher asked, echoing his own.

Kaden motioned for them to precede him out of the secret storage cellar. They exited through the door and climbed the narrow staircase to the room above. The four men gathered just outside the disguised door, built to look like a metal cabinet in the king's basement. "Would you consider joining my brother and Dayne in searching for the answers?" They continued up to the ground level floor above.

Kaden led them toward a room Draven had never set foot within, where, as king, Kaden held ceremonial appearances. His throne sat on the center of a dais, in front of a wall decorated with the most unique tiles Draven had ever seen. They were gold, three dimensional, and together formed a beautiful mosaic mural. "I've created a secret group of men, calling them the Cytherean Guard," Kaden said, motioning toward the gold tiled wall. "The Cytherean Guard's purpose is simple--to protect the secrets of the Sons of the Twilight, including your king, and to defend justice. Each man has been selected for a specific reason. You have been chosen, Draven and Asher."

Draven was speechless for at least a handful of seconds. "What would you need us to do?"

"Right now, our focus is on the tainted Eclipse. You would work undercover with the other Cytherean Guards to identify the person who poisoned our former king and queen and bring him to justice."

Draven met Asher's gaze then Dayne's and Marek's.

"No one knows about the Cytherean Guard but the four of us." Marek positioned himself behind his brother, on one side of the throne.

"Why us?" Draven stopped at the base of the raised platform, unsure what his king expected next.

Kaden waved him up. "We trust you."

With Asher at his side, Draven stepped onto the platform.

"And respect you," Marek added.

Asher and Draven swapped glances once again. "It would be my honor," Draven said.

"Mine too."

Kaden turned toward the wall behind his throne and revealed the purpose of holding this particular conversation in the formal throne room. A panel slid open, revealing an inner space. "Step forward and accept your new brothers," he said, motioning to Dayne and Marek. "Our two new Cytherean Guards. And you," he motioned to Asher and Draven, "will you swear your loyalty to your brothers? If so, step forward, join our brotherhood, and help us find out who is trying to keep the Sons of the Twilight in the dark."

* * * * *

"This is my last night of the blood-bond." Seated in the living room, Jasmyne fidgeted. She ran her hands down her blue jean-clad thighs. Then she went back to fiddling with the hem of her knit top.

It had been seven nights. Only seven. But it felt like it had been seven weeks. No, months. So much had happened. With the guys. Her mother.

Ironically, her mother had died sober, after spending roughly ninety percent of her adult life stoned. And she'd died trying to protect her daughter.

Jasmyne never would have guessed it would end that way. It was still impossible to believe. She half expected her mom to come staggering through the door any moment. She really hoped she'd come staggering through the door. A stoned mother was better than a dead one.

Gone. Her mom was gone.

After everything was over, and her guys had dealt with the Hawks, and the craziness had stopped, she'd spent the next couple of nights crying. Asher and Draven, bless them, had done their best to console her. They'd fed, or at least, that's what they told her. She had no memory of it. All she recalled was how they had held her, gently cradled her in their arms. She was grateful their venom erased her memory of the bite and any subsequent sexual activities that immediately followed. It was just as well. In her grief, she couldn't stomach the thought of carrying on with a couple gorgeous guys like a carefree girl.

She had no viewing for her mom. No funeral. Her mother was buried in a pretty little spot beneath an oak tree in a tiny cemetery. It was hard saying goodbye. Absolute agony. Her guys couldn't be at her side then, since the burial took place during daylight hours. But they returned later that night with her and listened to her talk about her mom for hours.

Draven, the man who'd finally learned to become vulnerable. And Asher, her rock, the man who lived and loved with more ferocity than any man she'd ever known. These two men had become her friends. No, more than that. She had begun to fall in love with them. So quickly. But then again, they'd been through so much together. Not to mention she'd had a huge head start with that very strange and yet-to-be explained magical connection she shared with Draven.

Draven sat beside her, stilling her restless hands by taking them in his. "Tonight we feed for the last time."

"Until when? How long until you take your next blood-bond?"

He kissed the back of her hand then lowered it, leaving both hers and his resting in his lap. "Asher and I are both very old by human standards. We require a blood-bond once a year."

"Every year?" The most scalding jealousy burned through her veins. Her guys would be taking another woman and feeding from her. Touching her. Stroking her.

Another wave of jealousy gripped her.

They couldn't take another woman. It wouldn't be the same with anyone else. No more than it would be the same if she took a new lover tomorrow. No. She couldn't. She wouldn't. Hell, she had no idea how she'd deal with everyday life.

Without her mother.

Without her purpose. What was left for her in Illinois? Her job, maybe. Nothing else.

"What's wrong, baby?" Draven asked, palming the side of her head so that the opposite side pressed against his broad, muscular chest. His voice hummed through her body like a low voltage electrical charge.

"I'm not sure. Maybe it's exhaustion. Or shock. Or insanity—"

"You're not insane," Asher insisted, sitting on her other side.

"That's debatable."

Draven kissed the top of her head then patted her back. "You're changing the subject."

I know! "This isn't easy."

That hungry, I'm-going-to-eat-you-up look all over his face, Asher kissed her fingertips. "What are you trying to tell us?"

That I've lost my mind. And I want to stay with you two, even though we're practically strangers. What am I thinking? "That...I'm going to miss you two. A lot."

"Oh baby," Draven murmured. "We're going to miss you too."

"More than you know." Her arm cradled in his hands, Asher kissed a trail up to her elbow.

The air in the room grew heavy as the weight of her unspoken words pressed down upon her shoulders. Inside, she was a bundle of mixed-up emotions, good and bad.

Because her guys were kissing, stroking and caressing various parts of her anatomy, she was physically feeling pretty darn good. But her heart was heavy. She felt like she was about to say goodbye to the two most important people in her life.

How could she possibly go back home and carry on like nothing had changed?

Her nose started burning. Her eyes too. Tears blurred her vision.

She'd lost her mother. The loss would hurt for a long time. But there was a positive side to it. Her mother's struggle with drugs was over. Her pain. Her sorrow.

Jasmyne hoped someday she'd find some comfort in that. For now, all she had was pain and sorrow and darkness. Uncertainty. Draven had been so right. She'd centered her entire life around her mother.

It would be so easy to shove someone else into that spot her mother had left empty. Or two someones. But in her gut she knew that was a stupid thing to do.

Her heart didn't give a damn about wisdom. Her heart wanted someone to love.

She cried while Draven and Asher held her close. They murmured words of comfort. They fed one last time. The memory of the pain and heat blazing through her body dimmed, flickered and finally disappeared altogether. Then they lay on either side of her, simply holding her until sunrise.

The alarm clock read 8:02 when Draven spoke the words she hadn't wanted to hear, "It's time for you to go home."

She didn't budge.

Asher sat up. "We can call a cab, but you know we can't accompany you to the airport."

She was kicking herself for not booking a redeye flight now. The airline she'd flown into Detroit on hadn't had a seat available on a nighttime flight. But she could have forked over the cash to fly another airline. Not that it would have done much. It was simply delaying the inevitable.

"I know," she said on a sigh. "It's time." It took Herculean effort, but she forced herself to get up and out of the bed. She donned her "Strong Jasmyne" face and gathered her clothes, placing them all back in her suitcase. Whether she was ready or not, it was time to go back and face reality.

She took the ring, Diana's Star, from her bag and handed it to Draven.

He accepted it with a look of sincere gratitude. "Thank you, baby."

"I figure it's safer with you than it would be with me. I don't know exactly what it's supposed to do, but I figure it shouldn't be out there, where someone else might get it."

"What about your job?" Asher asked.

She simply shrugged. Now that her mother was gone, she didn't care where she worked.

Her guys left her to herself as she showered, and their chitchatting filled what would have been painful silence while she dressed. Wearing sweats and t-shirts, their feet bare, they escorted her downstairs to the living room to await her cab.

She sat between them on the couch, her nerves raw. She was on the verge of crying. There were no words for how she felt. So she simply sat and stared at them, trying desperately to burn their faces to her memory.

If only she'd had more time just to enjoy her guys. There hadn't been enough hours.

"Are you okay, baby?" Draven asked, looking worried.

"Yeah. I'm tired. And it's going to be hard going home without my mom."

A horn outside sounded. The cab. It was time to say goodbye.

She hugged Draven first, sandwiched his face between her hands and kissed his cheeks, chin, nose, eyes. Then, tears flowing freely, she turned to Asher and did the same to him.

Eyes blurred to the point of near-blindness, she dragged her suitcase outside into the pink-skied morning. She got into the cab and waved a final farewell to the house she'd called home for some of the most confusing, terrifying, sad and wonderful days of her life.

She doubted she'd ever feel as close to another human being as she did Draven and Asher. Did she ever want to be that vulnerable again?

* * * * *

Three weeks later, when she returned home from work to find Asher and Draven sitting in her living room, she knew she did want to be that vulnerable. She needed to allow herself to be that vulnerable. She threw herself into Draven's arms.

"We wanted to give you some time," he said, catching her to him and swinging her around. He held her at arm's length and looking all serious asked, "Can you trust me now? You know I love you, that I want to spend the rest of my life, your life, all our lives, proving how much I love you."

"I'm just so glad you're here."

"So are we." Asher pressed up against her from behind and hooked his arm around her middle. "We missed you."

"I missed you too." She tipped her head to the side, shivering at the chills sweeping down her right side as he nibbled on that sweet spot on her neck. "Asher, I'm sorry we didn't share the same strange psychic connection I had with Draven—I still don't understand what that was all about."

Draven palmed her cheek. "I don't understand it either. It's never happened to me before, not with anyone. But I'm beginning to believe it had to do with my mother's secret, the one my father held over my head all my life. I don't know if we'll ever figure it out, but I'd like to try. Together."

"I'd like that." She nodded then let her head fall back against Asher. "And Asher, God, Asher. I could spend decades showing you how much I love you. You were always there for

319

me when I needed you. You were sincere and steadfast and genuine. My rock. You mean so much to me."

"You mean everything to me too," Asher said against her head.

She shivered, even though she was really, really warm all over. "So the three of us will be together? For how long?"

Draven said, grinning. "Four. Sometimes it'll be four. My daughter."

Asher added, "And you'll have us as long as you want. The rest of your life if you choose."

She really liked the sound of that. A lot. "But what about the next Binding? Will you have to find a new mortal? Can you take a blood-bond with each other every time?"

"It can be just the three of us from now on. We don't have to involve anyone else," Asher answered.

"Thank you." She pressed her flattened hands against the backs of Draven's, sandwiching them between her cheeks and hands. "That sounds wonderful." She kissed him and then she turned and kissed Asher.

She had a long way to go before she'd feel like she truly had her feet back under her, but Jasmyne was ready to step into the center of her own life, and she wanted Asher and Draven—and yes, Draven's daughter too—there with her.

Also by Tawny Taylor

ᘓ

Asteroid 6969: Siren's Dance

Blackmailed

Body & Soul 1: Pesky Paranormals

Body & Soul 2: Phantasmic Fantasies

Double Take

Ellora's Cavemen: Tales From the Temple IV (*anthology*)

Immortal Secrets 1: Dragons and Dungeons

Immortal Secrets 2: Light My Fire

Immortal Secrets 3: Spells and Seduction

Lessons in Lust Major

Mark of the Beast

Masters of Illusion

Passion in a Pear Tree

Private Games

Sexual Healing

Stolen Goddess

Tempting Fate

Touch of the Beast

Twilight's Possession 3: Everlasting Hunger

Wet and Wilde

Wrath's Embrace

About the Author

❧

Nothing exciting happens in Tawny Taylor's life, unless you count giving the cat a flea dip—a cat can make some fascinating sounds when immersed chin-deep in insecticide—or chasing after a houseful of upchucking kids during flu season. She doesn't travel the world or employ a staff of personal servants. She's not even built like a runway model. She's just your run-of-the-mill, pleasantly plump Detroit suburban mom and wife.

That's why she writes, for the sheer joy of it. She doesn't need to escape, mind you. Despite being run-of-the-mill, her life is wonderful. She just likes to add some...zip.

Her heroines might resemble herself or her next door neighbor (sorry Sue), but they are sure to be memorable (she hopes!). And her heroes—inspired by movie stars, her favorite television actors or her husband—are fully capable of delivering one hot happily-ever-after after another. Combined, the characters and plots she weaves bring countless hours of enjoyment to Tawny...and she hopes to readers too!

In the end, that's all the matters to Tawny, bringing a little bit of zip to someone else's life.

Tawny welcomes comments from readers. You can find her website and email address on her author bio page at www.ellorascave.com.

Tell Us What You Think

We appreciate hearing reader opinions about our books. You can email us at Comments@EllorasCave.com.

Why an electronic book?

We live in the Information Age — an exciting time in the history of human civilization, in which technology rules supreme and continues to progress in leaps and bounds every minute of every day. For a multitude of reasons, more and more avid literary fans are opting to purchase e-books instead of paper books. The question from those not yet initiated into the world of electronic reading is simply: *Why?*

1. *Price.* An electronic title at Ellora's Cave Publishing and Cerridwen Press runs anywhere from 40% to 75% less than the cover price of the exact same title in paperback format. Why? Basic mathematics and cost. It is less expensive to publish an e-book (no paper and printing, no warehousing and shipping) than it is to publish a paperback, so the savings are passed along to the consumer.

2. *Space.* Running out of room in your house for your books? That is one worry you will never have with electronic books. For a low one-time cost, you can purchase a handheld device specifically designed for e-reading. Many e-readers have large, convenient screens for viewing. Better yet, hundreds of titles can be stored within your new library — on a single microchip. There are a variety of e-readers from different manufacturers. You can also read e-books on your PC or laptop computer. (Please note that Ellora's Cave does not endorse any specific brands.

You can check our websites at www.ellorascave.com or www.cerridwenpress.com for information we make available to new consumers.)

3. *Mobility.* Because your new e-library consists of only a microchip within a small, easily transportable e-reader, your entire cache of books can be taken with you wherever you go.

4. *Personal Viewing Preferences.* Are the words you are currently reading too small? Too large? Too… ANNOYING? Paperback books cannot be modified according to personal preferences, but e-books can.

5. *Instant Gratification.* Is it the middle of the night and all the bookstores near you are closed? Are you tired of waiting days, sometimes weeks, for bookstores to ship the novels you bought? Ellora's Cave Publishing sells instantaneous downloads twenty-four hours a day, seven days a week, every day of the year. Our webstore is never closed. Our e-book delivery system is 100% automated, meaning your order is filled as soon as you pay for it.

Those are a few of the top reasons why electronic books are replacing paperbacks for many avid readers.

As always, Ellora's Cave and Cerridwen Press welcome your questions and comments. We invite you to email us at Comments@ellorascave.com or write to us directly at Ellora's Cave Publishing Inc., 1056 Home Avenue, Akron, OH 44310-3502.

erridwen, the Celtic Goddess of wisdom, was the muse who brought inspiration to storytellers and those in the creative arts. Cerridwen Press encompasses the best and most innovative stories in all genres of today's fiction. Visit our site and discover the newest titles by talented authors who still get inspired - much like the ancient storytellers did, once upon a time.